AL
And the Id

G. L. Keady

G. L. Keady

DREAMRAIDERS
SONS OF STEEL
CHANNELLING BO

Axis Stone Mysteries Series
SUICIDE BLONDE
LEG MAN
SMUGGLER'S HOLE

The Sons of Steel Saga
FUTURES END
CYBERWARS
DARK ENERGY
BLOCKCHAIN

Big Island Publishing
PO Box 3027, Tuross Head, 2537, NSW, Australia.
www.bigislandpublishing.au

ISBN:
Print: 978-06459738-5-3
Digital: 978-06459738-8-4

Edited by: Canon Doyle
Cover design and art: Brandon Evans-Keady

The Id: In Freudian philosophy, the division of the psyche that is totally unconscious and serves as the source of instinctual impulses and demands for immediate satisfaction of primitive needs. Another theory is that the Id is the mass of primitive instincts and energies in the unconscious mind that, modified by the ego and the superego, underlies all psychic activity. Is it either or? Alice certainly believes otherwise.

TABLE OF CONTENTS

CHAPTER 1
THE LAIR

THE **ALL-POWERFUL OCEANA** chapter of Zen Corporation, under the governance of a new Gorrick, wasn't about to tolerate any more interference from Black Alice. So Gorrick issued an edict to Honor, director of the newly established security division, ZEO (Zen Espionage Operative), to eliminate Alice once and for all and to destroy Kairos, the Oceana Time Travel wormhole-generating teleporter. A megalomaniac, Honor would pull out all stops to carry out the order, determined to succeed where her predecessor and former boyfriend Zanza Kew had failed. Gifted with a new face from cosmetic surgery performed by Doctor Lizzy Li, who had been appointed director of Zen's cybernetic development division, Zenesis, enabled Honor to be in disguise, which would better help her settle the score with the members of the Oceana Time Travel Division... in particular her nemesis Black Alice.

The shadow of a laugh is not distinct from the shadow of a scream of terror, but the reality of it is. A hunted man, Black Alice, lifted his blood-drenched hands and stared at them, wondering whether it was his blood or someone else's—he had no idea—he had only just regained consciousness. The only sound audible to him was a high-pitched whistle. Then the pain came... letting him know the blood was definitely his. He followed the crimson rivulet along his right forearm in search of the source and arrived at a deep gash in his bicep oozing blood.

Sound returned to normal, but the whistle was replaced by a much more sinister noise: the sound of crushing metal. He scowled, where the hell am I? It was dark, night... he was behind the wheel of a car, and it was moving... How the hell did I get here? But he wasn't driving it—the engine wasn't even running—the car he was on a conveyor belt. He glanced out of the shattered driver's side window; hmm, maybe that's how I got cut? I've got to get out of here. A feeling of dread was tying his stomach in a knot; he had to follow his instincts. He tried the door handle... but the metal wall of the conveyor channel prevented him from opening it wide enough to get out. He looked through the windscreen... there was a car ahead of him on the conveyor being fed into a crusher. It took only seconds for the massive metal claws to compact the car into a neat cube—his car was next.

Favouring his injured arm, he swivelled in the seat, brought both feet up higher than the dashboard, and then, glad he was wearing his Cuban heeled boots, let drive with a massive double-footed kick. The windscreen shattered, showering cubes of glass onto the bonnet. He was through it onto the hood in a flash, and then just as the metal claws opened up to consume him and the car, he jumped.

The two-metre jump was jarring, but his ankles and knees handled it. However, his jaw didn't handle the left hook he was greeted with on landing. The punch caused his knees to buckle, but driven by a powerful instinct to overcome adversity, he straightened up, looked his opponent square in the eye, and let fly at his face with a barrage of blows. The first two connected, but then a gunshot caused him to freeze mid-punch. His opponent hit the deck, cuffing a shattered nose... blood streaming through his fingers.

Unarmed, Alice knew it was a contest he'd assuredly lose if he were to continue the fight, so he slowly turned with his arms raised in capitulation.

There were three Zen agents, all armed.

"What's the beef?" Al snarled. He could tell by their calm, stony-faced behaviour they were mercenaries; he'd come across that look plenty of times before. It wasn't difficult to tell the objective was to execute him.

The guy with the broadcst build, a six-foot six commando type with a square jaw, eyebrows back-slashed with battle scars, and blond hair in a regulation army crew-cut, stepped forward with an automatic revolver held at his side. Obviously, the top dog, he strode over to Alice and, towering over him, glaring with abject disdain, growled, "On your knees."

"If you insist," Al said compliantly. He knew the next step in the deadly game would be a bullet in the back of the head.

With his fingers locked together behind his head, Al sank to his knees, wondering how the hell he was going to cheat certain death this time...

Then, everything shimmered—and he knew.

The rumble of the conveyor and crusher ceased, and the four mercenaries froze. Relieved that the cavalry had arrived to save the day, Alice lowered his arms and, chuckling to himself, rose to his feet.

"Down to the bloody wire... isn't it always the case," he grumbled, shaking his head.

It was time to make mischief. He took hold of the big guy's gun arm and aimed it at the leg of the guy he'd knocked down, who was still on the ground. He pulled the trigger. Then, while the vortex was forming, he sauntered over to one of the other two agents. Both of them were holding pistols. He raised the gun arm of the first guy, targeted the thigh of the big dude with the crew cut, and then pulled the trigger. Then he swung the same gun arm to aim at the second agent beside him and pulled the trigger again. Pleased with the crossfire concept, he then went to the second guy and deftly manoeuvred his gun arm to aim at the first agent's foot and then pulled the trigger. Satisfied that his manipulation of the scene would render the four agents out of commission for the next few months, he dived headfirst into the vortex.

"How did you get yourself into that predicament?" Doctor Secta asked, holding open a robe for Alice.

Naked, Alice struggled to his feet and slipped on the robe. "Thanks... I've got no idea, mate, but I'll tell you it was looking grim. Great timing to get me out."

"Thank Karzoff for that, he insisted on locating you with a sensor drone when you went missing. Once he found you and saw you were outnumbered by a bunch of Zen goons, he asked us to activate Kairos."

"Lucky Karzoff was on the ball. I was about to meet my maker," Alice said, making light of it but at the same time looking up with a thankful smile at the ten-metre circular particle accelerator they called Kairos II, that he'd just come through.

"I thought the Professor was going to fix this arriving in the nuddy thing... for goodness sake, man," Alice complained.

"He's written a new algorithm that Robert hasn't installed yet."

Secta was referring to Dr Robert James, the OTT physicist, and Kairos designer.

They walked across the event room floor and entered the control room. Just as they did, Karzoff burst through another door and erupted jubilantly, "Alice, you made it!"

Alice gave the man with the bright red hair a friendly pat on the back. "Yep, thanks to you bud."

Robert swivelled in his chair from the console to face them.

"And you too, Rob, the vortex arrived just in the nick of time," Alice said. "But how did the drone locate me?"

"The Professor has been working with Karzoff on a miniaturised version of the isotopic labelling detection device... the ILDD we use to detect your DNA marker," Secta explained.

"We only fitted the prototype to a drone yesterday... and then when you went missing we decided to give it a try," Karzoff said, enthusiastically.

"Lucky you did," Alice acknowledged.

"Lucky it worked... it looked to me like that big bozo was about to give you a head full of lead. You should have seen the chaos once time unfroze," Karzoff said with a snigger. "It was as though they had all been shot by a phantom sniper. The drone recorded it all."

"Ha! Ha! Wow! Dig to see that," Alice said with a devious chuckle. "So, time didn't freeze for you watching it?"

"No, but I could see everyone except for you on-screen freeze, quite bizarre," Karzoff said.

"And incredibly interesting," Secta stated, holding his chin, mulling it over.

"The quantum time bubble must have a specific distance around the vortex," Rob proposed.

"Yes, I wonder how far?" Secta pondered.

"How did you get trapped by them in the first place, Alice?" Karzoff asked.

"Dunno, last thing I remember I was walking down Bent Street on the way to meet my bass player Ratsso for a drink at the Fortune of War pub at the Rocks," Al explained, scratching his head bemused. "Next minute I woke up in the car headed for crushing jaws. Must've got jumped."

"I'll get Hope to take some blood to test, but I'll put money on a tranquillizer dart," Secta proposed.

"Probably shot from a vehicle," Karzoff added. "We will need to lift security to code red. We have already set up quarters for you here, Alice. Far too dangerous for you on the street now this has happened."

Alice snarled at the idea of being kept prisoner in his own town.

Secta detected Alice's change in mood, aware he was uncomfortable with losing his independence, caught his eye, and said reassuringly, "You'll only have to stay here until the heat's off, Al. It's for your own safety."

"Yeah, yeah, yeah… I can dig it… listen, I've been meaning to ask you… I want to go back and save Stain. I reckon if I went back to the hospital I could stop her from being murdered."

Secta stared at Alice, mentally seeking the means to gently dissuade him of the idea.

"I'm afraid that isn't possible, Alice. It would change the timeline of everything that has happened since. Everything we've done could be undone. Do you understand that?" Secta implored.

"You mean if she lived, it would alter things and change now?"

"Yes."

"Then what about bringing Sonoko back from 2047, wouldn't that be the same thing only from the future and not the past?" Alice argued.

Secta knew he was right to a certain extent. He'd originally proposed the idea to Alice when he first returned from the last mission to 2047. He figured they could have his Japanese girlfriend from that time link up with the older Secta in Sydney, possibly for him to send her through Kairos IV, back in time to join Alice now. But it had been a spur of the moment thing. Since then he'd thought it through and realised it would be crossing the line of the prime directive. What if she was to get killed, would that mean she wouldn't be born? It was a risk they couldn't afford to take.

"Yes, it would be a problem, Alice. I'm sorry I proposed it… I was out of line," Secta admitted.

"But there's no reason why we couldn't bring her here for a short period of time, provided she was pretty much confined to quarters," Robert proposed.

They all got the gist of his idea, and a pregnant pause resulted while it was contemplated.

Then Karzoff spoke up. "We should have a safe house somewhere precisely for that purpose… someplace nice."

"Top idea, Karzoff, that would have worked better for Mal than the Professor's pad did. It'd need a chopper service to the helipad on the roof here," Al proposed.

"Yes exactly, since the attack at the Professor's apartment, we have been keeping Mal confined here. He only gets to go out for Presidential campaign events and even then, under maximum security," Karzoff explained as he headed to the door. He stopped, turned, and added, "I will go now and propose it to Vice President Corowa."

After the murder of the President, the Vice President had assumed office as acting President of Oceana in lieu of the coming election.

"Are the Graphene lenses comfortable, Alice?" Robert asked.

"Don't even notice them… but I'd give my right arm to try them out on Gorrick, see if he fluoresces."

Alice had been fitted with Graphene thermal infrared and UV smart contact lenses so he could see Neon fluoresce. The OTT scientific team had determined that all Gorrick clones had Neon in their DNA and that under certain conditions, it could be detected. It was the only means they had of identifying the real Gorrick; the matrix of the clone they figured to be En-Lil. If the DNA failed to fluoresce, then it had to be En-Lil who was the object of Alice's quest.

Alice needed to find En-Lil, who had over time created two thousand clones in his image to further his drive for world domination and the ultimate extermination of mankind. It had been En-Lil thousands of years ago who'd killed his brother En-Ki and entombed his consciousness in an orb in the 5th dimension. Alice's quest was to unlock En-Ki, and to that end, he needed to locate the key, which En-Ki had told him was the Tablet of Destinies, held in some obscure place by the evil En-Lil.

Alice was keen to test the lenses on the new Gorrick, who had just taken over the presidency of the Oceana chapter of Zen after the former Gorrick had been assassinated by OTT. It was critical to determine whether he was En-Lil or not. It would be very convenient if En-Lil was living right on their doorstep.

Over the next week, Karzoff arranged a safe house for Alice and Mal on the Hawkesbury River, just north of Sydney. It was a stunning ultra-modern two-storey house, the only structure on tiny isolated Pelican Island. Fully self-contained with its own water supply and pelleted nuclear power, it boasted a helipad and was completely camouflaged from the air and water. With an impenetrable perimeter security system, its location remained so secret that it didn't even show up on military ordinance maps or local council documentation. They aptly named it "The Lair."

Both Alice and Mal were pleased with Rita, the live-in maid provided, who cooked, cleaned, and attended to their general needs. The view of the river from the second-floor lounge room and patio was so spectacular that they made a habit of having breakfast on the balcony.

One morning, while having coffee after a delicious breakfast prepared by Rita, Alice stretched and yawned. "What's happening with Vee?"

Wearing sunglasses and also topless in his shorts with his bare feet up on a spare chair, Mal inhaled the eucalyptus-enriched air before answering, "Karzoff said she's undergoing training... apparently, whether she's really your sister or not, she's an excellent candidate for the security team."

"Yeah? How so?"

"She's a black belt in taekwondo."

"How old is she?"

"Eighteen," Mal said, then sipped his coffee. A kookaburra laughed from a nearby tree.

"She'd have had to have done five years to get a black belt."

"I understand she got it in three. Pretty impressive."

Alice fell silent, bothered by the prospect of her being put in danger by him. The conversation ended abruptly when Alice's cellphone rang. He knew it was either Secta or Karzoff because, for security reasons, they were the only ones with his number.

Mal noticed an immediate mood swing in Alice. He had been rather dour since they moved into The Lair.

Alice put the phone down on the table and grinned at his friend. "Guess who just arrived through Kairos?"

"Who?"

"Sonoko."

"Well, it's no wonder you're beaming a big smile, mate," Mal said happily.

"Yeah, she'll be here in an hour."

Alice left to shave off his three-day growth and change. Mal chuckled, glad to see his mate back to his old self again.

Sonoko was greeted by the OTT team and taken from Kairos into the control room. Hope sat her down and offered a warm drink as she was still shaky from the ordeal.

"This is hot chocolate, Sonoko... the reconstitution of your atomic structure leaves you feeling cold. We don't want you catching a chill, so please drink," Hope advised warmly.

"Thank you, Doctor Hope. Alice told me so much about you... and the Professor."

Secta, the Professor, and Robert came in from Kairos, where they had been checking something technical.

"How's the patient?" Secta asked Hope.

"Just got the shakes, you know how it is."

"Secta, you don't look much different than your older self; you aged gently in the future," Sonoko said.

"You flatter me. Did you meet anyone else there?"

"No, Secta said it was best not to, so that I did not cross the prime directive line, he called it," Sonoko said, her shivering lessening.

"That makes sense," Vic said. "Oh, I'm the Professor, by the way, but you can call me Vic. And this is Doctor Robert."

"I know all about you from Alice. Where is he?"

"We'll take you to him soon, but for now, we need to run a couple of tests just to make sure you're okay," Secta said.

"Your future self told me to tell you he used this," she felt the back of her neck. "It is instead of injecting me with a formula."

Hope checked and found a round button made of an organic substance adhered to her first vertebra.

"It's like one of those round Band-Aid patches," Hope said, holding back Sonoko's hair for Secta and the Professor to see.

"He said you must take it off and reverse-engineer it... because it will give you an added advantage in teleportation," Sonoko explained.

Hope carefully peeled the patch off and handed it to the Professor.

He held it on the tip of his index finger for the three of them to study.

"The work is marvellous," Secta said, peering at it in awe.

"The circuitry seems to be crystal," Vic added.

"So, with it, anyone can travel through Kairos without the serum?" Hope concluded.

"Exactly. Hope, it's all yours to unravel and duplicate," Secta said.

"I'll get on it right away," she said, up to the challenge. "Look, it has something printed on it."

They looked closer. "Yes, it says clock drive," Hope read.

"Huh, that makes sense... a clock drive, it allows the projection through time. Clever," Vic proposed.

"Thank you," Secta said smugly, knowing he had invented it, albeit in the future.

The presidential election was only a week away, and Mal was having doubts as to whether he had made the right decision to run. So far, it had turned his life upside down, costing him the freedom he so valued. Now, he was beginning to wonder whether he'd ever get that freedom back.

As Rita poured him a fresh coffee, he stared in a trance at the sparkling sunlight on the blue waters of the Hawkesbury River, resigned to the notion that he was destined to be president and that he had to accept the loss of his freedom as the price for the highest office in the land.

Time skipped by like a fleeting shadow, and it wasn't long before he noticed a black speck in the sky, accompanied by the familiar thwop-thwop-thwop of beating chopper blades.

Minutes later, Alice and Mal were standing on the rooftop helipad, watching the Eurocopter AS 350 descending from the sky like a giant insect.

The downdraft from the rotors hammered them like a gale force wind, and when the big white-painted six-seater chopper touched down and the engine wound down, all fell silent, and the chaos of the moment dissipated like a puff of smoke in a breeze.

The side door slid open, and the fine, slight figure of the beautiful Sonoko stepped out. Upon seeing Alice, she raced across the rooftop with open arms as fast as her black Converse Chuck Taylor's would carry her and locked him in a passionate embrace. Mal smiled, seeing them together and recognising that they were a perfect match.

CHAPTER 2
PHANTOM

T HE FAILURE OF the mission to eliminate Alice had Honor nervous about meeting Gorrick. This was the first action of Zen Espionage Operative, ZEO, a security force she had painstakingly assembled from an international database of highly skilled and accomplished mercenaries. She hadn't expected four of the best soldiers on the market to be so badly outdone by Alice unaided. Restless in her seat alone at the boardroom table, she checked herself in her compact makeup mirror. The regrowth of her short-cropped hair, which she had dyed platinum blonde, looked neat. Her tapered black eyebrows, carefully sculptured, framed the long black lashes of her almond-shaped brown eyes. She had dispensed with the bright red lipstick that used to match the red piping of her Oceana uniform, opting for a classic dark red that better suited her new hair colour. Dressed in a grey business suit, she looked nothing like her former self. Doctor Li's surgery had transformed not only her face but also her entire personality. The door opened, and she quickly concealed the compact in her black Ostridge skin briefcase.

Gorrick entered the room carrying an iPad and quietly took a seat at the head of the table; his dark mood clouded the atmosphere like a noxious gas.

He deliberately placed the iPad on the table in front of him, reclined in his chair with a grave look on his chiselled face, and then said gruffly, "Good morning, Honor. I find it most disconcerting that the four members of your elite ZEO security force are out of commission due to wounds they received from having shot each other. Care to explain?"

It was the question she dreaded most. "Sir, they had Black Alice at their mercy, then in the blink of an eye, they shot each other, and Alice disappeared. It can only be assumed he had escaped through a wormhole. It is known that a period of time lapse occurs when a wormhole first opens. During that short period, only the time traveller is unaffected, so it is fair to conclude that Alice somehow tampered with our men—frozen in time—before he entered the wormhole to affect an escape. Then, once it closed, they awakened, and the incident occurred. It is the only explanation, sir."

Gorrick was slowly nodding his head. "So, you're saying he altered their aim and pulled the trigger while they were frozen, so that when they awoke, their guns discharged?"

"Yes, sir, none of them sustained a fatal wound, all of them were shot in a limb. That meant he was trying to demobilise them only."

"How did OTT manage to open a wormhole to him?"

"We don't know that, sir, unless they had surveillance tracking him."

"Hmm, that makes sense. Nevertheless, it is difficult to accept that no matter what we throw at him, he always manages to outdo us. It is a waste of resources trying to eliminate him... we need to change our tack," he said resolutely.

Honor was relieved he had accepted her theory—the shroud of darkness had lifted; her day was looking a little brighter.

"What's the update on the presidential candidate?" he asked.

"Malcolm Low, formerly Mal Function. We think OTT has moved him to a safe house until the election is over."

"Yeah, I get that. Again, a waste of resources trying to take him out; we need to focus on our own agenda rather than constantly worrying about theirs." He stood up and stared out of the window at

Sydney Harbour. "I have asked Professor Adamski to bring me up to speed on his progress... I want you to stay and listen."

Honor watched him open his iPad and press an app. Almost instantly, the door opened for a small, balding man to nervously bumble his way into the room.

Adamski took the nearest seat and with a trembling hand opened his iPad on the table in front of him, and then, peering through the thick lenses of his horn-rimmed spectacles at the others, his face twitched into something that resembled a smile.

"Your report, Professor?" Gorrick said fervently, still standing.

The Russian replied nervously, "I... I... have completed a budget to build a wormhole generator as requested. Many of the components are available to us from other Zen chapters."

Gorrick took a seat. "How long to build it?"

"Provided we can get the components I mentioned... six to eight months."

"Are you certain it will work?" Gorrick questioned.

"The computer modelling indicates so, I have no reason to doubt it... the premise is predicated on accurate science," Adamski said assuredly.

"Tell me, would there be any advantage in having the blueprint of the OTT teleporter?" Gorrick queried.

"No and yes, the science is the same, but it is always nice to compare, I expect... after all, Kairos is a working unit," Adamski said, with a shrug of his shoulders.

Gorrick rose to his feet, towering over Honor and Adamski, and said, "Thank you, Professor... please present your budget to finance and copy me."

Adamski had noticeably relaxed since presenting his report. Once he had left the room, Gorrick returned to the window, his back to Honor. "The budget won't be approved until we have compared his numbers and design with Kairos," he said, turning to face her. "We can't risk it failing; there is too much at stake. Get me the blueprint of Kairos."

Honor rose from the chair slowly, conscious of the difficulty in fulfilling Gorrick's request. "Will that be all, sir?" she said with unease.

"Yes, thank you, Honor," he said curtly, then turned back to face the window.

She left the boardroom, wondering how on earth to get her hands on the blueprint.

Her new office was on the same floor as the boardroom, only a short walk down the hallway. It was small, with a nice old-world styled timber-panelled reception area.

Seated demurely behind an antique office desk was her newly appointed secretary, Layla Migden. An attractive lass of nineteen, Layla had short-cropped blue-black hair worn messy with lots of product, black sculptured eyebrows, and square, grey-rimmed glasses that emphasised her azure blue eyes. Her bright red painted lips set her look off as more rock than roll than expected.

When Honor entered, she immediately noticed Professor Adamski standing, looking out of the window. "Professor, what can I do for you?" Honor asked curtly.

Adamski turned and, with a solemn look on his square face, said, "If you have time, could I have a word in private?"

"Certainly," Honor said, intrigued, with a raised eyebrow. "Layla, bring me a coffee... anything for you, Professor?"

"No, I'm fine."

Honor led him into her office and stopped just inside the room. Towering over him, she gestured at the small lounge setting. "Take a seat, professor."

"Please, let's dispense with the formalities, call me Uri," he said as he sat.

Honor sat opposite him and crossed her shapely legs, and he couldn't help but notice. "I thought it best to speak to you about this matter... As regards the report I gave Gorrick on the progress of the wormhole generator... there is a problem I failed to mention."

"Go on."

"All the technical aspects of my design will work without the need for the Kairos blueprint, which I am sure Gorrick has asked you to obtain. Having the blueprint will not make any difference to the problem I have, which, simply put, is the transference of a human through a wormhole generator. You see, the subject would first need to be broken down to atoms for transportation and then reconstituted at the other end, and... well, we do not have any such formula."

She detected a grimace of anxiety on the little man's angular face. "You are talking about Doctor Secta's dematerialising formula, I presume?"

He stammered, "Ah... Y... Yes."

"And you need it and not the blueprint?" she queried.

"Well, it would certainly be of benefit to have the blueprint of Kairos, but we cannot do without Secta's formula."

"You are right that I have been tasked with obtaining the blueprint, and let me tell you, I have no idea how—"

He sat forward in his chair and cut her off. "Perhaps I can help with that... I have friends in the Russian mafia, Black Hat hackers... I could put you in touch with them."

Honor reclined in her chair, finding the idea of a hack-attack appealing.

There was a knock at the door, and Layla entered with a mug of coffee. Adamski's eyes couldn't help but roam as she passed him to serve Honor the coffee.

When she turned to leave, she caught his eye, and he stared at her.

Honor broke the moment. "That might just work for the blueprint, but not for the formula."

"No, for that, I have another idea. Kew was vaccinated with the dematerialising formula. All we need do is free him, and I can isolate it from his blood."

Honor picked up her mug, and with a smug smirk on her face, took a sip. The idea that Kew was carrying the key to the entire Zen wormhole project had a certain ring of irony about it that appealed to her warped sense of justice. She knew that once she had obtained authorisation from Gorrick to free Kew, it would then give her control over the man who had cheated on her by having an affair with Lizzy Li.

"I think your plan is viable, Uri, but I will first need to run it past Gorrick."

"But if he finds out the project is dependent on the formula and that I failed to mention it, I—"

"Have no fear, Uri, I will calm the waters with him. Just put me in contact with your hacker friend and leave the rest to me."

It had been a night of celebration at The Lair, with Alice, Sonoko, and Mal trotting off to bed in the wee small hours of the morning, quite tipsy.

Alice woke with a start, feeling there was someone else in the room. Remaining motionless, he checked on Sonoko at his side and found her sleeping soundly. It was a large bedroom with a massive king-size bed. The crack of dawn was visible through the eastern bedroom window. A shadow moved in his peripheral vision. He froze and pretended to be asleep, but through squinting eyes, he watched the spectral shape of a man approach him. He readied himself. When the figure got near, he planned to jump up and confront the intruder. But what happened next had him even more perplexed. The shadow moved around the footboard of the bed then up beside Sonoko. Then, before Alice could react, it seemed to dive into Sonoko's body and disappeared.

Alice lay there for a time, wondering if he had been dreaming or if it were the effects of the boozy night. He sat up sharply, realising it was no dream. He had definitely seen a sketchy ghost slip into Sonoko's sleeping body.

A couple of hours later, Alice came out of the en-suite bathroom with a towel wrapped around his waist. Sonoko sat up in bed and yawned. Alice needed an explanation of what he had seen at dawn, and the only person who could provide it was Secta.

"Take a shower, babe. I've got an important call to make, then we'll have breakfast on the balcony with Mal, okay?"

She smiled, never making a fuss about anything, one of the things he liked most about her.

Sonoko hopped out of bed and happily made for the bathroom.

An hour later, Alice and Mal were seated under a big umbrella on the balcony, being served by Rita when Sonoko joined them.

Alice had phoned Secta and told him there was something important he needed to discuss. Knowing Alice wouldn't express concern without good reason, Secta agreed to fly to The Lair to discuss it in person.

It wasn't long before Mal sighted the chopper approaching. Alice went upstairs to the rooftop helipad to meet Secta, while Sonoko and Mal stayed on the balcony, chatting.

Secta stepped out of the chopper with Hope. Alice took them downstairs, leaving the chopper pilot with the aircraft to fill in flight plans, etc. Instead of taking them to the balcony, he took them to a study on the ground floor and locked the door behind them. They sat in a small lounge setting surrounded by an extensive library.

"All this cloak and dagger stuff isn't your game, Alice. What's up?" Secta asked, intrigued.

"It's no game, Secta. Last night, just before dawn, I woke up, and out of the corner of my eye, I watched a shadowy figure of a man in the bedroom. While I was keeping a sly eye on him, he slipped inside Sonoko's body and disappeared."

"What?" Secta and Hope said in unison, with looks of astonishment.

"Like a ghost or something?" Hope questioned.

"Exactly, only it had no features, it was a silhouette like a bloody cardboard cut-out... two-dimensional," Alice said, with a look of incredulity.

Secta thought it through and then asked, "I hate to suggest this, but it wasn't a dream, was it?"

"Absolutely not, that was the first thing I thought... nar, the thing came out of her and then returned... it's still inside her... spooky is what I call it... I can hardly look her in the eye without thinking of the damn thing."

Hope reached a comforting hand across the coffee table and patted Alice's shoulder. "You'll have to talk to Sonoko about it, Al. You can't let it get to you."

"Perhaps it has something to do with the Graphene lenses?" Secta posed.

"Could he be seeing something that exists in the UV or ultraviolet spectrum?" Hope queried.

"Possibly so," Secta said, getting to his feet. Even though it was a confined space, Secta still managed to pace the room.

CHAPTER 3
THE ID

S ECTA STOPPED PACING, having an idea. "What if
something came through the wormhole with Sonoko?"

"What, like a stowaway?" Al queried.

"Yes, a phantom." He had a revelation. "What if there are beings
who inhabit wormholes?"

"What a bizarre thought," Hope mumbled, bemused, "but then
again, we know so little about wormholes, it might be possible."

"Wait a minute, are you two saying this thing might be some sort
of alien species that lives in wormholes and has possessed Sonoko?"

"Couldn't have put it better myself, Alice. Yes, possibly made her
its host," Secta said with a look of scientific curiosity on his pale face.
"You're going to have to communicate with it, Alice."

"What, talk to the freaking thing? What makes you think it can
talk, let alone speak English?" Alice argued.

"It doesn't matter what language it speaks, Al. You'll understand
it; we just need to determine if it's benign or not, and the only way to
do that is to communicate with it," Secta stressed.

"He's right, Al... At the end of the day, if it was a threat, it would
have attacked you last night, wouldn't it?" Hope proposed.

"Yeah, I s'pose so," Al pondered. "Why don't we take her to the
lab and do it there, this morning?"

"How? Lock her in a booth and ask the creature to come out and
talk?" Secta chuckled at his own gag. "No, what you saw was a shadow.

I suspect it might only be able to materialise in the dark when it's safe for it to blend in with other shadows. I think it would be better if you were to ambush it tonight."

Hope asked, "Should he tell Sonoko?"

"No, not yet. Let's wait until he's has made contact. We wouldn't want to stress her unduly."

"Stress her? Hey, what about me?" Alice grumbled.

"Hope, are you a time traveller too?" Sonoko asked. She was seated at an oval table, having a post-dinner conversation with Hope, Secta, Mal, and Alice. The discussion was prompted by a quality pinot noir.

"No, I'm not tough enough. I steer clear of all the rough stuff; I'm just a lab-rat," Hope said dismissively.

"Oh yeah, so what about the two guards you belted when we escaped Oceana to stop the ferry?" Alice argued. "If that ain't tough, nothing is."

"That was self-defence," Hope admitted, blushing.

Mal took a swig of wine and then said, "Yeah, sure lady, if my memory serves me well, not long after that you drove a motorbike off the end of a wharf, leapt off it mid-air, and landed on the roof of a moving ferry thirty metres out in the water from the wharf."

"Yes, well, I'd missed the boat, hadn't I?" Hope admitted with a cute snigger.

Secta chimed in, "We wouldn't have any of this time travel technology without my sister here."

Now Hope was really blushing. It was rare to get such praise from her big brother.

"Way too much flattery, I'm overwhelmed," she complained with humility.

"Al, while you were with this beautiful woman here in Japan in 2047, I caught up with TC," Mal said. "You remember him?"

"Sure, the bloke to see when the band needed a gig," Alice chuckled. "The fixer... a serious character."

"Right-on. So, he tells me that old six fingers Charlie turned up at his place with a boat on a trailer... a brand new tinny with a twenty-horse outboard on the transom."

"Why is he called six finger Charlie?" Sonoko asked Alice in broken English.

Normally Alice and Sonoko would speak in Japanese, but with the others at the table, it was better manners to speak English, even though for Sonoko that meant it would be a little broken at times.

"Because he has six fingers on one hand, Sonoko," Alice explained, "An extra thumb, isn't it Mal?"

The idea of someone having an extra digit had Sonoko intrigued.

"Yeah, two thumbs on one hand," Mal explained, and then carried on with his story. "So, six fingers had obviously knocked the boat off and wanted to flog to TC to pay off a gambling debt. Apparently, a couple of Eastern Suburbs villains were after his butt for the bugs."

"What bugs?" Sonoko whispered to Alice.

"Bugs Bunny; money... rhyming slang," Alice whispered back.

"He wanted four grand for the boat, so TC offered him two and a half. After a bit of haggling TC got if for twenty-eight hundred," Mal said.

"What would TC want with a fricking tinny, he's got a gammy leg and definitely not the fishing type?" Al chuckled.

Mal topped up his glass and then continued. Secta, Hope and Sonoko absorbed by the story. Rita arrived with a fresh bottle of pinot and topped up the other glasses.

"Yeah, I know," Mal continued. "Anyway, about an hour later he gets a bell from Billy the Viper calling to say he'd been elected general manager of the Yarra Bay Yacht Club. Now the Viper, as you well know Al, is the classic tea-leaf."

"What tea-leaf?" Sonoko whispered to Alice.

"Rhyming Aussie slang again, tea-leaf; thief," Alice said.

Sonoko nodded her head with a furrowed brow, unconvinced, yet trying desperately to follow the story.

"So, for the Viper to be the general manager of a club there had to be a rort going on and TC wondered why the call. Viper said he was looking for something for a club raffle and figured TC might be in the know. So, TC said he had just the thing; a brand-new boat, engine and trailer. Impressed, the Viper asked how much and TC said five grand. The Viper could only do four but had an idea and they settled on it. On the day of the raffle TC turned up at the club towing the boat behind his car. It was a huge turnout loads of punters all buying tickets to try and win first prize: the boat and engine — touted at being worth six grand. When the Viper drew the winning ticket out of a barrel and announced the number, a voice shouted from the crowd he had it, and who do you reckon it was? TC. He collected the prize, hooked it back up on his car and drove home. The next day the Viper called around to TC's joint to collect a grand, his kick-back from TC for buying the boat for the raffle."

Alice was most amused and chuckled, "So, TC ended up getting the boat for free."

"Yep, and sold it a week later for three grand," Mal said.

"Viper had palmed the winning ticket. What a classic," said Alice.

"TC should be your minister for finance, Mal," Secta said with a snigger.

"You know that's a definite consideration," Mal joked.

"So, the election is in four days, what's your gut feeling Mal... will you win?" Hope asked.

"Hard to say. But there doesn't seem to be much opposition," Mal admitted.

"What is election for?" Sonoko asked.

"Mal is running for President of Oceana," Alice told her.

"Oh really, I think you make very good president Mal," Sonoko said with a big smile.

"I'll drink to that," Alice said, raising his glass. "To the next President of Oceana... Malcolm Low."

Secta, Hope and Sonoko raised their glasses in toast to Mal.

It was getting late and they'd polished off half a dozen bottles of pinot, so they were a wee bit wobbly. Secta and Hope would stay overnight in guest rooms. It had thus been secretly planned, so that in the morning they could discuss Alice's attempt to communicate with the phantom.

After all the wine she had consumed, it didn't take long for Sonoko to drift off to sleep, leaving Alice beside her in the dark with one eye open, waiting for a sign of the spectre. Time was creeping past at a snail's pace, and just as he was about to nod off, he watched a human silhouetted form slowly rising out of Sonoko's prostrate body.

The first thought that struck him was how to speak to it without waking Sonoko up, so he decided to whisper. "Hey you..."

It froze three quarters of the way out of Sonoko's body and looked sharply at Alice. The fact that it understood him sent a chill up his spine. Its face had no features... no eyes, nothing.

"Don't be afraid, I only want to talk with you, come with me to the bathroom so we don't wake Sonoko," Alice whispered bravely.

Hoping it understood him, he gently slipped out of bed and moved quietly to the bathroom, leaving the door slightly ajar to let some moonlight beam in from the bedroom window.

It was a large bathroom. Alice sat on the toilet, looking towards the door to see if the phantom had followed him. It manifested in front of him, shimmering slightly like a mirage.

"I am surprised you can see me," it said.

Alice wasn't sure if it was speaking English or if his translator chip was interpreting some other language, but it didn't matter; he understood anyway.

"I'm fitted with special contact lenses that see in UV and infrared."

"Ah, that explains it... UV is the bandwidth I have chosen," it said.

"Right... so who are you?"

"I am of the Id, and I am here to help you."

"The Id, what's that, a species?"

"We have been on Earth for thousands of years, brought here by En-Ki to hunt Dreamraiders."

The mention of En-Ki immediately clicked with Al, "Aha, now I get it... that means we have plenty to discuss."

"We do," it said.

"Why didn't En-Ki tell me about you?" Alice queried.

"Because, in his ethereal state, he wouldn't know if any of us have survived. We were originally twenty-four, brought here by En-Ki through a wormhole, but when he ceased to exist, the wormhole closed, leaving us stranded on Earth. Over time, Dreamraiders have killed most of the Id on Earth. Now I am the sole survivor. I detected wormholes opening some months back, but they closed too quickly for me to get to them, so I decided to hitch a ride with Sonoko to find you."

"How do you know about me?" Alice asked.

"I monitor my enemies, and they have become increasingly concerned about the threat you pose to them, Black Alice."

"By them, you mean Zen?"

"Yes, Zen, Gorrick, En-Lil, Amon, and the Dreamraiders."

With his eyes now adjusted to the dark, Alice could distinguish the features of the Id more clearly. For instance, he wasn't really just a black two-dimensional silhouette. In fact, he was dark purple and three-dimensional. He also noticed the Id was wearing a complete tight-fitted bodysuit, sort of like a Spiderman costume only deep purple. When the Id turned his head, Alice could see his facial profile. He had a square jaw, a prominent nose, but his eyes and mouth were indistinguishable. At about five eleven, he had a wiry but muscular physique. All the muscles were in the right places... Alice thought... this could be one tough dude.

They talked for hours, and then just before dawn, the Id told Alice he needed to return to a host, otherwise exposure to UVC in sunlight would kill him. It was then Alice got an unexpected shock; the Id wanted him to be the host.

"It won't hurt, Alice, you won't even know I'm there. However, if you want, you can communicate with me mentally, or speak to me out loud, and I will answer through you. Or if you want to summon me physically, I can do that where there is no UVC."

"This reminds me of when I possessed someone," Alice said, thinking of when he had materialised inside the body of Turk in 2087. So, the concept of having a conversation in thoughts wasn't foreign to him, even though this time round the roles would be reversed; this time he would be the one possessed.

"You need to understand you were destined for the quest, because you are gifted with the shine."

"The shine? Now that rings a bell. The first time I travelled in time, there was Ex and Djard... and the Shine... I gave it to a chick at a wharf... it was an amulet," Al recalled. A whole lot had gone on since then, but it was all coming back to him.

"You were gifted with it... it is the key to the future."

"You sound like En-Ki talking. Are you saying I was chosen for this gig?" Alice said.

"Yes, I've been waiting millenniums for you."

The Id took a couple of steps forward and melded into Alice's unsuspecting body. Al felt a little shiver ripple through him, and then nothing.

"You could have told me you were going to do that... Now that I've got you on-board, what do I call you?" Al thought.

"My name is Neit."

CHAPTER 4
TROJAN HORSE

HONOR KEYED SECTA'S email address, followed by the IP address of the OTT hub, into the dark net chat app on her computer. Adamski had given her the app to connect her with Lazarus, the Russian Mafia hacker group he'd recommended to obtain the blueprint of Kairos.

Honor had figured Secta's email address would be the best bet. She still had all the OTT email addresses and the IP details from when she was head of OTT security, and she hoped that Karzoff, the new head, would be consistent and hadn't bothered to change them after she had defected.

The services of the Lazarus Group weren't coming cheap; they wanted a million in crypto deposited in a nominated account before starting. Honor had cleared the amount with Gorrick, but it hadn't been easy. Gorrick wasn't happy that Adamski had failed to inform him that his wormhole generator design was dependent on more from OTT to function than he'd first maintained. It was why he'd resisted funding approval for the project, and his doubts had been confirmed. However, it was such an important undertaking that he gave his approval to use Lazarus and for Honor to determine a means to rescue Kew. He was now a critical element—they needed the dematerialising agent from his blood.

A million in crypto had been transferred. The Lazarus connection acknowledged receipt, and the hack commenced.

Honor sat back, satisfied with her efforts. Provided Secta's email address and the IP server address were still active, the hackers would be able to obtain all OTT correspondence over the last twenty-four months. She knew that was how long the data stayed on the OTT server. Now all she needed to do was work out how to nab Kew from the clutches of OTT. It was a challenge she would enjoy, an opportunity for revenge on Karzoff. She blamed him for the Anu Set suicide bomb terrorist attack on the Zen offices that had maimed her, wounded Kew, Doctor Li, and killed Gorrick and Doctor Chu.

Secta, Hope, and Mal were on the balcony of The Lair having breakfast when Alice joined them, looking worse for wear after minimal sleep.

"Al, looks like you could do with one of my eggnog bloody Mary's; best hair of the dog remedy on the planet," Mal boasted jovially.

"Damn right I could, mate," Alice groaned, flopping into a chair.

It was a warm sunny day with kookaburras and a tribe of magpies noisy reminders that The Lair was on an isolated island in the middle of a river.

When Mal hopped up and headed for the kitchen to concoct his legendary hangover elixir, Alice took the opportunity to chat privately with Secta and Hope.

Lowering his voice, he said, "The phantom and I are now the best of mates; in fact, I'm now possessed by him."

"You're kidding," Hope said, recoiling in shock.

"I'll fill you in on it all later... you'll find it very interesting. After breakfast, let's go to Kairos to continue talks with Neit of the Id in private."

Rita arrived to take Alice's breakfast order, and Sonoko followed her closely.

"The Id you say?" Secta queried quietly.

"Freud claimed that is the part of the human mind in which innate instinctive impulses and primary processes are manifest... the Id, ego, and superego... the model of the human psyche," Hope explained, as though reading from a psychology manual.

"Good morning," Sonoko announced as she took a seat beside Alice.

"Oh yes, oh yes," came a sexy, breathy cry from Secta's phone. He chuckled, "It's my new ringtone. Wonderful, isn't it?" He stood up and moved to the balcony railing to take the call. A few minutes later, he returned to his seat and said, "Karzoff has called an urgent OTT meeting in an hour."

Just then, Mal returned carrying a glass full of vegetation. He handed it to Alice. "Are you going back to town? I've got a television interview, so I can go with you."

Alice took a sip of Mal's elixir, and his eyes opened wide. "Blood-hell Mal!" he all but screamed, "What's in this?"

"Hmm, I might have been a bit heavy-handed on the Tabasco," Mal admitted with a wince.

Alice could only nod vigorously in agreement, busy preventing his head from exploding.

Sonoko was left on her own while the others left in the chopper for the city. She didn't mind; it presented her with the opportunity on such a lovely day to explore Pelican Island.

It wasn't long before Alice, Secta, and Hope were in the OTT boardroom sitting opposite Karzoff and Viktoria.

"There has been a cyber-attack on the OTT server," Karzoff said gravely. "That is the bad news, the good news is it was the old server... the one we used before Honor jumped ship, so they got nothing."

"Nevertheless, it tells us something. Firstly, the attack came from Russia, secondly, that someone is after something they think was on the server, and finally, there is only one person other than us who would've known the IP address... Honor," Viktoria said with a smirk.

"Honor?" Hope questioned.

"Yes, we think this proves she is still alive and functioning as a Zen agent," Karzoff explained.

Secta got up and began pacing. "What on Earth could they be after?"

Just then the Professor came barging into the room in a fluster. "Sorry I'm late, everyone, I've been in the Kairos control room all night installing the new software with Rob, you know how time flies there—pardon the pun. Oh Alice, you'll be happy to know you can now pass through Kairos without losing your clothes—the days of nude arrivals are over."

"Three cheers for that!" Al said.

The Professor took a seat. "What have I missed?"

"The OTT server has been hacked," Alice told him.

"I think Zen are after the design plans of Kairos," Secta posed.

"That makes sense, with Adamski there they'd have to be utilising his ingenuity to build a wormhole generator...otherwise they wouldn't be able to keep him," the Professor submitted.

"What have you done about the attack, Karzoff?" Secta asked.

"Nothing yet. They cannot retrieve any data because they cannot get through the new firewall."

"Okay, we'll leave that for a moment because there's another pressing matter. We've discovered that when Sonoko came through Kairos, a phantom came with her," Secta said.

"Are you serious?" Karzoff asked, bemused.

"Yes, it's confirmed, because this creature now inhabits Alice. I'll let him explain."

Karzoff jumped up. "Are you saying this thing is here? Now, in this room! That is a breach of security!" Karzoff asserted angrily.

"Sit down, Karzoff, chill-out, the dude's okay, his name is Neit, and he's of the Id... we had a long discussion last night," Al said calmly.

It took a little time for Alice to tell them all he could remember about the meeting with Neit. The picture was clear; Neit was on their side. In conclusion, he introduced Neit to them.

Speaking through Alice, Neit said, "It is important we understand one another. I am happy to answer any of your questions no matter how scientific, but first, you need to know something very important. When I first came to Earth with twenty-three comrades thousands of years ago, it was to hunt down and kill Dreamraiders. If you haven't heard of them, Dreamraiders are demons... at the time there were seventy-two of them on Earth. They are shape-shifters who occupy a host's posterior cortical hot zone, a region of the brain that includes visual areas as well as areas involved in integrating the senses. We know this because it is the same place we can occupy. Dreamraiders, as their name implies, enter the dreams of humans and from there they can jump from one person's dream to another's. They are the evil creatures from which the myths of vampires, gargoyles, the Mare, the Jinn, and others have evolved. When En-Ki and En-Lil clashed, En-Lil, known in the demon world as Amon, employed necromancy to summon the seventy-two demons of the Pantheon of Goetia to be his army. To counter this threat, En-Ki enlisted the aid of the Id. However, En-Ki was ultimately defeated, and his consciousness was imprisoned in an orb. As a result, our exit wormhole closed, leaving us stranded on Earth. I am the last surviving Id on Earth; the others have perished, slain by Dreamraiders. Over time, we, the hunters, became the hunted. As far as I know, there are no Dreamraiders left on Earth. However, while monitoring the enemy, I have learned that Dreamraiders have once again been summoned. This time, they are here to confront Amon's newest menace... Black Alice."

"So, you can jump from one person to another, and once inside that person, can you read their mind?" Secta inquired.

"Yes," Neit confirmed.

"That gives me an idea. Karzoff, feed the Russian hackers a bunch of useless data. Let's include an early blueprint of Kairos that didn't work. Also, give them an e-mail from you to me, stating that we'll move Kew by car to the old bunker in Avalon for safekeeping tomorrow at noon," Secta proposed.

"And will we actually do that?" Viktoria asked.

"Yes," Secta affirmed.

"So, you are giving Kew back to them. I remind you he assassinated the president?" Karzoff questioned, seemingly unimpressed.

"But we can't prove it," Viktoria stated.

"I reckon the president would endorse using Kew as bait," Al snarled.

"Indeed... as a Trojan horse," Secta added with a smug grin.

Honor sat at her desk, sifting through all the data she had received, forwarded by Lazarus from the hack. She struck gold when she found an email on the screen with an attachment containing the blueprint of Kairos. Just as she was about to call it a night, satisfied that the money had been well spent, she stumbled upon an email from Karzoff to Secta, dated today. Intrigued, she opened it and was surprised to find a notice that Kew would be moved by car from Oceana HQ to the bunker in Avalon tomorrow at noon. She leaned back in her chair, feeling as if the stars had finally aligned for her. It was an incredible stroke of luck to find this email. She immediately called Gorrick's secretary and requested to see him right away.

Fifteen minutes later, Honor breezed into Gorrick's office, feeling as if she was walking on a cloud.

Gorrick looked up at her from the computer monitor on his desk and asked sharply, "Honor, what's so urgent?"

She approached his desk and handed him a flash drive. "There are two files on this drive that you'll find interesting."

He inserted the drive into the USB port and opened the first file. "Aha, the blueprint of Kairos. Well, that's excellent... and," he opened the next file. "An email... well, well, it seems our friend Kew will be moved tomorrow. This is like music to my ears. Do you think it's a little too convenient to find this?"

"No, sir, they have no idea that we are planning to liberate him, and they are unaware of the hack," she replied confidently.

"Good. Then get the blueprint to Adamski. What is your plan regarding Kew?"

"I will deliver him to you by tomorrow night, I promise," Honor said slowly, savouring the moment.

Later that night, Secta paid Kew a visit, armed with a potent sedative. Once Kew was unconscious, Secta turned off the light and opened the door, allowing Alice to join him in the dark cell.

Secta locked the door as they exited the cell and headed for the elevator. "I think I should get fitted with graphene lenses so I can see Neit too."

"That'd be helpful," Alice agreed.

"Can he move around in the dark, or can he only jump from one body to another?" Secta inquired.

As they entered the elevator, Alice explained, "He said he can move around freely in the dark, but prolonged exposure to UVB can harm him."

"Yes, and full-spectrum fluorescent lights emit UVB as well. He'd have to be cautious, although they probably wouldn't emit enough radiation to cause significant harm—maybe just blister his skin if he has any. Did he mention where he's from?"

"He said he and twenty-two others were brought here through a wormhole by En-Ki, but I didn't ask about their origin."

"That would make him thousands of years old. I'd love to get a blood and DNA sample from him for study. Encountering another species is a rare opportunity," Secta mused with the curiosity of a true scientist.

The elevator doors opened, and they entered the corridor leading to the OTT head office.

"I'll head back to The Lair, unless you need me here."

"No Alice, go spend more time with Sonoko. She must be wondering what the hell is going on with you," Secta suggested.

"Yeah, I think I better tell her."

"Agreed."

CHAPTER 5
THE RIFT

T HE NEXT DAY, Karzoff received the expected call. The vehicle transporting Kew to Avalon had been ambushed, and the prisoner was taken without any casualties. He promptly informed the others.

Alice was preparing to depart from The Lair by chopper to OTT when he received the call. Delighted that their hunch had paid off, he headed down to the indoor swimming pool on the lower level of the opulent home to inform Sonoko of his departure. As he entered the well-lit, tiled room, he paused by the edge of the pool to admire Sonoko swimming gracefully in the clear azure water. When she spotted him, she swam over and, sleek as a panther, emerged from the water. Alice held her in his arms and helped her to her feet.

Just then, an incoming text alert sounded on Alice's cell phone, indicating that the chopper had arrived.

"A chopper's arriving, I have to go. I'll probably be back tomorrow morning... maybe sooner," Alice explained.

"No problem, my darling. I will wait for you," Sonoko replied sweetly before slipping back into the warm water.

A few minutes later, Sonoko heard the chopper land on the rooftop helipad and then take off again with its passenger. She got out of the pool and put on a robe. The clock on the wall at far end of the rectangular pool showed eight thirty; it was time for breakfast. As she headed towards the door, the entire room shimmered, and the lights flickered. She steadied herself against the wall, thinking it might be an earthquake.

She wondered, "I thought this only happens in Tokyo?"

Time froze—the clock on the wall stopped — all sound ceased and Sonoko became motionless mid-stride as though snap-frozen.

A jagged horizontal lightning bolt, about two metres in length, appeared in the air a metre off the floor, very close to Sonoko. It glowed along its leading edge, as if behind it was a wall of molten magma. Unlike a conventional lightning bolt, this one didn't disappear in a flash; instead, it hung in the air, pulsating like a living, breathing entity. Surrounding it, a swirling fury of arching blue and green electric energy rolled and crackled explosively, reminiscent of atomic fusion.

However, Sonoko couldn't hear it, nor could she smell the sulfuric stench that usually accompanies molten magma. She was frozen, and the existence of the tear in the fabric of time remained unknown to her.

The rift had intentionally been opened as close as possible to the last person who had been teleported through a wormhole, which happened to be Sonoko. The fracture stretched like an umbilical cord into another dimension, allowing a vile, evil demon to travel through.

Slime began to ooze out of the crack, and a clawed hand emerged, followed by a grotesque creature forcing its way out as though the rift was a birth canal. It flopped onto the floor, enveloped in slime, and slowly rose onto its clawed feet, snarling like a Velociraptor. The creature was naked, with dark olive-green, scaled reptilian skin, and a grotesque head reminiscent of the gargoyles seen on medieval European churches. Its dog-like muzzle was filled with pointed teeth, while its human-like arms and thighs were thickly muscled. Evil yellow eyes with vertical pupils, like those of a cat, darted around the room before settling on Sonoko, who stood motionless.

As quickly as it had opened, the rift closed, and all fell silent. But before Sonoko could regain consciousness, the grotesque creature dematerialised into a black vapor, which then entered her body. However, the crack in time had not entirely disappeared, leaving a small, luminous ten-centimetre hairline crack hovering menacingly in the air, a metre from the tiled floor.

Sonoko snapped out of her torpor and carried on, completely unaware that she had been possessed by a demon.

The entire OTT team had convened in the boardroom to hash over the next steps with Neit, Gorrick, and the quest in general.

True to form, Hope had researched much of what they had gleaned from the discussion with the Neit of the Id before he entered Kew. But most importantly, she had researched the name Amon, and the results were very disturbing. With the rest of them seated and sipping on mugs of coffee, Hope took the floor.

"Amon, an entity Neit had mentioned, is otherwise known as Marduk, whom we suspect to be En-Lil. According to Christian doctrine, Amon is the Grand Marquis of Hell. I'll read a little of what is written about him," she said, opening her notebook. "Amon telleth all things past and to come. Amon or Amun is the Egyptian supreme Sun God, Amon Ra, aka Merodach, and was represented with blue skin in human form. Amon, the Babylonian god Marduk, discerns the past and foretells the future. Amon or Marduk rose from an obscure deity in the third millennium BCE to become one of the most important gods and the head of the Mesopotamian pantheon in the first millennium. He was the patron god of the city of Babylon, where his temple tower—the ziggurat Etemenanki—the foundation of the heavens and the earth—served as the model for the famous Tower of Babel. Amongst other things, it is said Amon's function as a god of incantations may have been original to Marduk because he has a strong association with the city of Eridu and the god En-Ki, a powerful deity who did not belong to the original pantheon of the ancient Sumerian city of Nippur, now Nuffar in modern-day Iraq. One important artefact to know about in relation to Sumerian and Babylonian mythology is the Tablet of Destinies. The god who possessed the Tablet of Destinies was considered the supreme ruler by all the rest. Marduk or En-Lil and En-Ki fought over the Tablet. En-Lil won the battle and became the highest god. This confirms what En-Ki had told Alice and reaffirms that Amon is En-Lil, thus supporting Neit's explanation of his experience with the archdemon millennia ago. It becomes obvious that En-Lil has had many faces and identities over time, and these were to create confusion to provide him a safe haven from his enemies. We know another of his identities as Gorrick and how he has used clones to shield his own identity. In conclusion, I must agree with Neit that we are in grave danger of En-Lil, with his conjuring ability, to eventually summon a demon or more to oppose us. Oh, and by the way, just for interest, in Celtic mythology, Neit was a god of war."

When she sat back down, a shroud of foreboding had descended upon the others. It was the ominous feeling of being up against the supernatural, a feeling of helplessness, with no comprehension of how to deal with forces beyond the imagination.

Secta rose to his feet. "Well, thanks for that, Hope. We're all a little rocked by the revelation of what we might be up against, but at the end of the day, the unearthly nature of the quest and its subsequent challenges have always been confronting... but in saying that, nothing that we haven't managed to overcome. We will deal with these challenges as they arise, but for now, I think we should focus on what we have already put in progress."

Alice rose slowly from his chair, and with a look of purpose on his face, said, "But at the same time, we need to look over our shoulder because En-Lil is capable of a whole lot of bad shit... Look, I've had to deal with loads of crap we call supernatural... monsters like the Rooga... the Golem... cyborgs, virus-infected walkers, and now a phantom that's invisible to the naked eye. So, hey, demons... bring 'em on," he snarled. "If our plan succeeds today, we'll know if Gorrick here in Sydney is En-Lil. If he isn't, then we need to find the location of the real one. Find that out, and we'll be well on the way to completing the quest. You can rest assured to stop us he'll throw everything he has in his arsenal at us, but we need to stand as one and fight for what's right. So, do I have your support?" he said solemnly, glaring at each and every one of his confederates. "Speak up!"

Emphatic yeses erupted from all of them. Alice had stirred their spirit with his rallying speech. What lay ahead of them might be daunting, but they knew Alice had confronted the impossible before and won—they were loyal to the quest—they knew success depended on their skills and support, and that success would ensure a safe future for humanity—safe from the likes of Zen and Gorrick—safe from world domination—safe from an extinction event.

In the posterior cortical of Kew's brain, Neit instinctively knew a Dreamraider had materialised somewhere on Earth's current timeline. It was what he dreaded most because he alone understood the cleverness and ferocity of such an opponent, depending on which demon had been sent. For now, all he could do was keep his mind on the task ahead and deal with the Dreamraider later.

He was able to access all of his host's senses with the exception of touch and pain. He could see through his host's eyes, hear, even smell and taste, but more importantly, he could navigate the host's active, procedural, semantic, and episodic memories. Right then, he was being led by the two plainclothes Zen agents who had liberated Kew from the clutches of OTT. They were leading him through the underground car park of Zen HQ.

After a short elevator ride, he was met at the infirmary by a reception committee of four medical staff, which included Doctor Li and Professor Adamski.

"Nice of you all to turn out to greet me," Kew said facetiously.

Just then, Honor arrived.

"Wow, I must be of some value for you to be here," Kew snarled at her.

"Don't flatter yourself, Kew," she snapped back.

"Go behind the partition and strip; you will undergo a series of examinations to clear you of any OTT treachery," Adamski said, then nodded for the agents to act.

While Kew was being led behind a curtain, Honor approached Adamski and said, "I want a full psychological assessment as well as physical done, scans: the whole smear. Once you've cleared him, take your blood and DNA samples, and then bring him to my office. How long will it take before you can confirm you have isolated the dematerialising formula?"

Adamski was quite taken aback by her abrasive tone. "Not long, provided there are remnants present, which I'm sure there will be. From what I can gather, a traveller is injected with the formula before each journey, but the vaccine is not enduring," Adamski explained.

As Honor flounced out of the room, Doctor Li looked at Adamski with a scowl and whispered under her breath, "What a bitch."

"She must have got out of the wrong side of the bed this morning," Adamski said with irony.

Two hours later, Adamski brought Kew to the reception of Honor's office.

Layla, the secretary, was preparing to leave for the evening. She looked up from a compact still dusting her face with make-up powder. "You must be Agent Zanza Kew. I've heard plenty about you," Layla said while amorously giving the big ruggedly hunk of a man the once-over. He was her type, and she was making it obvious.

"And you are?" Kew quizzed.

"Layla, Her Majesty's new secretary."

"Tell her I'm here," he said coldly.

A moment later, the door to Honor's office opened, she came out, stopped at Adamski, and asked, "So, is he all clear?"

"Yes, and I have taken the samples. I will leave him with you and get on with my work."

"Fine, call me with the results. Kew, follow me."

Kew glanced at Layla, who responded with a raised eyebrow and pouted red-painted lips.

CHAPTER 6
HACKED

HONOR'S FACE HARDENED when, after delivering Kew to Gorrick, he told her dismissingly, "You can leave now." She felt her efforts had once again gone unappreciated, which was what motivated her to defect from OTT. Insulted, she stormed out of Gorrick's office.

"She didn't take being discharged well, did she?" Kew said snidely.

"It's something she needs to work on... she prefers being the authority rather than taking it," Gorrick said offhandedly. "Take a seat, Kew, explain to me what caused operation Dethrone to fail."

"It was a set-up, sir. They knew we were coming... I had plenty of time to think it over in solitary. I figure Black Alice overheard us while he was being prepped for Doctor Li's operation."

"But he was out cold?"

"It's the only explanation. He must have been foxing."

"Go on," Gorrick said.

"I entered the bedroom expecting to find Mal Function, but found Black Alice instead. He surprised me, and we fought, but he had a trick up his sleeve. A wormhole opened in the room... and time froze. Anyone unvaccinated with the demat formula is, therefore, rendered useless, so that immediately took out my accomplice. Alice forced me into the wormhole, and I ended up on the floor of OTT looking down the barrel of a waiting gun."

"They have obviously perfected teleportation to be capable of sending a wormhole anywhere in any time."

"I expect so," Kew agreed.

"Hmm, that makes things difficult," Gorrick said, processing it while getting up from his chair. He walked over to the window and looked out into the night. "This guy is always one step ahead of us."

"Black Alice? Yes, sir. Seems to have luck on his side."

"Maybe more than luck, I suspect."

"Do you suspect Honor of—"

Gorrick cut him off emphatically, "No." He ambled back to the lounge setting and took his seat deep in thought. "No, no, there's something else at play here. He knows far too much for a young musician with an overinflated ego."

Neit was finding the conversation intriguing but feeling it was drawing to a close, so he decided to make a move.

"Why did they take my blood?" Kew asked.

"Adamski is building a wormhole generator, but the hardware would be useless without the demat formula. He figures because you were injected with it to travel to 2047, it would still be in your system. If he can isolate it, he'll be able to replicate it," Gorrick explained.

"Ah, that's why the effort to get me released," Kew said discouragingly.

"Yes, but think of the positive side, you're still alive and you're free. Meet me in the morning, and we'll discuss your next mission."

Gorrick stood and then walked Kew to the door.

Kew stopped there, turned, and faced Gorrick. "I want the opportunity to redeem myself."

Neit noticed a light switch beside the door, reached out Kew's hand to lean against it, and accidentally flicked it off. The room fell into complete darkness long enough for Neit to jump from Kew to Gorrick.

Kew switched the lights back on, straightened up, and admitted awkwardly, "Sorry, my hand must've slipped, I'm still a bit wobbly."

"Go home and get some rest, Kew, you look tired," Gorrick said, patting him sympathetically on the back and thinking no more of it. He understood that solitary confinement would've taken a toll on him.

Gorrick closed the door after Kew, went back to the lounge setting, and flopped into his chair. Just as he was about to relax, there was a knock at the door.

"Come," he called out cantankerously.

Adamski entered flustered. "I'm sorry, sir, but I... I thought you should know immediately..." he stuttered nervously.

"What is it, Adamski? You look rattled?"

"The blueprint of Kairos is wrong... I suspect it is an early design and, therefore, has serious flaws."

"Are you telling me we paid a million to hack a redundant design?"

"Um, yes, sir," he admitted uneasily.

Gorrick pinched the bridge of his nose, closed his eyes, trying to restrain his anger.

"Give me something positive, Adamski, for God's sake... before I explode."

"I have successfully isolated the formula from the sample of Kew's blood."

Gorrick folded his hands in his lap, opened his eyes, and having curbed his need to blow up, said, "Good, how long will it take for you to replicate?"

"I can't be sure, sir, perhaps a month more or less, it depends—"

"Try for the latter. Get all of your department chemists onto it immediately. If you need more hands, then requisition them. That'll be all," he said tiredly. "Oh, send me Honor."

"Yes, sir," Adamski said, backing towards the door, feeling lucky to have escaped the wrath of his boss.

Neit had taken the conversation with Adamski on board; now he would wait for Gorrick to be alone before he could explore his subconscious mind.

A few minutes later, a knock at the door announced Honor.

Gorrick remained seated while watching her come towards him. "I've just heard from Adamski, the hacked blueprint of Kairos is useless," he said sternly.

Honor's face paled. She stopped short of him and fidgeted with the hem of her skirt. "We have a lot of data from the hack, perhaps there is a more up-to-date document... I—"

He cut her off, "I doubt that, Honor. You know what I think?"

"What, sir?" she said timidly.

"I think you have been set up by Karzoff. I think they knew they were being hacked and gave us a pile of redundant files. As a matter of fact, I would venture to say they even delivered Kew to us by providing you a convenient email— you, Honor, have been manipulated."

"Why would they do that?" she said, embarrassed, worried, and wondering where the conversation was leading.

"That is exactly what we need to determine." Once again, he was trying to restrain his temper but now suffering decision fatigue. He knew his team was inadequate, incapable of gaining the upper hand with their adversary, and he was running out of options. Why OTT had handed Kew over without a fight puzzled him.

"We scanned him for devices, he wasn't wired... we found nothing," Honor explained nervously. "He is psychologically sound, maybe they just don't have a need for him."

"Rubbish! Then why would they go to all the trouble of capturing him in the first place, and why transport him to the bunker? They know he assassinated the president. No, rest assured, there is more to this than meets the eye. Keep Kew under surveillance. I want to know his every move. This fiasco has cost us a lot... Adamski claims to have isolated the formula, if he's right, then the money will have been well spent, but you better hope he is right, Honor... Remember what I said, I want eyes and ears all over him... I don't trust this... it reeks of a set-up."

"Why are you going to so much trouble to isolate the formula when we have Kew to use as the traveller—he is after all, dispensable?" Honor asked curtly.

"I'm aware of that, but we need the formula," he said brusquely.

"Will that be all, sir?" Honor asked, sensing he was becoming more agitated.

Gorrick nodded dismissively.

Glad there was no more to it than an irate mood, she strode towards the door. When Gorrick had first mentioned the million in crypto bile had risen in her stomach with pangs of guilt. She quickly reassured herself that it was Adamski who had put her onto the Russian hackers in the first place, not that it was his or their fault, however using them had led to their predicament. But even more than that, she was pissed that Adamski had neglected to tell her the blueprint was useless before he squealed to Gorrick. She assured herself that she wouldn't fall for that again.

With Honor gone, Gorrick flopped back into his chair, well over what had turned out to be a tortuous day. He settled in for a power nap.

With the veil of unconsciousness enveloping his host, it was time for Neit to explore. It didn't take him long to discover he was in the mind of a clone. He found memory stems to a thousand more just like him: replicants—their social upbringing the only point of difference between them. It was obvious by his memories Gorrick had lived a long time, in fact, well over two thousand years as his memories went back as far as the fall of Babylon. But that wasn't what Neit was looking for... in a dark corner of his mind, he came upon a place reserved for special memories such as inherited memory—this was the place he was searching to find, and he entered.

When content with the information he'd garnered, Neit slipped out of Gorrick's sleeping body and moved like an illusion across the room. The purple spectre opened the door and escaped.

Gorrick sat undisturbed, cat-napping, totally oblivious that his memories had just been hacked.

As Neit stepped into the corridor on his way to the elevator, he noticed Honor's secretary Layla standing at the elevator doors with her back to him. The UVB from the fluorescent overhead lights in the corridor immediately began to heat up his skin, even though it was covered, he needed to get out of the radiation before it damaged him. He shot along the corridor like a dart and entered Layla's body. The elevator doors opened, and she stepped inside, unaware she had been possessed.

Instead of selecting the basement car park to collect her own car, Neit caused her to select the ground floor. In full control of her, she took her cellphone out of her pocket, and he caused her to dial a specific number he had been given. When it answered, she immediately terminated the call, and then returned the phone to her pocket, totally ignorant of having used it.

Layla stepped out of the elevator and was manipulated by Neit to walk out through a side exit into a laneway where she stood kerbside as if waiting for someone or something—she had no idea whom or why. After five minutes, an avocado green Volkswagen Beetle stopped in the laneway, and the passenger-side door swung open. If she had looked down, she would have noticed the shadow on the ground caused by the moonlight wasn't hers, and that it slipped across the pavement into the car. Snapping out of the trance, she realised she was standing in a dark laneway, staring at a green VW Beetle, turned, and casually walked back towards Zen HQ entrance doors, oblivious of what had occurred.

The rest of the OTT team was waiting for Secta and Alice to return with Neit from Zen HQ.

When they entered the boardroom, Alice lowered the lights for Neit to leave his body and join them physically. They all watched in awe as Neit emerged from Alice's body to take up a seat at the boardroom table.

"So, Neit, welcome back. We're anxious to hear about your experience," Secta said cordially.

"Firstly, Kew is a very dangerous, evil-minded man. When brought to the Zen infirmary, he met Doctor Li, Professor Adamski, and a woman named Honor, who seemed to be in charge of security."

"That confirms she survived the attack," Karzoff said, his face showing signs of distress at the revelation that his old nemesis was back.

"Carry on, Neit," Secta requested.

"After extensive physical and mental testing, Kew was released and then taken to Gorrick's offices by Honor, where she was dismissed for Gorrick to speak discreetly with Kew. He explained to Gorrick how Alice had pushed him into an open wormhole to capture him. After Kew had gone, a few minutes later, Adamski came into the office and told Gorrick that the blueprint of Kairos he had was redundant. It was then that Gorrick woke up to the fact that they had been set up, and he suspected OTT had given up Kew for a reason. Adamski told him he had isolated the demat formula from Kew's blood and would now attempt to synthesise it."

"Can they do that?" Karzoff anxiously queried.

"Yes, they can... we didn't think of that, did we?" Hope acknowledged.

"Go on, Neit," Secta prompted.

"Gorrick dismissed Adamski, and Honor returned. He told her she had cost Zen a million in crypto for an outmoded blueprint of Kairos."

Laughter erupted around the room, especially from Karzoff, who was almost hysterical. Getting Honor into trouble had always been a favourite occupation of his.

Neit waited for the laughter to subside before continuing. "Gorrick said he was worried that releasing Kew was far too easy and he figured there was more to it... his words were, 'I don't trust this... it reeks of a set-up.'"

"He is on to us," Karzoff grumbled.

"No, he just smells a rat," Alice countered.

"Yes, you are right, Alice. There is no basis to his suspicion other than instinct. I derived that from his mind. I can confirm Gorrick is an artificially created clone, more than two thousand five hundred years old. But the most important discovery I made in his mind was a direct route to his creator, En-Lil. He is on the planet Eris in the Tower of Futurum, defended by demons."

It was a jaw-dropping revelation, and it left them all, with the exception of Hope, stunned. She was busy researching Eris on her handheld device.

The Professor announced grimly, "Now we know this Gorrick isn't En-Lil... and what we're dealing with here."

"Yeah, demons, well, that's nothing new... been there, done that... it's all bloody science fiction or is it fantasy?" Alice said cavalierly.

"I wouldn't dismiss demons that easily, Alice. I have fought them, I have seen them kill better Id than I. They are a formidable foe."

"If they're so tough, then why doesn't En-Lil send them to Earth to deal with us instead of fighting us with limp-wristed clones of himself?" Alice growled.

"He probably believes they could get the job done, Alice," Secta submitted.

"No, I think it is more likely the real battle has not yet begun," Neit added gravely.

His proclamation triggered anxiety in all of them. The idea of an apocalyptic war to end time depicted in prophecies and religious doctrine since recorded history now seemed inevitable, and what made it even more terrifying was that if Neit was right, they would be at the coalface. This wasn't going to be a battle fought by soldiers, bombs, and politics; this was going to be a battle of good versus evil, of light over dark. This was going to be the endgame of a fight that had been unrelenting for thousands of years, though mostly fought in the underworld. It was a fight En-Lil thought he had won when he eradicated his brother, En-Ki. But his objective of world domination and the eradication of humankind had struck a new obstacle in Black Alice.

CHAPTER 7
DREAMRAIDER

HOPE READ FROM her device to her five colleagues seated around the OTT boardroom table. "The dwarf planet Eris is named for the ancient Greek goddess of discord and strife. With a radius of about 1,163 kilometres, it is about one-fifth the diameter of Earth. Like Pluto, it is a little smaller than Earth's Moon. Eris takes five hundred and fifty-seven Earth years to make one trip around the sun. The plane of Eris' orbit is well out of the plane of the solar system's planets and extends far beyond the Kuiper Belt, a zone of icy debris beyond the orbit of Neptune. As Eris orbits the sun, it completes one rotation every 25.9 hours, making its day length similar to ours. Eris has a very small moon called Dysnomia with a nearly circular orbit lasting about sixteen days. This moon is named after Eris' daughter, the demon goddess of lawlessness."

Secta was up pacing the floor. He stopped and, thinking out loud, said, "That leaves only one option, doesn't it?" He glanced at Alice.

Alice said gruffly, "Yeah, to find a way to get to Eris, knock over En-Lil, and nick the Tablet of Destinies."

"That is much easier said than done," said Neit emphatically.

"Why?" the Professor queried.

"To begin with, you would need to generate a wormhole to Eris, then find the Futurum Tower and ascend twenty-three levels to locate En-Lil. Many of those levels are guarded by powerful demons."

"Twenty-three levels, Eris, Discordia, next will be seeking the golden apple of discord that started the Trojan War... but right now, it sounds like Operation Mindfuck," the Professor said with a facetious chuckle.

"What on Earth is that?" Hope questioned.

"A concept developed by Robert Anton Wilson and Kerry Thornley in 1968 and given its name by Wilson and Robert Shea in the Illuminatus trilogy. Principia Discordia... the discordian society needed some opposition because the whole idea of it is based on conflict and dialectics. So, they created an opposition within the discordian society, which they called the Bavarian Illuminati, and thus built up the myth about the warfare between the discordian society and the Illuminati, vis-à-vis, good versus evil. The story contains the twenty-three enigma... the discordia part comes from Eris being the ancient Greek goddess of discord... and it seems there's some relevance to it with what Neit is saying," the Professor submitted.

Holding his chin thoughtfully, Secta agreed, "Yes, yes, truth is often found in myth... it's usually a case of unravelling a story to find what's at its core."

"And that's the golden apple of discordia metaphor," the Professor concluded.

"Well, I don't know about you, but it all sounds like myth to me right now," Alice said tiredly.

"It is just after 1 a.m.," Karzoff said, checking his wristwatch.

"Shall we call it a day and reconvene tomorrow at 2 p.m.? That will give us time for more research. Are you going back to The Lair tonight, Alice?" asked Secta.

"Yes."

The chopper touched down on The Lair helipad at 2 a.m., and Alice made his way downstairs.

Neit immediately said inside Alice's mind, "There's something wrong."

"What's up?" Alice questioned out loud.

"I sense an arrow of time."

That caused Alice to stop on the staircase. "Don't tell me that man, I was hoping to get some sleep tonight," Al complained. "So, what's an arrow of time?"

"An opening in the time continuum."

The house was dark, but Alice knew the sensor lights would come on as soon as he reached the next level. He whispered, "So what happens with this arrow?"

"It is how demons travel... it is similar to a wormhole."

"Are you saying there's one of them demons here?" Al whispered harshly.

"I cannot tell, only that a rift has opened."

"What if this thing... a demon... is waiting to pounce on me? What do I do? How do I kill it?"

"That depends on which demon it is. They can take three forms: a vapour, a human, or a beast."

Alice didn't like the sound of that, especially the beast part, and he continued down the staircase but with a lot more caution. He whispered emphatically, "Yeah fine, but how do we kill the damn thing?"

"A crystal ice blade can cut when it is the beast or when it is in human form but not when it is vapour... if you force the vapour into direct sunlight it will die. The most important thing is to not show fear because that is what it feeds on; fear increases its strength."

"Just terrific Neit, I'll just fearlessly leap into my wardrobe and drag out my trusty crystal ice blade to kill the bloody thing," Alice said facetiously.

"It is good that you have one there," Neit said unaware of Al's sarcasm.

When he reached the next level, the hall lights illuminated. He stopped. Sonoko would be asleep in the bedroom along the hallway, and he wasn't sure if he should go in and check on her or not.

"I sense your reluctance to go to Sonoko, is that because I am with you?" Neit asked.

"It's all a bit weird mate, don't you think?" Al paused and thought. "But no... but yeah, there's that, and you've got me nervous about a demon. What am I supposed to do?"

"Park me in a dark place so you can have privacy. I will not be bothered."

There was a walk-in linen press along the hallway. Alice opened the door. "Will you be all right in there?"

"Sure, no problem."

Alice stepped into the small room, leaving the light off, and waited for Neit to exit his body. The uncanny feeling shivered through his body as the purple shadow of Neit slipped out and then manifested at his side.

"I'll come get you in the morning then," Al proposed, staring at the strange spectre.

"Fine."

"Listen, if you sense anything more about this demon, feel free to come and wake me... but only if it's urgent, alright?"

"Got you," Neit affirmed.

Al closed the door behind him and then continued down the hallway to the main bedroom. He gently opened the door so as not to disturb Sonoko and crept inside. Within minutes he was beside her in bed drifting off to sleep. It had been a long day.

Al was dreaming of being in bed with Sonoko when Neit tapped him on the shoulder.

Al grumbled, "What are you doing here?"

"You told me to come to you if I found the demon. I tried to wake you but couldn't; you were out cold, so I had to enter you. We need to get out of here right now; I think the demon is in Sonoko."

"You sure?"

Alice looked sharply at Sonoko… she had begun to transform. Claws and pointed teeth, a monster in the making.

Moving quickly, Neit led Alice to a door through which they passed into a dark craggy forest. It was night, and there was a big blood-red full moon overhead. If it hadn't been for the moon, Alice wouldn't have been able to make out Neit in the darkness.

The branches of the denuded trees in the forest pointed at them like withered fingers. It was like a haunted, scary forest in a fairytale from the Brothers Grimm.

Alice stopped to take stock and asked, "What's this place?"

"I don't know, Alice. It is your dream. We have to find sanctuary; it will be coming after us."

"Wait a minute, explain this… am I dreaming?" Al complained.

"Yes, the demon has possessed Sonoko. It was waiting for you to dream of her so it can invade your dream. I told you, the prime objective of demons is to be a Dreamraider; it is the way they jump from one person to another."

"Okay, okay, I get that, so what is the demon?"

"I think this one is Gaap. If it is, I have fought him before. He is very shrewd and high up in the demon pecking order."

Neit knew Gaap was a cunning and evil adversary who had killed many Id over time.

"So how do I stop the thing?" Alice barked.

"We have to kill it. But for now, I suggest we get moving before it catches us."

"Wait, wait… how can it kill me?"

"Many ways, but what it will try first is to jump into you and then destroy your memory, and the only way it can do that is during a dream."

"Does Sonoko know this thing is in her?" Al asked a little panicked.

"Probably not."

"So, what if she dreams about me, can it jump into me then?"

"No, in someone else's dream, there is only a likeness of you. The Dreamraider can use it to jump through, the same as it can jump through anyone in a dream. But it can only jump out of a dream into reality through the original host or through a child."

"I'll need to get more on that later... but for now let's get the hell out of here."

"Fine, then dream up an exit for us," Neit said.

Alice woke with a start. Neit was sitting on the end of the bed. Al looked at Sonoko asleep beside him and whispered to Neit, "Is that thing still in her?"

"Yes."

Alice gingerly slipped out of bed and then crept out of the bedroom followed closely by Neit. Once in the hallway, he stopped to speak with the phantom. "How can I sleep without dreaming of her and then having this Gaap thing after me?"

"I need to possess you to keep guard. I can stop you from dreaming of her."

"Okay, do it."

Once Neit had slipped inside him, Alice headed for the spare bedroom to get some more sleep.

The next morning, Alice was gone before Sonoko woke, and when she did, she was totally unaware he'd been home at all.

"After Alice phoned me this morning, I asked Hope to research the demon Gaap. She'll be here in a minute with the details," Secta said.

Karzoff sat forward in his seat and said sternly, "Does Sonoko know this demon has possessed her?"

"No," Neit answered.

Secta's office had been deliberately dimly lit with no UV lighting for Neit's comfort. The Professor, Karzoff, Secta, Alice, and Neit were seated in the lounge setting. The door opened, and Hope entered.

"Sorry I'm late, everyone. It took a while to get all I could on this bloody demon," she said in a fluster, and then opened her notepad on the coffee table. "I'm sure you know everything I have on him Neit, but for the benefit of the others... Gaap, aka Tap, Coap, Taob, Goap, is a Goetic demon described as able to steal familiars from other magicians, make men stupid, and carry men between kingdoms."

"Ah, so us stupid blokes can blame Gaap?" Al quipped.

Neit cut in, "I'm sorry to interrupt you, Doctor Hope, but the information you have is incorrect. I expect it was composed by a religious order because it is naïve and far from the truth."

"I have no doubt you would be right, Neit. Yes, it was compiled by monks, as most of our written history has been. I expect your experience would be far more valuable to us than whatever I can research. Please go ahead," Hope said agreeably, and then took her seat.

"There is no real point in discussing Gaap's history. He is a prime demon, and we need to better spend our time on how to kill him," Neit started.

"Alright, now you're talking!" Alice barked, keen for action and put off by too much talking and not enough doing.

"I have fought Gaap once previously and lost. He is far too cunning. It is obvious that En-Lil, Lord of Demons from the Pantheon of Goetia, has conjured the fiend demon to kill Alice. That he can only achieve in two ways... firstly, to take possession of him in order to take command of his senses and thereby cause Alice to kill himself. Secondly, to occupy someone else and then drive that person to kill Alice. Conversely, there are only two ways to kill Gaap. The first is to lure him out of his host into physical form and then use a crystal ice blade to pierce his heart or brain—he can manifest in three forms: vapour, beast, and human—the ice blade will not kill him when he is vapour. The second way is to expose him as vapour to direct sunlight."

"For those of us who don't know, I've just Googled crystal ice blade... it's a knife or sword blade fashioned from quartz crystal," Hope said.

"That makes sense," the Professor chimed in. "Some types of quartz crystals have piezoelectric properties; they develop an electric potential upon the application of mechanical stress. We all know the old trick of charging a quartz crystal by rubbing it with a cloth so that it picks up a piece of paper."

Secta got up and began pacing the room holding his chin, thinking in his conventional manner. He stopped abruptly with an idea. "Quartz-tipped bullets."

"Now you're talking," Alice said excitedly. "Would that do the trick, Neit, or do we need a blade?"

"Both," Neit affirmed.

"I know a custom small arms manufacturer in Sydney, shall I get him to make up some crystal-tipped ammo and craft a crystal dagger?" Karzoff questioned.

"Absolutely," Secta agreed.

"And ASAP," Al added.

"What calibre shells?" Karzoff asked.

"9 mm would be the go," Al said. "How long for the blade, Neit?"

"It will need to penetrate its heart or be able to decapitate him, so it must have a razor edge and say this long," Neit demonstrated with his hands.

"A twenty-centimetre blade then," Al confirmed.

Karzoff got up and left the room to get on with it.

"So, how do we coax it out of Sonoko then?" Al asked.

"We hunt him in your dreamscape, Alice," Neit submitted.

"I have one other question for you, Neit. You say En-Lil is on the planet Eris holed up in the Futurum Tower," the Professor questioned.

"Yes," Neit acknowledged.

The Professor continued, "The only way we can reach Eris is to have a coeval organic item from there that would enable us to connect a wormhole to it through which Alice could travel."

He was right, and they all knew it. After killing Gaap, the main agenda would have to be getting to En-Lil on Eris; otherwise, he would continue to send more demons.

"Would a piece of Gaap's body work? He originates from Eris," Neit asked.

The Professor offered a smile with a nod, "It certainly would, Neit. Now we have another reason for killing it."

"It seems En-Lil might have dug his own grave sending Gaap to kill me," Al offered grimly.

CHAPTER 8
DRONE

GORRICK WAS SEATED behind his office desk when his new secretary, Miss Regina Fysh, knocked and entered. Dressed in an executive business suit with short-cropped black hair, rimless glasses, and hot pink painted lips, she exuded sophisticated charisma. She was tall, trim, with shapely legs, and walked with an impressive gait.

Regina stopped just inside the door and, after catching Gorrick's attention, said with a New York accent, "Sir, security asked if you could view some CCTV footage from last night; they found something weird about it."

"Certainly, Regina. Tell them I'll check it now."

"Fine, sir."

She turned on her high heels and left the room. Regina had been Gorrick's former secretary at the New York office of Zen and had joined him in Sydney at his request.

He hit a key that brought up the CCTV footage from the server to his computer monitor and then sat back with folded arms to watch it.

The footage showed the hallway outside his office with Layla waiting at the elevator. He noticed nothing peculiar about it. When the elevator arrived, Layla stepped in, and then the footage cut to the CCTV camera inside the elevator. Layla pressed the ground floor button and then made a phone call. Still, there was nothing odd about it. Gorrick was becoming anxious, thinking he might have missed something... or perhaps it was just a waste of his time. The next sequence showed her leaving the elevator and exiting the lobby through the side door. The final sequence was from an overhead exterior CCTV camera in the laneway outside Zen HQ. Layla stopped kerbside, as though waiting for someone. After a couple of minutes, a VW Beetle pulled up, and the passenger-side door opened. No one got out, Layla didn't get in, the door closed, and then the car drove off. Layla then re-entered the lobby, took the elevator to the basement car park, and left the building.

"Hmm, that was suspicious," Gorrick mumbled. He rewound the footage and froze the frame of the VW with the passenger-side door open. The angle from the camera wasn't the best to see the occupants, but there was enough of a profile of the passenger for him to zoom in. He took a still frame, printed it, and then immediately called Honor to come to his office.

Honor arrived minutes later, and after showing her the footage, he asked for an explanation. Honor had none. Then he handed her the still photo.

"Do you recognise the person in the VW?" Gorrick asked.

"Yes, it is Black Alice... but I don't understand... Layla, why?" she said, perplexed.

"We had best ask her, don't you think? Get her in here now," Gorrick ordered calmly.

It didn't take long before Layla was standing nervously before Honor and Gorrick, wondering why she was in trouble. The reason became apparent once shown the CCTV footage.

"Why did you meet Black Alice last night in the laneway?" Honor snarled at her.

"I have no recollection of doing that, Miss Honor. Please believe me; I only remember getting into my car, like I do every night, and driving home."

"Hand me your cellphone, Miss Migden," Gorrick said sternly.

She handed it over, and Gorrick checked the outgoing log.

"Here," he showed her the phone. "You called this number from the elevator."

"I didn't, sir, I—"

Honor angrily cut her off. "What a turgid pile of rubbish, girl. The footage clearly shows you making the call."

"Wait, the number has an odd prefix. Do you recognise it?" Gorrick said, showing Honor the phone.

"That is an OTT secure number prefix, sir... she called OTT from the elevator. Why did you call them? It was obviously to arrange the meeting. Why did you meet them?" Honor shouted.

Layla cringed and teared up. "I swear, I don't remember calling or meeting anyone," she pleaded.

"Okay, leave your phone and go back to your office, wait there until further notice," Gorrick ordered.

Sniffling, upset by the accusations, the teenager left the office.

As soon as the door closed behind Layla, Honor said, "I do not believe she is lying."

"I agree with you. Check the phone records to find out what was said."

"The call was not long enough; I think it was only a dial through as a signal. I will check the rest of her calls to see if she has called that number before or received any other calls from OTT. Could she be a double agent?" Honor asked.

"I doubt that. Have the CCTV vision analysed for foul play."

The OTT meeting had adjourned, and they were preparing to leave the boardroom. The resolution had been made that Alice would bring Sonoko to OTT, where she would be confined until Gaap had been dealt with. The plan was to avoid alarming Sonoko, and Alice would only bring her in if he remained possessed by Neit, ensuring protection.

However, a new problem had surfaced. Alice had informed Secta that Sonoko's birthday was due in two weeks, which meant she would have to return to her own time. Having two Sonokos coexisting on the same timeline was too dangerous, and they couldn't risk pushing the limits of the prime directive this time. It was imperative to act swiftly and eliminate Gaap.

Just as they were about to depart the boardroom, Viktoria entered, paused just inside the door, and announced, "Everybody, Karzoff has gone to meet his special weapons contact. He spoke with him on the phone, and it will take some weeks to produce crystal-tipped 9 mm ammunition, but his contact does have a crystal dagger, so Karzoff went to take a look."

"Did Karzoff update you on the plan for Al to bring Sonoko here?" Secta inquired.

"Yes, but not all of it, especially the part about Alice doing it," Viktoria replied, surprised.

"The resolution was passed after he left," Alice explained.

"I'm sure Karzoff wouldn't have agreed with that, nor do I. Under the circumstances, it's too big of a risk to take with you, Al," Viktoria stated firmly.

Alice, Neit, the Professor, and Hope sat back down to consider her objection.

"I think you're right, Viktoria," Hope chimed in. "No one knows how this thing with Gaap is going to pan out... it's dangerous."

"The whole catastrophe is dangerous, Hope," Al rasped.

"When has this quest we're on never been dangerous?" Secta added, pacing the floor.

"In Karzoff's absence as acting head of security, I cannot approve your plan. I propose taking two troopers to The Lair to bring Sonoko back here," Viktoria asserted.

"We were worried about frightening Sonoko," Hope said.

"I can handle that... I'll tell her there has been a security breach, which, in fact, is true. I just won't tell her that the breach is her," Viktoria proposed.

"Clever, that should work. Don't you agree, Al... Neit?" Secta questioned.

"I agree it will be easier to handle what needs to be done from here. I see no real problem with what you propose, Viktoria, though I do not trust Gaap," Neit admitted.

"Do you want to accompany me?" asked Viktoria.

"No, it would be too dangerous in daylight," Neit explained.

"Then it's done. It's now 0945... I will need time to prepare. I will leave in the chopper at 1400 hours. Alice, please call Sonoko and inform her we'll pick her up at 1430... tell her she'll be staying at HQ for a couple of days. Don't elaborate. Say I will explain everything when I see her," Viktoria said.

"No sweat," Al confirmed.

They were comfortable with Viktoria's organisation; she was good at her gig. Secta walked her out of the boardroom.

In the corridor outside, Secta startled her with a kiss.

"Safe trip," he said meaningfully.

"Piece of cake, Hon," she replied playfully.

After lunch, Honor returned to Gorrick's office with the findings of the CCTV analysis and handed him a flash drive containing the results.

"The lab found some anomalies when the footage was filtered through UV," she reported.

Gorrick brought up the video files on his computer. The camera in the hallway outside his office suite showed a phantom shadow moving through the frame along the hallway and entering Layla Migden's body while she was waiting at the elevator.

"You can see it again on video four," Honor explained.

He opened video four and watched the same shadow leave Layla's body and enter the waiting VW.

"Did you see it? It's very quick," she said.

"Yes, I will just slow it down," Gorrick said studiously.

He slowed down the vision and then froze it just before the phantom entered the VW.

Reclining in his chair, lacing his fingers together behind his head, he said, "Seems we are dealing with a lot more than just Black Alice."

"What is it?" Honor queried.

"I suspect a chimera... some sort of phantom. OTT must have recruited it to do their dirty work. The question is, why did it come out of my office?"

"There is no CCTV in your office, sir, so we can't check," Honor said.

"But there is in the reception area. Have them check if that thing actually came out of here."

"Yes, sir." Honor turned and headed for the door, then stopped and turned back to Gorrick. "Oh, by the way, sir..." She took her cellphone out of her pocket and ambled back to him. "I ordered drone surveillance of OTT, and this morning at 0700, it picked up something on the daily chopper trip to and from the Gosford area north of Sydney. I have some still frames here."

She handed Gorrick her phone, and he peered at the stills on the device.

"If you zoom on the chopper on the OTT helipad once it has landed, you will see something interesting."

He zoomed and enlarged the passenger disembarking from the chopper.

"Is that Black Alice?"

"Correct, sir. I checked the radar, and the chopper came from Pelican Island on the Hawkesbury River. The take-offs and landings are from a residential helipad on a house on the island. I'm convinced Black Alice is staying there."

Gorrick rose slowly to his feet with a look of elation on his face, thinking, "At last, a positive." "Excellent work, Honor," he said, handing the phone back. "Assemble your troops."

"Yes, sir," Honor said with enthusiasm, glad to be back in the good books.

Twenty minutes later, Gorrick received a notification on his computer that the CCTV footage from the reception had been treated with a UV filter and was ready to be viewed. He opened the attachment.

His greatest fear was immediately realised; the spectre had indeed come from his office. He watched it flash through the room and out of the door into the hallway. Further spectral analysis had been done on the footage by the technicians. An infrared filter was applied to reveal the spectre had body heat, confirming it was a being of some description. Gorrick cursed not having a CCTV camera in his office because the footage had him begging the question: what was it?... and what had it come for?

Alice was walking along the corridor toward the Professor's office when Viktoria came out of a doorway, followed by two troopers. The troopers were dressed in assault gear—grey overalls, flak jackets, helmets with heads-up comms, and waist belts packed with weapons.

"Hey Vik, you guys look like you mean business. You'll scare the hell out of Sonoko dressed like that," Alice reasoned.

"Did you call her?" she asked.

"Yeah, she's expecting you... pretty timid about it, though."

"Don't worry, I'll put her mind at rest when we get there. See you in an hour or so."

"Cool, good luck," Al said.

As she moved off, one of the troopers stopped and patted Alice on the shoulder.

"Hi Mr Alice, remember me, Trooper Dicks?"

Alice looked him up and down and said jokingly, "Face rings a bell, can't quite pick the nose."

"Last time I saw you, it was standing on the bow of a speedboat racing after a ferry in Sydney Harbour," the trooper said.

The penny dropped for Alice. "Oh, that Trooper Dicks. Didn't I sign a graph for your daughter?"

"Yes, that's right."

Alice slapped him on the back. "Take care, Trooper Dicks. Good to see you."

He followed them a short distance down the hallway, then turned off to the Professor's office.

CHAPTER 9
BLADE OF SLAUGHTER

ALICE ENTERED THE professor's office and found him and Doctor Hope with a hot coffee waiting for him. He took an armchair in the comfy lounge setting.

"Have you heard from Mal?" Hope asked him.

"No, I guess he's on the campaign trail with the election only a week or so away," Al said.

"Where's Neit?"

"I'm in Alice," he spoke through Alice.

"That's really weird," Hope reacted.

"Imagine what it's like from my side," Al said with a chuckle. "I just caught Vik and her team on their way to the helipad. How are we going to handle Sonoko when we get her back here?"

The Professor got up and lowered the lights. "Low enough for you to come out Neit?"

Al shivered as shadowy Neit slid out of his body.

"Brrr, I'll never get used to that," Al said with a shiver, then took a sip of coffee.

Neit took a seat beside Alice.

"Coffee Neit?" Hope asked.

"No thank you Hope, though I'd like to taste it, I have no need to consume fluids. Thank you for the lighting, Professor... I think I should explain a little more about Gaap now that we have the time."

He recalled when he'd fought Gaap at the battle of Nineveh in 612 B.C.

"There was no problem with UV in artificial lighting back then... the Id could move freely under the cloak of darkness. I was with the Chaldeans led by King Nabopolassar father of Nebuchadnezzar II when they besieged Nineveh, at that time the greatest city on Earth. The sacking of the city and the killing of King Sin-shar-ishhun led to the destruction of the Neo-Assyrian Empire and the fall of Assyrian rule. The soldiers of King Nabopolassar were pillaging for treasure in the bowels of the palace of Nineveh when they came upon a hidden room they believed to be the treasury. Word was immediately sent to the King that a demon was guarding the treasure and the soldiers couldn't get past it. I was summoned by the King and asked to deal with it. He requested it of me because along with my fellow Id, we had successfully killed the demon called Baal-Peor prior to the siege. Baal-Peor was an Assyrian god associated with licentiousness and orgies and worshipped in the form of a phallus, but in reality, he was a demon brought to Earth by Amon or En-Lil called Ashur by the Assyrians. En-Lil had ordered Baal to infiltrate the court of King Nabopolassar in the guise of a beautiful young woman, to seduce his generals and thereby uncover the attack plan. When one of Id caught sight of her, he immediately recognised she was a demon. We alerted the King and then on his orders captured her and burned her at the stake. As she burned, she laughed hysterically and then manifested into her true form: a monstrous, bearded demon with horns and sharply pointed claws... then, right before our eyes, Baal vanished. Though we knew we hadn't killed it, the King was impressed and so ordered me to vanquish this new demon, so he could get the treasure.

Soldiers led me accompanied by another Id, Jaith, through a labyrinth of dark slimy tunnels down into the wicked bowels of the palace and the room they had discovered.

Peering through the grate in the big wooden door, I could see the guardian beyond. I recognised it right away as Gaap in the form of a grotesque human. After we got the door open, Gaap realised the threat and immediately transformed into its beastly self. The metamorphosis was so chilling it scared the soldiers off, leaving me with Jaith to fight it. Its new form was well over two metres tall. Imagine the classic gargoyle found under or above the eaves of Gothic Churches, put there to ward off evil spirits... well, that's what Gaap looks like: a monster... part beast, part man, long neck, large hands with three strongly curved claws. Its eyes are like those of a cat, yellow and set deep in its elongated reptilian muzzle. Its jaws were filled with sharp pointed teeth and its skin dark green scales."

The description reminded Alice of a scaly version of the Rooga, the horrific creature he'd fought and killed in another dimension. Neit's story had him intrigued because it was only twenty-five years prior to him being in Jerusalem in 587 B.C. The Professor and Hope were also totally absorbed.

"We were both armed with crystal swords, and though our opponent was formidable, we were confident that between us, we could kill it. But we had seriously underestimated Gaap's cunning. At first, it snapped at us like a cornered animal lashing out with vicious swipes of its claws. One swipe could easily knock the head off your shoulders or unzip your belly to gut you. We vaporised to be less of a target. The idea was to manoeuvre into position to strike with the blade and then manifest from vapour into solid form to make the blow."

"How can you hold a sword when you're vapour?"

"Good question, Alice, we can't, so I had to time passing the sword to Jaith just before I vaporised, then he'd do the same and pass it back to me... that way we could work in closer to make a strike... otherwise, with its long reach, it would have got us. We left one sword on the ground and worked passing the other one back and forth.

I got in close, solidified, and Jaith threw me the sword, but just as I was about to catch it Gaap swung around and knocked it out of the air. He then hit me with a powerful backhander that knocked me across the floor. The sword smashed up against the wall and shattered into pieces.

Flat out on the floor and only half conscious, I was an easy target for Gaap. He rushed at me to make the kill. Jaith chased after him. I was so dazed I couldn't concentrate to vaporise. Jaith needed to get to the back-up sword on the floor before Gaap could get to me. Just as Jaith collected it, Gaap grabbed me, picked me up, and flung me like a rag doll through the air... I just managed to vaporise just before I hit the wall otherwise the force would have killed me.

Jaith attacked Gaap... but then Gaap did something totally unexpected, he jumped at Jaith, and disappeared inside him.

Jaith stood perplexed unsure what to do next. I struggled to my feet. Jaith walked towards me with the blade raised in the air. Possessed, he had been turned by Gaap to kill me. I quickly vaporised and slipped behind him. When I materialised, I watched it end."

Neit fell silent, leaving the others on the edge of their seats.

"What happened?" Al eventually asked.

"Something I will never forget... Jaith sliced open his own throat."

The moment was filled with the realisation that Jaith had made the ultimate sacrifice. Though they couldn't see Neit's face, shadowy tears dotted the arm of the lounge chair in which he sat, testament to the magnitude of the dark memory.

"Can Gaap control the host?" Hope asked.

"The Id can only occupy, while a demon can possess," Neit explained.

"So, was Gaap dead?" the Professor queried.

"At the time, the Id believed when the host died the occupant died as well, but we learned over time that not to be the case."

"So Jaith died in vain," Al said.

"Yes."

The discussion went on for an hour or so with Neit recounting his battles with demons over the years that eventually led to the depletion of the Id forces down to him. His stories only enforced that they were up against a formidable foe.

Secta arrived with bad news. He was worried. "There has been no contact with Viktoria. Even the chopper pilot isn't responding. I checked with flight control, and the chopper is still on the helipad at The Lair. Something is terribly wrong... I can sense it."

The door opened, and Karzoff entered carrying a long thin case. He put it down on the coffee table and observed, "You are all looking glum, matches the gloomy lighting... what's wrong?"

When Secta explained to him that Viktoria had gone to fetch Sonoko and all contact had been lost, Karzoff flopped despondently into a chair.

"Damn, she should have waited for me to return. Impetuous youth," Karzoff complained.

"I fear the worst," Neit said gloomily.

"Gaap?" Al asked.

"Yes," Neit confirmed.

Regina Fysh showed Kew into Gorrick's office. Gorrick came out from behind his desk and took a seat in the lounge setting.

"Sit down Kew, there's plenty to discuss," Gorrick said easily.

Kew was looking rested. He took a seat opposite Gorrick. Miss Fysh waited.

"Something to drink, Agent Kew?" she said casually.

"I'll take a coffee... standard double, no sugar."

"A doppio, and you, sir, the usual?"

"Thank you, Regina," Gorrick said.

Gorrick waited for Regina to leave the room.

"We've had a serious breach of security, Kew. Look at this." He handed Kew a notepad. Kew watched an edited version of the filtered CCTV footage.

"What—is—that?" Kew reacted, astounded.

"We don't know. But what we do know is it came out of my office. It is a sentient being and it infiltrated us for and on behalf of OTT.

See it getting into the VW at the end… you can clearly see Black Alice in the vehicle."

"So, whatever it is, it had possessed the girl," Kew posed.

"Exactly, Honor's secretary Layla Migden. But she remembers nothing of it. The creature even made her call OTT from inside the elevator to arrange the damn pick up," Gorrick said in an almost full-throated roar.

"I can see why you're pissed, I would be too. If they've got some sort of phantom working for them, then we're in real trouble."

"That goes without saying. Now look at this." Gorrick showed Kew the series of photographs taken of the OTT helipad by the drone. "Zoom number three on the passenger that just got out of the chopper."

"Black Alice."

"Right, that was 0700 this morning. The chopper brought him from Pelican Island in the Hawkesbury River… and it is not the first time."

"So, he's staying there… is it a safe house?"

"We believe so. I've ordered Honor to come up with a plan to hit Black Alice there."

Kew chuckled, "Good luck with that," he said facetiously.

Gorrick reclined in his chair and massaged his chin thinking, "Hmm, are you sceptical?"

"I should say so. It will take more than some tin-pot plan of Honor's to nail this bastard, plenty better than her have tried and failed."

"I hear you," Gorrick agreed.

"You send a bunch of agents charging in there, and none of them will come out. He's there for a reason—they'd have it locked down like a fortress."

"I expect that would be quite right."

"I've given it a lot of thought, and we need to use their own weapon against them," Kew said.

"How is that?"

"We need a wormhole generator."

"We are building one."

"That'll take too long. Surely Zen Japan or some other chapter is working on one. Look, if Zen was capable of dropping a spacecraft through one into Japan in 2047, they must be working on one somewhere now. That's only a couple of decades away."

"True. I will look into it. In the meantime, I want you to put together an elite force of operatives. Find me six of the best. Do you have the contacts?" Gorrick asked with urgency.

"I do."

"They will be trained to ultimately become the Zen time travel force. We will screen them together. You know the enemy, Kew, and you know the sort of fighter we need. We are in a war we must win. I have asked Honor to do the same but expect from previous experience for them to be only usable under certain circumstances and not to be relied on. From you, I expect much more. Do you get that, Kew?"

"Yes, sir," he barked enthusiastically, like a GI to his commanding officer.

"Good. You report directly to me."

Miss Fysh brought coffees.

"How long do I have, sir?"

"No time like the present, Kew. I'll arrange new offices for you… nowhere near Honor. Regina, tell Professor Adamski I want to see him in fifteen minutes."

After putting the coffees on the table, she stood beside Kew and told Gorrick, "Yes, sir."

She was close enough for Kew to inhale her perfume and give her the once over. He liked what he saw; nice legs, thin ankles.

She caught him mentally undressing her, turned, and with her back to her boss raised a sly eyebrow at Kew. He took it as confirmation of mutual attraction.

Oblivious of their little interplay, Gorrick was determined to uncover which Zen chapter had progressed most on the development of a wormhole generator. He already knew there was a competitive race between chapters to be first. Once he knew, he could set Adamski on the path of importing it. He was aware Adamski wouldn't approve because it meant using another physicist's blueprint, and his kind were known for being possessive. But that didn't bother Gorrick in the slightest. The issue was to get a wormhole generator up and functioning as quickly as possible in order to compete with OTT, and nothing was going to prevent him from achieving that.

It was Karzoff's turn to be pacing this time in the Professor's office with his cellphone up to his ear, desperately trying to contact the chopper pilot or members of the assault team. "I cannot raise anyone," he growled despondently and then flopped into a chair. "I will have to order another chopper."

"The helipad can only take one chopper at a time, mate, it wouldn't be able to land," Al said, picking up the box Karzoff had left on the table. "What's this?"

"Open it," Karzoff said.

Alice unlatched the small clips on either side of the fifty centimetres by ten grey leather upholstered box. "Beautiful craftsmanship," he said admiringly.

Inside, he found a majestic Gothic dagger in a hard leather scabbard. The hilt was carved with fine leather thonging. Treating it with the reverence of a holy relic, Al slipped the blade out of its scabbard and held it up. It was made of quartz, so highly polished he could see his reflection in it.

"Now this is a blade," Al said. He felt the edge with his thumb. "So sharp I could shave with it. Tell us about it, Karzoff."

"It was a prop made for a movie shot here about thirty years ago called Demon Hunter. It's called the Blade of Slaughter. It took my friend six months to craft it. I persuaded him to sell it to me," Karzoff explained.

"It is a seraph blade," Neit said, full of admiration. "It will cut a demon's flesh whereas nothing else will, and if plunged into its heart or brain, it will kill it."

"Alright! One of my songs is called Blade of Slaughter. You carry the blade of immortals... bathe in the serpent fire. You toast from the cup of the unvanquished, your thunder will shatter the quiet... Blade of slaughter," Alice sang, while slicing the air with the blade. As he swiped, it produced a whistling note. He stopped, "Did you hear that? A harmonic comes from the crystal." He sat back down. "When do we get the crystal-tipped bullets, Karzoff?"

"I am afraid they are a problem... it will take him months to make them," Karzoff said dispiritedly.

"That's okay, mate, you did well... this blade is unbelievable... I get what you were saying, Neit, you'd have to get in real close to the demon to use it, and the monster's long reach would make that seriously difficult," Al admitted.

"Yes, that problem proved fatal for many of my fellow Id."

"Neit, is that a costume you're wearing?" the Professor asked out of the blue.

"We don't have time to go into that now, mate," Alice said, trying to keep the focus on the problem at hand. He knew only too well how the Professor's enquiring mind could easily drift off the track.

"I know how curious you humans are, so no problem Alice... Yes, this costume protects me from UV radiation and absorbs neutrinos, Professor."

"Hmm, will you ever show us your face?" The Professor probed deeper.

"No, but if it helps you to understand... I am invisible to your eye. I exist in a different bandwidth than you."

"What do you eat... drink?" asked the Professor.

"Sometimes you're like a tuba in string selection, Professor," Al groaned facetiously, annoyed that Neit was being interrogated.

"It's a fair question, Al," Secta intervened.

"My energy is derived totally from the absorption of neutrinos, Professor."

"What the stuff are neutrinos?" Al asked.

"Tiny neutral particles nicknamed ghost particles because most of the time they pass right through stars, beings, and other matter without interacting with it," Secta explained.

"When we have more time, I will explain further and tell you about the world of my origin… but for now, we need to attend to the more urgent matter of getting to The Lair," Neit said.

"But how?" Karzoff posed.

Alice got up, pointed the dagger at Secta, and declared, "Fire up a hole, Secta."

"A wormhole?" Karzoff said incredulously.

"Yep, a wormhole… we're going in!" Al snarled.

CHAPTER 10
THE DEVIL INSIDE

❝ I AM ONLY responsible for what I say, not for what you understand," Gorrick chastised Adamski.

"But sir, you gave me the authority to develop my design... I presumed—" he appealed.

Gorrick cut him off, "Wrong, I gave you the opportunity to come up with a design, I did not say we would necessarily implement it. Look, take the Japan chapter offering us a near-working generator as a positive. You will be able to get it up and running using your software much sooner than if you had tried to construct your own. The hardware will arrive here by air transport in a matter of days, we won't have to wait months or a year."

"But sir—"

Gorrick eyeballed him. "This is not a debate, Adamski... Go and prepare. I expect now that you have the paradigm, the schematics, and the technical drawings, you will be able to concentrate on adapting your pioneering software to run it. I remind you that what you have is exactly what Japan and other Zen chapters haven't been able to write, error-free controlling software. Now, can you see the advantage in this?"

Adamski acquiesced, "Yes, sir, I... I can focus on the driving software without the distraction of having to construct the hardware."

"Correct."

"Now, while you're here, can you please take the time to explain to me in layman's terms, how your wormhole generator will function?"

Adamski perked up a little, he enjoyed talking about his work. "The unit is a circular titanium pipe twenty metres high. At sixty-centimetre intervals around it are positioned powerful electromagnets. Protons or electrons or other particles are injected into the accelerator and induced to speed around it at close to the speed of light."

"Are you describing a condensed particle collider?" Gorrick asked.

"Yes, more or less. We then activate a collision event with a minuscule organic object that originated from the target destination... it must be organic to register an exact date. This presents the target timeline. Once the target collides with the accelerated particle, a wormhole the size of a Higgs boson opens for a nanosecond. If we can reduce a human to atoms then when the wormhole opens, we can inject those atoms through dimensional space to the target time. The entry point of the clockwise rotating wormhole has a positive charge and at the other end it rotates counter-clockwise with a negative charge. When the atoms pass through the negative charge, they reconstitute and the time traveller materialises intact."

"Brilliant, is that how Kairos functions?" Gorrick asked.

"Fundamentally yes. The critical factors are the timing and, of course, the serum Doctor Secta invented. Without it, time travel wouldn't be possible."

"As much as I hate to admit it, he is a brilliant man," Gorrick said.

"Yes, he, his sister Doctor Hope, and Professor de Luz are equally ingenious. It was de Luz who came up with the process of injecting a time traveller's atomic structure into a wormhole," Adamski explained.

"Thank goodness you've managed to isolate the serum; otherwise, it would have taken us years to develop."

"Longer, I think. But it still might not work… however, should it fail, I have a card up my sleeve."

The word "fail" isn't in a Gorrick's vocabulary. His distaste for the word registered on his face and in his tone. "What do you mean by that?"

Adamski recognised the bad reaction and sought to correct it. "I… I mean to say, sir, that as a back-up in case of a problem, we have our own time traveller in Kew. All I need to do is create the activation formula so he can be reduced to atoms. He already carries enough of the serum in his system for it to work."

Gorrick thought about it a moment and then his expression suggested he'd come to terms with it in a positive manner. "And is that something you can do sooner rather than later?" he questioned calmly.

"Oh, yes, sir, much sooner. It will only be a matter of days before I have the activation formula synthesised."

"Good. What more do we need?"

"The next most important part, sir; the drive mechanism."

"Explain."

"Fortunately, the blueprint that was hacked of the early model Kairos wasn't completely useless. It showed the computer system OTT have employed to drive the entire process… It is a Cray XC 70 Supercomputer with Dragonfly network topology. The software I have written will be more efficient than theirs. The supercomputer locks everything together. It drives the accelerator… it determines the collision point and locks in the exact nanosecond to deliver the traveller's atoms into the wormhole with absolute precision, something that couldn't be achieved without it. Plus, it stores the telemetry to activate a reverse wormhole for the time traveller to return."

"This Cray XC 70 Supercomputer sounds expensive."

"About three million dollars, sir," Adamski said tentatively.

Gorrick wasn't rattled by the amount.

"I expect they are not available off the shelf?"

"Nearly, only a few minor customising adjustments, and we could have one up and running in a week."

"Have you submitted the costs to accounting?" Gorrick asked.

"Yes, sir, they're awaiting your approval."

"Thank you, that was very informative, Adamski... keep me up to speed."

The little man trudged out of the office, leaving Gorrick satisfied. The prospect of having a wormhole generator up and running sooner than later had him excited.

Gorrick got to his feet, walked over to the window, and looked out at Sydney Harbour sparkling in the afternoon sunshine. Provided Adamski could get his act together, he would soon be able to compete with OTT in time travel. The challenge now lay in obtaining intelligence on future OTT missions, and to that end, he needed Honor to concentrate on cyber-espionage. He strode back to his desk and phoned her. It would mean taking her off pursuing Black Alice and focusing on mining the intel required. That was fine by him, as he preferred to have Kew deal with Alice for the time being.

At first, Honor took it badly. She was keen to make amends for her recent failure and felt the opportunity of redemption had been removed. However, when Gorrick suggested that her expertise might be better directed at obtaining intel on prospective OTT missions, her mood lightened. During the course of the conversation, to avoid any petty jealousies, Gorrick avoided mentioning that Kew had been given the task of eliminating Alice.

Alice stepped out of the vortex that was still rotating counter-clockwise around him. It shut down seconds later, leaving him standing alone in the lounge room of The Lair.

"I do not like this," Neit said with dread inside Alice's mind.

Alice instinctively felt for the sheathed crystal dagger strapped to his belt.

Because it was growing dark outside, the sensor lights switched on.

"We should cut the power to the lights so I can come out and help you," Neit suggested.

"Okay, there's a mains switch in the kitchen," Al said.

He moved through the corridor commando-style, only to stop when he came to the kitchen door.

"Would it know you're here?" Alice queried.

"No. I will not come out of you until you have located it. We should not lose the element of surprise," Neit said.

"Fine," Al agreed.

Al drew his blade and holding it ready, carefully pushed open the swinging kitchen door. A light immediately illuminated the L-shaped room. He opened the fuse box fixed to the wall behind the door, took out the emergency flashlight, and then flicked off the mains switch. The kitchen fell into darkness. He turned on the torch and noticed something on the floor in the beam. As he approached, a gruesome sight was revealed: a severed arm. On closer inspection, he could tell it belonged to Rita, the maid.

"What the hell?" he said shocked.

He proceeded, shining the torch ahead of him, slowly, cautiously, expecting the worst, and then the flashlight revealed it. On the floor, in a massive pool of blood, lay the dismembered body of Rita, wide-eyed staring in a lifeless rictus of death. He had to hold back throwing up. As he flashed the torch around, it uncovered the rest of the shocking scene. The white-painted cupboards were drenched in blood it was like a slaughterhouse.

"She's been ripped to pieces," he groaned. It was his first encounter with the barbarous monster, and its handiwork had chilled him to the bone. "This is insane," Alice mumbled.

"I feel your anxiety, Alice… but we will need all of your strength to get through this," Neit cautioned.

"I'll be right, just a bit of a shock, that's all."

He shined the torch back down at Rita and highlighted clawed footprints in the blood on the floor leading towards the other exit door.

"It went that way," he said, shining the torch at the door and the doorknob drenched in blood.

Only the sound of Alice taking a deep breath for courage before moving on permeated the deathly silence. His steps towards the door were less confident than they had been when he first entered the kitchen; his legs were now trembling.

He opened the door and shined the flashlight at the bloody footprints that continued across the living room floor towards the staircase to the bedroom on the next level.

"It went up there?" he whispered. "Feels like it could jump out from anywhere."

He felt the darkness closing in on him, and with it, the fear caused a knot in his stomach.

"You need to find Sonoko; he would not have killed his host," Neit advised.

Aware this mission was never going to be pretty, he started up the staircase. By the landing of the second floor, the footprints had become faint but still obvious enough to see they were headed for the main bedroom. The torch lit up the hallway and another body. This time, a trooper. He was laying facedown spread-eagled on the floor. Alice got to him, turned him over, and was somewhat relieved to find it wasn't Trooper Dicks. He knelt down and felt for a pulse.

"He's dead, neck's broken." He shined the torch on the trooper's right hand holding a pistol. "S'pose that was useless."

"It could wound but not kill it," Neit said.

"What if you shoot it in the head?"

"I do not know... we did not have such weapons when we fought demons."

"Surely if you had the technology to build wormholes, you would've had guns?"

"We did not build wormholes, Alice, that was En-Ki."

Alice removed the pistol from the trooper's grip and checked the magazine. It was empty, so he took a fresh clip from the trooper's belt and loaded it. He felt better having a gun and figured that maybe Neit hadn't mentioned using a gun because he'd never used one.

Neit read the thought and said, "Perhaps you are right, it is certainly worth a try."

With his legs trembling less now that he was better armed, he pointed the torch at the floor. Though they were faint, the torch lit up bloody claw prints leading to the bedroom door. There was no doubting Gaap had gone inside.

With a shaky hand, Alice slowly turned the door handle and then pushed open the door. He shined the torch at the bed and spotted Sonoko curled up, either asleep or dead. Then he caught something out of the corner of his eye. There was a body on the floor near the bathroom door. The torchlight revealed it was Viktoria. He quickly went to her, knelt down, felt for a pulse in her neck, and was relieved to find it weak, but she was alive. Shining the torch along her body, there were no wounds. She was facedown, so he carefully and quietly turned her over. Her face was badly bruised, her mouth bleeding. She had been badly beaten and probably knocked senseless. But at least she wasn't dead.

Neit's voice resounded in his mind, warning, "Alice, turn around quickly."

CHAPTER 11
TORN

IN THE DARKNESS of the bedroom, Alice rose to his feet from Viktoria flat out on the floor and turned towards Sonoko on the bed. The torchlight lit up a grotesque beast rising out of Sonoko's body. Neit had been spot-on with his description of the foul thing. It looked like it had climbed down from the eaves of Notre Dame. A gargoyle, with a dog-like muzzle filled with snarling teeth, pointed ears, powerful shoulders with muscly arms, and massive claws. Its torso was cut like a bodybuilder but covered in dark olive scales. A loud guttural purring, like that of a big cat, a tiger, or a panther, rumbled from it, and its evil yellow cat-like eyes glared menacingly at Alice. As its big powerfully built legs stepped out of Sonoko onto the floor, Alice aimed the pistol.

The monstrous two-hundred-centimetre beast took one look at the pistol and in the blink of an eye morphed into vapour. Alice had missed the opportunity to shoot.

"Now we are in trouble," Neit cautioned in Alice's mind.

With the torch held in one hand aimed at the vapour and his pistol aimed in the other, Alice tracked it moving like black smog pushed by a breeze towards him.

"Retreat, Alice, now!" Neit shouted.

Alice obeyed and raced out of the room with the vapour trailing him.

On the run along the hallway, Neit said hurriedly, "We need it solid to kill it... use the light... the vapour is affected by light."

Alice knew exactly what to do. He charged back down the stairs headed for the kitchen. The vapour shadowed him, gliding over the floor like a waft of inky smoke.

"It cannot hurt you while it is vapour, and it cannot enter you while I am here," Neit advised.

It didn't matter, Al was having no part in it catching up with him. He crashed through the swinging kitchen door, opened the fuse box, and flicked on the mains. The kitchen and lounge room lights illuminated immediately. He left the torch behind and with the pistol up and ready pushed back out through the door. He stopped in the lounge room holding the gun in two hands, scanning the room. There was someone sitting at the breakfast table on the balcony with his back to him.

Alice moved slowly, vigilantly towards the open sliding glass patio doors.

He stopped before entering the balcony and fiercely ordered, "Stand up with your hands raised!"

The person turned sharply in his seat to face Alice.

He instantly recognised him. "Trooper Dicks?" Alice questioned.

"Yes, Mr Alice... I was knocked out by someone and only just came around," he said rubbing his head.

Alice lowered his gun.

"I think it's him, Alice," Neit said in Al's mind. "You must get close and kill him with your blade."

It was a concept Alice found difficult... how could he stab and kill Trooper Dicks, one of his own men?

"He who hesitates is lost, get in close and stab him, Alice," Neit advocated forcefully.

But Alice was hesitant. Neit hadn't known about using a gun; how could he be sure Gaap had possessed Dicks?

"Are you one hundred percent certain it's in him?" Al thought.

"No... but if you want to be sure, ask him something that only you and Trooper Dicks would know."

That seemed sensible. Alice recalled signing an autograph for Trooper Dicks in the street on his way to Oceana HQ, for that fateful interview with Honor ages ago. He slid the pistol into his belt but hovered his hand over the hilt of the blade.

"Hands down, Trooper, it's okay, I thought you were the enemy," Alice said amiably.

Trooper Dicks remained seated while Alice approached him.

"Wouldn't your family be worried you're not home?" Alice queried, standing close to the trooper.

"Oh, they won't worry, they're used to me being late."

"What's your daughter's name again?" He remembered signing the autograph to Dorothy.

"Dorothy, you signed the graph to her," Dicks recalled.

"Gaap has accessed his memory," Neit said. "He cannot jump into you while I am here; you need to trick him."

Alice thought for a moment, then said, "Who hit you?"

"I don't know... it came from behind. I've been laying on the floor out cold for I don't know how long."

"Is the pilot upstairs?" Al asked.

"I guess so."

"Okay, call base now on your implant and tell them we have one officer down, and we're leaving now," Alice said, figuring Gaap might not know how to access the trooper's implant. "Come on, we'll go to the helipad."

Trooper Dicks got up slowly from his chair, then in a quick movement went for his side gun. Alice drew the blade in a flash and plunged it into the trooper's lower stomach. Then, in a quick action, he belted the gun out of the trooper's grasp onto the floor.

Trooper Dicks slumped to his knees, holding the bleeding wound in his gut.

"Kill him!" Neit almost screamed in Alice's mind.

Al hesitated, and it was just enough time for the black vapour to escape from the trooper.

Dicks collapsed. The lights inside were too bright for Gaap to enter in his vapour form, so he morphed back into the beast. Alice and Neit had achieved their goal; Gaap was now in a form that could be killed... but even so, by the look of it, Alice knew he was in for one hell of a fight.

Alice raised the pistol and was about to pull the trigger when Gaap unexpectedly jumped at the prostrate body of Dicks, re-entering him. Then, moving like a macabre man-sized marionette, Dicks, with eyes closed, obviously unconscious, rose awkwardly to his feet, then flopped into a chair with his chin on his chest. In a sharp, unnatural movement, his head jerked up to face Alice, his eyes opened wide, and he spoke with a bizarre and raspy voice.

"End this futile pursuit, Black Alice. It will only result in death and destruction."

With his pistol aimed at Dicks, he snapped, "Destruction is your master's goal anyway, isn't it, Gaap?"

"If you know my name, then you know what I am capable of... nothing can stand in my way," Gaap snarled.

"Be careful, Alice, he is cunning. You have him where you want him; you have to shoot Trooper Dicks. The death of one to save many," Neit urged.

Alice was torn; he didn't want the Trooper's death on his conscience. A patina of sweat broke on his forehead as he kept the gun trained on the target with both hands, a nervous finger on the trigger.

"I know your boss, En-Lil, sent you here to kill me... there is no easy way out of this... it's either you or me," Al argued.

"You can't kill me, little man, you can only kill him."

"That's what you think," Alice snarled.

"It would take more than just you, Black Alice," Gaap growled.

Not expecting it, Alice's body shuddered when Neit stepped out of him, snatched the knife out of his hand, and stood at his side holding the blade threateningly at Gaap.

"We meet again," Neit exclaimed.

"So, this is how you know my name... an Id! I thought all of you were dead," Gaap snarled, a string of thick saliva hanging from his chin.

Alice sensed a change in his tone and figured the arrival of Neit had the monster worried.

"The last time we fought, I thought I had killed you," Neit said coldly.

"Ha! Just goes to show how gullible the Id are, or should I say, were. All you managed was for your friend to kill himself... for nothing!" Gaap roared with an ironical laugh. In a display of sheer strength, he picked up the solid wooden six-seater breakfast table in one hand and threw it like a feather six metres across the balcony. It hit the wall and smashed into kindling.

Neit lunged at him with the knife, but with a sharp wipe of his hand, Dicks knocked it out of his grip.

"Out of the way, Neit!" Al yelled.

Neit ducked, and Alice fired four shots into Dicks' chest. As he slumped forward in his chair, dead, Gaap erupted from his body as the beast. In a rage, he grabbed Neit and then held him as a shield, backing slowly towards the patio doors.

"Shoot, Alice, shoot! Do not worry about me!" Neit pleaded.

But Alice wasn't prepared to risk it. Neit was far too important. Instead, he dived for the knife on the ground and charged Gaap, slashing at him with it, narrowly avoiding cutting Neit held tight in Gaap's clutches.

A slash caught Gaap's extended hand and severed a finger. He growled like an angry lion and unceremoniously cast Neit hard against the wall. The force was so fierce it knocked Neit out cold.

Al kept slashing at Gaap but couldn't get close enough to inflict any serious damage. Then, timing it between desperate lunges from

Alice, the beast turned sharply and fled into the living room. Al hadn't expected him to be so quick on his feet. He chose not to chase after Gaap but to attend Neit.

"Neit, Neit, are you with me?"

Neit came around. Holding his head, he said, "Yes, yes... what happened?... where is he?"

"He took off inside."

"Did you wound him?" Neit asked, taking Alice's hand up.

"I don't know, it all happened so fast but..." he checked the floor, "I think I..." he found what he was looking for and picked up Gaap's severed claw, "Got this."

"Just what we need, keep it safe," Neit said.

Alice slipped the bloody digit into his pocket.

"Which way did he go?" Neit asked.

"He ran back inside."

"He has probably gone back to his host; it would be the safest place for him. We should get Sonoko back to HQ; it would be easier to deal with him once she's confined."

Al nodded affirmatively, pulled his cell phone, and dialled Secta.

Alice had brought the Clock Drive for Sonoko. A short time later, a vortex opened for the three of them to pass through back to Kairos.

In the interim, a chopper was dispatched to rescue the survivors, which turned out to be only Viktoria. A commando and a forensic officer were lowered from a hovering chopper onto the helipad at The Lair and soon discovered the remains of the missing pilot; Gaap had also torn him to pieces.

Alice and Sonoko emerged from Kairos, greeted by Karzoff, two guards, and Hope. Alice chose to act as if nothing had happened at The Lair and Gaap hadn't possessed her, so she kept quiet.

As Karzoff led them into the control room, Sonoko mentioned, "I feel very strange not being connected to my i-Keeper."

Alice knew that Sonoko's odd feeling probably stemmed from Gaap's possession. He also knew that in her time, Sonoko's life had been managed by an organic cochlear stem-cell implant behind her right ear. The VV, as it was called in Japan, kept her constantly connected to an Internet-like system known as the i-Keeper, providing access to a vast database of information for her daily needs. Consequently, she had become highly dependent on the i-Keeper, and without it, she would undoubtedly feel insecure.

"I suppose it'd be like being off the teat," Al joked.

Sonoko nodded, not entirely understanding the reference, but Hope chuckled, fully grasping the joke.

The pneumatic door hissed open, and once inside, Karzoff took charge. "Sonoko, we brought you back here because it was too dangerous for you to stay at The Lair. We will provide you a room here. Let me take off your Clock Drive for now."

Sonoko glanced at Alice, worried about being separated from him.

"It'll be alright, babe," Al reassured her warmly. "It's only temporary."

"Come on, Sonoko. I will take you there now," Karzoff said.

Sonoko gave Alice a sad look that tugged at his heartstrings, but he tried to comfort her, saying, "It's okay, kiddo. I'll be with you soon."

She reluctantly followed Karzoff and the two troopers out of the control room.

"How's Viktoria?" Alice asked Hope.

Hope grimaced, "Secta has been beside himself with worry."

"She was out cold when I found her, but she had a pulse. I couldn't see any physical damage."

"I saw the photos you sent of the maid and the troopers. It must have been terrible," Hope said sympathetically.

Alice sat on the edge of the bench. "There wasn't much left of poor old Rita."

"So, is it in Sonoko?" Hope inquired.

"Neit thinks so, but he can't be sure. I had to shoot Trooper Dicks because the mongrel thing possessed him," Alice admitted, feeling disheartened.

Hope placed a consoling hand on his shoulder. "I'm sorry, Al. That must have been awful."

"Yeah, he's got a daughter, Dorothy. I signed a graph for her..."

Secta walked in and said, "Alice, glad you're okay. I heard it was pretty rough..."

"Yeah. Any word on Vik?" Alice asked, disconsolately.

Secta nervously wrung his hands. "She's still in a coma... The doctor says she took a heavy blow to the head."

"Head trauma can take some time," Hope said sympathetically.

Despite Hope's positive spin, Secta continued pacing the floor.

Alice shivered as Neit stepped out of him and asked, "What is the next step with Sonoko?"

Secta stopped and exclaimed, "Oh, Neit... we were waiting to ask you that."

"Well, provided he is in her, I would suggest you erect a magnetic force field around Sonoko; otherwise, Gaap will simply turn to vapour and escape under the door," Neit explained.

Hope jumped out of her seat, as if on a mission. "I'll go find the Professor and get him onto it."

As the door closed behind her, Neit admitted, "You know we cannot be certain Gaap is in Sonoko."

"What do you mean?" Secta questioned.

"I was only guessing that Gaap would return to his host."

"There must be a way of finding out?" Alice probed.

"Sooner rather than later. We don't want that bloody thing on the loose around here," Secta declared firmly.

"You're telling me!" Al snarled, then remembered something, reaching into his pocket and pulling out the severed claw. He held it up for Secta to see. "But we have this."

CHAPTER 12
ENTROPY

❝ I REQUIRE AN agent to infiltrate Oceana, so you will apply for a job there," Honor said decisively to a suited-up, skinny Chinese man seated opposite her. "I have prepared references for you to submit."

He scanned Honor's office as though valuing it for an auction.

"I understood my job at ZEO was to be proactive, not undercover," he said gruffly without any noticeable accent.

"Take it from me, Mr So, cyber-espionage takes many forms. Yes, I originally spoke of you leading a tactical commando force, but my orders have since changed, which is not uncommon here at Zen," she said sardonically.

"Call me William or Will. I'm not one for formality. Look, I get what you're saying, but being a spook isn't my cup of tea. I'm combat-trained." His eyes drilled into Honor's, unyieldingly. For a thin, unassuming frame of a man, he punched above his weight. His stare caused the tiny hairs to rise on Honor's forearms. Will So's military record, prior to him becoming a mercenary, was exemplary. He didn't look like much, but as a mercenary, he was the entire package: technical, cyber, and combat-ready.

"Your SAS record suggests otherwise... Will," Honor said coolly, reading his record displayed on the computer monitor in front of her. "Seems you have a penchant for volunteering for black missions."

"I did, but things are different in a war zone."

"Well, consider this a new kind of war zone. We are engaged in an undeclared war with Oceana. Right here," she handed him a flash drive. "On this, you will find a brief and a number of videos I have compiled on OTT. You should binge-watch them. My secretary will submit your application to Oceana HR today once you have completed the online forms. They advertised for security officers, and you have all the necessary qualifications. The position is effective immediately."

He took the flash drive, stood, and glared at her expressionlessly.

"As incentive, if you succeed in the mission, I will personally give you a substantial bonus."

The promise of financial reward brought a smirk to his otherwise sullen face. Honor watched him leave, feeling confident that the scrawny, unremarkable-looking Australian-born Chinese would get the job done.

Layla poked her head in the doorway. "I'm leaving for the day, ma'am. Is there anything else?"

"Yes, come here."

Dressed in a cute red polka-dot A-line knee-length, sleeveless dress, Layla breezed into the room. Her blue-black hair was short-cropped, advertising her classic tapered neck.

"Gorrick has absolved you of complicity in the recent penetration by OTT."

"Thank you, ma'am," Layla said with relief.

"But that does not mean you're completely off the hook."

"Sit down opposite me, Layla."

Layla complied.

"Before you leave, Layla, have Mr So, who should be waiting at your desk, complete the Oceana employment application on the flash drive I gave him. Then submit it immediately to Oceana HR over the secure network. I don't want them knowing where it came from." Her tone changed to sultry. "I like you, Layla. I fought for you with Gorrick, who wanted to let you go," she lied. "You owe me."

Layla responded with a curt smile.

Secta and Hope had left the Kairos control room to analyse Gaap's claw in the laboratory. The Professor, Alice, Karzoff, and Neit were still debating how to deal with Gaap should they have him confined.

The Professor questioned, "I don't understand why Gaap left Viktoria and Trooper Dicks alive?"

"I agree, it seems out of character with what he did to the maid, the other trooper, and the pilot," said Karzoff.

"A valid point, I suspect he heard Alice arrive through the vortex, and it interrupted him," Neit proposed.

Al was seated at the console, peering through the large studio window at Kairos, thinking. He swivelled his chair round and said, "Nar, the pilot was killed on the helipad, and the trooper on the second floor... the maid in the kitchen, all too far apart. He left Trooper Dicks and Vik alive for a reason, I reckon."

"You might be right, Alice," Neit conceded.

"Wait a minute... so if he got what he needed from Trooper Dicks and then let him die, why did he let Viktoria live?" Karzoff queried.

Reality struck them all when they realised what might have happened.

"Are you thinking what I'm thinking?" the Professor queried.

"I reckon," Alice confirmed. "The bastard only left Vik alive to be his backup host. He might not be in Sonoko at all... he could be in Vik!"

The possibility had them on their feet and worried.

"He could have jumped from her into anyone visiting the infirmary by now," Neit asserted anxiously.

"Wait, there is no need to panic... not yet. Can we confirm which of them is hosting him, Neit?" Karzoff asked.

"No, we have no way of knowing if he has jumped... all we can do is wait until he reveals himself," Neit explained.

"But he might kill in the meantime," the Professor warned.

Karzoff posed, "Even if we could identify the correct host, how would we deal with it?"

"Alice would have to go to sleep and dream during which we could hunt down Gaap... but Alice would first need to know whether to dream of Sonoko or Viktoria. Gaap knows he is most vulnerable in a dream, but while it is day, he has no choice but to hide in his host and wait," Neit explained.

"So, let me get this straight... Alice needs to dream of, say, Viktoria, in order to connect with her. Is that what you're saying?" the Professor questioned.

"Yes. Once connected with the host, we can hunt down Gaap because he has possessed her... he would be hiding in her subconscious mind," Neit explained.

"Right, now I see why we need to know which is the right host," Karzoff admitted. "But how then do you kill it?"

"Only he or I can be killed in a dream because we both occupy the host, Alice would only be a visitor like an avatar... but he is vital because it is his dream, and he can change it to suit him," Neit explained.

"So, Alice can support you by altering the terrain or circumstances for you to hunt Gaap down, and what, stab him, is that right?" the Professor asked.

"No, I cannot take a weapon with me into a dream, I need to jump inside of him to destroy him," Neit said.

"But wouldn't that kill you as well?" Al queried.

"Not if I'm quick enough to get out in time," said Neit.

They pondered the ramifications for a moment, and then Karzoff jumped into action. "Okay, first, we need to isolate Viktoria to stop people from getting near her."

He was right. The more people exposed to Viktoria, the greater the risk of Gaap jumping into one of them and escaping, if he hadn't done so already.

"Wait, Karzoff, I must occupy you to prevent possession by Gaap," Neit said.

"How does that work?" the Professor asked.

Neit explained, "He is unable to enter what is already occupied."

Karzoff stopped at the door and turned back to Neit, looking flummoxed. Neit didn't wait for any more debate and slipped inside Karzoff.

Alice chuckled at Karzoff shivering, his eyes opened wide in surprise.

"Feels weird, doesn't it?" Al scoffed.

When the door closed behind Karzoff, the Professor told Alice, "Logically, you should dream of Sonoko and then Viktoria. That way, we'd know soon enough where Gaap is."

"It's not as easy as that, Professor. It takes time to find Gaap in the dreamscape... and let me tell you, it's weird inside someone's dream... spooky as hell. When I went into Sonoko's dreamscape, it was like being on the set of a sixties Hammer horror flick... a craggy forest of wicked black trees pointing at me like clawed fingers, doors that opened into completely different places. I mean, like you're in a living room, and you open a door to find a cemetery or something strange on the other side... and distorted stuff, like you're in a Salvador Dali painting or on acid."

"Hmm, there seems to be a lot of rules, difficult to keep up with them, but it's so fantastic. What I'd dang-well give to experience consciously exploring someone's dream," the Professor said enthusiastically.

Gorrick awakened abruptly from a power-nap and glanced around his office, somewhat startled and disoriented. It took him a few moments to re-establish the year, day, and place. It was a side effect of having lived so long. Sometimes during a power-nap, he would be cast back to another time... but this instance was different... he had connected with the clone hive: a psychic force similar in a way to the link that often connects identical twins, providing a nexus between all the living Gorrick clones.

While unconscious, he had found the hive alive with news: an arrow of time had opened in Sydney through which a demon had materialised.

Gorrick stood from his armchair and walked to the window, looking north and muttered, "Gaap is here." He had learned that his master, En-Lil, had sent Gaap. The hive was so active because this marked the commencement of the war between Zen and humanity. This was what the clones had been created for... to reach a point in time when humanity had managed to harness the power of mass destruction and then for Zen to turn it against them. Now he could freely focus on the wormhole generator and leave the all-powerful Gaap to rid the world of his nemesis, Black Alice.

Special lenses in his eyes allowed him to see a faint radioactive light in the northern sky. It was a light that only his hive and demons could see. The faint light beyond the Sydney Harbour Bridge, at a low trajectory on the horizon, was the radiance from the arrow of time: the rift.

The tiny hairline singularity at The Lair, Gaap had emerged from, had opened a little wider since his killing rampage. Within it, entropy stretched all the way back to the planet Eris biding time to wreak havoc on Earth. The rift would grow in proportion as an esurient parasite feeding on the terror of the brutal slayings perpetrated by Gaap. Each time he would take a human life in a barbarous fashion, the arrow of time would expand, and high-energy oscillations increase. Ultimately, it would transform from a singularity to a black hole capable of drawing everything from the surface of Earth into its ravenous vent.

With the Gorrick clone experiment failing and his plan of world domination derailed at every turn by his nemesis, Black Alice, the black hole was En-Lil's counteroffensive. Though Alice was Gaap's primary target, ultimately the more of a maelstrom that could be generated by human suffering, the larger the black hole would become until it finally devoured the entire world.

The secondary objective was to destabilise world peace through nuclear war. The suffering on such a massive scale caused by such a war would fuel the singularity far beyond what Gaap could achieve alone. Thus, it was the grand design for the Zen Corporation under the auspices of Gorrick to incite a world nuclear war.

Right then, Gorrick was staring at the radiance from the epicentre of hell: a tiny undisclosed hairline fracture in the fabric of time hovering next to an indoor swimming pool inside The Lair on Pelican Island, north of Sydney.

As the main provider of nourishment to the singularity for the time being, Gaap needed to keep killing to facilitate its growing demands. As he killed, he absorbed the élan vital of his victim, which he then remitted by electromagnetic oscillation directly to the singularity.

While in its infancy, the singularity was most vulnerable.

CHAPTER 13
SO

WITH VIKTORIA SAFELY contained in a negative pressure room, Karzoff made his way from sickbay to the elevator.

"Where are we going now?" Neit asked Karzoff mentally.

He wasn't expecting a voice in his head, and it gave him a jolt. "Huh Neit! That is a new experience. Um, I… I am going to HR. We are running seriously low on well-trained agents since one was killed, and another injured when Alice was ambushed by Zen agents a short while back. As a consequence, I have ordered a recruitment drive. I want to check the results."

"Fine, but we need to get back to Alice quickly. We have little time to waste."

"I understand. It is on the way and will only take a moment," Karzoff assured Neit.

There were three men sitting in the waiting room at Human Resources. The HR officer, forty-year-old hyper-efficient Kyleen Hern, dressed in a dignified business suit with short-layered blonde hair, displayed her pleasure at seeing Karzoff with an amorous smile.

He approached her desk. "Miss Hern, how are you?"

"Well, thank you, sir. These three gentlemen are to be interviewed for the position in security. Do you wish to attend?"

"Unfortunately, right now I am dealing with a crisis," Karzoff said, giving the men a once-over. "I just wanted to check the response."

She handed Karzoff three folders containing a dossier on each recruit.

"If you could check through these while you're here, it would be very helpful," Kyleen said, with a warm smile.

"She is fond of you, Karzoff," Neit whispered.

"I know that, thank you," Karzoff said stiffly.

"I'm sorry, sir. I just thought that while you're here..." Kyleen said, shocked by Karzoff's gruff response.

He looked up sharply from the documents, realising the confusion.

"Sorry, I... I was not talking to you, Miss Hern," he stammered and stuttered, awkwardly attempting to make sense of his statement to her.

"Best not to try and explain yourself, Karzoff, just continue reading. She will just put it down to your obvious eccentricity," Neit advised, highly amused.

Karzoff changed the subject. "How is Vee going in her training?"

Kyleen checked her computer, "Ah, another week or so, sir. She is an excellent candidate."

"Good," he acknowledged cheerfully, then glanced again at the three men. It was obvious to him that out of the candidates, one stood out like a sore thumb. William So's biography read like it was purpose-written for the job.

"Which is William So?" Karzoff muttered to Kyleen sotto voce.

"The Asian gentleman," she replied, with a wrinkled brow, thinking the name So should have made it obvious to Karzoff.

"His credentials are impeccable... after you've confirmed them and interviewed him, if he passes, sign him up, give him interim security clearance, and let me know. I have an immediate task for him."

"But we normally screen for—"

Karzoff cut her off, "Bypass the formalities this time, Miss Hern. We are in crisis control here, as I intimated, and we are understaffed."

"Yes, sir."

"Thank you, Miss Hern."

"You're welcome, sir," she said with another amorous flutter of blue painted eyelids.

As Karzoff moved off, headed for the elevator, he caught a steely-eyed glance from William So seated sandwiched between the other two applicants.

"You are thinking of having him guard Sonoko. Do you not think he should first win your trust?" Neit asked.

"I have had enough of you, Neit," Karzoff grumbled, irritated. "That was embarrassing back there. And no... he has better credentials than I."

"To quote Nikola Tesla: 'Every effort under compulsion demands a sacrifice of life-energy. As we grow older, reason asserts itself and we become more and more systematic and designing. Those early impulses, though not immediately productive, are of the greatest moment and more often than not shape our very destinies,'" Secta said, reading the quote from his cellphone.

"It was the same for me at Uni," the Professor admitted. "If I only had that time over again, there are things I should have pursued."

"Well, keep perfecting Kairos, mate, and you might get the chance to go back and make that correction," Al concluded with a chuckle.

"Listening to you guys, I'm fortunate to have been given the opportunity to see my dream realised at my age," Robert admitted, talking about Kairos and the opportunity to make real what was ostensibly a theoretical design.

They were waiting for Karzoff to return from containing Viktoria. The door to the control room opened with a hiss, and Hope entered.

"I have the results on the claw, guys. The DNA is alien, blood type unknown... eighty per cent of the alien RNA in its nervous system has been edited from an outside source. Twice a portion of the sample transformed to vapour after I touched it with a foreign object, such as a probe or pipette, which seems to be an auto-defensive reaction. Its morphing ability is astonishing... I would suggest it can mimic almost anything in nature for an amount of time I'm yet to establish. Similar to the manner in which an octopus can camouflage at will, only Gaap's entire physical being can restructure. Quite amazing."

"Phew, some kind of adversary," the Professor said, ending with a cynical sigh.

"You didn't come across a way of killing it, did you?" Al asked.

"Yes, actually... a particular helicase enzyme does separate the DNA double helix molecule."

"What the stuff's a helicase?" Al questioned.

"Motor protein enzymes that utilise energy from nucleoside triphosphate hydrolysis in order to unwind the two annealed nucleic acid strands of a DNA," Secta explained.

"Yeah, right," Al grumbled, "now for all us dunces?"

"The enzyme unwinds the DNA helix, killing it," the Professor clarified.

"There are a lot of different helicases... but in this instance, pure hydrogen worked... broke it down completely," Hope said.

Al was intrigued and asked, "What happened when you used it... the hydrogen?"

"The sample burst into flames," Hope said, playacting an explosion with her hands.

Secta jumped up and began pacing the floor. It was the breakthrough he was hoping for, a scientific means to defeat the demon beyond a gun, a dagger, or crystal-tipped bullets.

The door opened.

"Karzoff," Secta said. "Where did you put Viktoria?"

"In the negative pressure room, no air can get in or out. Provided the demon has not jumped from her already, she is safely contained."

"What about Sonoko?" Al asked.

"She is guarded and monitored 24/7 on CCTV," Karzoff reported.

"But we know that isn't good enough, the room isn't airtight, is it?" the Professor queried.

"No, we only have the one negative pressure room," Karzoff admitted.

Hope dimmed the lights for Neit to emerge.

Karzoff shivered as Neit stepped out from him.

"What do you think Neit?" Hope asked.

"I do not know if Gaap is here, but I do sense another presence that is far more dangerous," Neit said gravely, and that got their full attention. Secta stopped pacing the floor and took a seat to listen to what could be worse than a rogue demon.

"The arrow of time has re-opened. The same one that Gaap had entered through. I sensed something when at The Lair, but it must have been too small to identify. Since the killings, it has grown in proportion," Neit explained.

"What is an arrow of time?" Al questioned, worried that a new obstacle had reared its ugly head.

"Asymmetry in time, or easier to understand, an imbalance," Secta explained.

"Like a wormhole?" Alice proposed.

"Similar, only far more destructive. An arrow of time is virtually a baby black hole," the Professor said gravely.

"And why's that so bad?" Al asked.

"Because of entropy... it can ultimately cause the collapse of time," Secta boomed. He was up and pacing again, his face paled by the threatening disclosure. "This will be by far our most prodigious battle. It's now quite obvious that this singularity is how En-Lil intends to destroy the world."

"Once open, it can only be closed at its origin," Neit added.

"Are you absolutely certain of that, Neit?" Secta asked fervently.

"I have no doubt, Secta."

Alice got up and joined Secta, pacing about, only he was pacing like a big agitated cat. "Never bloody rains, it pours," he almost hissed.

Neit summed things up. "There is only one option remaining, Alice. You must kill En-Lil soon before the arrow of time enlarges to the point of no return."

It was clear what needed to be done, but there were some serious questions to be answered first. To begin with, will the claw provide a tight enough lock on the bearings for them to send a wormhole to the Futurum Tower on Eris? Then, would the atmosphere of Eris be hostile to a human? And... what is the gravity?

Secta, Hope, the Professor, and Robert went off to the Professor's study to research the answers to those three critical questions, while Alice, Neit, and Karzoff stayed in the control room concerned about how to deal directly with Gaap.

"Wait, what if Gaap has not possessed Sonoko or Viktoria? What if he was using them as a diversion, and that is why he let Viktoria live?" Neit proposed.

"I don't get it... why?" Al queried.

"Because he might not be here only to kill you, Alice, but to guard the arrow of time," Neit asserted.

Alice slowly nodded thoughtfully and then said, "In the same way he guarded the treasure? Tell me, is the Tablet of Destinies one of the treasures?"

"I have no idea, Alice, why?" Neit asked.

"Because that might be how En-Lil got to use them on En-Ki."

"You might be right, Alice," Neit confirmed. "That would surely explain why Gaap was guarding the treasure. I presumed it was the value of the gold and jewels."

"Had an arrow of time opened then?" Alice asked.

"It must have, for Gaap to be there."

"So maybe Gaap escaped back through it to Eris with the Tablet of Destinies," Alice reasoned.

Karzoff received a text message. "I must go to orient a new recruit," he told them. Alice was too preoccupied with the notion he could go back in time to get the Tablet of Destinies from the treasury to notice Karzoff leave. Then he decided no, he needed to put an end to this once and for all... he needed to kill En-Lil.

"We must confirm Gaap is not in possession of either Sonoko or Viktoria before we can assume he is guarding the rift at The Lair. Alice?" Neit said, trying to snap Alice out of his musing.

"What's that?"

"We need to confirm Gaap's location," Neit repeated.

"Yes, but how? Where's Karzoff?"

William So was waiting at HR for Karzoff. Miss Hern got up from behind her desk to introduce the new recruit to his boss. "Senior Inspector Karzoff, this is William So, the only successful applicant."

"Has he been processed?" Karzoff asked.

"Yes, sir, I saw to it myself," Kyleen said modestly.

"Good. Welcome, Mr So," Karzoff said stiffly. "Thank you, Miss Hern. Follow me, So."

Karzoff led So to the elevator, which they took to sickbay. A brief walk along an austere corridor with their footsteps the only sound took them to an agent guarding a door. A brute of a guy in his late twenties, he looked more like a Rugby player than an agent.

"This is Agent Hooper, he is guarding this room. It is shielded by an electromagnetic field. An alert will sound should anything leave the room or enter it. You will relieve Agent Hooper and guard the door. I repeat, nothing or no-one is to enter or come out."

"Who or what's inside?" So inquired.

"That is classified. The mobile you were issued with has my number under direct dial one hash. Call if you need me, otherwise

Agent Hooper will relieve you in three hours. Any questions, So?" Karzoff asked firmly.

"No, sir."

As Karzoff and Hooper were leaving Agent So at his post, Alice arrived.

"Ah, Karzoff, Miss Hern said you might be here. I need to see Sonoko."

"I was just on my way back to Kairos, no problem." He pulled his cellphone from his pocket and punched in a code. "Disabling the field and..." he pressed more keys, "unlocking the door. There you go. Phone me when you have finished, and I will lock it back up."

"Thanks, I'll only be a few minutes."

"Black Alice, this is Agent William So, a new recruit," Karzoff said by way of introduction. "Black Alice is your superior, So."

"Will So... I think I know a relative of yours, Will Not, ha, ha," Alice joked in his normal cavalier manner. The look on Agent So's face said he wasn't impressed: he'd heard the gag before.

Alice opened the door and stepped inside. It was more like a hotel suite than a remand area. There were three rooms, a living room with kitchenette, a bedroom with an en-suite bathroom. Over the sound of the TV, Alice could hear Sonoko taking a shower. He went into the bedroom. The lights were dimmed.

He shivered as Neit left his body and then whispered so as not to be heard by Sonoko. "I'll come back and collect you in an hour. Is that long enough?"

"I presume so," Neit said.

Alice shut the door behind him, leaving Neit to do his job.

"Later, Will," Alice growled, passing the agent on guard to head for the elevator.

So wondered why this Alice character was so feared by Honor; he looked like he was only a few years out of high school and acted like a punk.

Once the elevator doors had closed on Alice, So pulled a small cellphone from his pocket. It wasn't the phone he'd been issued by

Miss Hern; it was an encrypted phone Honor had given him. He sent her a text explaining what he was doing and that he'd just met Black Alice. He also explained a person named Sonoko was in the room he was guarding. Within seconds of sending the text, a reply came. Honor ordered him to go into the room and get photos of the interior and the occupant. She advised if he is seen to claim he was just doing his job checking.

Agent So opened the door and slipped into the room. Sonoko was just finishing her shower. He stealthily snapped a few shots of each room, and then when Sonoko came out of the bathroom in a robe, got a shot of her in the dim light just as Neit was entering her.

"Oh, who are you?" Sonoko said abruptly, a little shocked at someone being there.

"Security ma'am, just checking you're all right," So claimed nonchalantly.

"I'm fine, thank you. What is your name?"

"Agent William So, ma'am... it's my first day on the job."

"Thank you, William."

Agent So made it back into the corridor just in time because the door locked behind him, remotely activated by Karzoff.

William wasted no time in sending Honor the pictures he'd taken.

Sitting behind her office desk, Honor peered at the photos on her cellphone. A smug look spread across her face like a virus as she asked herself, "Who is this Asian woman, Sonoko?"

She typed a message for So to find out more about Sonoko; where she is from, her nationality, and why she is there? In the meantime, she would show Gorrick the photographs.

An hour later, Alice and Karzoff approached Agent So in the corridor.

"Everything all right, So?" Karzoff inquired.

"Nothing that a coffee wouldn't fix, sir. I need something to break the monotony," he said, imperiously.

That didn't go down too well with Karzoff. "I would have thought a man with your military training would better understand what is required of a sentry," Karzoff snapped.

Alice sought to calm the waters. "I'd need a coffee myself, having to stand around like a Brown's cow. He could grab one now while we're inside, couldn't he, Karzoff?"

Karzoff eased off. "Yes, I suppose he can. There is a kitchen with a coffee machine at the end of the corridor. Take five."

"Thank you, sir," So said and scooted off.

Four minutes later, as he was walking back from the coffee machine, So heard voices in the corridor. He stopped around a corner to eavesdrop on a conversation between Alice, who had just come out of the remand room, and Karzoff, who had waited outside the door to give Alice and Sonoko some privacy. It seemed like a bizarre conversation to So because it was between three people, but there were only two present.

"I found no presence in Sonoko; we must check Viktoria now," Neit said from Alice.

"That's a relief," Alice sighed.

"Well, at least it narrows it down. Let's go," Karzoff said.

As they headed for the elevator, Agent So stepped out from around the corner, holding a mug.

"Agent So, take your post; the door is locked," Karzoff ordered.

"Yes, sir."

Alice and Karzoff carried on along the corridor to the elevator. Inside, Neit said, "I have a bad feeling about Agent So." The elevator doors closed.

Agent So immediately sent Honor a text about what he had overheard.

115

Honor was in Gorrick's office, showing him the photos she'd received from William So when a text came through. She read it and then showed it to Gorrick.

"A three-way conversation between two people? Hmm, get the boffins in security to test these photos in the same way they did for the CCTV footage... I think you might've stumbled upon something here."

Honor immediately dispatched the photos from her phone to the technical division at security, accompanied by an explanatory text.

CHAPTER 14
ACHILLES HEEL

O UTSIDE THE NEGATIVE pressure room, Alice and Karzoff sat waiting for Neit to complete his search for Gaap in Viktoria's mind.

"It'll be a relief to let Sonoko out; I feel guilty for locking her up," Alice admitted.

"If Viktoria is clear, then take Sonoko out for something to eat, maybe show her some sights of Sydney," Karzoff suggested.

"You reckon it's safe?"

"It will give me a chance to try out my new recruit on field work. Besides, things are likely to get crazy once we decide on the next move... I suspect you might soon be taking a trip off-planet."

"I've been off the planet for years, mate," Al said with a cheeky chuckle. "I'll check on Neit."

Alice pulled the pressurised door open, slipped in, and closed it behind him. Inside, Viktoria lay unconscious in a hospital bed with a multitude of medical gadgetry hooked up to her and beeping. Alice felt a shiver as Neit occupied him.

"You can have her released from here, Alice. There is no sign of Gaap, but she needs medical attention," Neit said in Alice's mind.

He went back outside to Karzoff and said, "She's all clear, mate. Better get the doctor; Neit reckons she needs immediate attention."

"I have arranged for you to take Sonoko out for something to eat. Secta has called a meeting in two hours, so you have time as long as you do not venture too far."

"Good-o, I'll go get her."

Honor was thrilled to learn from So that he had been assigned as a bodyguard for Alice for the next two hours. It was an opportunity not to be missed, so she wasted no time in informing Gorrick.

"It would not be difficult to slip Agent So a weapon and have him dispense with Alice once and for all," Honor said emphatically.

Sat behind his office desk, Gorrick pinched his bottom lip, mulling the idea over. He had put Kew on the case, but to avail of this opportunity, they didn't have much time.

"I agree, this is too good a chance to miss. What's your plan?" Gorrick asked.

Walking hand in hand through the city amidst the plethora of lunchtime pedestrians, Alice was taking Sonoko to the Bennelong Restaurant at the Sydney Opera House for lunch. With the harbour sparkling from the noonday sun in a cloudless blue sky, it was a perfect day.

"Sydney is very beautiful," Sonoko said.

"Yeah, it has its moments. If we had more time, I would take you to one of my favourite restaurant in Watson's Bay."

"I'm happy to go anywhere with you, Alice."

Every so often, a member of the public passing by would recognise Alice and say hello, something he prided himself in acknowledging.

Inconspicuously tailing them was Agent William So.

They crossed over Albert Street to make their way along Macquarie Street to the Opera House, passing only a block from the

Zen Building. It was then that a man in a conventional run-of-the-mill business suit covertly handed something to Agent So, who was on his cellphone receiving instructions from Honor.

"Sorry you haven't had the greatest of times here," Alice told Sonoko warmly.

"Oh, it's okay. I have not seen as much of you as I wanted, but I know you have been very busy."

Agent So quickened his pace until he was within earshot of Alice and Sonoko.

"I'll be leaving on a time travel mission in a couple of days. I wanted you to stay, but because your birthday is coming up, you'll have to return to your time."

She squeezed his hand a little tighter. "Why?"

"Because apparently two of you can't exist at the same time."

"But that was no problem for Secta when he came to 2047," Sonoko claimed.

"You're right of course but we needed to take a risk then. We can't afford to take a risk with you."

Agent So was holding his phone, eavesdropping on the conversation. Honor was recording it back at Zen Headquarters. Once the exchange was made, she would amplify the signal and filter the extraneous noise to hear it more clearly.

Sonoko was upset, tears traversed her pallid cheeks. Alice sought to lift her spirits.

"When I get back, I'll come to your time and we'll take a holiday somewhere... you plan it. Can you get more time off work?"

The idea cheered her up a little. "I have a few weeks of leave still owed to me, so yes, no problem," she said, wiping tears away. "Would you like to go to a warm place or a cold one?"

"You tell me, I'll be lobbing back from a pretty strange place, so I'll be happy to go somewhere safe and relaxing with you... anywhere."

Alice couldn't tell Sonoko his destination, and she knew not to ask.

"Okay, leave it to me," she said happily.

"Spare no expense, we can go anywhere on Earth or send a wormhole to another planet if you like," he joked.

The Opera House was in view now, and they reached the promenade leading to it.

So terminated the call; out in the open, he was far too conspicuous to be on the phone. He had his orders, pushed up through a crowd of tourists ascending the stairs, stealthily slipped a small syringe out of his pocket, and with it aimed at Alice, lunged to inject him in the back.

Just as he was doing it, an elderly lady slipped on the stairs directly in front of Alice, and he made a grab to catch her. In doing so, he knocked So's hand holding the deadly injection. It missed Alice and stabbed Sonoko in the thigh, causing her to stumble.

"You alright?" Alice asked, thinking he'd knocked her.

"Yes, yes, I'm fine."

Alice helped the old Korean lady regain her balance. "Are you okay?"

She nodded. "Thank you." And then carried on with her tour group.

Alice gave Sonoko a hug and then, holding her at arm's length, peered into her big, beautiful almond-shaped brown eyes. Standing on the Opera House esplanade with the warm breeze flagging her shiny, long black hair out behind her like a banner, she was an absolute picture. He wanted to kiss her. But just as he was about to, her eyes rolled back in her head, and she collapsed on the ground.

Agent So was quick to break from the covert position he'd retreated to after injecting the wrong mark, and he went to Alice's assistance. Down on one knee, holding Sonoko in his arms, it was all déjà vu for Alice... it was a replay of what had happened to his former girlfriend, Stain, when she collapsed from an overdose on his bathroom floor. With his brain swimming in confusion, he could tell by the colour of Sonoko's cheeks and her shallow breathing that whatever it was, it was life-threatening.

In the chaos of the moment, Alice recognised Agent So and deduced he'd been assigned by Karzoff to follow them.

"William, quick… phone Karzoff, tell him I need a doctor here fast, it's life and death."

A crowd had gathered around them. While Agent So was on the phone to Karzoff, a man in jogging gear pushed through the onlookers.

"I'm a doctor," he shouted in a strong British accent. "Let me through, please."

While Alice was holding Sonoko's limp body in his arms, the doctor checked her vitals.

"Have you called an ambulance?" the doctor asked urgently.

"Yes, my friend is calling now."

The doctor looked up at William on the phone and shouted at him, "Tell them to bring Atropine and to get here within ten minutes, or we'll lose her."

Alice glared at the doctor, "What are you saying, doctor?"

"I've seen this before in London. She's been injected with a nerve agent. Are you with her?"

"Yes."

"Is she a special government agent?"

"No, a scientist."

"Well, someone has tried to murder her, and unless the antidote gets here quick smart, whoever did it will have succeeded."

"It was fortunate the British doctor was there with the knowledge on nerve agents," Karzoff said.

"Yeah, visiting on holidays, staying in a hotel and taking a jog… serendipity maybe?" Alice pondered. "What was it anyway?"

"A VX-type nerve agent called Novichok administered intravenously. It works by inhibiting an enzyme called acetylcholinesterase at the nerve junction… effectively an off-switch.

It acts mainly on the body's involuntary nervous system, which controls things such as heart rate, respiratory rate, salivation, digestion, pupil dilation, and urination. The symptoms are white eyes as the pupils are constricted, convulsions, drooling, and in the worst cases—coma, respiratory failure, and death. We won't know how well Sonoko has responded to the antidote for at least forty-eight hours... much depends on the amount of time the nerve agent had to work and unfortunately that was longer than it should've been because of the difficulty we had in getting hold of the antidote: Atropine," Hope concluded with a sympathetic glance at Alice who was seated at the far end of the board table with his head in his hands. "I'm so sorry Alice."

Also present were Neit, the Professor, Secta, and Karzoff.

"I doubt Sonoko was the mark; it had to be you, Alice... There was no strategic value in hitting Sonoko. Anyhow, with what you told us about preventing the Korean lady from hitting the ground after tripping, I would say the commotion caused the assassin to miss his target... you," Karzoff observed. "This was Zen trying to kill you. We were fortunate agent So was there to call for help; otherwise, we would have lost Sonoko right there on the steps of the Opera House," Karzoff explained.

Alice looked up from his hands and snarled furiously, "We need to end this now!"

An eerie silence came from the cloak of contemplation that had descended upon them from Alice's outcry. They knew he was right; no-one was safe from the tyranny of Zen, and that needed to change.

Alice rose slowly to his feet. "Look, they assassinated the president, and they have tried every which way to kill me. They killed our agents, and as Secta and I witnessed in the not too distant future, they will be responsible for a devastating world war. We can't let that happen... Zen, Gorrick, and En-Lil must be destroyed, and now! It's solely up to us to prevent the horrible future we've experienced from eventuating," Alice argued passionately.

"And the arrow of time. It must be closed from its origin before it gets any bigger," Neit warned."

Al glared at the Professor. "Tell me my friend, will Gaap's claw give us a time lock to send a wormhole to Eris?"

"Yes, it will," the Professor said emphatically. "But the atmosphere of Eris will not support human life."

"So how does En-Lil survive there?" Al queried.

"The Futurum Tower might be contained inside an atmospheric bubble on Eris, similar to the force field you described surrounding the UFO in Tokyo. It could also provide gravity similar to Earth," Hope explained.

"So, the three questions have been answered... I can get there, breathe the air, and handle the G's... so Neit, next is to devise an attack plan," Al said.

Secta stood up. "I've modified a Salt gun to what I call a Gallium gun. It's designed to fire pepper spray bullets that explode on impact. It uses CO_2 cartridges similar to a paintball or airsoft gun. But it has limitations."

"Such as?" Alice asked, still standing and seriously pumped.

"It's only accurate six to ten metres from the target. The shells don't penetrate the target; they explode on impact, releasing the hydrogen... so if Hope's right and hydrogen is the Achilles heel of the demons, it should do the trick."

"How long before you have a working model?" Al asked.

"I've ordered a gas charging device to load up the projectiles; it will arrive today, so in answer to your question... by tomorrow morning."

"How do we get it through the wormhole?" Al queried.

"I've used 3-D bio-printing to produce the gun and cartridges... basically it and the ammo are manufactured from synthesised bone that I've gallium-coated," Secta explained.

"What's gallium?" Al probed.

"An organic metal that binds stronger than any other, a meta-material that takes the shape of any item its applied to that had been magnetically charged. So, the bone gun is exposed to electromagnetic radiation along with gallium, the latter acts as like a metal laminate or a skin if you like, which renders the gun impervious to most known forms of destruction, heat, cold, etcetera." Secta explained.

"Brilliant," Al said with a positive grin.

With twenty-three levels to negotiate to the summit of the Futurum Tower and the possibility of a demon guarding each level, Alice and Neit would need to be well-armed with plenty of ammo. But most importantly, Alice needed to be assured the Gallium gun with its hydrogen projectiles could kill any demon they encountered, no matter how tough or high up in the demon pecking order it was.

"So, first, we'll need to test it on a demon," Secta said.

"Well, there's one I know…" Alice snarled.

"Exactly," Secta said. With Viktoria still in a coma, Secta, as much as Alice, wanted revenge on the demon Gaap.

CHAPTER 15
THE DREAMING

G ORRICK WAS STUDYING the test results of the photographs taken of Sonoko at OTT by Agent So. He could see quite clearly the purple silhouette of Neit seated on the edge of the bed facing the open door of the en-suite bathroom. The next shot was even more revealing because it had captured Neit entering Sonoko's body after she'd come out of the bathroom.

The phone rang. It was Honor. She reported the mission to assassinate Black Alice hadn't gone to plan. Another failure was the last thing Gorrick wanted to hear, and the fact that So had not only missed Alice but injected Sonoko compounded his frustration.

"This could have serious consequences, Honor," Gorrick snarled into the phone.

"Should I abort Agent So's mission?" she said nervously.

"No, he is expendable… get as much dope on OTT as you can before he is captured. I want to know the nature of their next time travel mission. Make it a priority… and Honor, see if you can get it done without messing it up," he grated.

There was no comeback for Honor; she had to cop the jibe on the chin. Once again, she had been left with egg all over her brand-new face. Experience in the espionage game had taught her that things didn't always go to plan and that someone always needed to be the scapegoat, which in this case was her.

"Have you seen the results of the photos?" Gorrick questioned.

"I have only just received them. It looks to be the same phantom that came out of your office."

"Undoubtedly. Get So to do some digging, find out who or what the goddamned thing is! Get him to work fast; it's only a matter of time before they get the CCTV footage from the assassination attempt and recognise So played the starring role."

"Not if it goes missing… leave that to me," Honor said curtly.

After hanging up, determined to make amends for the failure of the mission, Honor immediately texted Agent So to give him a new brief and to hurry him up. She then called an acquaintance at Sydney Opera House security and offered an inducement to obtain the CCTV footage covering the promenade area where the Alice/Sonoko incident had taken place. To beat Karzoff to the punch and obtain the footage was her personal vendetta.

With Sonoko in a critical condition in the ER, Alice was working with Neit in the Professor's office on an assault plan for The Lair. Karzoff entered the dimly lit room.

"Something very strange has just happened," Karzoff announced with a perplexed look on his craggy face.

"What now Karzoff, it's tough to believe that anything could get any weirder round here?" Al grumbled.

Karzoff flopped into an armchair. "When I ordered the CCTV footage of the incident from Opera House security, they told me there is none."

"That's weird all right, makes no sense, there are bloody cameras everywhere around there. It's a terrorism hotspot for heaven's sake," Al complained.

"There goes any chance of identifying the assailant," Karzoff protested.

"I smell a rat," Al moaned.

Karzoff leaned forward in his chair. Alice had given him an idea and said excitedly, "Maybe you are right, what if Zen got to them with a bribe?"

"Now that'd make perfect sense, especially if your old mate Honor was behind it," Al hinted.

Karzoff flopped dejectedly back in his chair. "That bitch... yes, you are probably right on both counts Alice. I should have known. Perhaps I should give the head of security a personal call."

"That's what I'd be doing," Al agreed.

Karzoff got up to leave.

"Hey Karzoff, where's Mal?" Al asked.

Karzoff stopped at the door. "His campaign ends today... the country goes to the polls tomorrow. Newspapers say it will be a landslide."

"Where's he staying?"

"Here, in the penthouse suite. I will be back in an hour," Karzoff said closing the door behind him.

"Speaking of photographs, what is that device you use to call people?" Neit said.

"A cellphone," Alice said impatiently, frustrated from sitting around.

"Yes, when I was occupying Sonoko, Agent So came to the doorway and aimed a cellphone at her."

That got Alice's attention.

"And then what?"

"Sonoko asked him to identify himself, he told her and left."

"I'm pretty sure he wasn't authorised to enter the room... and what was he doing with a camera? They're banned in high-security areas," Al snarled.

"I sensed there is something about him that is not right," Neit admitted. "I should have gone with you to the Opera House instead of staying here talking to the Professor."

Alice was deep in thought, recalling the incident at the Opera House. He had been aware Agent So was tailing them as the appointed bodyguard, but why, when the incident happened, had he been so close to them?

"He's a new recruit..." Alice thought out loud.

"Yes, and Karzoff ordered Miss Hern to drop some of the induction formalities."

Alice glared at the purple silhouette sitting opposite him and said, "Maybe he's a Zen spy? The assassin!"

"There is a way of finding out for certain," Neit said.

Karzoff and Agent So were driving back from the meeting with Opera House security. Karzoff wasn't satisfied, "I cannot believe the footage has gone missing."

"Seems odd their surveillance system went down right at that critical point," So said. "How is she anyway?"

Karzoff turned into the entrance of the underground car park of Oceana Headquarters.

"Still critical, I doubt she will make it. When a nerve agent as volatile as that is injected, there is little hope of the antidote beating it. Such a shame, a lovely girl Sonoko."

"How long has Alice and her been an item?" So carefully probed.

"He met her in Tokyo on his last mission."

"Did he meet the phantom then as well?"

"Phantom? Oh, you mean Neit... no, he came through with... Wait, how do you know about Neit?" Karzoff asked, becoming suspicious of So's line of enquiry.

"Oh, you know... word gets out," So said cautiously.

"Well, you have only been here a day, and already you are up to speed on the gossip. We will make a spook out of you yet," Karzoff said with a chuckle, brushing off the suspicion.

"Sorry, it comes with the territory. I think I found out more about any SAS mission when I was in service from the ground staff than I ever did from official briefings. What's the next mission?"

Karzoff pulled the black SUV into his designated car space.

"For you?"

"No, Alice," he said pushing it.

Karzoff hopped out of the SUV and locked it with the remote. The lights blinked. He led So to the elevator. Inside it, he inserted his finger in the identification module, looked up at the new facial recognition camera, and then typed his password into the keypad.

"Look up for FR, insert your finger, then swipe your card," he told So. "I think it will be an off-world mission. But you will be briefed when the time is appropriate."

So was content with the information Karzoff had leaked but needed to know more about Neit and prodded a little deeper.

"This guy Neit, what exactly is he?"

"An alien working with us capable of all sorts of amazing things."

They stepped out of the elevator en-route to the offices of OTT Security. Upon entering, they found Alice sitting in a lounge chair reading the newspaper. The headlines read:

MAL LOW PRESIDENTIAL LANDSLIDE VICTIORY INEVITABLE

Alice lowered the newspaper and said, "Karzoff, I need a word with you in private."

"Wait here Agent So," Karzoff said.

Alice handed the newspaper to So and said, "Here... enlighten yourself." It was a cynical remark, and only Alice knew why.

Being led into Karzoff's office, Alice asked, "Any luck with the footage?"

"No, apparently the cameras in that particular section were out of commission." He closed the door behind them. "Take a seat, Alice."

"Last time you told me that, I was tortured by Secta in his old lab, remember?" Al growled.

"Those days have long since passed, Alice."

"Tough to believe the CCTV happened to be down right then, I reckon Honor beat you to the punch mate."

"I suspect you might be right. Now what is on your mind, Alice?" he said curtly, dreading the thought that Honor more than likely had got one up on him.

A few minutes later, the door to the office opened, and Karzoff invited So inside. It was quite a large square room with a mahogany desk at one side, a lounge setting in the centre of the room, tall ceiling-to-floor windows, but the view was obscured by opaque vertical blinds. The room was dimly lit, and Agent So wondered why.

"Sit down, William," Karzoff ordered cordially.

As So sat in the lounge chair, he felt a strange sensation and shivered.

"This is a debrief of the assassination attempt. As the bodyguard, it was your responsibility to avert the incident. Should that have been inescapable, then we expect a summary of the situation."

While William gave his account of the events leading up to the assassination attempt, Neit was inside his mind, reviewing his recent memories. A few minutes later, Alice saw Neit slip out of So and stand behind him. Alice stood and walked around behind So for Neit to enter him.

"He is the assassin, all right," Neit told Alice mentally. "A Zen agent, he was personally assigned the hit by Honor. He was charged with killing you, determining the next mission, and identifying me... This was derived from the photos taken by So of Sonoko, and CCTV they captured of me at Zen using UV filters."

Alice took it on board and then sat back down. He gave Karzoff a nod of affirmation.

"Thank you, So, wait outside, please," Karzoff said.

As So headed for the door, Alice said, "Where's Candy, your secretary, Karzoff? I'd kill for a cup of coffee."

"As I keep telling Miss Hern at HR, we are hideously understaffed. She claims to be recruiting a new receptionist for me today."

"Let's hope she does a better job than she did of recruiting agent So from Zen."

Karzoff's expression froze with the confirmation that So was a spy.

"And what makes it worse is that he was briefed to assassinate me, find out our next mission, and determine who Neit is, by your friend Honor."

At the mention of her name, Karzoff practically threw up.

"What are we going to do about it?" Karzoff groaned.

"That scumbag out there tried to kill me and might have murdered Sonoko. Right now, I feel like blowing the bastard's head off," Alice snarled.

The phone on Karzoff's desk rang. He answered it. "Hello, yes... he is here. Oh dear..." he glanced at Alice sorrowfully. "I will let him know, thank you."

He walked solemnly back to Alice, put his hand sympathetically on his shoulder, and said softly, "Sonoko just passed away, Alice, I am so sorry."

Alice looked like he was about to explode. Neit immediately jumped out of his body.

"You can't do that, Alice, not yet," Neit warned him.

Karzoff was flustered and stammered, "What? What is it, Neit?"

"He wants to kill Agent So."

Alice's face was flushed. He put his head in his hands and groaned, "No!" Every time he gets close to a woman, it ends the same way — those he loves die.

Honor received a text from So saying: "I think they're onto me, what should I do? Next OTT mission is off-world. The phantom is an alien working with them. Sonoko is from Alice's last mission to Tokyo. Please advise."

She looked up smugly from her phone, thrilled to have beaten Karzoff. Keen to impress Gorrick with her success, she got up from behind her desk and headed for his office.

Regina Fysh permitted Honor entry to Gorrick's inner sanctum. After explaining the situation to Gorrick, it was time to come up with an exit strategy for Agent So.

"You did well, Honor. I presume So knows little of our business?" Gorrick asked.

"Correct, but I think it would be best to withdraw him."

"But what if they send him back occupied by the alien?" Gorrick proposed.

"Then we would have the alien."

He knew she was right. The concept of capturing the alien appealed to him. He got up from behind his desk, walked over to the window, and peered out. After a pause to think, he turned back to her and said, "We need to use this situation to our maximum benefit."

Alice stepped out of the elevator into the corridor that led to Kairos control.

"It is a far better ploy to use the situation for our benefit," Neit mentally told Alice.

"I should've wrung So's neck right then and there," Al muttered furiously.

"He would be of no value to us dead, now would he?" Neit proposed.

He stopped before entering through the security door into Kairos and lamented sorrowfully, "I can't believe she's dead." He pondered the thought a moment then brushed it aside, as he was capable of doing, and said probingly, "What is death anyhow, Neit? Got any alien ideas?"

"Well, on several occasions, I have been in occupation of someone who died, and I can tell you this, the life force leaves the body at the moment of death."

"By life force, do you mean spirit?" Al asked.

"Not in a religious sense. It physically leaves the body behind."

"And goes where?" Al quizzed.

"I think death is a process... the door if you like... through which the spirit passes into another dimension... we say we return from where we all derive: the dreaming."

Alice pulled open the pneumatic control room door and stepped inside, "An interesting observation, Neit... I like it. The dreaming is culturally significant to me."

CHAPTER 16
A SWITCH IN TIME

THE STAGE WAS set for a showdown between Alice and Gaap, while only a few blocks from Oceana HQ, at Zen, Kew was assembling his new recruits. There were six in all, hand-picked by Kew from known ranks of mercenaries, soldiers of fortune, and hired guns. Each of them had extensive combat Special Forces and technical backgrounds. They were prepared to go the extra distance, do anything, and kill anyone if so ordered. They would never win best looks in a line-up, but any one of them would certainly win the title of most formidable. It was now up to Kew to train them for forthcoming missions. The objective of time travel would be kept secret from them until they had succeeded in passing the rigorous endurance tests he had conceived. These tests would convince him that they were made of the right stuff to deal with the supernatural nature of future missions. He had no doubt they would cut it.

The election was over, and the results were in. The official ceremonies had concluded, and Mal was in residence at the office of the president in Oceana HQ.

"Are you happy for me to continue as your private secretary, sir, or shall I begin a recruitment program?" Miss Rita Vallins asked the president-elect politely.

Mal was sitting back in the big comfy lounge chair the former president favoured, reading the morning tabloid that sported the headlines:

MALCOLM LOW WINS PRESIDENCY WITH AN UNPRECEDENTED MAJORITY

He lowered the newspaper and smiled, "Don't be ridiculous, Rita. There's no way I could do this gig without you... I wouldn't trade you for the world."

Rita blushed. "Oh, thank you, sir."

"Call me Mal between us, okay?"

"Yes, Mal. Do you want coffee? Alice is booked in to see you, should be here any minute."

"Yes, please, better make it a couple of cups of that fantastic brew you're famous for... and a bunch of cookies. You can bet Al will be starving—he always is. Tell him to come in when he lobs. Oh, by the way, Alice, Hope, Secta, and the Professor can cold-call me any time they want, okay?"

"Yes, sir."

Rita liked her new boss. He was friendly and honest. He'd only been in office a few hours and had already lightened the mood with a fresh and positive approach to the office of the president.

Mal went back to reading the newspaper, and seconds later, Alice cruised in.

"Hey, dude!" Al said with a friendly chuckle.

"Al!" Mal got up and embraced his friend.

"Congrats, mate. You slayed them... told ya yer would."

"Sit down, mate. Rita will bring us some of that great coffee."

Al flopped into the chair opposite Mal. "I hope she brings some of them biscuits. I'm so hungry I could eat the arse out of a skeleton."

Mal chuckled at Al's gag. "No worries, I ordered them."

"Beauty," Al said with a sigh.

"Did you vote for me?" Mal said with a cheeky grin.

"Don't be ridiculous," Al quipped. "Mate, I haven't seen you in a while with you on the campaign trail and all."

Mal's mood changed to sorrowful. "Al, I heard about Sonoko. I'm so sorry, mate—the news blew me away."

Al nodded slowly, his eyes tearing up, still not over the shock. "She was a great kid. Mate, I feel so responsible. Her birthday was coming up... ah, what a waste of a life."

"Mate, why can't you just go back and stop it from happening? Grab her before it happens and then ship her back off to her own time where she'll be safe?"

"Can't, Secta reckons it's to do with the prime directive... you know, can't radically change the events on the timeline or something."

"But that's not really relevant in this case, is it? Her being here is already breaking the prime directive, and now that she's been killed before she was born makes it totally wrong. Leave it to me, we'll talk with Secta and get it done, alright?"

"See, mate, told you you'd make a great president."

"Might be but from what I heard Karzoff has a lot to answer for putting a novice bodyguard on you. If it had been one of our best it might not have happened."

"All that's been going on with protecting you on the campaign trail and the casualty rate fighting Zen and with Viktoria still in a coma, poor old Karzoff has been left short-handed. I don't blame him mate, besides, Agent So came with top credentials. We know now he's a skilled assassin," Al said sternly.

"What? The killer is walking free amongst us?"

"Yes, it was me he was after. He's a Zen plant, Neit probed his mind to find out."

"And what are we going to do about it?" Mal asked, sitting forward in his seat, still shocked the culprit was free.

"Use him to our benefit. We don't know how yet but if we need to we can send false information to Honor at Zen."

"I thought she was dead."

"Apparently not."

Miss Vallins arrived with a tray upon which she balanced two mugs of coffee and a plate of cookies. She popped it on the coffee table between Alice and Mal.

"There you go gentlemen. Will there be anything else, sir?"

"Yes, have Secta join us please."

She nodded and then left the room. Alice hoed into the biscuits.

"Rita's a keeper Mal," Alice said, munching into a biscuit.

"Absolutely," Mal agreed, relaxing back in his chair and taking a sip of coffee. "Ah, a perfect brew... Mate, I'll have to leave all this espionage stuff up to you blokes for now, I've got stacks on my plate..."

"I can dig it. Let's change the subject... how are you handling it so far?" Al asked.

"I'm already regretting leaving behind those halcyon days of gigging. You ever feel like that?"

"Sometimes," Al said forlornly. "But I plan to sit in on the band whenever I get the urge. You could do that as well."

"Yeah, that's an idea. I could go in disguise. So, back onto the dreaded subject, where are we up to with all this Zen stuff? I've been out of the loop so long you'd better fill me in."

Mal sat wide-eyed like a kid being told a wicked fairy-tale, while Alice brought him up to speed on all that had transpired over the past few weeks, and there was plenty to tell: the arrival of Neit, Gaap, Viktoria, Trooper Dicks, Agent So and the planned mission to Eris. He'd only just finished when there was a knock at the door.

"Bloody-hell Al, that's incredible and I thought I had plenty on my plate... That'd be Secta. Come in!"

The tall skinny man entered the large office. Mal stood up and shook hands with him.

"Secta! Take a seat, want a coffee?"

"I ordered one from Rita. So, celebrations are in order... well done Mal," Secta said genuinely.

"Thank you... Al just finished filling me in on everything. I'm glad he did, if I'd read it, I doubt I'd believe it. Look, one thing sticks out at to me... the prime directive was broken in bringing Sonoko here was it not?"

"Yes, but under special circumstances—" Secta mumbled, glancing at Alice.

Mal cut him off. "I understand that mate, but wouldn't you say we have a problem with her sad demise, in that now she has died before she was born?"

Secta thought it through held his chin and admitted, "Yes, that does present us a bit of a pickle."

"So, here's what I reckon; we send Al back in time to just before the incident... he knows the perpetrator... so he can prevent it. He could swap the syringe with a sedative so it can still play out that she died on the time line for everyone else involved to believe... but instead we'll send her back to her own time. What do you think?"

"That's a brilliant idea Mal. You're going to make a fine president... but there's one problem... it can't be Alice," Secta said.

"Why?" Mal said. He and Alice were perplexed.

"Because Alice is already there and that would make two of them in the same space and time... however..." he paused for effect, "I do have an idea."

"Spare no expense, we can go anywhere on Earth or we can send a wormhole to another planet," Alice joked to Sonoko. He stopped her, took something from his pocket and peeled the back off it. "It's your clock drive." He adhered it to the back of her neck.

The Opera House was in view and they walked onto the promenade leading to it.

Agent So terminated the call to Honor, out in the open he was far too conspicuous to be on the phone. He had his orders, pushed up through the crowd of tourists ascending the Opera House stairs and stealthily slipped a small syringe out of his pocket. There was shimmer and he froze.

Alice and Sonoko stopped in their tracks.

With everyone around him bar Sonoko frozen in time, Alice knew a vortex was opening.

Neit stepped out of the vortex and without saying a word to Alice moved like greased lightning directly to Agent So standing behind Alice, swapped syringes in his frozen hand, and then popped the deadly syringe into Alice side pocket. He gave Alice thumbs up and then dived back into the vortex that closed rapidly behind him. It all happened in seconds to avoid UV damage to Neit.

Time unfroze... Agent So aimed the syringe at Alice and lunged to inject him in the back. Just as he was doing so an elderly lady slipped on the stairs directly in front of Alice. He made a grab to catch her. In doing so he knocked William's hand holding the syringe. It missed Alice and stabbed into Sonoko's thigh causing her to stumble.

"You all right?" Alice asked thinking he'd knocked her.

"Yes, yes, I'm fine," she said.

Alice helped the old Korean lady to regain her balance. "Are you okay?"

She nodded, "Thank you."

She carried on with her tour group.

Alice gave Sonoko a hug and then holding her at arms-length he peered into her big beautiful almond-shaped brown eyes. Standing on the Opera House esplanade with a warm breeze flagging her shiny long black hair out behind her like a banner, she looked an absolute picture. He wanted to kiss her. But just as he was about to her eyes rolled back in her head and she collapsed into his arms.

Agent So was quick to break from the covert position he'd retreated to after injecting the wrong mark and went to Alice's assistance. Down on one knee holding Sonoko in his arms, it was all déjà vu for Alice... it was exactly like what had happened with his former girlfriend Stain, when she collapsed from an overdose on his bathroom floor. With his brain swimming in confusion, he could tell by the colour of Sonoko's cheeks and her shallow breathing that whatever this was that had harmed her was life threatening.

In the chaos of the moment Alice recognised Agent So and deduced he'd been assigned by Karzoff to follow them.

"William, quick phone Karzoff, I need a doctor here fast, it's life and death."

A crowd had gathered around them. While Agent So was on the phone to Karzoff a man in jogging gear pushed through the onlookers.

"I'm a doctor," he shouted with a strong British accent. "Let me through please."

While Alice was holding Sonoko's limp body in his arms, the doctor checked her vitals.

"Have you called an ambulance?" the doctor asked urgently.

"Yes, my friend is calling now."

The doctor looked up at William on the phone and shouted at him, "Tell them to bring Atropine and to get here within ten minutes or we'll lose her."

Alice glared at the doctor, "What are you saying doctor?"

"I've seen this type of thing before in London, she's been hit with a nerve agent. Are you with her?"

"Yes."

"Is she a special government agent or something?"

"No, a scientist."

"Well someone has tried to murder her and unless the antidote gets here quick smart whoever did it will have succeeded."

The timeline had been altered, but nature itself had compensated for it. A new timeline had formed, the old one lost to time, and everything altered from then on accordingly. Agent So still believed he had injected the wrong mark with the nerve agent and dumped the evidence (the syringe) in a trash bin before entering Oceana HQ.

Sonoko was given the antidote, but it didn't matter. Alice knew she was safe; the thumbs up from Neit had confirmed that, though he wouldn't find out until later exactly what had taken place. But because the vortex had opened, he had a fair idea.

At the next OTT meeting, Alice handed the syringe Neit had put in his pocket to Hope. She took it immediately to be analysed.

Alice was amazed at how the Professor and Secta had managed to produce a syringe to withstand the rigors of teleportation. The Professor had come up with a carbon fibre needle attached to a syringe made entirely from silicon so it could pass through Kairos. It wasn't something he simply conjured up from his imagination; the two components were actually currently being tested in a medical laboratory in Sydney.

There had been no need to inject Neit with the demat formula because he simply vaporised to facilitate teleportation. The critical factor Alice learned was for Neit to exit the vortex, swap over the syringe, drop the nerve agent syringe into his pocket, and then get back through the vortex before it closed. If he'd missed it, he would have been left out in the open on a sunny day at midday, where the UV radiation would almost certainly have killed him. Neit was the only individual on the planet with the knowledge of the old timeline.

Sonoko was safe. They could now proceed with sending her back to her own time.

Alice visited Sonoko at sickbay and found her confused by what had happened. He told her, "It was a rift in time that caused you to pass out," he lied. "Secta told me it was because your birthday is coming, therefore your mother is pregnant right now in Tokyo, and there are two of you actually living at the same time."

"Oh, I understand. It crosses the prime directive line, doesn't it?"

"Yes. To make sure you're safe, we need to send you back, baby, today."

She started to tear up. He hugged her. "Not to worry, love. As soon as I get back from the next mission, I'll come to Tokyo and we'll take that holiday like I promised," he said warmly.

CHAPTER 17
CHAA!

" DID YOU FEEL that?" Kew asked.

Gorrick turned from his office window, which looked out across the sun-drenched skyscraper skyline of Sydney and the harbour, and said, "No, what was it? A tremor?"

"No, I think it was a ripple in time. Since I was injected with the demat serum, I can feel when a wormhole opens and closes. Some sort of temporal distortion."

"Hmm, interesting." He sat down opposite Kew, spoke on his OSCI, "Miss Fysh, send me Adamski... oh, she is... send her in."

Honor breezed into the room. Before noticing Kew sitting with his back to her, she said, "You told me to come up with an exit strategy for Agent So, sir."

"Yes, sit down Honor, you know Kew."

She grimaced.

"Hello Honor," Kew said smugly.

"Zanza," she said curtly and then took a seat.

"Go on Honor," Gorrick requested.

She pursed her red lips, annoyed that he was forcing her to disclose her intel to Kew. "Agent So told us that Sonoko, the woman he accidentally injected with the nerve agent, is from the future—"

Kew cut her off, "I remember her. She's the scientist Black Alice was having a fling with in Tokyo. They must have brought her through a wormhole."

"Yes, well, they will be sending her back in a coffin now... she's dead," Honor said, well pleased with herself. "As I informed you, Agent So also learned there will be an off-world mission soon and has since told me there will be an assault on something that has occupied their safe house."

Gorrick immediately knew Agent So was alluding to The Lair, the rift, and Gaap. The door opened, and Regina Fysh showed in Adamski.

"Adamski, take a seat, you know Kew," Gorrick said.

"Yes, sir." Adamski's tight thin lips curved into what resembled a smile.

"Sorry to drag you away from the construction, but I have a couple of important questions for you. Do you think a side effect of Secta's demat formula could be the ability to sense a wormhole opening and closing in time?"

Adamski pondered the concept. After a moment's contemplation, his bushy grey eyebrows lifted above his black thick-rimmed glasses with an epiphany. "Yes, that makes sense. I'd say more precisely when time has been altered or changed from its given path. In quantum astrology, it is called particle-wave duality or, in laymen's terms, the creation of parallel timelines. This would generate a ripple that only those encoded with the serum would feel or sense... why?"

"Because I felt two of them a while ago," Kew said.

Gorrick was nodding. Honor was flummoxed by the explanation.

"Does that mean time changed?" Gorrick questioned.

"Yes, most likely... two timelines are generated when the original timeline is altered, say after a wormhole opens. Then the timelines converge when the interrupter—the wormhole—closes again. We could safely assume Kew felt a wormhole open and then close somewhere," Adamski explained.

Gorrick was intrigued; however, the explanation only raised more questions. He moved on by handing Adamski his cellphone.

"Flick through those photographs... Kew, take a look at them over Adamski's shoulder."

Both men peered at the pictures of Neit entering the body of Layla Migden and then Sonoko.

"That is the phantom or spectre we have learned from Agent So is an alien working with OTT. A UV filter was used to uncover it in the photographs," Gorrick explained.

"It must exist within the UV bandwidth... extraordinary," Adamski concluded.

"Can you explain the phenomenon?" Gorrick asked.

"No, I can't, but I can do some research."

"Good, do that sooner rather than later and let me know, it is important. We cannot have OTT any further ahead of us," Gorrick barked.

Realising he was being dismissed, Adamski got up and made his way out of the office.

"This assault on the—" Kew started.

Gorrick interrupted him, "The safe house is called The Lair. In it is a rift that is not unlike an open wormhole. It extends to another place in time. It is critical to Zen that it does not fall into the hands of OTT. Currently, to prevent that happening, an alien creature is guarding it, but now Honor has warned us that an OTT assault team will try and take out the guard and capture the rift. We will need to launch a counter-offensive."

Both Honor and Kew were even more astounded by what they'd been told. It was nightmarish, unthinkable: a hole in time being guarded by an alien.

"Is this alien on our side?" Kew asked.

"Yes."

"Honor, we need So to determine when the assault will take place," Gorrick ordered.

She pulled her phone and said, "Now, sir?"

"Absolutely," Kew said.

Honor glared at him, offended by being given orders by him, but she got over it and punched in a text message to So. Seconds later, her phone rang.

"It's him," she told Gorrick.

"Take it," he approved. "Put it on speaker."

She pressed a button then spoke. "Agent So... when is the assault scheduled?"

"It will be within the next 48 hours," Agent So said.

"Where are you now?"

"I am in the pantry on level 7. The Japanese girl Sonoko is dead... they have no idea it was me," he said in a harsh whisper and then terminated the call.

Honor could barely wipe the smirk of satisfaction off her face. She instinctively knew that having So on the inside of OTT provided such critical intel it had put her back in favour with Gorrick.

"With what Neit explained, a high degree of radiation derives from a rift, far more than from a wormhole," the Professor claimed. "This morning we flew a drone fitted with a Geiger counter over the Lair, and we got a fix on the arrow of time. It is in the indoor swimming pool area."

"Could there be a conflict opening a wormhole close to it?" Neit asked.

It was obvious from the Professor's expression he hadn't considered it.

"A good point, Neit. I think you might be right," Secta said, pacing the control room floor. "We can't risk that."

"The assault needs to be in daylight. Though it will hinder my ability to help Alice, it will contain Gaap. There is no need to transport there through a wormhole."

"What's the latest on the Gallium gun, Secta?" Al enquired.

Secta was pacing the floor, deep in thought. Hope knew Viktoria's condition was playing on his mind.

"Secta?" Al repeated a little louder.

AL and the Id

"Oh, sorry Alice. It's in the last stage of the 3-D printing process. I'll test fire it tonight, and if it goes well, it will be ready for you tomorrow."

Alice was holding the crystal blade and a couple of handguns. Everything was hanging on Secta finishing the Gallium gun. The update meant the assault would proceed tomorrow.

Karzoff came into the room.

Alice put the guns and blade on the bench and asked, "Okay, now you're here Karzoff, how about we make a decision on what to do with Agent So, because if I see his head around here, I'll probably knock it off."

But Karzoff had what he considered a more important announcement. "The doctor just called to say that Viktoria is out of the coma and talking."

Secta very nearly burst into tears. Hope caught his reaction, quickly moved to him, and gave him a hug. "Go on, go see her... off you go."

Secta gave a silent nod to the others and took off in a hurry.

"What great news," the Professor said. His relief that Viktoria was back in the land of the living was echoed by each of them.

Karzoff's expression hardened. "I have just eavesdropped on a phone conversation between Agent So and Honor."

"Shouldn't he be in jail?" Al snapped.

"I have eyes and ears on him... he warned them of our impending assault on The Lair."

Alice was shocked. "How did he know about that?"

"We've only just agreed on a course of action?" Neit added.

"A ball park prediction, I would say," Karzoff said, "anyhow, we can have him provide disinformation to Honor. I have heard on the grapevine that Kew has been assembling a crack team of mercenaries we can assume will be used to defend Gaap and the rift."

"Well, that at least confirms the rift, Gaap, and Zen are connected," the Professor stated emphatically.

"I think Gorrick would have a sensory connection to the rift seeing it connects back to his maker, En-Lil," Neit proposed.

Robert swivelled in his chair from the console to face them and said, "Alice, I've brought up the coordinates of Sonoko's lab in Japan from the computer's memory, I'm all set to go. I believe the Professor has fitted her with the new Clock Drive?"

It was obvious by a sudden change in his attitude Alice was rattled by the realisation the time had arrived to send Sonoko back.

"I'll um, go get her then," he said, getting up from his seat forlornly.

Hope stopped him on the way out. Always tuned into the emotions of her friends, she was the champion of tempering them in times of trouble. "Think of it as a positive Al," she said supportively, "she'll be safer back home, and you won't have to worry about her."

Alice locked eyes with her. "S'pose you're right, mate... I'll be okay once she's gone... you know how much I hate goodbyes... a hangover from my youth."

Hope wasn't aware of Alice's turbulent youth, in and out of orphanages and bounced around from one foster home to another like a proverbial tennis ball. The oppression of being first nations in a white-man's city. She flashed a faint smile at the Professor, knowing that along with Neit but not Robert, they were the only three in the room without a partner to worry about.

A series of gauges blinked to life on the console displaying a virtual constellation of tiny coloured lights as Robert engaged the computer drive to Kairos. A lover of technology, Neit watched over Robert's shoulder the process of tuning the complex array of components that enabled the Kairos particle accelerator to perform its teleportation miracle.

A low hum came from the adjoining computer room as it stepped up a gear.

"That sound is from a series of fans kicking in to keep the mainframe cool," Robert explained.

"How dangerous is this?" Neit quizzed.

Standing beside him, the Professor chose to answer. "Very, especially at the critical point when the particles collide to form the muon that opens the portal."

"A muon?" Neit probed.

"An elementary subatomic particle similar to an electron but not composed of other particles. It only has a fifteen-minute lifetime. When it decays, it produces an electron and two neutrinos. We create a negative muon using helium which allows it to bond with other atoms," Hope explained.

"And that generates the wormhole. I'm currently working on how to keep the wormhole open for longer than fifteen minutes," the Professor explained.

Robert turned from the console and added, "We're thinking a pion might be the answer. It's the building block of neutrinos and consists of a quark and an antiquark. We think it might under certain conditions have a longer decay."

"All this talk of neutrinos is making me hungry," Neit joked.

The three scientists laughed; they hadn't realised Neit had a sense of humour.

Hand in hand, Alice and Sonoko walked the corridor leading to Kairos in a hushed silence. Neither was capable of finding the words to adequately describe their feelings. Finally, when they stopped at the control room pressure door Sonoko looked up at Alice with teary eyes and said, "Will you remember me Alice?"

He held her shoulders looked into her eyes and said warmly, "The image of your face is tattooed on my mind love."

Somehow, it was the answer she expected from him, and it worked for her. They kissed passionately and then Alice turned the handle on the big door. A loud hiss erupted from the seal breaking and an indicator light flashed green for them to enter decontamination. Once completed, the control room door hissed and opened. Alice led Sonoko inside.

Hope immediately went to Sonoko took her hand and asked, "How are you love?"

"Very sad to be leaving thank you Hope," she said politely.

Hope walked her to the door of the dispatch cubicle with Alice in tow.

Neit joined them. The sight of him shocked Sonoko.

"I feel like I know you well, Sonoko," Neit said taking Sonoko's hand in his. "I am Neit of the Id. I came through the wormhole here with you to help Alice."

"Neit is our friend Sonoko, he helped protect you against an enemy that seeks to destroy us," the Professor told her.

"Is that why I must return to my time?"

"Yes, that and because we can't have two of you on the same timeline," Hope explained.

"Engagement T minus five minutes and counting," Robert warned.

The time to leave was upon them. Fresh tears welled up in Sonoko's beautiful brown eyes.

Alice gave her a passionate hug. "Say hi to Shintaro when you see him. I'll see you soon — I promise."

Hope opened the cubicle door. Sad and dejected, Sonoko ambled into the small room.

The pressure door was closed behind her. Alice gave her a wave through the small window. "Chaa!" he mouthed. Unlike him there was a noticeable emotional tremble to his voice. It was a sad moment. Hope was tearing up... the Professor patted Alice affectionately on the back.

Robert fired up Kairos with the touch of a key and then announced, "Counting down... ten, nine, eight..."

Alice couldn't watch Sonoko in the despatch booth it felt too terminal, so he left that to the others. Hope because she had to and Neit because he was curious.

"Five, four, three, two—"

A shrill sound lasted a second, and then the lights flickered ever so slightly with the sudden power surge, and Sonoko was gone.

CHAPTER 18
WASP

IT WAS DECIDED the assault team would deploy in conventional transport rather than a wormhole. It was planned a chopper would drop them on the helipad at The Lair. The team would consist of six SAS commandos, Agent So, and Alice, the team leader. Neit would accompany Alice. Scheduled for 0600, they had sixteen hours to prepare.

Alice briefed the commandos on the mission while Karzoff briefed Agent So separately in another room. Alice had at first resisted taking So on the mission for obvious reasons, but once Karzoff had explained he could be utilised to lure the Zen attack team that Kew was known to have recruited—at their convenience—and that made sense. The mission now represented an opportunity for Alice to kill several birds with one stone: Gaap, Agent So, and Kew.

Karzoff made sure So was given every opportunity to pass the details of his briefing on to Honor. He had given So an incorrect deployment time to ensure Alice had a buffer to neutralise Gaap, secure the rift, and then set an ambush for Kew and his team.

Gorrick was pleased when Honor breezed into his office to outline the details So had passed on regarding his OTT briefing, so much so that he came clean about the special unit he had covertly ordered Kew to assemble. Honor reacted surprisingly well to the news. It made perfect sense for her to look after the cloak-and-dagger operation, while Kew led the strike force—she wasn't a risk-taker when it came to her life.

They agreed to leave Agent So in place at OTT for the time being because of the invaluable information he was providing.

Kew was immediately summoned to Gorrick's office and ordered to prepare his task force for the assault. There was a lot to prepare, but they had time. So had instructed them that the OTT sortie would be carried out at noon the next day.

Honor was worried; she knew OTT protocol required the mission to go dark from a given time, which meant Agent So would drop out of communication with her. But Gorrick didn't share her concern; he was confident Kew and Gaap would be able to handle the situation without any further involvement from So.

With preparations for the mission complete and a special announcement to make, Secta called a meeting of the President and the rest of the OTT members. The President invited them for happy-hour drinks at his office. He planned for it to also be an executive celebration of his presidential win and an opportunity to wish Alice well on the forthcoming mission.

The lights in the presidential offices had been fitted with anti-UV filters and dimmed for the benefit of Neit. It was the first time Mal had met the alien and was fascinated by him. They were standing near the huge windows that looked out over the city, which was bathed in the orange afterglow of sunset.

"What about this guy Alice, he seems different than others?"

Mal took a sip of beer and smiled at the strange purple phantom that had asked him the question. "He's one special bloke Neit... the kind any man or woman would consider fortunate to meet in a lifetime. You know at times individuals are literally born heroes, characters that would without question stand up against injustice and give voice to the underdog... the downtrodden. Think of a person that can be incontrovertibly relied upon... who would take a bullet for you... a winner with an extraordinary intellect that can be so easily underestimated... that person my friend... is Alice."

"You know, I think he might say the same of you," Neit said.

"Nice of you to suggest that Neit but I tell you, I'm not in the same league. You know there was a time when I doubted him... when he was hell-bent on stopping a protest ferry we were on from colliding with a U.S. nuclear submarine in Sydney Harbour. He risked his life that night to save the world from a catastrophe that would have annihilated mankind, and in my doubting ignorance, I was trying to stop him." He shook his head and rolled his eyes at his own idiocy. "Since that night, I've never doubted him again," he said peering with admiration at his mate across the room chatting with Secta, the Professor, and Hope.

Alice had a bug in his bonnet and laid it on Secta. "Why the hell can't I just go through the rift like it's a wormhole?"

"That's a question better answered by Neit... but I'd say it acts in a completely different manner than a wormhole... perhaps even an unconventional oscillation," Secta posed.

"We need to study it to make sure," the Professor added.

"We need to capture it first," Hope said, always armed with a logical assessment of a problem.

"By the way, how's Vik?" Al asked.

"Keen to get back to work," Secta quipped, followed by a sigh of relief, grateful she was out of the coma.

Beer in hand, Karzoff joined them. "Talking about Viktoria, when I visited her earlier all she could think about was getting back to work. Selfless girl, that."

They all nodded at the accuracy of the statement.

Karzoff continued, "Did you hear that Mal was asked in a TV interview to disclose the truth about alien visitations?"

"Wow, how did he answer that?" Hope asked.

"He promised to provide full disclosure by the end of the week," Karzoff said.

"If he's up front, then he'll be the first world leader to do so," Secta said with a doubting raised eyebrow, suspicious of any politician's ability to be honest without a political agenda.

"Do you doubt him, Secta? Let me tell you if there's one thing I can say about Mal is he prides himself on telling the truth," Al professed.

Mal and Neit joined them.

"Hey guys, I was thinking about taking Neit along with me to a TV interview about alien disclosure. What do you think?" Mal asked.

Alice shot Secta an 'I told you so' glance.

"I think it would cause mass hysteria," the Professor theorised.

Overhearing the discussion, Robert left Rita Vallins and Kyleen Hern to hear more.

"As damage limitation, it might be wiser to disclose the truth incrementally," Secta suggested.

"Good advice Secta, how about you write the disclosure for me?" Mal said by way of invitation.

"I'd be happy to do that Mal," Secta said agreeably.

"You wouldn't be able to handle the studio lights anyway Neit," Hope joked.

Alice pulled Karzoff aside and muttered to him conspiratorially, "Where's Agent So?"

"With two of my best men... they will be keeping eyes on him. He still has a secure phone to Zen that he will need to hide somewhere before we go black in the morning."

"I'm still not sold on taking the bloke along, you know that Karzoff," Al grumbled.

"Something I learned from Honor, if anything goes wrong then the prisoner becomes insurance," the red-haired man said tapping the side of his nose with his forefinger to show his smarts.

"I'll tell you something... your insurance will be coming back from the mission in a body bag," Al snarled.

"I expected that from you Alice," Karzoff said, with a macabre grin. "Why do we not just get a priest to banish the demon, is that not what they do in the movies?"

Alice ignored Karzoff's wisecrack and re-joined the conversation between the others.

Hope asked Alice quietly, "Are you worried about tomorrow Al?"

"Hard not to be nervous, but that'll go once we're into it... Sort of like going on stage."

"I guess you'd be used to that."

"Always get a gut full of butterflies before a gig—nervous as a cat—feel like I could throw up but it all goes away as soon as I get to the mike centre stage."

"Do you miss performing?" she asked.

"I was talking to Mal about that earlier. He regrets giving up his freedom. He loved doing gigs."

"What did you advise him?" she probed Alice.

"Just to think of the presidency as a different kinda gig... besides, he can still moonlight with the band whenever he gets the urge."

"Alice?" Secta butted in. "I asked Neit about going through the arrow of time."

Neit was standing next to them, listening and explained, "Yes, no-one knows how it is generated, and I do not know of anyone who has tried to go through it... but I get the impression passage through it is meant only for demons. I don't believe even En-Lil can pass through it."

Hope nodded in agreement, and then added, "After studying the anatomy and chemical composition of Gaap's digit, I'd have to agree with you Neit... there isn't anything known that can match it... I'd venture to say it's resilient to a lot of conditions that would totally destroy a carbon-based life form."

"Speaking of the demon, I'll be test-firing the Gallium gun in a couple of hours Alice," Secta said.

"Let's hope it's a success... we're committed to the assault now whether it works or not," Alice grated. He didn't like having to rely on an experimental weapon in such a circumstance where confidence was everything.

The door opened, and a couple of Secta's lab workers manhandled a crash test dummy into the room. Secta went over to them and instructed them where to place the man-sized figure.

"What's this?" Mal questioned Hope and the Professor.

"This is guaranteed to blow your mind, Mr President," the Professor said resolutely.

Once the two lab assistants had left the room, Secta tapped the side of a glass with a ballpoint to attract the attention of the others and then spoke up like a keynote speaker. "Mr President, my friends and peers... I requested this gathering to introduce something that has been in development and is now ready for operations. We have utilised the amazing Core i20 organic chip that we brought back from our recent mission to Tokyo in 2047. It is a twenty-core organic processor with a clock speed of 20.5 GHz that requires no liquid or air-cooling. It has two terabytes of memory and is so tiny it can fit on the tip of an index finger. To my knowledge, there is nothing comparable anywhere in the world at present... a first for Oceana." He gently placed his glass on the coffee table, reached into his side pocket, produced an item the size of a matchbox, and then held it in his open palm for them all to see. "This is the NSD-Wasp. Nanotechnology—a swarm drone... artificial intelligence or Ai that driven by the organic chip can react a hundred times faster than a human. It has stochastic motion as a built-in anti-sniper feature. It has cameras and sensors and just like your phone is equipped with facial recognition. But that's where the comparison with a cellphone ends—inside the Wasp is three grams of shape explosive... watch."

With a sudden unexpected move, Secta cast the small item into the air. It buzzed like a hornet and hovered just above the heads of the audience. "You hear the buzz?" Secta said, "Scary isn't it?... threatening, but what's even more scary is that it also has stealth mode."

The tiny drone turned sharply… it had identified a target. It shot off at lightning speed and homed in on the crash test dummy—bang! The shock of the sound caused some in the audience to flinch.

Though the Wasp had disappeared it had left behind a hole the size of a bottle top in the forehead of the dummy.

"That little crack you heard was enough to penetrate the skull and destroy the contents, the subject is now brain-dead."

A murmur of amazement buzzed around the room.

Secta continued, "This little fellow doesn't get emotional, doesn't disobey orders, and doesn't miss. The weapon makes the decisions for an airstrike of surgical precision. It can be programmed to act in a team with a hive mentality… it can penetrate cars, trains, and planes. It can evade people, bullets… pretty much any countermeasure… the Wasp cannot be stopped," he said fervently.

An even stronger murmur went around the room. They were astounded by the brilliance of the technology and the potential of it. Mal led the applause.

Secta held up a hand to stop it. "Thank you… thank you… the Wasp renders nuclear war obsolete. It can take out an entire enemy army virtually risk-free, just characterise him, release the swarm, and rest easy. This is a smart weapon… it can discriminate between friend or foe, and locate the enemy using data, or even a hashtag. It provides the capacity to target any evil ideology right where it starts." He pointed his finger at his head. "In the mind. I thank you."

Alice glared at Mal and then professed out loud, "That, is one hell of a game changer!"

"So how does this thing guarding the portal know we're on the same side?"

Gorrick leered at Kew and replied stiffly, "It's a demon… it knows… don't concern yourself with incidentals."

"I think you need to explain what's going on. I still don't get it?" Kew complained.

Gorrick was in Kew's new offices to look over his attack plan. It was quite a small space, just two rooms. The briefing room they were in and Kew's private office. It was furnished Spartan but adequately.

Kew wasn't comfortable with the plan; far too many questions remained unanswered. Gorrick realised if he didn't come clean about everything, he would risk losing Kew's trust.

Kew could feel the unblinking stare from Gorrick drilling into his brain.

Half an hour later, Kew knew all about En-Lil, Gaap, the ultimate plan, and the mission of the Gorrick clones. He also knew how he was expected to fit into the diabolical scheme.

"What I have told you is confidential, there will be no mention of it to anyone... do I make myself clear?"

"Yes, sir," Kew said resolutely.

"Put a tap on So's phone. I want him tracked. I don't want that left up to Honor."

"What about her, how am I expected to deal with her?" Kew asked.

"Leave her to me. She provides important insight into OTT. Concern yourself with the mission. The rift cannot fall into the hands of the enemy."

"That's all well and good, but what's in it for me?" Kew said smugly.

"What do you want?"

"It's not about money, it's about power."

Gorrick smiled. Kew was a man after his own heart — greedy and imperious.

"When we win the ultimate battle, I will give you your own country."

It was an answer Kew hadn't expected, but it was music to his ears. The stakes had just been raised—the spoils were there for Kew's taking.

It was clever manipulation by Gorrick, conscious as he was of Kew and Honor being imbued with massive egos and an insatiable hunger for power.

CHAPTER 19
RACE AGAINST TIME

I**T WAS A** morning Major Jack Jackman was never going to forget. Since his retirement, it had become a tradition for him to relax back in his favourite comfy chair on the outdoor balcony of his cabin with a mug of freshly brewed coffee in hand, watching the sun rise over the lake at the end of his street. Even after a lifetime of early morning rises in the U.S. Military, living alone in the log cabin he had crafted with his own hands, and witnessing the day begin, gave him a sense of satisfaction and contentment. However, this particular day was going to be unforgettable.

Hovering over the water above the rickety old timber wharf at the end of the street was something Jack had never seen before. It was a crack in the fabric of time, and it was unlike anything he had ever witnessed. He estimated it to be a ten-metre long jagged line, glowing from within like a furnace from hell, suspended about ten metres above the water, making no sound. Its presence was all-encompassing.

With no other houses around and no joggers or dog walkers at that time of day, the enigma was for Major Jack Jackman's eyes only. He hopped up from his rocking chair, darted inside, and returned seconds later with a pair of military-grade M-25 14 x 40 image-stabilised binoculars. Peering through them, he could clearly discern a violent fury of black clouds of smoke rolling around the open lips of the rift, and inside it, what appeared to be molten lava. A pelican flew into view right near the anomaly and was instantly vaporised.

"Holy mackerel!" he cursed loudly, bringing down the binoculars. "What is that Goddamned thing?"

He rushed back inside to fetch his Nikon D-45 camera. Zooming the 50 mm lens, he took a rapid-fire series of shots of the irregularity.

The Professor was preparing to leave the office for the evening when his cellphone alerted him to a message. He opened it and immediately identified what his old friend JJ had sent him from Bachman Lake, in Irving, Texas.

By the time he got through on the phone to tell Secta, he was already aware there were other rifts opening up around the world.

Secta immediately called an emergency meeting of OTT staff members.

Assembled in the executive boardroom, eyes were on Secta, referring to a map of the world on the large monitor.

"So far, there are reports of seven open rifts, including ours. As you can see by the red dots on the map, each rift is in a strategic position in close proximity to an active particle collider: Cern in Geneva, Irving in Texas, Brookhaven in New York, U-70 Proton Synchrotron Ihep in Protvino Russia, Rutherford Applet in Chilton UK, and Cosy in Jülich, Germany, and of course, our very own Kairos. So, I ask, why is this the case?"

"Are there any more active colliders?" Neit asked.

The Professor peered over the top of his eyeglasses at Neit, "No, not that we are aware of."

Alice was battling with an explanation. "So, what do you reckon? Have they opened up for more demons to come through or what?"

"I do not think so, Alice," Neit proposed grimly. "It is more likely they are part of a stratagem for the elimination of humanity."

"En-Lil?" Al advocated.

"Yes," Neit affirmed.

They knew there was no point debating it any further; it was time to act. The only thing that could stop this was the plan they had agreed on. The only new factor was that it was now a race against time.

The President came into the room, stopped, and announced, "I've just had the Whitehouse on the phone." He glanced at the monitor. "I see you're already acquainted with the issue. Do we know what it is, Secta?"

"Yes, Mal, they're duplicates of the rift we already have here."

"Is this some kind of alien invasion?"

"Speculative, but yes, you could say that," Secta affirmed.

"What should I tell world leaders who are on the edge of panic?"

"It will need to be kept from the media," Secta said gravely.

"And they'll have to trust us to deal with it," Alice added.

Mal caught Alice's eye and said solemnly, "Seems the protection of mankind is once again in your hands, old buddy."

"Ha! They won't like that much," the Professor piped up assuredly.

"Who won't like it?" Alice questioned.

"The Whitehouse... they have a penchant for being in charge. Control freaks... next this place'll be crawling with CIA agents, they're probably in the air right now. No, I suggest you keep quiet about what we know and our plans, Mr President; at this stage, the less interference the better."

Mal was all ears. He bowed to the Professor's experience in dealing with U.S. bureaucracy. Remaining standing, Mal nodded at de Luz, "Good advice, Vic, we'll play our cards close to our chest then."

"I have a question," Robert said. "Why is the centre of all this right here in Sydney? We're only a backwater in the whole scheme of things compared with the U.S. or the UK... why here?"

"Because of those two," the Professor said.

"Alice and Secta, why?" Robert queried.

"They are a thorn in Zen's side... Gorrick's Moriarty if you like," the Professor explained.

"I didn't ask for the quest to wipe the floor with Zen... but if it wasn't us, it would be someone else," Al snarled.

"Just means the battlefront is at our doorstep," Secta said, echoing Alice's sentiments.

"This invasion of sorts on such a scale now begs the question: what do we have planned to counter it?" Mal challenged.

It was a question with no conclusive answer. At this stage, they were totally reliant on Neit's solution of taking out the rifts at their origin on Eris by eliminating En-Lil in his refuge, the Futurum Tower. It seemed logical when they decided on the plan, and they had no reason to doubt it now; however, the stakes had increased with more rifts opening around the world, there was extra pressure on their plan to succeed.

Hope got a text. Her face paled. "I just got a message from our techies. They overflew The Lair with a drone an hour ago, and the radiation from the rift has increased substantially. They recommend evacuating the area for a radius of at least five clicks."

"That will require the military, and that... will attract attention," Mal said grimly.

"Neit, will taking out Gaap shut down the rift?" Alice asked.

All eyes focused on Neit—the question was germane.

"I cannot answer that question, Alice," Neit admitted.

Though their backs were to the wall, they knew they had no alternative but to try.

"Will we be safe from radiation going in there?" Al asked Hope.

"It's at eighty Rad now; if it gets over a hundred, it will cause acute radiation syndrome for anyone within a hundred metres of it. I'd say now you have much less time to get the job done than you originally had planned, Al," Hope said solemnly.

It wasn't what Alice wanted to hear.

It was still dark when Alice, six commandos, and Agent So, all fitted out in black fatigues and armed to the teeth, assembled on the Oceana rooftop helipad. The chopper was on its way from the airport and due in five minutes.

Secta was there. He handed Alice the Gallium gun.

"The test firing was successful, but the range is limited. Here —" He handed over half a dozen bullets. "It's single-shot. You load it from the breech."

Alice studied the gun and the bullets in his hand. He didn't look confident.

"It feels a tad fragile, like a toy," he judged, feeling the weight of it.

"You could say that," Secta acknowledged.

Standing with the six commandos and Karzoff, Agent So glimpsed Secta handing something else over to Alice, which he furtively slipped into the side pocket of his black flak-jacket.

"I would feel a lot more confident if I was armed," So told Karzoff.

"The reason you are participating in the mission is to assist Alice. Follow his orders… it will be invaluable experience for you."

Just as Karzoff finished speaking, the sound of the approaching Airbus ACH-160 filled the air. The white chopper with no livery appeared out of the inky night sky and with the thwop, thwop of its rotors resounding off nearby buildings, touched down on the heliport target.

Secta offered his hand to Alice and yelled above the engine noise, "Good luck, my friend."

Not one for formalities, Alice shook his hand without saying a word, turned, and walked briskly across the tarmac to board the chopper.

Inside, it was configured for eight passengers. Alice took a seat, strapped up, opened the breech of the Gallium handgun, loaded a shell, and then slid it into his waist belt next to the crystal blade and a 9mm Glock. He felt well-armed.

With an uneasy silence aware that the safety of the planet rested firmly on the shoulders of the assault team, Secta and Karzoff watched the chopper lift off and head north.

News was breaking of people witnessing the appearance of strange volcanic fissures around the world. An interview with Major Jackman, featuring several photos he'd taken of the oddity hovering over the finger wharf at the end of his street, had made the headlines. The area had since been cordoned off by the military. There was scientific conjecture as to the nature of the strange anomaly, with explanations ranging from a new weapon being secretly tested by the military to the arrival of some kind of alien craft. Governments had been unable to shut down the reporting. News was spreading via social media at a phenomenal rate. Major Jackman's photos had gone viral, and conspiracy theories were spreading like wildfire. The world was abuzz with conjecture. As the Professor had predicted, panic was taking a grip on society. Within the hour, reports came in of more rifts, one in Germany and another in the UK. Blame was being levelled at Iran, sectarian religious orders… any ideology or country perceived to be a threat. In reality, the governments or the secret agencies connected to them had no idea what the rifts were or how to deal with them. All they could do was isolate them, surround them, and then watch and wait.

The massive number of munitions the U.S. military had assembled in such a short time, encircling the rift at the end of his street, amused Major Jackman… surely it was overkill. But the sardonic smile was quickly wiped from his face when a couple of men-in-black turned up and, ignoring his former military status, ordered him out of his premises to a safe-house miles away from the scene. Jack sent the Professor a text to tell him.

The Professor was in the Kairos control room with Secta, Hope, and Robert, preparing to monitor the assault on The Lair when the text came through. Robert had Kairos locked-in on standby to send an exit wormhole to Alice should it be needed.

Karzoff burst into the room with a face like thunder. "There is a report of a Russian airstrike on an anomaly that appeared very near to the new klystron critical particle accelerator in Siberia."

The Professor was reading the text and immediately read it out loud to the others.

Robert switched his computer to online news reports.

After hearing the text Jack had sent the Professor, the others quickly crowded around Robert to take in the latest news reports.

"There's a YouTube video of the airstrike," Robert said. "Wait... here it is." He hit play.

There was a wide shot of a rift that had formed over an icebound lake. It was picturesque: a small lake surrounded by lush forest. But then there was the rift... a strange, angry-looking oddity suspended above the lake, bubbling magma. It was only about three metres in length but striking: a red-hot jagged volcanic gash in the atmosphere with turbulent black smoke rolling around its molten lips. A MiG-27K fighter-bomber swooped into the shot, delivered a missile, hit the afterburners, and then climbed skyward at Mach one. The missile hit the target and exploded. The radiance from the explosion highlighted a force field bubble surrounding the rift and protecting it. The missile had no effect.

"What the devil is going on?" Karzoff bellowed.

"It's a similar force field to the one that protected the UFO over Tokyo in 2047," Secta observed.

"Why did they hit it... bloody fools?" Karzoff growled.

"How do you expect the military to act rationally when they're confronted with something completely irrational?" Hope posed.

"The Russkies must be paranoid about the theoretical particle studies they're doing there... it's cutting-edge stuff... probably the most powerful of all the collider experiments. Otherwise, they wouldn't have ordered the strike," Robert submitted.

"What's the nature of the experiment there?" the Professor asked.

"Glueball theory," Robert said.

They exchanged looks of concern; it had to be relevant that the rift had opened close by such a potentially dangerous facility.

When the smoke cleared from the explosion, the rift had expanded to double its size. The video finished.

"Was I seeing things, or was the rift bigger after the explosion?" Hope said.

"I think we just learned something," Secta said, pacing the room and clasping his chin. He stopped, turned, and faced them. "It feeds on violence."

The revelation had them more worried than ever about the pending assault.

Hope raised a question. "What would happen if one of these countries nuked one?"

There was a sharp intake of breath around the room. The thought was Earth-shattering... literally.

"We need to tell Mal... the U.S. or any of the others mustn't use nukes," Secta said intensely.

"Mal also needs to brief his generals ASAP," Karzoff said sternly. "If Alice fails, he will need to have the military on standby."

"This is what he wants!" the Professor bellowed, having an epiphany. "En-Lil is trying to provoke a nuclear attack... with the nature of the rift, I suspect the reaction of a nuke would be an antipode causing the rift to evolve into a malefic black hole that could effectively consume every living thing on Earth!"

CHAPTER 20
HEAD-TO-HEAD

THE EIGHT PASSENGERS on the chopper were sitting in silence as soldiers do going into battle. Each of the six commandos carried two handguns. They were dressed in matching black fatigues, flak-jackets, and MICH 2000 Kevlar helmets with headsets and flush-mounted Mohoc cameras beaming back via satellite to OTT.

Agent So was in civvies. Compared to the commandos, he appeared nervous. On the other hand, Alice was calm. Dressed identically to the commandos but wearing a red beret in preference to a helmet, he was staring out of the starboard side window at the rays of dawn lighting up the azure Pacific Ocean in all its majesty. Its sheer beauty had him wondering whether this was his last day on Earth or whether it was just another page being turned in the weird book of quests he was on. He cast his mind back to En-Ki's all-encompassing voice and was reminded he was doing all this stuff risking his life and that of others on the basis of a voice that emanated from a glowing orb. It seemed ridiculous right then, sitting in a chopper, armed to the teeth and headed for a battle with a demon over a rift in time. The idea of it was off the planet: surreal—but then again, he was getting used to that. Gone were the days of being a simple heavy metal singer, when all that was asked of him was to dress up like a rock star, remember the lyrics and sing. Now it seemed that at every turn the fate of humankind rested on his young shoulders.

"What'd I do to deserve this?" he mumbled to himself.

Sitting opposite him, Agent So saw Alice's lips move but couldn't hear him over the engine noise.

"Were you talking to me?" he shouted.

His voice snapped Alice out of his reverie. "No," he grated. Secta's voice erupted in his headset.

"Alice, are you there?"

"Yes, Secta. Go ahead."

"There is news of other rifts opening around the globe. The Russians bombed one only hours ago, which caused it to grow in size. We think the rifts feed on violence."

"Yeah, so?" Al growled, not in the mood for scientific jargon.

"We believe the demon is trying to provoke a battle with us to grow the rift."

"Yeah well, there's little we can do about that other than take him out as quickly as possible."

"Remember the force field bubble around the UFO over Tokyo?" Secta reminded him.

Alice pictured the huge UFO hovering above the Zen dome in Yokohama Bay being fired upon by Japanese warplanes, the missiles deflecting off the massive force field bubble.

"Yeah, I remember."

"Well, the rift has the same protection, so watch out that Gaap doesn't use it as cover."

"Roger that," Al said.

"Okay, good luck, Alice. Out."

It was feasible they were being provoked into a fight with Gaap just to feed the rift? It meant nothing they could throw at it to destroy it would do any more than make it grow bigger and more powerful. It was a paradox; they had to destroy Gaap, but it would make the rift stronger.

The pilot came online to Alice. "ETA two minutes, sir."

"Copy that," Al said and then switched to the team comms. "Two minutes, men, lock and load."

Gaap's evil yellow eyes looked sharply up at the natatorium ceiling as soon as he heard the sound of an approaching chopper. He knew instinctively it was carrying the enemy. Its muzzle full of V-shaped, sharp teeth forged into a macabre grin, knowing the mission he'd been given by his master would soon be executed.

As the chopper descended towards the bullseye target on The Lair helipad, Alice ordered the squad to activate cameras for streaming live to OTT. They were out of the chopper in seconds after it touched down, assembling at the entrance to the house to watch the chopper depart. Then, with only the occasional distant sound of magpies and kookaburras, they were enshrouded in a deathly silence.

Ignoring the disquietude, Alice ordered Agent So to stay at the helipad while they reconnoitred the house. So wasn't impressed by being left alone unarmed and tried to argue the point with Alice, but it fell on deaf ears.

Alice led the commandos down the staircase to the landing on the top floor. Their destination was the natatorium two floors down in the basement. Drone recon had already established it was where the rift was located. The nagging question was whether Gaap was at the rift or waiting somewhere along the way to ambush them.

"I sense your conundrum… but there is now enough light in the house to force Gaap into the darkness. It will be within the safety of the arrow of time," Neit informed Alice mentally.

But Alice didn't trust Gaap, so he sent three men to check the three bedrooms on that floor. The commandos moved stealthily with clinical military precision and within a couple of minutes returned with an all-clear sign for Alice. He led them down the staircase to the living area. As he reached the landing, he was reminded of what he'd found in the kitchen last time. A vivid picture of the bloody dismembered body of Rita flashed in his mind's eye. Neit got the picture, and it was so graphic it even sent a shiver down his spine.

A swift silent hand motion from Al had his men fan out. After checking the balcony and kitchen, content it was clear, they assembled to move on. It meant Gaap was waiting for them down below in the basement where he was safe from exposure to sunlight. Al stopped the squad at the dark stairwell that led down to the basement. He thought about turning the lights on and then decided against it, not wishing to alert Gaap.

"No, turn them on, it knows you're here," Neit said psychically.

Al flicked the switch, and the spiral staircase lit up. He started down.

Back at base, they were on the edge of their seats with bated breath, eyes glued to a pair of TV monitors mounted on the console. One was displaying a full screen from Alice's helmet camera, and the other a screen split into six windows with a feed from each commando. The audio made it even creepier with the rustling of body movements, footsteps, and heavy breathing. The limited commentary from Alice kept them guessing.

When Alice stepped from the alcove into the spacious natatorium, he was greeted by a horrific growl that was so loud and unexpected it almost jolted Hope out of her chair. She recoiled with a hand over her mouth to suppress a startled yelp. The control room fell silent.

The seven-foot monster was at the far end of the room, its clawed hands shaped defensively. A seething sound like laboured breathing wheezed from its wolf-like muzzle and reverberated throughout the tiled room.

Alice stood his ground and raised a hand to stop the squad behind him.

"What the hell is that?" The commando immediately behind Alice muttered.

The reaction was to be expected. Alice anticipated how tough it would be when reality struck the men that a monster, the stuff of myth and legend, a powerful beast, a colossus, savage and formidable, the enemy, confronted them. No matter how well they'd been briefed, seeing it right before their eyes was always going to be a shock.

"Okay, fan out both sides of the pool," Al ordered.

Three commandos with guns held up trained on Gaap filed quickly into position. With the Gallium Gun held out in front of him, Alice edged towards Gaap.

It was nail-biting stuff for the four of them watching the monitors in the Kairos control room.

"Alice needs to get close to use the Gallium gun," Secta said uneasily, aware that was far easier said than done.

As the commandos on the far side of the swimming pool closed to within three metres of Gaap, the leader propped to cover Alice.

Gaap let out another loud earth-shattering growl and then crouched into a pose to take on Alice.

"Is he close enough to shoot?" Hope asked nervously.

Secta grimaced, "Any second now."

Alice stopped. There was a deathly pregnant pause. Those in the control room held their collective breaths.

Alice took a steady aim... and then fired. The shot was right on target but exploded in a flash when it hit and lit up a force field bubble enveloping Gaap.

"You won't get through the force shield. It is emitted from the rift," Neit told Alice. "You need to lure him away from it."

"Yeah, well how do you recommend I do that?"

Secta's static-enriched voice shrieked through the headset, "Alice, he's protected by a force field."

"I know Secta... I know, Neit wants me to lure him out of it. Any ideas?"

Neit and Secta didn't have time to answer because the monstrosity came at Alice. The commandos opened fire. A hail of bullets simply bounced off the force field protecting the monster.

Backing up, Alice holstered the Gallium gun and then drew the crystal blade. As Gaap moved, the rift could be seen behind his huge frame. It was suspended two metres above the floor, a metre long with black smoke rolling in a thunderstorm-like fury around its molten lips. It was menacing.

In an unexpected move, from a standing position just short of Alice, Gaap sprang six metres through the air across the pool and landed on the other side right next to the three commandos. Before they had time to react, he attacked them. Alice and the other three commandos watched helplessly while Gaap tore the men limb from limb. Soon the pool was crimson from the dismembered limbs the monster had torn from them and cast irreverently into the water. It was a bloodbath.

Alice and his men opened fire, but the bullets were deflected by something. He yelled to Secta, "Something's still protecting it!"

Back in the control room, Hope averted her eyes from the monitors unable to stomach the brutality of the assault.

The three remaining commandos were still firing at Gaap, but the bullets were ricocheting off him.

"It's the temporal distortion of the force field; it's wider than we thought and intuitive. That means Alice won't be able to get inside it," the Professor said with urgency.

There was nothing left of the men it had butchered, so Gaap turned his attention back to Alice and his three comrades. In one almighty move, it crouched down and then sprang up into the air, across the pool, and landed right in front of Alice. By then, Alice had his pistol out and, along with his three support troops, emptied their magazines into Gaap... all to no avail. The weapon spent, Al cast it aside and then, with all his might, struck out at Gaap in a last-ditch effort with the crystal blade. It wasn't deflected by the shield and sank into the deltoid on Gaap's left shoulder.

The creature let out a deafening howl and then, in a reflex action, belted Alice with such a powerful blow that it sent him careering into the wall. Alice slid down the wall onto the floor out cold.

Gaap turned on the three remaining commandos.

Through the haze, Alice could just make out a voice way in the distance calling his name: Alice, Alice. It took a moment for him to recognise it belonged to Neit. He opened his eyes and didn't like what he saw. It was what he imagined the floor of an abattoir would look like: blood, guts, and body parts everywhere. The pale blue wall tiles had been sprayed red—nothing remained of his commands—every one of them dead. And cowering over him, ready to strike a death blow, was the perpetrator, Gaap.

Alice looked down at the crystal blade still in his hand. He would wait for the right moment to strike. "You demonic piece of crap," Al spat at the beast. "Come on, have a crack at me... take me out... come on... give it your best shot!"

Immune to the ferocity of Alice's verbal assault, Gaap leaned in real close only half a metre from Alice's face.

Alice recoiled from the snarling rows of shark-like teeth and the drool hanging in strings from its hideous jaws.

Back in the control room, they were glued to the close-up of Gaap's drooling muzzle and its evil yellow eyes glaring at them from the monitor.

Aware of how close it was to the camera on Alice's headset, Hope erupted, "Al, no! It's going to kill him!"

Trapped on the floor with his back to the wall and Gaap cowering over him, Alice gagged from the foul stench of its putrid sulphurous breath. Gaap was so close the drool was slopping onto Alice's lap and forearms. But Alice waited patiently for the right moment. Then, when Gaap's face and gnashing teeth were only thirty centimetres from him, he struck, driving the blade upwards with all his might at Gaap's exposed throat. But with the sharpest of reflexes, Gaap caught Alice's hand, rag-dolled him to his feet, and then, with the strength of ten men, flung him through the air into the swimming pool.

Alice plunged into the water with so much force, the wind was knocked out of him when he hit the bottom. Thrashing about, he desperately tried to reach the surface, but Gaap was in the water with him, holding him down.

Neit panicked, knowing it was a fight Alice had no chance of winning.

CHAPTER 21
ATROPHY

THE LIVE FEED from the camera on Alice's tactical headset was severed the moment he hit the water. Secta immediately shouted Robert an order, "Now!" Robert knew exactly what to do.

Alice violently and desperately thrashed his way to the surface, but only long enough to take a badly needed gulp of air before Gaap's huge claw came plunging down onto the top of his head to push him back under. Through the chaos in the water, Alice caught sight of Gaap's thigh and plunged the crystal blade into it. The water quickly clouded crimson with the demon's blood, but the injury wasn't enough to stop him. Intent on drowning Alice, he held him down with all his might.

Wielding the blade underwater, trying to inflict more damage on Gaap's legs, was too strenuous for Alice. His strength was sapped by lack of oxygen. His arms felt like lead weights, and he was losing the fight. Then, through the ferment of bubbles and swirling water, he saw a familiar sight—a vortex was forming underwater only a couple of metres from him. The thought of salvation reenergized him, but would it be enough for him to reach it? He wasn't sure, but it was all he had. In a last-ditched effort, he slashed at the claw holding his head down and felt the blade hit the mark in the creature's wrist. A severed claw floated down past him, trailing blood. It had worked— he was free. He kicked off the floor of the pool with all the strength he could muster, surged up to the surface, filled his lungs with a massive gulp of fresh air, and then dived back down to swim as fast as he could towards the open vortex. But it was like swimming through a tank of gel. With time frozen, the water's viscosity had changed. While he was at the surface, Alice had failed to notice that Gaap, unaffected by the time freeze, was standing waist-deep in the pool holding up its bleeding stump, staring at it disbelievingly, and bellowing in agony like a crazed wolf with its leg ensnared in the jaws of a trap.

A huge gush of water spewed from Kairos with Alice in it. He flopped onto the floor like a beached dolphin and lay there gasping for air. Hope held open a towelling robe into which he struggled.

Shivering, he stuttered, "Just in the nick of time, I was a goner for sure!"

Hope rubbed his back, "Come inside and warm up. You're safe now."

"I feel like a drowned rat," Alice said, rubbing his hands together to warm them.

Secta, the Professor, Karzoff, and Robert were waiting in the control room.

"Alice," Secta almost shouted, so glad he was safe. "Did the Gallium gun work?"

Still shivering, Alice shook his head. "Nar, only the crystal blade could get through the force field."

"What about the Wasp?" Karzoff questioned.

"Didn't get a chance to use it... wait a minute," Alice froze. "Where's Neit?"

The others looked concerned.

"Isn't he inside you?" Hope asked.

"No. He must have jumped. You've gotta send me back... Now!" Al roared. "Get me back to stop my men being killed."

"We can't do that, Alice. There would be two of you in the same time... you'd cancel out," the Professor said gloomily.

"You mean I can't stop it?"

"I'm afraid not, Alice," Secta said. "We can only send you back to after you left."

"What good is all this if it's going to cost the lives of those men?" Alice snarled.

"What's done is done, Alice, it is what it is," Secta said.

Alice snapped, "Send me back to finish off that thing. Now!"

"No, Alice, it would be suicide," Secta argued.

Alice had boiled over and wasn't about to take no for an answer. "It wasn't a request, Secta!" he growled.

Secta backed off; he knew Alice well enough not to push it.

"That thing has killed six of my men and just might kill Neit... unlike us humans, it kills anything that gets in its way."

"I wouldn't say that, Alice. Us humans kill tons of creatures every day from bacteria to insects underfoot."

It was the wrong thing for Robert to have said. To Alice, he had trivialised the death of his men, and the others knew it.

Alice exploded. "Don't give me any of your cryptic scientific blag, dude... hear me?"

The young man cringed at the ferocity of Alice's tirade. "Send me back, right now!" he ordered in no uncertain terms. "If the mongrel kills me, then just pull me out, and I'll go back in again... and I'll keep going back till I've done the bastard!"

"But that defies—" The Professor started, but Alice stopped him mid-sentence with a wicked eyeballing.

"Just do it, Secta... hear me?" Alice snarled and then stood defiantly with arms folded stoically, demanding the team's acquiescence, and he got it—they knew better than to question him, and all except Hope jumped into action.

Trying to calm the tension, Hope spoke warmly to Alice. "Take it easy, mate, remember you're not into violence... we need to think this through." She was worried Alice was beginning to show signs of anxiety. He needed to be in control for what lay ahead.

"We glorify and damn violence at the same time," he snarled reflectively.

"Should we not be sending in a backup team by chopper?" Karzoff questioned.

"No, what I need to do, I'll do alone," Al snapped.

Secta heard him and shot Hope a sceptical glance. They would send in backup no matter what Alice said.

Rob had the mainframe online. The standby button was locked into place with a satisfying click, and the control room lights dimmed automatically.

"Do you still have the Wasp?" Secta asked, as an afterthought.

"Don't know if it made it through the vortex," Alice said quickly checking through his jacket pockets. "Ah yeah, here it is. Not much use though, it can't penetrate the force field."

"It's made of organic material, so there's no problem with time travel. See the little button on the top?"

Alice checked the tiny drone in the palm of his hand and acknowledged, "Yes."

"That releases it from preprogramming. If you then throw it at a live target, it will lock onto it."

"Cool," Alice said, slipping it back into his pocket. He checked his weapons. The pistol was missing from his belt. "Nine mil didn't make it."

"It is probably at the bottom of the pool," Karzoff muttered.

With his checks done, Alice announced, "Okay, I'm set. Let's get this show on the road."

Unconvinced that Alice was one-hundred percent, Hope queried, "You haven't convinced me you're okay, Al."

He turned to her with a smug look and snarled facetiously, "Next time I'll bring a note."

"I'm sorry, Al," she cried, stepping away from the console with her hands held out in apology. "But you're no good to us dead, love. I'm worried that all the breaking down and reconstruction of your atomic structure might be taking a serious toll on you."

"What, like side effects?"

The Professor added, "Yes, Alice, it is indeed probable that in your reformation, some of your bits may be malformed."

"Some might reckon I've always had a screw loose, Professor, so it probably wouldn't matter anyhow," Alice joked.

"It's not funny, Al. We're dealing with unknown territory here... There are signs in your temperament causing me concern," Hope reiterated.

Alice calmed down noticeably in an effort to keep the lid on any concerns they might have. "I'm with you... I'm with you... look, we should do some tests when I get back, okay? But there's no point in worrying about it now. I feel fine, just a bit edgy, that's all. It isn't every morning you have to get your head around fighting a demon to start the day, is it?" He touched Hope's shoulder affectionately. "I'm alright, kid."

She studied his eyes and was convinced he was telling the truth. "As my dad used to say, if you're going through hell, then just keep going," she smiled.

Alice grinned in the cheeky manner that so much endeared him to them. "See this attitude... it's rusted on."

Secta turned from beside Robert at the console to watch Alice enter the dispatch cubicle.

They all knew what Alice meant by his last statement: his resilience was unrivalled.

Again, Hope and Secta exchanged looks of concern for Alice's well-being, aware the opportunity had now passed to do anything about it: the countdown for dispatch had begun.

"I share your concern, Hope," the Professor admitted quietly. "The ravages on his body and mind are unimaginable. I'm surprised we haven't seen more side-effects."

"We're at fault here, Professor, it is up to us to monitor his health."

"Yes, Hope, I think his toughness... his do or die bravado deflects the attention that should be routine. It's easy to lose sight that we have no idea how the effects of time travel might atrophy the physiology."

The discussion caught Secta's attention. He turned from the console and said, "I totally agree, you can begin by running tests on me while Alice is busy on the mission. I'm used to being a lab rat."

The entire time travel process was still in its infancy. What they had achieved till now was profound, worthy of a Nobel Prize, but questions remained of the repercussions such as the effects of the process on time-space distortion and on physiological endurance. Being able to generate a wormhole and keeping it open long enough to enable the transfer of matter was ingenious; however, the physics of the dematerialisation and then the reconstitution of the atomic structure they'd pioneered, remarkable as it was, could still have consequences over time and was always going to be the biggest challenge.

"Chaa!" Al said, stepping into the cubicle.

At the same moment across town, Kew was in his office on his computer. A message flashed on the screen. It was the surveillance team reporting that a drone with eyes on Oceana had sighted chopper traffic to and from the target. He knew that meant Alice's team had gone in ahead of schedule and that they'd probably been leaking disinformation to Agent So. He immediately leapt onto the phone to marshal his team.

Agent So was restless after having sat at The Lair helipad for the last two hours, nervously listening to gunshots from the floors below, followed by a deathly silence permeated only by the laugh of a kookaburra that he figured was cackling mockingly at his predicament.

The tedium of waiting like a recalcitrant schoolboy for the next order from his superior officer, had gotten the better of him. The time for insurrection had arrived. He gingerly made his way down the staircase on a reconnaissance mission, all the while hoping he wouldn't run into Alice coming up.

Under normal circumstances, the relatively instantaneous journey through time felt like nothing more than an astral-flash to Alice: one second, he was in the cubicle, then the next he was at the destination. He felt no obvious ill-effects from the experience, perhaps a moment of disorientation, a little giddiness, a dry taste in his mouth, and tinnitus—that was the most annoying aftereffect, the tinnitus in both ears that lasted a couple of minutes after arrival. And this time it seemed to be louder.

He was prepared to confront Gaap as soon as he materialised in the natatorium, but Gaap was nowhere to be seen. The tinnitus in his ears was as loud as microphone feedback at a sound-check, only constant, so constant it was playing havoc with his thinking. His left ear felt hot—he touched it and found blood on the tip of his finger. The conversation with Hope and the Professor in parting was ringing home—perhaps they were right—what if he was beginning to suffer side effects from the process?

In his inimitable fashion, he brushed off the thought and got on with the gig at hand. He looked around—the pool water was stained red with blood. Torn limbs, heads, and torsos of his men were scattered about the tiled floor as though they had been put through a combine harvester. It was a gruesome nightmare. He leaned down and pulled the headset off a severed head and panned the camera for everyone back at the control room to see.

"This is what that mongrel monster did to our blokes," he snarled and just got it out in time before he bent over and puked. A few deep breaths, and he was ready to move on, but first he aimed the headset camera at the rift.

"It's bigger, guess it fed off the slaughter."

The tear in time was now two metres long. A bright orange jagged pulsing cut in the air that looked like the gateway to hell. Around the white-hot lips of the blazing gash swirled dark angry clouds, and for the first time, Alice could hear a low evil rumble coming from it as though it were a guttural murmur from the devil himself. Even six metres from it, Alice could feel its intense heat on his face.

He turned the camera on himself. "You were right, Hope, I am getting side effects... nausea, dizziness, and tinnitus in both ears that's so way too loud... the symptoms only lasted a few minutes, I'm okay now. I'll wear this to keep you up to speed... I'm going to find this mongrel and get back Neit."

Karzoff's voice bellowed through the small speaker. "Back-up is on its way by chopper, Alice."

"I said—"

Before he could finish protesting, Secta cut him off. "The boss ordered six commandos to support you, Alice, ETA fifteen minutes."

Alice was pissed off, but he wasn't about to argue. After a sigh, he growled, "Alright, alright... but tell them to wait on the helipad for my word to enter and put them through to me as soon as they're in the air."

He leaned down, wrenched a Glock from a severed hand on the floor, and then snarled into the mike, "Right, over and out."

The bloodbath had struck a nerve with Al. He wasn't going to rest until he had the demon's head on a block. But where is the foul thing? He questioned mentally... but there came no reply from Neit. Then his mind flashed on Agent So waiting at the helipad. It's gone to kill him. Pistol in hand, at the ready, in his usual swagger, he headed up the stairwell.

CHAPTER 22
THE SOURCE

A BLACK KAMOV KA-60 in Zen livery sped through the clear blue sky over North Sydney, bound for The Lair. On board, Kew and his six-man strike force were dressed up and ready for the assault. Cruising at a casual one hundred and fifty km/h, the fifteen-seater turbo-powered Russian-built chopper would reach the target in ten minutes.

At the same time, a chopper manned by Oceana troopers took off from the rooftop helipad of Oceana Headquarters in Sydney, heading for the same destination. The pilot spoke to Karzoff in the seat beside him. "Radar has picked up a bogey headed for our target, sir."

"Can we identify it?"

"I'll check with ADS-B."

"What is that?" Karzoff queried, not up to speed with pilot-speak.

"Auto-dependent surveillance broadcast, sir: geo-positioning. All aircraft transmit an ID signal to satellite," he said, flicking a switch on the dash. The response showed immediately on the control computer screen. "Zen Corporation, sir."

"Right... then we have company," Karzoff said, as he nervously placed a hand on the grip of his sidearm. Dressed in commando fatigues with a green beret covering his red hair, he looked the part. It had been a while since he had been in action, and that was making him feel a little anxious. He wasn't confident with guns — "you're a lousy shot," Honor used to chide him. Gazing out of the window, he reminded himself that his aim had been accurate enough to drop the Zen Agent, Anu Set, in Jerusalem a while back, and that thought spiked his courage.

"We need to beat them to The Lair, Captain," Karzoff said resolutely.

"Roger that, sir."

Karzoff switched to Alice, "Karzoff here, can you hear me, Alice? Alice? Come in..."

There was no response because Alice was online to Secta while ascending the staircase.

"I'm alright, I'd tell you if I wasn't," Alice said, with a lowered voice to avoid alerting the enemy. He was at the landing to the living room, surveying the scene before entering.

Secta's prattle was distracting him, so he switched off the headset. Karzoff would now have no hope of warning him of the impending Zen assault.

Alice tightened up when he noticed William So sitting at the table on the patio with his back to him. The living room looked clear—with the pistol held in both hands, he scurried commando-style through the living-room out onto the balcony and stopped a few metres from So.

Sunning his face in the morning rays with his feet up on a chair, So sniggered offhandedly, "I take mine black with two sugars."

"You'll be taking a bullet in the back of the head if you don't face me," Al growled.

So slowly got to his feet and faced Alice.

Steadfast, Al kept his pistol trained on him.

So's expression changed, and he bellowed in a slightly different tone, "Shoot him, Alice!" Looking surprised that the voice had come from him, So quickly cut it off, "Pay no attention, that was just—"

"Neit, is that you?" Al queried.

"Alice, I..." So squawked, and again took over to suppress Neit, "Yes, he's in occupation, but he'll be dealt with."

Alice took a step forward.

So's face darkened to an evil grimace. "Stay where you are, or the Id dies," he roared demonically.

Alice realised it wasn't So talking; it was Gaap. Even though he had the upper hand with Gaap trapped inside So, unable to escape in the sunlight, the threat of Gaap killing Neit, who was also trapped, made for a Mexican standoff.

"What's to stop me shooting you?" Al threatened.

"You'd be killing the Id as well."

"He's lived a long time; I reckon he's prepared to martyr himself to rid the universe of the likes of you," Alice argued.

"That might be, but will you pull the trigger?"

"In a heartbeat."

"I don't believe that... I call your bluff." He stood, faced Alice, and threw open his arms. "Take your best shot," he snarled defiantly.

"Before I do, answer me this... why are you here?"

"Ah, there is nothing more certain in life than death for a human. A pitiful species, poorly designed—second-rate genetics—you need to be culled to make way for a superior race."

"And I suppose that's you... had a look in the mirror lately? Is your gig from En-Lil to cull the human species?"

It was a loaded question.

"I obey my master's orders."

"Why here then... why Australia?" Al snarled.

"To eliminate you."

"Let me get this straight... you were sent across the galaxy to this little blue planet to take me out because I represent such a huge threat to your despotic master. A touch of overkill, isn't it? Am I that much of a threat?"

"That's not for me to say, the master has his reasons... I have my orders," So spat back.

Out of the corner of his eye, Alice caught sight of a chopper on late final approach low, just above the tree-line at the back of So.

So heard it as well and looked up in time to see it descending directly overhead. Blocking the sun, its shadow was cast over the patio. Alice recognised an opportunity and moved quickly to block the patio doors to the living-room and yelled, "Jump now, Neit!"

A black wisp of vapour shot out of So's body and entered Alice. So looked back at Alice with surprise. He'd been outfoxed. Alice raised the Glock and fired. The shot was precise... though the bullet made only a small hole in So's forehead, the exit wound took the back of his head off and painted the patio floor a grisly crimson. So's eyes rolled back in his head, his knees buckled, and he crumbled to the deck. As he did, Gaap slipped out from him, manifested into his gruesome demonic form, and snarled maniacally at Alice.

The shadow from the chopper was retracting quickly as it landed on the helipad. Alice needed to keep Gaap where he was to let the sun finish the job and kill him. He noticed Gaap's hand had regenerated the same as the finger he'd severed. Brushing that aside, he raised the Glock and emptied the clip into Gaap, but the hail of bullets had no effect. He was still protected by a shield.

Alice ditched the empty Glock and drew the crystal blade from his belt. He snarled, holding it up for Gaap to see. But Gaap wasn't intimidated and charged Alice with claws raised. It was on.

"Strike at its throat!" Neit's voice thundered in Alice's mind. But that was easier said than done; right now, Alice wished he had a tyre lever or Ex's katana, something with a bit more reach and grunt than the flimsy dagger.

A loud rumble of footsteps from behind Alice stopped Gaap just short of Alice, and Kew's distinctive voice rang out urgently. "Drop the blade, Alice... Now!"

"Go to hell," Alice muttered to himself, and then swiftly darted around behind Gaap, using the monster as a shield from Kew.

Kew was standing in the middle of the living-room, his pistol aimed at Alice. He quickly motioned for his men to fan out. Alice counted six of them.

The beating sound of a chopper's rotor alerted Alice that the cavalry had arrived.

In one sharp, unexpected move, Gaap twisted his upper body around and let fly at Alice with an almighty backhander that collected him on the side of the head, propelling him across the patio on his backside. He skidded to a halt, cushioned from hitting the wall hard by the dead body of Agent So.

Gaap wanted to attack Alice while he was on the deck trying to regather his senses, but the shadow had moved, leaving him in direct sunlight. He ducked under the big patio umbrella for protection.

All hell broke loose in the living-room as Karzoff's men rumbled down the staircase and engaged Kew's forces in a gunfight.

Dazed, Alice shivered when without saying a word, Neit withdrew from his body and entered Agent So. Then, to Alice's surprise, the dead man convulsed awkwardly, and like some kind of twisted zombie marionette, clumsily struggled to his feet. Alice sat up and watched the corpse stagger like Frankenstein's monster taking its first few steps towards Gaap. With the back of his head missing, the remnants of his brain were oozing like a glutinous slime down the back of his neck.

What are you doing, Neit? Alice thought, and then all of a sudden, it dawned on him.

Kew fired two shots at So to try and stop him. One bullet blew his left cheek off, and the other forged a gaping hole in his chest that Alice could see through. But So kept moving.

When he reached Gaap, he grabbed the shaft of the umbrella, wrenched it out of the table, and cast it aside. Gaap was exposed to the sunlight, causing his body to begin degenerating. Smoke was rising from his skin. In a rage, towering over So, he belted him in the face. The blow was so hard it left his head hanging by only a few sinews from his neck.

So collapsed onto the deck.

Then, with one great swipe of his arm, Gaap demolished the wooden table and then, angry that the sunlight had prevented him from finishing off Alice, roared like an angry lion and charged through the patio doors into the mayhem of the living-room battle.

Kew stepped out onto the patio with a menacing grin on his sullen face, pistol aimed at Alice, who was still struggling to get up.

"Finally, the chance for me to finish the job that others couldn't... and what a pleasure it will be."

Alice returned serve, "Nothing's going to paper over the cracks in your personality, Kew. You're just Gorrick's glove puppet. Zombie So here has more brains than you."

Alice slipped his hand surreptitiously into the side pocket of his jacket and grasped the Wasp. He had to keep Kew talking to stop him from peeling off a shot.

"It all ends here, Alice," Kew barked, relishing the moment.

Without warning, Agent So reached out and grabbed Kew by the ankle. The unexpected shock caused Kew to look down sharply, providing Alice the opportunity to press the button on top of the Wasp and fling it at Kew.

He looked back at Alice just in time to see and hear the Wasp skyrocketing towards him with a wicked buzzing sound like an angry hornet. It homed in on Kew's forehead, and even though he managed to duck, it corrected mid-flight and slammed into the target.

A crack like a stick breaking sounded as the three grams of shaped explosive detonated. The drone had discharged its deadly payload, and Kew's days were over. His hand went limp... he let go of the pistol, it dropped onto the titled floor as he crumbled in slow motion to join Agent So.

Just as Alice got to his feet, a black vapour slipped out of So's lifeless body and entered him.

"We make a good team," Alice said mentally.

"It is not over yet," Neit reminded him.

"Alice!"

His name being called caused him to look at the living-room. It was Karzoff; he and his team had Kew's men contained. Two were dead, and two were wounded. Alice strode into the room.

"One of ours is down and another with a serious wound. I will get them and the prisoners back to base," Karzoff said hurriedly.

"Which way did Gaap go?"

"That thing scared the life out of me. We fired at it, but bullets just bounced off... it went down the staircase over there," Karzoff said, pointing a trembling finger in the direction of the staircase down to the pool.

"I don't know what to do, Karzoff. I've thrown the kitchen sink at the bastard, and nothing works." He held up the blade, "And this thing is useless; you need to get too close to use it... it should be a sword."

"Did you get Neit?"

"Yep."

Karzoff looked past Alice onto the balcony. "Is that—?"

"Yeah, what's left of Agent So and Kew. What do you reckon, Neit?"

"We cannot capitulate, Alice... the arrow of time is increasing in amplitude."

"What?" Karzoff queried.

"He means the rift... Every time Gaap does something violent, it gets bigger."

Karzoff looked nervously at Alice. "What is that supposed to mean? It is going to swallow us up?"

There was no simple answer to that except a probable yes—they really had no idea, but it seemed the most logical explanation as to why the rift was there.

"Wait." The command base had called. "Yes, he's here, one moment." Karzoff took off his headset and handed it to Alice. "Secta, he is with the President."

Alice put the headset on. "Yeah, Secta, what's up?"

"Is Gaap dead?"

"No, but Kew and Agent So are, plus a couple of their troops and one of ours."

"You're on loudspeaker; the President is here with a message."

"Al, glad you're okay," the President said.

"What's going on, Mal? I can tell by your voice there's trouble."

"I got a call from the CIA, they've got a tactical team arriving here in about an hour... they want to take over the situation with the rift."

Alice thought about it a moment. When he didn't respond, the President asked, "You there, Al, did you hear me?"

"Yeah, sorry, Mal, I was just thinking. Look, Gaap is a distraction... I'm gonna need a lot more than a toy gun and a toothpick to kill it... let the CIA take over. Secta, we should concentrate on getting me to Eris. The fight needs to be waged against En-Lil at the source... fighting this thing here's just a waste of time."

CHAPTER 23
SUITCASE BOMB

GORRICK WAS PACING his office, mad as a cut snake when Honor came in. He faced the window with his back to her, hands clasped tightly behind his back and thundered, "I suppose you've heard?"

She tentatively took a seat in the lounge setting. "Yes, Kew and Agent So are dead."

Gorrick turned from the window with a grave expression on his chiselled face and eyeballed her. "We've lost all of them! What can we do to defeat this guy?"

"I think we need to reconsider our strategy, sir... it isn't working."

He strode over and sat down facing her. "You're quoting the obvious, Honor." He paused to calm down, took a deep breath, and then continued. "At the end of the day, he has overcome everything we have thrown at him. The only thing he has been unable to defeat is the demon guarding the rift... but then again, Gaap failed to beat him as well." He lowered his head and clasped his forehead, eyes shut, thinking: a man with a conundrum he was struggling to solve. "We need to secure the damn rift," he mumbled.

"Why?" asked Honor.

Gorrick slowly raised his head, realising she was right to question him. He stood up and in a more positive mood said, "You're right, Honor... why? This entire episode with the rift has been a major distraction and has cost us lives. Oceana cannot defeat Gaap... All we need to do is leave him as the rift gatekeeper while we get on with the job of building the wormhole generator."

"And the RF android development program, sir," Honor added.

"Exactly, and with your insider knowledge of Oceana, you can focus on destabilising them."

Ten hours later, two CIA agents led a crack tactical team of seven U.S. Navy SEALs into The Lair. Their mission was to deploy a suitcase bomb into the rift. U.S. Military intelligence proposed the detonation of the small nuclear device would cause the irregularity to implode and collapse upon itself; an action Secta and the Professor hotly refuted, claiming the explosion would only increase the rift's volatility.

The CIA agents had arrogantly refused their intelligence, which included field footage of the rift, Gaap, and detailed reports. As a result, the nine-man assault team ignorantly stormed The Lair inadequately prepared for the terror awaiting them.

The President was in the control room with the OTT team, waiting anxiously for word of the assault. The operation was commanded from a U.S. Frigate in Sydney Harbour. OTT had been denied a streaming feed from the assault team: the Whitehouse had classified the CIA mission top secret.

"They've made a massive mistake ignoring our intel," Al grumbled.

The dark purple shadowy form of Neit was seated beside him. "This is not going to end well. I have been in its mind, I know what is going on in there, and it is not pretty... that thing is programmed to kill."

"Wait, you said programmed... what do you mean by that? Are you suggesting Gaap is artificial intelligence?" the Professor queried.

The idea of Gaap being an android of some kind had pricked the ears of the others.

"Yes, it is a genetically modified alien creature re-programmed by En-Lil."

Secta stood up abruptly and began pacing the floor, intrigued by the idea. He stopped and said, "That might explain the force field... maybe it's artificially generated by the creature itself, perhaps an implant of some description."

"What does it matter if it's a bloody robot or not?" Alice all but complained.

Hope had the answer. "If it is an android, Ai, it means we've been using the wrong tactics to defeat it."

Alice nodded slowly; it was beginning to make sense to him.

"Then it's highly likely the demons guarding En-Lil in the Shadow Tower would also be Ai," the Professor added.

"Yes, that would probably be the case," Neit affirmed.

"So En-Lil has been building androids for donkey's years to protect him, including all the Gorrick clones."

"Yes, Alice, his objective is to replace mankind with Ai, which fits in with what we discovered in 2087 with Turk and the others... If you remember, Gorrick was busy turning humans into Cyborgs," Secta said.

"We saw the same thing with Anu Set," Alice added.

"En-Ki genetically altered Neanderthals to produce Cro-Magnon man forty thousand years ago. His brother En-Lil and his father Anu didn't agree with him starting a new race, they wanted a race of androids totally under their control," Hope hypothesised.

"Are you saying that's at the core of the war between En-Ki and En-Lil and that it's only just now coming to a head?" the Professor sought to have clarified.

"Yes, it just might be," Hope said.

"So, we know by 2087 that En-Lil hasn't succeeded... in fact, we know that in 2047, he was having a crack at creating a race of alien human hybrids then," Al said.

"Which you stopped. So, both times on two different timelines you've prevented him from achieving his goal," the Professor proposed.

"Which is why he wants you dead," Neit concluded.

"In all those thousands of years, he hasn't been able to perfect the perfect android," Alice said.

"The two of them must have been thought of as gods by less-informed people of the past," Hope submitted as she got up from her chair and headed for the hot water jug to make a brew.

"That is true, Hope," Neit said. "But En-Ki was always benevolent, while En-Lil is notoriously malevolent."

"Good versus evil, light versus dark, it has always been thus," Secta preached.

Cradling a cup of hot chocolate in her hand, Hope resumed her seat. "People like to say that the conflict is between good and evil, but the reality is the conflict is between truth and lies." She took a sip of her drink and grimaced. The hot chocolate was rubbish.

"It seems by what you're thinking, one of them was a better scientist than the other," Mal posed.

Neit knew the answer to that from personal experience. "Yes, En-Ki was the scientist, En-Lil the warrior. It was the reason for the falling out; En-Lil never understood En-Ki, he was jealous of his brother's genius."

Hope put down her mug, stood up, and announced, "This could take a while. I'll take Alice and start running some tests on him. Buzz me if you've got any news. Come on, Al."

"You staying here, Neit?" Alice asked the shadow seated alongside him.

"Do you need me, Hope?"

"No, Neit."

The pressure door hissed with Hope opening it for her and Alice to pass through.

The natatorium resembled a scene from a zombie apocalypse movie rather than a swimming pool. A thin mist of smoke from gunfire veiled the scarlet water of the pool like a shroud of death.

Bodies were strewn everywhere, the aftermath of the destruction caused by both the OTT troops earlier and now the Navy SEALs. The tiled floor around the oblong swimming pool was awash with gore and blood.

Only one man remained standing, and he was Calvin (the Jet) Cole. A former quarterback for the Detroit Lions turned CIA agent, he possessed a lightning arm as he gripped the small bomb, the size and shape of a gridiron football. Nervously, he activated the timer on it, realising he had only two minutes to get the bomb past the monster that had just annihilated his assault unit and into the rift before it exploded.

Warm blood gushed from a deep wound in his shoulder, running down his arm and dripping from his fingertips. He wavered unsteadily on his feet, the loss of blood taking a toll on him.

When they first encountered the monster guarding the rift, they had no idea that their weapons would be rendered useless against it. A force field surrounding it caused their bullets to bounce off harmlessly—they had never encountered anything like it before. Then, in a rage, the monster came at them, grabbing men and tearing them to pieces like they were mere toys. There was no defence against the ferocity of its attack.

Calvin's CIA team leader, Reagan Gillard, ordered him to stay clear of the thick of the battle to protect the weapon. On his order, he would dispatch the bomb. The order never came. When Reagan led the first attack, the monster reached out and ripped his head clean off, casting it into the pool like a beach ball. Then, one by one, as the rest of the men attacked, they were virtually shredded by the marauding colossus with its voracious appetite for butchery.

A ricochet bullet cut into Calvin's bicep, and though it caused him intense pain, he ignored it. It was nothing compared to the carnage his comrades had suffered.

He found himself at the other end of the pool from the monster. The creature stared at him, challenging him to come close enough to be ravaged. He needed to get within throwing distance, and he only had a minute and a half to do it.

Inching along the side wall, he moved closer and closer towards the rift and its terrible guardian.

Aware of what Calvin was doing, the brute let out a roar like a wild animal but stayed planted right in front of the rift as its sentry.

Calvin cursed to himself, "Why didn't I throw it at the rift before it wiped them all out?" The answer was obvious—he had been under orders to wait. It wasn't the first order of this mission he disagreed with. Why they had snubbed the intel from the Aussies was beyond him. Doing so had resulted in them walking directly into an ambush. But it was all too late now.

A static-enriched monotone voice crackled through his headset, requesting an update. He didn't have time to tell them much more other than he was the lone survivor and about to deploy the weapon.

Calvin the Jet Cole was within range… the LED timer was counting down from 15 seconds—it was now or never. He sucked in a deep breath and stepped out from the wall only four metres from Gaap and the rift. His mind was cast back to ten years ago when he threw the winning pass to get the Lions home over Arizona—10, 9, 8, 7—his throw needed to be even more accurate this time because there was only half a metre opening in the rift… 6, 5, 4. He let fly… his lightning arm launched the ordnance like a cannonball… it zipped right past Gaap's left ear and into the rift. He hit the deck, rolled into a ball, and covered his face, knowing full well he was dead meat.

The explosion shook the house right down to its very foundations. But to Calvin's surprise, it was all over in a couple of seconds, and he was still alive. He slowly unfurled and looked up at the rift. The monster had gone, but the rift had doubled in size.

A tremor resulting from the small nuclear detonation shook Sydney. The increase in size and power of the rift, a result of the bomb, sent a shiver up Gorrick's spine, causing a wry smile to crack on his otherwise unemotional face. He went over to the window and looked north to see if the magnified presence of the rift was in view. Instinctively, he knew it had just fed on something most fulfilling, something that had boosted its size at a far greater rate than the consumption of human souls ever could. He gazed in awe at a spiralling column of fire that now shot a hundred metres into the sky above Pelican Island, resembling a red glowing twister. The spectacle lit up the northern part of Sydney as though it were an erupting volcano. Even at twenty-five storeys up, he could hear the sirens of many fire engines rushing to the scene.

"Now that we've thrown a cat amongst the pigeons," he muttered happily to himself. "Gaap can now move on to phase two."

Doctor Hope gave a comic snort of derision. "Great, so all of a sudden you haven't got time for this, huh?"

Alice sat up on the gurney. "Something bad just happened, didn't you feel it?"

Hope rolled her eyes. "Regardless of whatever it is, I'm going to finish these tests. You're far too important, and I'm worried about you."

She was holding his arm, ready to take a blood sample. A cold stare from her got acquiescence from Alice. She jabbed him with a syringe.

By this time, Alice had become accustomed to being jabbed, so he didn't even bat an eyelid, just carried on with the conversation. "Why?"

"What do you mean, why?" said Hope, focused on the job.

"Why am I so important to you? Is it purely from an OTT perspective or what?"

She removed the needle and went to a nearby bench to test the blood sample in a haematology analyser. Her lab was equipped with many chemical and immunoassay analysers central to clinical diagnostic testing.

After smearing a blood sample on a glass slide, she slipped it into the unit and then studied the results on the monitor connected to it. Instantly she noted an abnormality. "That can't be right?" she questioned herself, concerned. Without looking at Alice, she asked, "Have you been suffering headaches, tinnitus, blurred vision, dizziness, or fatigue?"

"Yeah, but that comes with the territory, don't it?" Al grumbled.

"My God!" she exclaimed, glancing up at the ceiling with distress.

"What is it now?" Al said dismissively. He really wanted out of there.

Hope quickly prepared another slide to confirm her prognosis. "Just give me a minute, Al," she said worriedly. The results came up the same. Now moving even faster, she prepped another slide and went to a different analyser: a spectrophotometer, it counted platelets in blood cells.

After five minutes, she read the print-out, her worst fear confirmed. She got up and, moving back to Alice on the gurney, noticed he was dozing. She gently touched him on the shoulder. What she had to tell him wasn't going to be easy; it was serious news.

"Al... Alice?" she said warmly.

He didn't stir.

She gave his shoulder a little prod with her finger. "Al? Wake up."

He was unconscious. She took his pulse. It was slow. A tear rolled down her cheek; she knew his condition was due to the dematerialisation and re-materialisation process, and he had finally succumbed to it. She bent down and gently kissed him on the lips. "To answer your question, yes, it is more than an OTT perspective... I, I love you, beetlehead," she said, her eyes misted with tears.

CHAPTER 24
SAGE

" **I CAN'T BELIEVE** you just said that, Secta!" Hope all but screamed at her brother, incensed by what she thought was an insensitive comment. "The preliminary tests show Polycythemia vera, a mutation in the JAK2 gene that regulates the production of blood cells."

The Professor weighed in on the argument. "When the body makes too many red blood cells, it leads to a thickening of the blood. It can be associated with an elevated platelet count and an enlarged spleen. It could be caused by exposure to intense radiation... I expect it's a side-effect of the process."

Secta was pacing the control room floor.

"Seems to me the old Secta has returned," Hope snapped irritably.

"Look, Hope, we don't even know how badly he's infected. You're overreacting," Secta said emphatically.

"He's in my lab unconscious, Secta. We've witnessed a deterioration of his wellbeing over the last few missions... it was only a matter of time before—" she broke down.

The Professor wrapped a consoling arm around her. "Take it easy, girl. We'll solve this. I think you're taking what Secta said a little out of context."

"You need to take a look at what the world is up against, Hope. A swirling inferno: a flaming tornado several hundred feet into the air. One more careless bomb from the Yanks, and I believe its polarity will be reversed, causing it to revolve in the opposite direction and suck everything into it, which would be the entire population of Sydney, including us. Already, there is pandemonium on the streets, Hope. This is also happening in other places around the world... and there is only one way to stop it, and only one person on Earth to stop it: Black Alice. You know that, Hope... he must go to Eris to shut this evil thing down, or it will be all over for humankind."

Sobbing, she slowly, reluctantly nodded her head. "I know, Secta... I know... but it will kill him."

"Not if we can get SAGE to work," the Professor said with a smug smile.

Secta stopped pacing and locked eyes with the Professor. "What the heck is SAGE, Vic?"

"Subatomic gene extraction... SAGE: a formula for curing diseases like cancer and leukemia by removing genes. I was working on it back in my Desertron days but couldn't perfect it due to one vital component... the means to dematerialise the atomic structure."

Hope wiped the tears from her eyes, her scientific mind racing to process the Professor's hypothesis. "Our formula does that," she barked.

"Yes, it does... your formula was the component I needed. So, it works like a filter. Once the subject has been dematerialised and is progressing through the injector to the wormhole, it passes through a filter encoded to remove the said gene. In Alice's case, it would be the JAK2 gene. When he is rematerialised at the other end of the wormhole, it would be minus the said gene."

"Brilliant," Secta expounded.

But the Professor's face looked doubtful. "You must remember it's only theory... it needs further refinement to work..."

"Then, what are you waiting for, Vic? Go to your lab and get started," Secta said blithely.

"I'll need Robert to help," Vic said.

Robert turned from the console and said, "At your service, sire."

"Hope... Alice we will need to be stabilised before we can do anything," Secta said, turning to Robert, who was just about to leave with the Professor. "Robert, is the telemetry locked in for Eris?"

"Yes, Secta."

"Right, we'll check the patient and do some research. Karzoff is monitoring The Lair, and the President is supposedly keeping in touch with the Yanks. Let's move," Secta said encouragingly.

"I'll join you," Neit said. He had been keeping quiet, trying to interpret what all the fuss was about.

It didn't take Secta and Hope long to determine a course of treatment for Alice. Their research revealed complications of Polycythemia vera or PCV may include cardiovascular events such as a stroke, mini-stroke, or heart attack, or problems in the veins, including deep vein thrombosis, pulmonary embolus, and blood clots. The progression of the disease varies with each patient, as does the treatment. Lowering the hematocrit (HCT), a measure of the red blood count, to less than 45 has been shown to improve survival and is the treatment goal. Alice's blood count was 14; if it got down to less than 13.5, he'd be diagnosed with anaemia.

The course of treatments recommended for PCV were: Phlebotomy, the removal of blood to reduce the overall number of blood cells... with fewer cells, the blood thins and flows more easily, and symptoms generally improve. And a low-dose of aspirin to prevent platelets from sticking together: Aspirin can prevent life-threatening blood clots causing heart attacks and strokes.

Secta prised open Alice's left eyelid and pulled down the lower lid. Then he shined a torch into his pupil to check the response. "Anaemia... Hope, get onto sickbay and inform Doctor Wilson that Alice will require immediate dialysis: a transfusion. Give him Alice's blood type and our prognosis. Ask him to confirm that it's PCV."

Star Lord, your footprints in the sky
Star Lord, show us peace of mind
You hold, the key to our time
Star Lord
We can fly
Like a shooting star we're far away from your galaxy
All the worlds you see live in a peaceful dream
I hold the only key
I, I can offer peace of mind
I'm the Star Lord
We can fly

Singing quietly to himself, sitting at the top of the stone staircase at the front of the Hyde Park War Memorial, Alice gazed up at the massive ceiling enclosing the cavern. There were fissures in it through which the sun, being directly overhead, sent rays of light, giving the cavern a mystical otherworldly appearance.

"The rays tell us it is noon," Zule said, sitting down beside Alice.

He glanced at her long trim bare legs and sexy sandaled feet, then up into her glorious face and long blonde hair. "You're a sight for sore eyes," he thought.

"Was that the song 'Star Lord' you were singing?" she asked.

"Yes, I wrote it a long time ago... back when I first started a band in Perth. I was only a kid. I recorded it a few years later... but now with all that's happened, it makes me wonder about the significance of the lyrics. 'You hold the key to our time'... what is the key?"

Zule snuggled up to him, her blue eyes showing wonder. "Don't you know the meaning when you write it?"

"Sometimes, but not in this case. It was like I was channelling someone or I was just off my face... can't remember which," he chuckled.

"Show me being off your face," she said almost childishly.

He went cross-eyed, pulling a funny face that cracked Zule up. She kissed him passionately. He closed his eyes, enjoying the sensual moment, the taste, and feel of her warm full lips. Her lips were gone. He opened his eyes and found Ezekiel sitting opposite him. From A.D. 2134 or thereabouts back to 587 B.C. in an instant! What's going on? He wondered.

"The question is what is the key to the future? How do we find it? Is it a physical thing or only perceived? The key may be you, Daniel... I think you are the key to the future," Ezekiel said.

Alice recalled how Ezekiel called him Daniel, perhaps mistaking him for the biblical figure he later wrote about. He stared at the wise old sage, wondering whether his disclosure was prophecy or just the ramblings of a geriatric who'd experienced so much in life that it had rattled his senses. He was just about to speak when he suffered another flash. When his vision cleared, this time he was sitting beside Morrigan Hud in the Zen boardroom in Angel City. At the end of the long table was Gorrick. Alice remembered he was conscious inside Turk, similar to what Neit does with him.

"He looks like one of those tall white Nordic aliens the ufologists talk about," he thought to Turk.

"Maybe he is," Turk started, but Alice spoke over him with his voice out loud, locking eyes with Gorrick. "What do you say to the accusation that you're an alien and that Zen is trying to take over the planet?"

Gorrick thought long and hard about it, then replied with a smirk, "I'd say it's a load of rubbish. I'm the key to the future, not you. You're a dangerous man, Turk. You did time for stepping out of line in the forces; if you don't watch yourself, you'll be doing time again here."

The image of Gorrick looking exasperated flickered like a bad TV signal and then strangely began to repeat, as though being replayed, with Gorrick's voice crackling and echoing, "I'm the key to the future, not you... the key to the future... the key to the future." Another flash of light, and when his vision cleared, he was in Tokyo in 2047. Gorrick was standing in front of him, straight-backed like a general inspecting troops on parade. By his mannerisms, it was easy to tell he wasn't impressed with Alice's arrogance.

"I don't think you get the picture, Black Alice. Your SAT team is right now being annihilated, and you are about to meet your death."

"Yeah, yeah, yeah, I've heard that shit before, Gorrick... your clone in 2087 gave me pretty much the same rave. What is it... a prepared speech or something? You megalomaniacs are all carved out of the same block of rubbish. The population of this planet has been putting up with your trash since biblical times, and you've never won, with or without your superior technology. Little ole insipid mankind seems to always knock you over, and let me tell you... it won't be any different this time... mark my words. You'll wish in the end that you'd never laid eyes on me."

"We'll see about that hubristic fool. You're not the key to the future, Alice, I am!" Gorrick snapped. He'd said it again... "You're not the key to the future, Alice, I am!"

Alice blinked. His vision was blurry. It cleared for him to see a giant eye staring at him only centimetres from his face. He realised it was enlarged out of proportion because it was studying him through a magnifying glass.

"Ah, we have you back, Alice."

He heard the eye speak, but it was Gorrick's voice repeating over and over in his mind that had him spellbound: "You're not the key to the future, Alice, I am!" He snapped out of it and barked, "Who are you?"

"Doctor Wilson. You've just regained consciousness."

"How long have I been out?"

"Three hours or so."

"Three hours?" Al snarled, struggling to sit up.

The doctor gently forced him back down on the hospital bed. "Now, now, just relax, Alice. You've been through quite a procedure; you require rest to recover."

"What procedure?"

Hope's smiling face popped into frame. "We've given you a grease and oil change, Al. New blood."

"Ah, Hope," he was relieved. "Where am I? What's happened?"

"You're in the sickbay, and you've been given a blood transfusion."

"What, like Keith Richards?"

"Yes, but not infants' blood," Doctor Wilson croaked with a bedside chuckle, trying to lighten things up.

Alice's confusion showed on his face. "I don't get it... what could I have wrong with me? I feel fine."

"Access your implant and search Polycythemia vera. While that keeps you busy, just relax here until Doctor Wilson lets you go, alright?" Hope said matronly.

"Yeah, yeah, yeah," Alice said agitatedly. "Where are you going?"

"To help the Professor and Secta develop a cure for you," she said.

Calvin the Jet Cole disembarked an MH-60 R Seahawk Lamp chopper that landed aboard the USS Zumwalt, a guided missile destroyer anchored in Sydney Harbour. The warship was visiting Sydney in convoy with the Georgia class nuclear submarine that had caused so much controversy only months before. Though the sub had only just departed, USS Zumwalt had remained behind for extra duties and then was ordered by the Executive Director of the CIA to hold in support of mission: Operation Lair.

Calvin was immediately escorted from the helipad to the ship's Combat Direction Centre below deck, the CDC, for debriefing.

A three-way video conference call was established with Dianne Fisher, Director of the CIA, and her executive agents at Langley, Virginia, headquarters of the CIA, and half a dozen scientists from the CIA Directorate of Science and Technology, also at Langley.

Calvin gave an account of the assault and the combat performance of the SEALs support unit and then said, "We had no effective counter to the power of the alien enemy. It was guarding the rift protected by an impenetrable force field of some description. I've never seen anything like it; bullets just bounced off it."

"After you deployed the bomb, what happened to the alien?" Miss Fisher asked.

"I hit the deck, certain the force of the explosion was going to kill me... and covered up as best I could only fifteen or so feet from ground zero. The effect of the blast was surprisingly minimal... not what I expected. When I looked up... the alien had gone."

"Where?" Fisher asked.

"Inside the rift, I guess."

"How long was it before you noticed the changes in the rift?" asked senior CIA scientist Dr Stein.

"Immediately after the explosion, it started to pulse like a slow heartbeat and then began to expand. All my comms were down... I had to get out of there, I felt it was going to blow."

"But it didn't," Stein suggested.

"Well, no, not in conventional terms anyway. It sprouted a spiralling column of fire that burnt right through the ceiling like it was cling wrap. I got the hell out of there, and by the time I reached the rooftop helipad to trigger my GPS for pick-up, the spiral was about a hundred feet in the air, spinning like a blazing twister, making a terrible whooshing sound. It was like all hell had broken loose."

"Yes, so the chopper pilot reported. Apparently, his instruments went wild on late final approach to The Lair," said Commander Curtis, head of helo-operations.

"We have satellite data that confirms since the explosion, the rift has been emitting a transient disturbance, an electromagnetic pulse or EMP," Doctor Stein said.

"And what affect do you expect from that, Doctor?" asked Miss Fisher.

"It will knock out power grids. At this stage, we expect within a five-mile radius of ground zero," Stein concluded.

"That will cause havoc in Sydney. Have we informed Oceana, Dwight?" Fisher inquired.

Dwight Williamson, 3rd captain of USS Zumwalt, spoke up, "Not yet, Miss Fisher, but we expect them to be monitoring the situation."

"Why has there been so little liaison with Oceana?" Fisher asked.

"We were ordered to proceed on a need-to-know basis... a black op, ma'am," Curtis said, somewhat reservedly.

"So, Agent Cole, based on your personal experience, what is your recommendation to proceed?" Fisher asked.

What he said surprised the hell out of them. "We need to knock it out before the EMP emissions shut down the city and cause chaos. The suitcase bomb was only partially effective. An MQ-1 Predator UAV armed with six Hellfire air-to-surface missiles fired in succession would, I think, be more productive."

CHAPTER 25

FIRE DEVIL

T HE DOOR TO the Professor's study slid open, and Hope entered, taking a seat in a vacant armchair beside Neit's.

The Professor said, "It's strange to realise I'm now the same age as old people."

Hope chuckled, "That's it, off you go to academic aged-care."

"I thought that's where I was," the Professor responded.

Secta chimed in, "You probably are. Dementia is apparently like that. This is all just an illusion."

Joking aside, he changed to a serious tone and asked, "How's the patient, Hope?"

A relieved smile broke on her face. "His haemoglobin is back up to 17.5. The transfusion worked. How are you getting on with SAGE?"

The Professor was about to answer when the door slid open again, and Karzoff breezed in, looking all flustered. Remaining standing, he announced, "I've just come from a meeting with the President and chiefs of staff. We have a problem."

"If it's about the EMP emissions coming from the rift, then we already know," Secta said.

"What EMP?" Hope queried.

"We'll tell you in a minute. Go on, Karzoff," Secta said.

"Well, aside from the mayhem going on in the streets outside, the CIA decided to inform us of their failed mission and that they are considering hitting the rift with more bombs. Their scientists are claiming it to be the only way to shut it down."

"Silly fools are treating it like an oil rig fire. What did Mal say to that?" Secta asked.

"He asked me to run it past you," Karzoff said.

Neit jumped in, "It will only make it worse."

"We're all in agreement with that. After what happened with their last effort, you'd think they'd be wise enough to see the explosion only intensified it," Secta said, getting up and pacing the floor, visibly irritated.

"I know the U.S. Military, and that's how they think, all gung-ho, worse than the bloody Poms. They think blowing the crap out of something will fix it... they tried the same damn thing in Vietnam, and history recounts what happened," the Professor sounded off.

All eyes were on Secta for an answer, but there was none forthcoming. He was too busy pacing the floor, holding his chin, deep in thought. The conundrum for him was perplexing. If they were to allow the U.S. to proceed with the bombardment, the twister would most likely reverse and suck the population of Sydney into it.

Knowing Secta was processing the information to come up with a solution, Karzoff turned to Hope and asked, "How is Alice?"

"We've stabilised him with a blood transfusion."

"When will he be back on deck?"

Secta stopped pacing and said, "We have issues in getting Alice to Eris to shut down the rift from its source. Firstly, Alice is ill, and secondly, we have no idea if he could survive the conditions there. We can't send a probe through to find out, and SAGE, well..."

With a very serious expression on his face, the Professor said, "It's Catch 22. We can use SAGE, but we won't know whether it worked until he gets back, and if it doesn't work, the process might well kill him."

"Then send me," Neit said. "I can survey the scene, analyse the atmosphere, and buy you more time to repair Alice."

All of them exchanged a raised eyebrow glance at Neit's suggestion, knowing full well he was right; it was the obvious solution. The trick, however, would be in delaying the Americans from bombing The Lair.

"Hey, what was the zombie thing you did with Agent So's dead body? I didn't know you could do that! Man, that was seriously creepy," Al told Neit, who was sitting on the edge of his hospital bed.

"Ah, a little trick I picked up over the years... not quite perfected yet, still a little awkward," Neit replied.

"You're telling me. Anyhow, it worked. Hey, Karzoff dropped by a little while ago and said you offered to go as an advance party to Eris."

"Yes, well, someone has to do it... look at you, in bed," Neit said.

"Hey, you're being facetious. That's a happening thing, you picking up on good old Aussie sarcasm."

"It ain't difficult around here, Alice."

"Now you've used a contraction! Listen, no going inside the Futurum Tower without me, right? I'll be set to go as soon as you've sussed whether I can survive there or not."

There was scepticism in Alice's tone. He wasn't totally in agreement with Neit going on his own. The reasons were understandable, but he hated the thought of him risking his life up against the sort of threats that could exist there—especially with Gaap as an indication.

"Listen, when they bombed the rift, what happened to Gaap?"

"Word is he simply disappeared," Neit said.

"Nah, that doesn't wash with me... after all he caused? Unless the bomb knocked him out... no, he wouldn't have just split."

"I agree with you. I figure there is more to it than meets the eye."

"The President of Oceana said his scientists don't agree with another assault on the rift. They claim it will only serve to increase its power. Essentially, we have no jurisdiction there... so I can't press the issue... diplomatically," Dianne Fisher, Director of the CIA, told Agent Curtis Cole over speakerphone.

Cole was in the captain's cabin of USS Zumwalt with Captain Dwight Williamson 3rd. They exchanged looks of concern.

"My scientific advisors have requested more data, so you'll need to fly a UAV through the funnel of the twister and take readings. You'll get the specs in 12 hours. We're already analysing what we can from satellite imagery, but we need actual data. Once we have the data, we'll confer again with Oceana."

Calvin was apoplectic. "That's not good enough! Your scientific advisors haven't experienced this thing. They're sitting in plush offices in Langley sipping barista coffees and eating donuts," he yelled angrily. "We don't have the time to pussyfoot around because the Australian's haven't got the balls to act. They've had plenty of opportunity and have come up with zilch. We need to act now before this gets out of hand."

Captain Williamson was shocked by the ferocity of Cole's tirade, as was Dianne Fisher at the other end of it.

She stammered and stuttered before saying, "I understand how the horrible personal experience would have you riled up, Agent Cole, but there are protocols we must follow."

"Argh! Damned the protocols... political babble!" he growled, and then jumped up from his seat and stormed out of the cabin.

There was a pregnant pause while Williamson and Fisher contemplated Cole's discontent. Then Fisher spoke up. "Well, that there is one angry Agent."

"Troubled by the loss of his team, I've seen it before... he might require some counselling."

"He might also be right in his assessment. Give me a few hours to run the options past the government."

Calvin Cole was standing at the bow of the USS Zumwalt, leaning on the handrail, staring north at the twisting, seething, white-hot firestorm tornado that cut the night sky as though sliced open by a flaming knife. The rift was holding static over Pelican Island.

Dubbed by the media a Fire Devil and then explained away by a government spokesperson on the evening NEWS claiming it to be the result of an open fissure in the Earth's crust known in scientific terms as a Phreactic volcanic eruption: when cold surface water comes into contact with hot rock or magma generating an eruption of steam. It was far from the truth but plausible enough a white lie for the public to buy for the time being though it failed to explain why the entire northern sky glowed red. The last time the Sydney skyline had looked anything like that was when raging bushfires surrounded the city.

The air was alive with the sound of sirens from emergency vehicles. Numerous fire trucks and support vehicles were rushing to the scene expecting to have to contain the spreading of fire to the drought-stricken forestation in the area. None of them had any idea they were dealing with a supernatural phenomenon.

The city of over five million people was in absolute chaos: rapidly turning into a war zone. Panicked residents were being evacuated in a five-kilometre radius of the rift epicentre. But fear of the unknown was the real interloper here—there was no known precedent. Prophets of doom were proclaiming Armageddon: the end of time. Religious zealots warning it was the beginning of the end... hell on Earth, pay-day for sinners, and they weren't that far off the pace with the hell on Earth analogy. It sure looked that way.

Calvin grinned macabrely. Possessed by Gaap, he thought the view was spectacular, but was at the same time anxious to hit the rift with a barrage of missiles to feed its voracious appetite for maleficence. But now that it was dark, he could do as he pleased and get up to some mischief.

"It's convection... the rift generates convection, creating the gigantic equivalent of a dust devil, only it's static and fire, not dust. Dust devils form from the bottom up, whereas a tornado forms from the top down. The intense heat from the core of the rift rises, and when it hits cooler air, convection is generated," the Professor explained.

The members of OTT were in the office of the President. The meeting was to brief him so he could continue a dialogue with the CIA.

"So, in order to extinguish this thing, it would need to be at the bottom... we need to shut down the rift," Mal said.

"Yes, but that would mean cutting off its source, and we believe that is on Eris," said the Professor.

"If the rift is linked to a wormhole from Eris, how does it stay open when we can only keep one open for sixty seconds or so?" Viktoria asked, showing her enthusiasm to be back at work.

"That's exactly what we hope to learn from this," Secta answered.

"I don't believe the arrow of time is a wormhole, I think it is conjured," Neit suggested.

None of them were expecting him to say that; they all thought of the rift as a physical anomaly.

"Are you saying it's nothing more than wizardry, Neit?" Al quizzed.

"So would it burn if you stepped into it?" asked Hope.

"Yes, it would burn," Neit said. "It is a living entity."

That rocked them.

"Are you suggesting it's alive?" Secta questioned.

Neit nodded, "Yes, but as a conjured entity."

"Like a genie or a spirit," Alice submitted.

"Yes, or a demon," Neit added.

Secta was up and pacing.

Mal leaned over to Hope and whispered while watching Secta, "Does he always do that?"

"It's how he thinks," she said.

Mal pulled a quizzical face, "Makes me nervous."

Secta stopped, he had it together in his mind. "It makes sense. All this has been conjured by En-Lil to distract us from Zen's activities. Don't get me wrong, we still have to defeat it because even though it's only for want of a better name, an illusion, it exists in our space and time, and if we don't make it go away, illusion or not, it threatens to throw the entire world into total chaos. That, I presume, is the plan, which would then open the door for Zen to do its dirty work. So, from what Neit has explained, En-Lil has focused his powerful wizardry on manifesting the rift and Gaap. That is why the connection is staying open; it is not reliant on a wormhole. Shut down En-Lil, and you shut down every rift on the planet."

"That makes complete sense, Secta," Mal said. "The question for us is how do we put the brakes on the CIA to stop them from feeding the rift more energy from bombs?"

There was a pregnant pause as they all contemplated the conundrum. Then Neit spoke up.

"Tell the Americans the truth."

They all exchanged a look of surprise.

"He's right," the Professor said. "It's time we laid it on the line. They'll eventually find out about Kairos anyhow. This way, it will kill two birds with one stone. It will stop them from bombing The Lair again, and it will force them to trust us... because they wouldn't have any alternative. We've got Kairos, and we've got Alice."

"Isn't that putting it all at risk?" Hope asked.

"I think under the circumstances we have no choice," Karzoff countered.

"I agree," Mal said, getting to his feet. He began to pace, which amused Hope. Secta watched Mal pace past him, deep in thought. Mal stopped, turned back to them, and said, "I'll go directly to the U.S. President, avoid all this messing about with the CIA. Secta, Professor, I'll need you both for a conference call to help explain it all to her... most of it is way beyond me."

Alice got up and said, "Right, so what's next? I'm hungry."

Hope had the answer, "We send Neit to reconnoitre Eris."

"Neit, are you positive you're okay with this?" Al queried.

"Yes, Al, no problem."

"So where are we up to with SAGE, Vic?" Hope asked, noticing changes in Neit's vernacular: using contractions and calling Alice, Al.

The professor said, "Robert will install the new algorithm in Kairos once Neit has completed his mission. A series of virtual tests proved successful, but there's no guarantee it will remove the JAK2 gene from Alice's DNA—it is, after all, experimental."

"Isn't everything around here?" Alice said, waggishly.

Vic eyeballed Alice. "We can but only try."

"Okay, good enough for me. Now, time for some grub," Alice said, his mind on his tummy.

Mal was still at work in his office, signing documents, when his secretary, Miss Vallins, opened the door and poked her head in. "Sir, I have a strange call from the CEO of Zen Corporation, Gorrick. Do you want to take it?"

Mal looked over his square-framed reading glasses at her quizzically. "You're right, that is odd. Alert Karzoff, give him a link to the call, and have him record it."

"Yes, sir." Her pretty face disappeared back behind the door.

Mal got up from his comfy armchair, moved into the high-back leather chair behind his desk, and stared at the hands-free phone on his desktop, expecting it to ring at any moment.

He yawned; it had been a long day. Under normal circumstances, he would have left for home by now, but the fewer interruptions after the close of the day's play had given him the opportunity to catch up on a few things that had been left unattended.

The phone rang. He took a deep breath and answered it. "Gorrick, you're the last person I expected to hear from."

"We've not met, President Low," said the ice-cold voice at the other end.

"No, and I don't see any reason why that should change. What do you want?" Mal returned serve with equal venom.

"Is the view worth it from your high moral ground, President Low?"

"You didn't ring to discuss the view, surely?"

"I certainly did. If you look due north, you will see the view to which I refer."

"You're talking about the eruption."

"You and I both know the arrow of time is no eruption. We also both know you and your allies have no idea how to handle it."

Mal was getting worried; it was sounding as though the conversation was leading to a threat.

"That, of course, is only your opinion," Mal said resolutely.

"It would be an opinion if it weren't for the fact that I am in control of the arrow of time... so here it is, President Low... surrender Black Alice to me within 24 hours, or the arrow of time will begin consuming your constituents."

The expression on Mal's face said it all; it reflected his worst fear: Gorrick's threat was ubiquitous—if he did have control of the rift, then it meant his clones had control over the other rifts open around the world. He decided to call him on it. "You insult my intelligence, Gorrick... surely you don't expect me to believe you can control the rift."

"I stand corrected, President Low. I don't have direct control over the rift as you call it... I have control over the demon Gaap, who is in control of the rift. You have my demand. Enjoy the view from your high moral ground... goodbye, President Low."

Gorrick terminated the call. Mal stayed on the line and asked, "Did you get that, Karzoff?"

"Loud and clear, sir."

"I have a conference call scheduled with the President of the United States for 0600. Be in my office at 0500 to go over Gorrick's threat... may as well make that all of OTT."

"Neit will be off-world, sir, and Al has been ordered to take R&R," Karzoff reminded him.

"Yeah, right. Just the others then."

CHAPTER 26
DEVIL INSIDE

BACKSTAGE AT A Black Alice reformation gig, designed as a planned distraction for the public from the anomaly north of Sydney, chaos ensued. The live podcast had attracted a swarm of film crew, rolling up leads and dismantling equipment. The band had just finished their third encore and was now being led by the stage manager to the dressing rooms. Meanwhile, the support band, Cried Wolf, was in the process of loading out of their dressing room.

In passing, Lemmy, the lead singer of Cried Wolf, stopped Alice and said in a gruff voice, "Hey Al, you were hot tonight."

"Picked up a few pointers, did you Lemmy?" Al replied, bantering as usual.

Lemmy, the front man of arguably the best thrash metal band in the country, was an imposing figure. Standing at six foot six, with long dreadlocks, a bearded face, and hardly a spot on his exposed skin that wasn't tattooed or pierced, he truly lived the rockstar lifestyle, reminiscent of his deceased namesake from Motorhead.

Being a huge fan of Cried Wolf, Al had chosen them to open the gig, and Lemmy was grateful for the exposure.

The big man gave Al a bear hug and said with a thick Glaswegian accent, "Bud, can't thank you enough. There's a big piss-up tonight at Kronno's bunker to celebrate the gig, with stacks of biker gangs. Should be mighty. Bring the boys."

"I'll tell 'em, Lemm, but I've got stuff to do. Thought you were real good tonight. Loved that third song, what was it? Get a Rat Up Ya!"

Lemmy beamed a mostly toothless smile, with one gold tooth at the front that gleamed in the lights. "My fav mate, wrote it meself."

"Hey, dig the tooth," Al said.

"24 carat gold, mate. I'll be gettin' the rest done when I get the dosh. Take it easy, Al."

"Man, you know me. I'll take it any way I can get it," he cracked, and then opened the door to his dressing room.

The gig served two purposes for Al. First, his undying obligation to his band members and fans; second, a distraction and a chance to unwind from the weight of the world.

Intentionally, Al had kept it a small gig compared to other Black Alice concerts. He wanted to reconnect with his audience, so he chose a six thousand-seat auditorium. Nevertheless, the revenue from net rights and tickets was enough for Alice to donate a sizable amount to a children's charity.

Inside the change room, he found his sister Wyetta helping herself to some of the food laid out on a long table.

"Hey Vee, how goes it?"

Dressed in Gothic fashion, as expected, she looked stunning. She gave Al a peck on the cheek and said, "You were magnificent tonight… and the band… wow!"

Ratsso added, "Yeah, so good to have you back, Al, even if only for one gig."

Alice picked up a roast chicken leg and dug in. "Wasn't bad for only one rehearsal on the day. Has Slut hit you up yet?"

"He tried to flash at me, but that was all," Vee admitted with a giggle.

"Hey, Slut, did you flash at my sister?"

Slut turned around from talking to Ratsso and peered at Alice from behind a mask of long black hair. "Yeah," he growled. "She was totally impressed."

"He flashes it at everyone," Blue the drummer scoffed, "even the road crew."

Al smiled, relishing the backstage banter of his band that he'd so missed.

"Hey Al, they say you donated the take to charity?" Ratsso said while packing up his Fender Precision bass.

"Don't worry Ratsso, you guys will still get your dosh," Al promised.

"Nah, wasn't worried about that, mate. Just wondering why?" Ratsso inquired.

"Because he's an orphan, stupid. He donated it to a children's charity, didn't you Al?" Blue explained.

Al nodded in affirmation, then grabbed a handful of M&M's from a bowl and poured them into his open mouth.

"That was a kind gesture, Al," Vee said.

Ratsso stopped on his way out and gave Vee the once over. "She's got better legs than you, Al."

"Yeah, but they're hairy," Al joked.

Vee put her hands on her hips and said smugly, "How would you know?"

"She's got you there, Al. See ya," Blue quipped facetiously as he passed by.

Al went back to studying what to treat himself with next from the mass of food left on the table.

"We should be donating all this tucker to charity, what a waste," he complained.

Blue poked his head back inside the door. "Hey Al, there's a stack of press outside waiting to interview you. If you want to give 'em the slip, I'll create a diversion."

"Yeah, do that Blue. Don't feel like talking to 'em."

Blue nodded and closed the door.

"We better slip through the concert hall while Blue holds 'em off. Come on, let's bail. See ya, fellers."

Alice and Vee slipped out the door and then hurriedly meandered through the dark stage area towards the front entrance.

On the street outside the gig, Al was looking to hail a cab when a cub reporter jumped out from the shadows and jabbed his phone in his face, demanding, "Alice! Do you admit to being a time traveller for the Oceana Government?"

Al angrily brushed the phone away and growled, "Don't know what you're talking about… get outa my face."

The reporter aggressively shoved the phone back in his face, hitting him on the eyebrow and splitting it open. A trickle of blood ran down his cheek.

Vee sprang into action, throwing a flurry of karate punches and kicks that smashed the young feller's nose and decked him.

Alice looked down at the smitten reporter. He was holding his bleeding nose but okay. Recognising he wasn't badly injured, Alice hailed a cab. They hopped in, and it sped off.

Sitting on the back seat, mopping his split brow with a tissue, Al said, "Bloody hell, you made short work of him. Think it was necessary? He was only a cub reporter?"

"Give me that," Vee said, snatching the tissue off him and wiping the wound. "Not up to me to suss him out… the threat required a response, so I neutralised it."

"Sure did. Nice left hook…" he said, with a sarcastically raised split eyebrow.

She shrugged her shoulders. The wound had stopped bleeding, so she handed him back the bloody tissue. "What's this about you being a time traveller?"

"Argh, just press bullo, forget it."

"Well, that's not what's been going around the office."

"Doesn't pay to listen to rumours, mate," Al growled. But it wasn't working, Vee had him sussed out.

"Yes, it does. I know all about OTT."

Alice told the cabby to pull over in front of Café Epiphany. Though it was close to midnight, he knew his favourite haunt would still be open.

Inside, Alice grabbed his usual table. There was only one other punter in the place.

"I'm gonna have French toast and an espresso," he said, handing Vee the menu.

A quick scan of it had her say, "Same."

Alice went over to the front desk and ordered. When he sat back down, Vee had more questions loaded.

"Look, everybody knows you're the traveller in the OTT setup."

"Yeah, who told you that?"

"Kyleen Hern... HR."

Alice grizzled, "She's a mouth on a stick, that one."

"So, what'll be bro... you going to come clean with me or what?"

By now Alice was convinced she wasn't a Zen spy; however, he still wasn't one hundred percent sold on her being his sister... though things like them both ordering the same food and having the same taste in clothes had him wondering. He glared at her as though trying to peer into her soul.

"You're still not sure if I'm really your sister, are you?" she said perceptively.

With two fists propped under his chin and his elbows resting on the table supporting his head, he let out a deep sigh. He was weary from the performance and not really in the mood for a debate, but at the same time, he knew he needed to clear the air so they could get on with life. He groaned, reached into his pocket, produced a pill, and dropped it.

"What was that? You on something?" Vee complained.

"Just a pill, what are you, my mother?"

"No, just don't want to miss out," she giggled.

That made him smile. It was exactly what he'd think. "Nar, just meds. Tell me, what do you remember of mum?"

She glared at him, knowing he was trying to catch her out. "In a prison hospital bed, dying."

"You visited mum in prison when she was dying?"

"Yes," she mumbled, tears welling up in her eyes. "Never met dad, he was long since dead."

The waiter arrived with the food and drinks. Once he'd gone, Al refocused on Vee, a tear trickling down her cheek.

"You're my sister, all right," Alice admitted. "I feel it, and that's enough for me."

Sniffling, she tentatively reached across the table and took her brother's hand.

Holding her warm hand melted his heart. Something in his life had changed right then... he felt fulfilled, complete—he was together again.

"You do know mum was a ten-pound pom, immigrated with her folks from the UK to Fremantle."

"I know we are white blacks, well, I'm a bit more tanned than you, but I didn't know that about mum. I was born in prison and taken from her when I was only six months old, then fostered out... it was a series of foster homes after that abuse and all."

He studied her eyes, then said passionately, "We've travelled the same path, sis."

"Let's eat... I'll tell you all about OTT."

Secta and the Professor were in the control room, standing behind Robert, who was seated entering data into the mainframe.

"Karzoff called," Secta said. "Mal has a conference call with the U.S. President at 0600, wants us there at 0500."

"5:00 am, he's got to be kidding?" Robert grumbled.

"You don't need to attend," Secta said.

"Know what it's about?" The Professor queried.

"I'd say a heads-up for the conference call with the Whitehouse."

"Where's Hope?" the Professor asked.

"She and Viktoria needed a break, so they went to a gig," Secta mumbled on his way to the booth to check on Neit.

The purple-shadowed figure of Neit was seated there, waiting to be dematerialised. They had agreed he would only stay long enough on Eris to gauge the atmosphere: air quality, temperature, etc., and examine the terrain. Hopefully, he would also see the Futurum Tower.

"If only we could send a camera to record this history-making event... this'll be the first time a person has been teleported to another planet," Robert said.

"Neit isn't a person... are you?" Secta joked.

The concept of a camera had the Professor all fired up. "Once we can get over the hurdle of only being able to reduce organics to atoms, sending material things will happen, but it's a little way off yet. Did you know Fujifilm has developed an organic camera sensor with a phenomenal dynamic range... and a Russian mate of mine is working on a camera with no metal parts... it's made of glass, carbon fibre, and rubber."

"Fascinating," Robert said. "And—"

Secta cut him off. "Neit is set, let's go, Robert."

That ended the conversation. Robert swivelled on his chair back to the console and commenced the countdown.

Secta opened talkback to Neit in the small room. "Remember, Neit, you will have no longer than three minutes before the vortex closes. If that occurs and you miss it for whatever reason, stay where you are, and we'll get a new link to you."

Neit nodded with a thumbs-up, hip to the game plan.

The Captain's cabin on the USS Zumwalt consisted of two rooms, a bedroom with an en-suite, and a living room that doubled as an office. It was austere yet functional, resembling a blend between a ship's cabin and a three-star hotel room. Seated at his desk, Captain Dwight Williamson 3rd poured himself two fingers of JD and was just about to savour the drink when the door opened, and Cole poked his head in.

"Want some company?" Cole asked politely.

"Why not? Pull up a chair, son. How about a JD?" Williamson chuckled mirthfully in a Southern accent, holding up the half-full bottle.

"Don't mind if I do," Cole responded, pulling a seat up opposite the seasoned man.

Dwight had a high forehead, a prominent white moustache, and matching white hair in a military cut. A tall, moderately-built man with broad shoulders, he bore a striking resemblance to the legendary American Civil War Confederate General Robert E. Lee, evident from the framed sepia-tone photograph of Lee hanging on the wall behind him.

"Things got a little heated when you were talking with your superior, but much to my surprise, she came around after you stormed out like a spoiled brat. I'm surprised she took it so well. You can gather from that I wouldn't take such insubordination from any of my men." The Captain said in all seriousness while offering Cole his drink.

Cole wasn't about to engage in an argument over military convention. He had purposely crafted the act to force the CIA Director's hand. He pulled a smug look at the comment and then downed the two fingers of bourbon in a single gulp.

The Captain reacted to the look. "Do you have a problem with authority, son?"

It was a loaded question, and Cole knew it. "Not really, only stupidity."

The Captain's face grew dark. Forty years of service in the U.S. Navy had made him intolerant of insubordination. Right now, Cole represented everything Dwight Williamson 3rd loathed about the rebellious youth of the day.

Just as he was about to launch a tirade at Cole, he noticed the young man's face twist into a terrified expression, as though he'd been poisoned. Cole grabbed at his throat and contorted awkwardly in his seat.

"You alright there, son?" The Captain inquired worriedly, suspecting an allergic reaction to the bourbon.

Cole leaned back in his chair, both hands clawed in agony, his eyes wide with terror. He let out a gurgling scream, staring down at his chest with wide eyes, his body trembling uncontrollably. A grotesque clawed hand burst out of his chest, gripping his bloody beating heart.

Williamson sprang out of the chair in sheer panic.

The claw opened, dropped the heart on the floor, and then retracted inside Cole's chest. His body slumped limp in the chair, with blood and gore oozing from the cavernous chest wound.

Williamson stood there behind his desk, stunned, frozen. Everything had fallen silent except for the sound of his own heart pounding like a bass drum from the massive surge of adrenaline. As he poured himself a large slug of JD, he noticed a black vapour exuding from apertures in Cole's limp cadaver.

If what he'd just witnessed wasn't bizarre enough, Williamson was completely astounded by the unnatural phenomenon of the black vapour moving in the air like a living entity. The stringy, smoky, black substance floated towards him and, though he struggled not to inhale it, couldn't prevent it from entering his body through his ears, nose, and mouth. His eyes rolled back, and the whites turned pitch black. An uncontrollable nervous tremor vibrated through his entire body, and he flopped back into his chair, contorting... then he slumped with his head bowed as though unconscious. After a couple of seconds, his head lifted sharply... his eye colour reverted from jet black back to powder blue. The transformation was complete; Gaap was now in control of Captain Dwight Williamson 3rd and the USS Zumwalt.

Neit materialised in a strange world. The ambient light was blue, and the sky was dark, indicating night-time. A day on Eris lasted 25.9 hours, not too different from Earth. Eris' large moon, Dysnomia, appeared on the horizon, crimson like blood, occupying a significant portion of the sky, much more than Earth's moon.

Eris, larger than Pluto, was sometimes regarded as the tenth planet in our solar system. It was once referred to as Planet X.

Neit checked the topography. The rocky surface was formidable, but what surprised him the most was the temperature and atmosphere. He had expected it to be around minus 217 to -410 degrees Celsius, as scientists had predicted... but it wasn't. Instead, it was quite pleasant. Scientists had also anticipated the air to be methane, but he had no trouble breathing. It seemed to be a mix of oxygen, nitrogen, and carbon dioxide, with even water vapour in the air.

The mountains were ice-capped and reached skyward much higher than any on Earth. However, there were no signs of plant life, which raised the question: where does the oxygen and carbon dioxide come from? As he turned around to look in the other direction, he realised the reason behind its habitability and was surprised by what he found. The great valley he stood in was dominated by a massive structure, a gigantic pyramid similar in size to the Great Pyramid at Giza, glistening in the reflected light of Dysnomia. It generated a force field, evident from the blood-red reflection of Dysnomia on the perimeter of the massive force field bubble inside which he stood. This bubble obviously contained an artificial atmosphere. Neit assumed the pyramid was the Futurum Tower.

It was an awe-inspiring structure, and Neit's mind boggled at how something so massive could have been constructed in this environment. Then it dawned on him that it differed greatly from the Great Pyramid. Instead of being constructed from sculptured blocks of pink granite, basalt, and limestone, this pyramid was fabricated from metal, solid gold.

"He's taking longer than expected," Secta said with a hint of panic in his tone. His pacing of the control room floor was unsettling Karzoff, the Professor, and Robert.

"Why don't you sit down and relax, Secta? There is nothing we can do but wait," the Professor said reassuringly.

It was a ground-breaking mission. This was the first time they'd tried Kairos off-world and over such a distance: 14,062,199,874 kilometres. There were a lot of technical doubts that had become more concerning as the time lag caused stress. Not that Secta was doubting the process or that he was agitated; tense would be the right description, and the manner by which he relieved that tension was to pace the floor.

"We have confirmation the wormhole reached Eris... that's a success in its own right," Robert said.

"If there was a problem with the atmosphere, he would have come straight back," the Professor added.

"So, what's keeping him?" Secta urged.

"It's not time to panic yet, my friend. He's only been gone a few minutes," the Professor said with just a tickle of humour to lighten the mood.

The XO tapped on Commander Williamson's cabin door with his knuckle and then pulled it open. He found the CO sitting at his desk.

"Sir, pardon me, but operations have had notification from HQ to prepare a UAV for a recon mission," Executive Officer Kyle Carter said.

Carter was in his early forties, a tall, slender man with a moderate mid-west accent. He paid no attention to the suit-bag on the floor.

Dwight had been busy cleaning up the mess from the slaughter of Cole. He'd done a thorough job and stashed the dismembered body in the suit-bag, ready for disposal into Sydney Harbour, if and when the opportunity arose. Dwight opened his laptop and read the order.

"Okay, make it so, Carter. I'm sure they won't order the flyby until first light. Have Lieutenant Ferguson call me directly when he gets the green light; I'll want to speak with him before launch," Commander Williamson replied.

Lieutenant Ferguson was the operations manager responsible for all off-ship operatives.

"Here, sir?" Carter asked, standing stiffly to receive his orders.

"Yes, no matter what time. Oh, and tell him to ready a Tomahawk anti-sub missile in the vertical launching cell," Williamson said.

"Armed, sir?"

"Yes, high explosive incendiary."

"GOT or GOLIS, sir?"

"Fixed target GOLIS, command off line of sight... GPS target: The Lair. I'll clear it with Oceana and HQ," Williamson concluded.

It wasn't for EO Kyle Carter to question his orders, even if they were to enable a Tomahawk Block IV anti-sub, subsonic, network-centric missile carrying a 450-kilogram high explosive warhead, capable of sinking a submarine or any naval ship, for a strike on a civilian target. The power of the specific warhead would completely take out Pelican Island, but more importantly for Gaap, it would trigger the rift to reach its optimum capability to annihilate Sydney.

"Deployment will require an authorisation code, sir," Carter said.

"Thank you, Carter. I'll see to it. Dismissed."

The scene was set... all he needed now was the code.

In the control room, Secta, Karzoff, the Professor, and Robert were becoming more worried about Neit. It was now well past the return deadline, and the vortex was about to close. The angst was causing the Professor and Secta to question whether they'd been a little too ambitious, risking Neit's life on such a speculative mission.

Across town, Honor was in her office, angry that Kew was dead.

On the floor above, Gorrick was at the office window, marvelling at the finger of fire illuminating the northern sky in a crimson glow. Content he now had the upper hand on Oceana, he would soon relish finally settling the score with his arch-nemesis, Black Alice.

Sitting back in his chair with his feet up on the desk, Captain Dwight Williamson 3rd was grinning from ear to ear because he would soon be set to deliver his killer blow and seal the fate of the population of Sydney: a Tomahawk Block IV anti-sub, subsonic missile. Not only that, but it would cause irreparable devastation at other locations around the planet because the arrow of time had a hive mentality, and each location fed off the other. Each rift connected just outside Earth's atmosphere to the main core that snaked like an umbilical cord through space, all the way to Eris. The final explosion he would deliver would provide enough energy for the main core to generate a ripple effect that would feed a massive power surge to each rift. He was aware that his master, En-Lil, was right now dispatching a demon to guard each of the other six open rifts. The end of mankind was nigh.

CHAPTER 27
THE KEY

THERE WAS MASSIVE relief when, after a third wormhole had been dispatched to Eris, with hope diminishing, Neit materialised. Secta and Karzoff rushed into the advent room to help Neit to his feet after he had popped through the big circumference of Kairos and landed on hands and knees.

"Neit! Neit! You don't know how glad we are to see you!" Secta exclaimed. "We really need to do something about this hard landing," he added, mumbling indifferently.

Karzoff placed an arm around Neit's shoulders and walked him towards the entrance door to the control room. "We can hardly wait to hear about it, are you all right?"

Neit nodded, still trembling and trying to regain his senses after the ordeal.

"Welcome back," Robert swivelled on his chair and said jovially.

The Professor was busy texting. He looked up, pocketed his phone, and said, "Just letting Hope and Al know you made it. Good to see you, Neit. Sit down and tell us all about it."

Just then Alice, Hope, and Viktoria entered through the pressure door. Al's face broke into a big smile upon seeing his shadowy friend, "Neit! Alright!"

"Sit down, guys, Neit was just about to tell us about Eris," Secta said.

After delivering a graphic description of the terrain of Eris, with its dark sky and the magic of the moon Dysnomia rising huge and crimson on the horizon, he described the force field... and then came the big surprise: the Futurum Tower. His description of the golden pyramid literally blew them all away—it was not what they were expecting.

Feasting on a handful of walnuts, Alice stopped Neit. "Wait a minute, mate, are you saying this golden pyramid is bigger than the Great Pyramid in Egypt?"

"Yes, Alice."

"But how... how could a thing that big have been built there?"

"It is made of gold, Alice. I suspect it is not a monument such as the replica here on Earth at Giza but a gigantic spacecraft."

The statement stunned his audience. He continued, "But what delayed me from returning was I decided to approach the pyramid to find the entrance... but couldn't find one. All I found on one side of it was a small slot near ground level."

"What, like a letterbox?" Al said, smirking while crunching nuts.

The idea of a massive golden pyramid with a letterbox slit at its base generated a light-hearted chuckle from them.

"Did you see any sign of the rift?" Secta asked enthusiastically.

"Something was being emitted from the apex of the pyramid, but it was too high up for me to see clearly... but it looked like... what do you call it... oh yes, a laser beam."

"That would be it, all right," the Professor confirmed.

"Great," Alice said, his spirits somewhat dampened by the description. "So, how the stuff am I gonna get inside the thing?"

There was a pregnant pause while they all pondered Alice's question. No matter how crudely he put it, he was right.

"Does anyone know what Futurum means? It sounds Latin," Hope pondered.

"Hang on, let me look it up." Alice accessed his mental database. "Yeah, it's Latin all right, means exactly what it sounds like, namely; the future."

Hope nodded. It made sense. "Right, so we're looking for the key to the future. The way to open it, assuming the letterbox is a keyhole... I think—"

Alice looked up sharply. "Wait a minute, what did you just say? The key to the future?"

"Yes, that does sound familiar, doesn't it?" Hope said, struggling to remember where she'd heard it before.

Alice got up from his seat and, still munching walnuts, began pacing the floor. "That's it... that's it!" He stopped and theatrically threw his arms open wide. "Everyone from En-Ki to Neit, even Gorrick, has mentioned the key to the future... remember Hope... The Shine... the key to the future?" he said animatedly.

"The amulet hanging on the wall of the motorbike display at St. James Station. You took it and—"

"Yeah, I gave it to the pregnant chick at the wharf that night, the one that looked like Djard from the future... it was the night of the collision between the ferry and the sub. I was wearing it... I took it off and handed it to her and said, 'take this, it's called the Shine, give it to your child, it's the key to the future... it was the talisman Djard was wearing around her neck in the future that Ex wanted so bad... it was part of a vision I'd been having and hearing the words The Shine...'"

"Yes, Alice, I told you I know about the Shine, you thought it was a motorbike, but I told you it is something completely different, something more," Neit explained.

The revelation was of such enormity it had Alice totally gobsmacked. With his synapses firing up big-time, images of the past flashed through his mind.

The others waited for him to arrive at a conclusion, and then he finally said, "It opened the sarcophagus in the future, and the bike came out... the Shine was a key. Maybe..." Alice looked up at the others, the words frozen within the realisation.

Secta said it for him. "Maybe the Shine is the key to open the Futurum?"

"Through the letterbox opening... it must be a keyhole," Neit agreed.

Alice's expression turned dour. He flopped into a chair and groaned, "Yeah, but how the stuff are we going to get it back? I gave the damn thing away, didn't I? All we can do is send me through a wormhole to get it back..."

"It would be no good to us anyway, Alice, it was metal, wasn't it?" said the Professor.

"Yes, but..." Al sighed.

"We don't need it... all we need is a drawing of it, the design, so we can 3-D print it in an organic substance, maybe resin," Hope said brightly. "If we call Harley Davidson, they'll surely still have the artwork... it was, after all, their display."

"Sons of Steel ride the Shine, of course it was! Great thinking, Hope." Al said positively.

Given the report from Neit of the conditions on Eris and the success of his mission there, they agreed Alice and Neit, once equipped with an organic replica of the Shine, would transport to Eris to shut down the arrow of time and expel En-Lil from his refuge. The ETD would be fixed following the scheduled meeting with the President. After that, the Shine artwork would need to be secured... they thought they had time, but they didn't know the President had been given a deadline by Gorrick to deliver Alice to Zen.

They were all looking a little rough around the edges when they filed into the President's office: it had been a long night refining and testing SAGE, and planning the assault on Eris.

The orange horizon line of sunrise was just visible through the east-facing window, whilst through the north-facing window, the sky could be seen ablaze with the sinister crimson glow of the rift.

Mal turned from the north window, his face grave, surprised to see Alice there. He smiled at his friend. "Al, didn't you do a gig earlier tonight? You must be knackered."

Al flopped into one of the comfy lounge chairs and sighed, "You know me, Mal, hate missing out on anything."

Secta, the Professor, Karzoff, and Viktoria took seats. Miss Vallins brought coffee and cookies. Hope was the last to arrive.

Mal ambled over to them and took his seat. "I won't dilly-dally... aside from the fact that I'll be speaking to the President of the United States at 0600 hours, at which time I want both Secta and the Professor present, I have some news that may spoil the party. But before I tell you, it's important you understand the gravity of the situation here. As you're no doubt aware, there's chaos on the streets. Folks are panicking. There have been riots, looting... it's apocalyptic, and if something isn't done to shut this thing down real soon, we'll have a coup on our hands." He paused to eyeball each of them sincerely. "We all know the Yanks won't be able to beat this thing. I trust you guys to get it done, but you have to be upfront with me because the clock is ticking. Now, the real bad news... Gorrick phoned me last night and threatened that if I don't hand over Alice 12 hours from now, he will unleash hell on Sydney through the rift, which he claims to be in control of."

A deathly silence fell on the room while each of them contemplated the threat.

Secta was the first to break the silence. "He probably is indirectly in control, but Gaap would be running the show."

Alice shivered as Neit emerged from his body. The purple shadow took a spare chair in the discussion circle. "That is correct," Neit said. "There would be a telepathic link between Gaap and Gorrick."

"But how? When the Yanks rescued the sole survivor of the assault on The Lair, he reported no sign of Gaap... anywhere... he'd gone," Mal exclaimed.

"I would be worried, Mr President, that the survivor of which you speak is possessed," Neit said gravely.

Mal's face drained of colour, and then he asked hesitantly, "Are you saying that Gaap might be on board USS Zumwalt?"

"If that is where the survivor is, then yes," Neit confirmed.

"It's going from bad to worse," Mal admitted.

Just as Mal had requested, OTT gave him an honest appraisal of the probability of pulling off the assault on Eris. Taking into consideration the threat that En-Lil and his demon guardians posed, factoring in Alice's physical condition, they rated a less than fifty-fifty chance of succeeding. But in his usual swagger, Alice brushed the odds aside, opting for a more pragmatic approach.

"One, we're out of options, and two, I'd rather take on En-Lil than be handed over to bloody Gorrick."

None of them were going to disagree with him. It was resolved the mission would go ahead once everything was ready. If the deadline to give Alice up to Gorrick breached, then Mal would somehow buy time with him. In the meantime, he would mobilise the armed forces to police the streets but would keep a declaration of martial law as a last resort.

Secta and the Professor stayed behind after the meeting had adjourned.

"Tell me about this SAGE gadget you've invented, Professor?" Mal asked just after requesting from Miss Vallins for another round of coffees.

"It's not really a gadget; it's an algorithm. A block of code, if you like, through which Alice's atoms will pass on their journey through the collider to the wormhole. It's actually positioned at the event horizon. What happens is quite simple: the algorithm weeds out the nasty JAK2 gene and disposes of it."

"Brilliant... and how does it recognise that gene from the others?" Mal asked.

"Good question... by its unique banding. Every gene has its own discrete set of patterns called G-Banding or Giesama bands."

"Fascinating," Mal said. "Won't that affect Neit as well?"

"No, we won't activate it until after Neit has passed through."

Miss Vallins delivered three mugs of coffee. "It's time for the conference call to the Whitehouse, Sir."

Mal took a swift, nervous gulp of coffee. "I hope this is strong coffee; I should lace it with whiskey, I could do with a settler, look," he said, displaying trembling fingers.

"Just take a deep breath, Sir, think of it like you're about to go on stage. I'll put the call through," she said, with a cute, encouraging smile.

"Ah, that girl certainly has the most calming manner about her," Vic muttered admiringly.

An iPad on the coffee table signalled an incoming call.

Time was ticking away. Secta and the Professor hadn't returned from the meeting with the President. They'd been gone two hours.

Alice, Karzoff, and Neit were in Hope's office. Hope was on the phone.

"That's the one, would it be possible to email me the design? It's rather urgent. Thanks." She put down the phone and beamed a smile at Alice. "Got it... a copy of the original artwork of the Shine."

"That-a-girl."

"What material will you use to produce it, Hope?" Neit asked.

"Secta has been experimenting with organic resins that would pass through the wormhole. We can 3-D print it directly from the artwork. He said he's already 3-D printed a new resin handgun for you."

"Yes, he has," Karzoff confirmed. "He asked me to send off some resin cartridge cases he made for my friend who supplied the crystal blade to fit with quartz-tipped resin bullets... very clever stuff. They should be arriving soon; I better go and check."

As Karzoff left, Hope retrieved the email from Harley Davidson and printed the artwork of the Shine. She handed the A4 printed sheet to Alice. "There you go, Al, your old friend."

"The Shine," Al said, staring at it almost mystically.

Neit chuckled, realising he was only joking.

"Do you know, Neit, I find it weird that after all these years of astronomical observation, a fly-by from the New Horizon spacecraft in 2006, and subsequent imagery from the Hubble and Webb telescopes, as well as loads of technical analysis, you found that Eris had none of the features that have been discovered there," Hope reasoned.

"You must remember what I experienced was enclosed in a force field, Hope: an artificial environment. But I must say I have noticed that much of the analysis of planets in our solar system made by your scientists is inaccurate. For example, you are yet to realise there are exterior or surface planets such as Earth and geothermal underworlds such as Europa, Enceladus, and Mars."

"Are you saying there could be life on these underworld planets and moons?" Hope queried, quite astonished by Neit's claim.

"Indeed, there is. Charon, the moon of Pluto I come from, is such an underworld planet."

"I just Googled it: in Greek mythology, the souls of the dead, both good and evil, were faced with the journey to Hades the Underworld across the River Styx on the boat of Charon the Ferryman."

"A metaphor, the Greeks were good at that," Neit said.

"Charon was also the son of the primal gods Nix, the Goddess of night, and Erebus, the god of darkness. The word Erebus was also used to indicate a region of the Underworld where the dead would go immediately after dying."

"Yes, Erebus is a crater on Mars, the portal entrance to the Underworld there. There is a lot of truth in Greek mythology, like a lot of humanities recorded history of Earth, a mix of the imagination and fact, much like Sumerian, and of course, the many religious myths worshipped here still. Most of what is regarded as myth is, in fact, a metaphor; it was the only way your ancients could explain things beyond their comprehension or knowledge base."

Hope wanted to continue the discussion but was interrupted by the arrival of Secta and the Professor.

Secta announced, "The mission is on, Alice and Neit, you now represent the interests of the entire human race."

"Yes, the U.S. President wished you Godspeed, as U.S. Presidents do," the Professor said facetiously; he had no time for suits and bureaucracy.

"As they do..." Alice mumbled, with the realisation that the fate of mankind now rested firmly on his shoulders. "The key to the future."

"By the way, Neit, as the six rifts have opened in close proximity to particle colliders around the world in Geneva, Texas, New York, Russia, UK, and Germany, it has been reported a demon is now guarding each of them, just as Gaap has been defending the one here."

"That is good news, Secta," Neit said encouragingly.

Secta was surprised. "Why is that good news?"

"That is six less demons we have to deal with on Eris," Neit said.

"Seven if you count Gaap," Al added.

CHAPTER 28
INSIDE OUT

IS THE FUTURUM internally homogeneous with the Great Pyramid of Giza? That was the burning question. Neit didn't seem to think so. He had gleaned from Gorrick's mind that there were twenty-three levels, each guarded by a demon. The Great Pyramid was known to have only ten levels or sections, possibly eleven, with a new cavity recently located using muon radiography.

"The interior of the Great Pyramid is still a mystery; there could very well be twenty-three levels. We just don't know," the Professor said, answering Alice's question.

"So, should we use it as a model for our assault plan?" Alice queried.

"I understand what you're thinking, but that might be a mistake," the Professor concluded.

They were stuck with a ten-centimetre, letterbox-sized aperture in the wall of a 147-metre-high pyramid and nothing more.

"Talk about flying by the seat of your pants," Al groaned.

The more they discussed it, the more foreboding the mission became.

Alice had put up with enough talk, got up, and headed for the door.

"Let's just get on with fitting me out with as many weapons as possible; this is going to be a suck it and see mission. My guts are rumbling; I'm going to the canteen for some food... give me a whistle when we're ready to go. Alright?"

The Professor was quite surprised by Alice's laissez-faire approach to the mission, but it came as no surprise to Secta and Hope; they had gotten used to Alice's bravado and admired it.

With so much depending on the success of the mission, the tension was mounting, and Alice needed to escape it.

Viktoria had been sitting quietly listening to the discussion. Once Alice and Neit had left, she posed the question to the others, "Are we convinced Neit is on our side? I mean to say a lot of what we are doing is based on his hypothesis. Just throwing it out there, we're taking him on his word only, do we have any reason to doubt it, after all, we don't really know him... do we?"

It was a valid observation.

"I don't think now, at the eve of the mission, is the right time to be casting aspersions on Neit," Hope said irritably.

"Look, I'm only asking if we can trust him? He was on Eris longer than expected... longer than it would take to collect the info he returned with. The thing of it is, the fate of humanity rests on his shoulders as much as it does Alice's."

"Doubting Neit's integrity is irrelevant," Hope snapped.

"It's my job, Hope," Viktoria returned with interest.

Secta and the Professor were listening intently, weighing up the debate.

"Okay, give me one good reason to doubt him?" Secta finally said, buying into the controversy.

"Fine, one, he's an alien, and two, why didn't En-Ki ever mention him to Alice? With such a critical role to play in the quest, surely he would have said something about him."

She had a point.

"If he was against us, he's had plenty of opportunity to obstruct our plans and hasn't," Hope argued.

"What if the objective is to deliver him to En-Lil?" Viktoria asserted.

That stopped them in their tracks.

But Hope was on a roll of supporting Neit. "We can't just go around being suspicious people; it's important to trust," she appealed.

"We trusted Honor, and where did that get us?" Viktoria advanced. "The question is, are we prepared to risk Alice's life with Neit?"

Secta got up from his seat and paced the small room, thinking. He came to a conclusion, stopped, and said, "I think that's better left up to Alice. Now come on, we've got plenty to do, and precious little time to do it."

Time had flown by, and before long, all of OTT were assembled in the control room, preparing for departure. Decked out in commando gear and wearing a red beret, Alice was loaded up with weapons. He had concealed a dozen WASPS in pockets and had a brand-new resin pistol holstered on his waist belt. Spare clips were loaded with crystal-tipped ammo and stored in other pockets.

As Alice was picking up the crystal blade from the bench table, Karzoff took it off him and said, "You won't need that."

That won him a quizzical look from Al. He knew it was practically useless, but it was better than nothing.

From behind his back, Karzoff produced a green velvet metre-long sheath.

"This arrived with the crystal-tipped shells from my friend, the armourer," Karzoff said, handing it to Alice.

Inside the sheath was a Katana in a scabbard. Alice gripped the hilt and drew it out. It was a crystal sword. He held it in an attack pose and then swished it through the air.

"Now, this is a weapon," he said with confidence. "Happening!" Now he felt more confident being better armed. He slid the katana back into its scabbard and then slipped it over his head so it hung off his back.

Secta handed him a brown object. "Recognise this?"

Alice took it and smiled. "The Shine... not quite as shiny as before—the original was chrome."

"It's resin and will teleport. Besides, it seems from the properties of the original that it's more about its shape that makes it functional than its composition," Secta confirmed.

Alice nodded and slipped the leather thong it was attached to over his head. "Let's hope it works."

"We'll open a wormhole to you every 10 minutes from your departure time. So, there will be one there for you whenever you want to return," Secta said.

"Good, but keep it guarded in case we lob back with a bloody demon on our butt!" Al said with a cheeky chuckle. It might have been a joke, but Secta and Karzoff took it seriously.

"Done," Karzoff confirmed.

Neit was to be dispatched first and was already in the departure cubicle waiting.

While he was out of earshot, Secta approached Alice and said covertly, "I know this is not the best time, but we need to be assured that you trust Neit one hundred percent."

Alice gave him a surprised look. "Why, you got doubts?"

"Not really, it's just that everything is depending on you two, and, well, En-Ki never did mention him, did he?" Secta said awkwardly.

"I reckon that's just the way En-Ki does stuff. Lets it happen. Look, I've been at the coal-face enough times with Neit to trust him. When everything's on the line as it is this time, we all start having doubts. It's a bit like standing at the altar, watching your bride making her way down the aisle, all you can think of is: heck, am I doing the right thing... and then all of a sudden you realise how beautiful she is and it all makes sense. Well, Neit and I won't be tripping down the aisle, but when the poo hits the fan, I'll be sure as hell glad to have him at my side. Does that answer your question?"

"Adequately," Secta said with a nod, having been in the same situation and counting on Alice. He turned to Robert at the console. "Start the countdown, Robert."

"Yes, sir. T minus 10 and counting," Robert said.

Hope went over to the cubicle and waved at Neit. The purple shadow seated on the departure stool offered a shy wave in reply.

The Professor was on standby, holding a printed circuit board.

"What's the Professor got there?" Viktoria whispered to Karzoff, sitting beside her.

"That is the SAGE card. He will insert it into the mainframe once Neit has been dispatched."

The pressure door opened, and Mal entered with Miss Vallins. Recognising the countdown was underway, he went to the cubicle window and gave Neit a thumbs up. "Good luck, mate."

Neit acknowledged him and then, in a blink, was gone.

The Professor moved quickly into the computer room to insert the card into the Cray mainframe.

In the meantime, it was time for goodbyes—the time Al hated most.

Mal went first. He pulled Alice into a bear hug, and they slapped each other's backs. Then Mal stood back from Alice, and they performed the ritual greeting that they had so often shared. To the chant Oct-a-gon, a couple of hand slaps, a hip bump, then with hands on hips, a quick pelvis grind, and then in unison, they chanted, "Happen-ing!"

The others found it most amusing.

Mal eyeballed his friend and then said in all seriousness, "You be careful, Al, no getting killed, alright? Promise?"

"Yes, you turd. I promise."

"Turd, eh! Dare to call the President a turd?" he said, and jokingly shaped up.

"Yeah!… Okay, enough of all this goodbye rubbish, I'm out of here," Al grumbled as he headed for the cubicle.

Hope stopped him at the door. "See you, Al. You should feel like a million bucks when you get there, with that horrible JAK2 gene gone from your DNA."

"Sounds good to me," Al said, reaching for the door handle of the cubicle. He stopped, turned to face his friends, and giving his customary wave, shouted, "Chaa!" He went back to opening the door, but before he could get it open, Hope tapped him on the shoulder, swung him around, and hugged him. Then, before he could avoid it, she planted a big, passionate kiss on his lips. Though taken aback, he obliged, as Al would. They kept their eyes locked when they'd finished kissing—something special had passed between them— something quite unexpected as far as Al was concerned. It felt a little like whenever Neit possessed him. A little stunned, without uttering a word, Al wrenched open the cubicle door and stepped inside. Hope forlornly placed an open palm against the small glass window. A tear traversed her cheek, doubts flickering through her mind: is this the last time I will ever see him? Can Neit be trusted? Will the SAGE algorithm work? And the biggest question of all: will he survive a battle against an enemy as powerful as En-Lil?

Robert commenced the final countdown.

Captain Dwight Williamson 3rd received Lieutenant Ferguson in his cabin. The straight-backed, tall, skinny officer, who looked like there was a coat hanger left in his jacket, was in his late forties. He stood at ease in front of the Captain's desk.

"Sir, I have orders from HQ to deploy an observation UAV. Do you copy, sir?"

Gaap had other ideas. "No, Lieutenant," the Captain said gruffly.

Taken aback by his Captain's veto of his orders, he stuttered in trying to respond, "Bu... bu... but, sir—"

The Captain cut him off. "It would be a waste of time."

"Er, um, EO Carter said you'll have a deployment code for me, Sir."

"No, that would also be a waste of time."

Before Lieutenant Ferguson had time to react, Captain Williamson's entire body exploded in a shower of blood, guts, and gore, leaving a horrific monster sitting in his place.

Gaap's reptilian green lips parted into a macabre sneer filled with pointed teeth. Then, as quick as a flash, before Lieutenant Ferguson had time to react, Gaap leapt out of the chair and slipped inside him. Now in his new capacity as operations officer, he could launch the missile without having to concern himself with a stupid confirmation code.

Alice fingered the dark slit in the golden wall of the pyramid. Satisfied it would take the Shine, he took it off and held it up to show Neit, standing beside him. "Well, the old Professor got it right with SAGE, 'coz I feel terrific... let's hope this works as well." He slipped the bat-shaped talisman into the crack. The fit was perfect. They waited, but nothing happened. Alice sighed, pulled it out, and then re-inserted it with a bit more gusto. This time there came a whirring sound, and the Shine spat back out like an ATM returning a card. Alice withdrew it... and then, to his astonishment, the slit magically enlarged into a dark cavity large enough for them to enter through.

"Well, if En-Lil didn't know we'd arrived, he'd sure as hell know now," Al muttered, looping the leather thong of the Shine around his neck.

The darkness inside the pyramid became dimly illuminated as soon as they stepped inside. Alice stopped and looked about the corridor for the light source but couldn't find it. He drew his pistol.

"Reckon it would be better if you climbed on board, Neit," Al said cautiously.

Neit didn't argue and immediately melded into Alice.

"Now, I guess I should expect the unexpected," he said. Leading the way on instinct alone, Alice proceeded tentatively along the passageway that sloped on a gentle incline. The walls he observed were made of black glass or obsidian, shiny, reflective... alien-looking. Two metres high and a metre and a half wide, the tunnel was narrow, so much so it was giving Alice claustrophobia. "I hate this," he mumbled.

"There's a demon up ahead, I can sense it," Neit said telepathically. "Not everything you see will be real, Alice. Some of it will be a spectre conjured up to unnerve you. Remember that En-Lil is the master of illusion."

Lieutenant Ferguson left the gory, bloody mess that was formerly his commanding officer slumped in the chair and made for the door. He stopped and peered back at Dwight.

"You look inside out," he scoffed, enjoying his handiwork. As he reached for the door handle, he was struck frozen.

Across the harbour in the penthouse suite of the Zen building, Gorrick was seated behind his office desk, frozen in mid-motion of signing a document, looking like a department store mannequin.

In six other locations around the world where there were rifts, the demons guarding them were also struck frozen. At exactly the same moment, every clone of Gorrick on the planet froze. It was the hive thing... all connected, they had been rendered immobile because they were simultaneously receiving a telepathic message transmitted by their grandmaster, En-Lil.

In a frosty tone, En-Lil's voice rasped inside each of their minds. "Black Alice is on Eris and has entered the inner sanctum of my Futurum. Gaap will release a weapon to provide the power for the mass destruction of humanity. Stand clear... the time has come," he said with maniacal superiority.

With the message received and understood, they all reanimated.

"I have commandeered USS Zumwalt. You have four hours to evacuate Zen personnel to your sanctuary," Gaap said clearly in Gorrick's mind.

"What of you, Gaap?" Gorrick replied mentally.

"My force field will protect me from the blast."

Gorrick was forced to drop his threat to the President; he now had new orders to act on and so stood down the twenty snipers he had positioned on the rooftops around Oceana HQ to take out Alice.

For the past twelve months, Zen had been constructing a new headquarters near the New South Wales country town of Goulburn. They had bought enough land there to build their own city, which they expected would ultimately annex Goulburn. They called it Angel City. It would ultimately become Zen's global nerve centre with Gorrick as the President. It didn't matter to him that this would happen sooner rather than later. The plan for evacuation to the sanctuary had been formulated; now it was only a matter of executing it.

Within minutes, the first chopper landed on the rooftop helipad of Zen to transport principal staff to Angel City. Among them were Honor, Layla, Doctor Li, Professor Adamski, Gorrick, and his secretary Regina Fysh. At 250 km/h, the six-passenger Mercedes Benz EC 145 Eurocopter would have them at the Angel City heliport in less than twenty minutes.

From 3,000 metres above Sydney in the clear blue sky, Gorrick marvelled at the awesome sight of the flaming rift glowing in the north, knowing that in four hours it would engulf Sydney in an immense fireball and annihilate it, including his nemesis Oceana and all of its staff at Kairos. A ghoulish grin broke on his face... it was the countdown to ecstasy.

CHAPTER 29
THE LIVING DEAD

A LICE CAUTIOUSLY APPROACHED the end of the narrow tunnel. It was a T intersection with a larger tunnel left and right: the left sloping upwards, the right sloping down.

"Which way?" Alice asked Neit mentally.

"Up. But the demon guarding this entrance is close by."

Alice took the left and started up the forty-five-degree gradient. His claustrophobia disappeared as soon as he entered the much larger tunnel.

"There's something up ahead that looks like a room."

As he stepped into the dark room, there was a flash of light, and the glassy black walls shimmered. When his eyes adjusted, he found himself in a forest. It was night. A large crimson full moon overhead had the tall rainforest trees casting long eerie shadows on the ground.

The sharp sound of a stick breaking underfoot alerted Alice to someone or something off to his right. He peered into the shadows and sighted a pair of yellow luminescent eyes staring back at him only twenty metres away.

"That must be the demon. Is this forest one of En-Lil's illusions?"

"I expect so. Tread with caution, Alice; he is as cunning as a fox."

Alice drew the crystal katana and crept bravely towards the yellow eyes. When only a few metres from them, he could tell they belonged to a young man standing naked two metres off the ground inside the V of a big double-trunked tree.

Alice stopped. He expected his universal translator to allow him to converse with the alien, but then thought perhaps the language might be unknown. Nevertheless, he decided to give it a try.

"Hey there, what's your name?" Alice asked in English.

"Yaotl, warrior of the night winds," the young man answered.

Alice was relieved they could understand one another. He quickly researched the name Yaotl and found it was the name of an Aztec demon of the Underworld, sometimes called Night Sun. Known as a shape-shifter, it could take the form of a human or a Jaguar.

"This Yaotl is very dangerous, Alice. He is a cunning guardian. The talisman around his neck gives him his power. Look at his left foot."

His foot was only skeletal bone, no flesh.

"He lost it in a battle against the Earth Monster. When smoke emanates from the amulet, it is a sign he is about to shape-shift."

"You walk in my forest without seeking my permission," Yaotl snarled arrogantly.

"Yeah well, I didn't see any signs," Al chirped casually.

The young, wiry, but powerfully cut youth hopped down from the tree. He was taller than Alice had expected, over two metres. He limped closer to Alice and stopped short of him, looking him over like he was lunch.

Yaotl raised his hands sharply and shaped them into threatening claws.

Alice was taken aback by the sudden movement and then watched the fingernails on Yaotl's hands extend as if by magic into vicious talons. Dark smoke began to discharge from the amulet hanging on the leather thong around his neck. Alice realised he was about to transform and held the sword ready for a fight.

Neit was right; Yaotl shape-shifted into a strange meld of animal and human. His skin shimmered and then transformed into the spotted coat of a Jaguar. His skull morphed into the head of a Jaguar, sort of, with pointed teeth and wild animal eyes, grotesque. With saliva drooling from its muzzle, it crouched down on all fours and prowled towards Alice, teeth bared, a big angry cat stalking its prey.

"It will pounce to try and rip out your heart, Alice!" Neit cried out loud to get over the full-throated snarling of the monster.

He was on the money. Yaotl sprang at Alice. In the air, he looked twice the size. Unhampered by its skeletal leg, it was a good two metres off the ground, flying towards him. Alice timed his blow accurately. With a powerful swipe of the crystal blade, as sharp as a razor, he sliced right through the throat of the Jaguar while it was airborne, and severed the head clean as a whistle. Head and body parted company and landed on the ground. Immediately the scenery reverted to the glossy cavernous walls.

Alice reached down, picked up the amulet from the carcass, and shoved it in his side pocket.

"Might come in handy," he said almost mockingly while sheathing his katana.

"You did well, Alice," Neit said with a sense of relief.

Alice was content but concerned. If Neit was right and the guardians were going to get more powerful than this guy with each level they progressed, then he was in for a long night. He knew it was a lucky blow that severed Yaotl's head. If it had gone the other way, he'd be dead meat by now. The question bothering him was whether that sort of luck would hold out.

"I'm starving, I'm going to lunch," Robert told the others.

But what about Alice don't you have to watch for him?" Viktoria asked.

"No, I've programmed the computer to open a wormhole to Eris every ten minutes."

"Off you go then, see you in an hour or so," Secta said.

Karzoff got up from his chair, "There is no use us sitting around growing cobwebs...the guards are posted, we have other work to do. Come on Viktoria."

"I'll let you know as soon as anything happens."

"Thank you Secta," Karzoff said, leading Viktoria and Robert out of the control room.

"If SAGE did the job on Alice could you program it to eliminate cancer cells from the blood or body?" Hope questioned the Professor.

"It is possible, that's what I was working on in the first place, years ago. But it's a little more complicated than simply removing genes like the JAK2. I wish I had more time, age is beginning to creep up on me," he said forlornly.

"Well then why can't we just remove the aging gene?" Secta queried with a chuckle.

"Oh, to exist is to survive all the unfair choices. Heterochromatin disorganisation," the Professor responded.

"The bundling of DNA found inside the cell's nucleus. Controls the activity of genes and helps the molecular machinery inside cells to function normally. Accumulated alterations in the structure of heterochromatin may be a major underlying cause of cellular aging," Hope professed.

"Begging the question can we reverse the alterations by removing that gene from DNA?" Secta posed.

"That is precisely the question, but it would take dedicated focus and plenty of modelling trials before we could try it on a human," the Professor put in a nutshell.

"What if we could speed up the modelling by using the 20.5 GHz processor we brought from the future?" Secta queried.

"Now you're talking... that's teleology," the Professor agreed with a big grin. The idea had cheered him up no end.

"But, first, we need to see if it worked on Al," Hope reminded them, perpetually pragmatic.

"I have no doubt it worked, Hope," the Professor said confidently.

The ramifications of what they were casually discussing could be ground-breaking for humanity: a possible cure for cancer... the fountain of youth. Secta knew the longevity formula he'd trialled on himself had preserved him, but he wasn't sure if there would be side effects. So far, he hadn't experienced any but he was aware a rebound could happen at any moment. Hope caught Secta's eye, sympathetic to his concerns.

There was a hiss from the sliding pressurised door and the President entered looking worried. "I got a call from the U.S. President. Something has gone terribly wrong... they've had no confirmation of a launch code sent to the commander of the USS Zumwalt. Apparently, the CIA ordered a UAV recon mission of the rift, it required an approval code, and then a confirmation receipt but all comms to and from the destroyer went down... now they're asking for us to intervene to determine what the hell's gone wrong."

"What, after they denied our offer of help, typical," Hope grumbled.

"Hard to believe with all the technological might of the U.S. forces they could lose contact with a damned destroyer anchored in Sydney harbour," said the Professor.

"Maybe Neit was right, Gaap might have possessed the agent that survived the assault and has run amok aboard the USS Zumwalt," Secta speculated, pacing the floor.

Mal flopped into a chair. "Just when I thought it couldn't get any worse, this is a goddamned nightmare." He looked up at Secta, "Did Al make it to Eris?"

"Yes."

"I reckon this will all come down to him succeeding," Mal groaned.

"That's why Gorrick threatened you... because Gaap has control of the warship," Secta hypothesised.

Mal nodded, "You're absolutely on the money Secta."

The door slid open and Karzoff barged in. Puffing out of breath he said, "Zen is evacuating their headquarters. They are being airlifted to their Angel City set up near Goulburn."

"Huh, well doesn't that just make complete sense... so it begins," Secta said reflectively.

Secta was referring to the Zen Angel City facility Alice and he had engaged in 2087 on his first-time travel mission. He was hoping that by fixing things with Zen concurrently it would positively change the future. But this news meant the apocalyptic dimension in which Turk and Morri battled for survival against Zen oppression could be inevitable. Was destiny lending a hand to Zen and Gorrick to establish a global powerbase at Angel City? And another question; is this the same Gorrick they encountered in 2087? Both possibilities were nagging him, his thoughts drowning out the conversation.

"Secta, Secta!" Hope repeated in an effort to snap him out of his reverie.

It worked. "Oh, sorry... what were you saying Mal?"

"He was saying that if Alice were here we could open a wormhole to USS Zumwalt for him to sort out the problem," Hope said.

"Yes, well, we know that's not on... and I've got no idea how we can help them," Secta concluded.

"What if Gaap has seized control of the Zumwalt so he can fire a missile into the rift to further activate it?" the Professor proposed.

"That makes perfect sense! It would be why Zen is evacuating... because that is the plan?" Karzoff postulated.

A cloak of disquiet descended upon them... they knew if it was the plan—and it had to be—there was nothing they could do about it.

Mal ran his fingers through his short blond hair and said with an agonising groan full of dread, "Our problems are coming in spades. What the hell are we gunna do?"

"Sink it," Secta almost screamed. "Sink the Zumwalt before he can fire the missile."

Mal looked at Secta wide-eyed, "Are you crazy, that thing sitting in Sydney Harbour is loaded to the gunwales with nuclear warheads!"

"It'd be the lessor of two evils to let Gaap fire the missile Secta, at least then there's a slim chance Alice might be able to stop it... we need to buy him some time," the Professor said.

Mal jumped up, "Okay, okay..." he said emphatically, "I'll speak with the President, tell her there is nothing we can do but bite the bullet. In the meantime, I'll order the immediate evacuation of Sydney."

The further Alice progressed along the corridor, the narrower it became, and that was beginning to bother him.

"Don't worry, the entrance to the next level must be nearby," Neit said in an effort to calm him.

"You'd expect with all this bloke's genius it'd be more modern than looking like a bloody medieval dungeon. Speaking of that..."

He arrived at an alcove with a narrow staircase. "I guess we go up." Not waiting for an answer, he ascended the twenty or so stairs.

The landing at the top was inside a large empty cylindrical room. The wall, a good twenty metres high, was capped by a domed ceiling. Alice twirled slowly around, looking up into the dim light of the dome. The entire surface area of the floor, walls, and ceiling was made of that same shiny black glass that was on the wall back where he'd fought Yaotl. The entire glass area shimmered.

"What the...?"

"I sense a demon," Neit said warily.

A flicker from the wall followed by a bright flash like from a camera blinded Alice, and then when his eyesight had adjusted, he was standing in the middle of an arena: a gladiatorial arena. "Not again?... How many times have I—"

Before he could finish the sentence, a door slid open in the wall, and from out of the darkness stepped a monster of a man dressed only in string budgie smugglers. Flexing in a most muscular pose, he stood at least seven feet, had a big square jaw, a Neanderthal brow, a shaved head, and a M. Universe physique that glistened like gold in the light.

Alice had an awesome build, but this bloke was something else.

"Who's this poser?" Alice grumbled.

"Ask him," Neit suggested, almost comically.

"I'm Black Alice, who are you?"

"Antaeus, son of Poseidon," he snarled and then pointed at the wall, which zoomed. Alice saw that it was constructed of human skulls, all the way up to the ceiling. "My victims," Antaeus bellowed boastfully.

Alice wasn't impressed; he was more interested in searching his database for a reference on him and found it. A quick review found that Antaeus would challenge all passers-by to a wrestling match, which he always won, killing his opponent. He had built a temple to his father fashioned from the skulls of his victims.

Before Alice could finish absorbing the information, the huge man came at him.

Alice went for his sword.

"None of your weapons will have any effect on this demon, Alice. He is a spirit demon—the living dead. I'm reading your search; you have to wrestle him," Neit said grimly.

"It's a mismatch mate!" Alice snarled, out loud.

Antaeus stopped and, towering over him in a fighting pose, yelled with a voice like resounding thunder, "Fight, Black Alice... defeat me to pass."

CHAPTER 30
THE BITE

ALICE SCANNED THE arena. It was reminiscent of the one in which he'd fought the Golem back in 587 B.C. In fact, he was sure it was the exact same arena. The only difference was no gallery of spectators, and Antaeus was the giant instead of the Golem.

"Hey, I reckon En-Lil has somehow accessed my memory for this stage setting; it's all too familiar."

"That is correct, it is in your memory. We need to use it as a weapon somehow. Buy some time... let me think it through," Neit said in Alice's mind.

"Yeah, well, better make it quick, mate. This bloke's got plans of ripping my head off."

Alice quickly unhitched his belt and put it with his weapons on the ground. As he straightened up to face his opponent, he made the conscious decision to use a similar method to the one he'd used to defeat the Golem: his agility. He began circling around the towering seven-foot man, who didn't like being spun around at all. To counter Alice's tactics, Antaeus tried to manoeuvre him up against the wall.

Backing away, closer and closer to the wall, with things looking grim, Alice soon found himself pressed hard up against it, with Antaeus standing over him like a colossus. Thinking quick before the giant could get a grip on him, Alice crouched down and dived through the big man's legs, and then, just as he had done with the

Golem, scurried up onto his back. He threw his arm around Antaeus' throat to secure himself, and then while the giant was growling in protest and thrashing about angrily trying to flick Alice off his back, he reached over the giant's head, found his left eye with his fingers, and then ripped his eyeball out. That unleashed fury from the wounded fiend. With gunk from his gaping eye socket oozing down his cheek, he wheeled around and flung himself hard against the wall. The collision winded Alice. Crippled, he slid down the wall onto the ground.

"Alice, I found it!" Neit yelled in his mind. "His power comes from the underworld. Hercules defeated him by locking him in a bear-hug and lifting him off the ground."

Alice heard him but was too busy trying to clear the stars from his vision to say anything. His senses were just coming back online when a gigantic hand appeared through his foggy vision and grabbed him by the face. It lifted him off the ground like he weighed nothing—he knew what was coming next—the big mug was going to slam him into the deck.

Not one for ranking with losers, Alice grabbed hold of the monster's massive forearm and swung his legs up to lock a scissor-hold around his throat. Alice compressed his powerful thighs, and his adversary's face began to turn red from the blood rushing to his head.

Antaeus swung his upper body wildly, and Alice held on with his legs like a trapeze act. Then, when he felt the moment, Alice reached down, slung his arms around the big man's knees, and with all his strength pulled them together. The giant toppled over backward and hit the deck hard, his head bouncing off the stony floor. Alice knew he had him dazed. Now recalling Neit's advice, he fastened his cut arms around the downed man's waist and, reminding himself that he had bench-pressed 200 kilograms in the gym, strained like hell but managed to lift him up off the floor. Then, using up all the strength he could gather, he bear-hugged him.

After thirty seconds or so, Alice could hear a cracking sound inside the giant's body... then Alice was completely blown away... with a bang, Antaeus exploded into dust. Left standing in a cloud of powdered body, Alice watched the walls return to shiny black obsidian.

"What just happened?" Alice exclaimed out loud to himself.

"I guess it worked. You disconnected him from his power source," Neit said.

"He was a lot lighter than I expected."

"It's the gravity, less than that of Earth."

"Forgot I'm here on another planet. Right-o, two down, let's move." He collected his weapons.

The President had instructed the OTT team to assemble in the Kairos control room.

A cold silence had descended on the room; they were all on edge. Even though they were immune to it by their location, they knew the world outside the Oceana complex was in chaos. The military was struggling to contain the mayhem in the streets caused by the panic of compulsory evacuation. Though people could see the threat in the northern sky, they didn't think it was threatening enough for them to leave their homes and possessions. The lack of warning given by the authorities meant the evacuation was nothing but a mad rush. There had been broadcasts over all media that it was time for self-preservation: that a terrible peril was imminent. However, there had been no official explanation of exactly what the peril was or a prediction of what might happen should people choose to stay...because no-one knew.

A loud hiss when the pressure door opened heralded the President's arrival. He entered, flanked by two secret service bodyguards.

Karzoff immediately stood and acknowledged the two guards he'd ordered to protect the President.

"Sit down, Karzoff," Mal said calmly. "I think you all know that what's going on above us is terrifying." His body language showed deep concern. "I called you here to inform you I'm about to order the total evacuation of Oceana HQ to Canberra."

Secta stood ready to interject, but Mal held up his hand to finish. "For executive staff, choppers will leave from the helipad at ten-minute intervals, and below at the rear car park, buses will leave in fifteen-minute intervals. For the science staff, there is always the bunker at Avalon if that's your preferred option."

He cast his eyes at Secta for him to respond.

"We can't leave Kairos unmanned, Mal, not with Alice and Neit off-world," Secta appealed.

"Yes, I know, I've factored that in. It's the main reason I chose to talk directly to you. Whoever stays runs the risk of being trapped seven floors underground should Sydney be levelled by that rift thing... so you will need to decide who stays and who goes."

"There is no debate, I'll stay... the rest will leave," Secta said assertively.

"You're the last person I can afford to risk, Secta," Mal said emphatically.

"If Sydney goes up and I get stuck down here, I can simply transport myself through Kairos to the bunker... I'm the only one other than Alice and Neit with that capability. It's a lay-down misere, Mal... and, to be frank... there is no other option. Besides, this is like déjà vu. If you recall, I've been stuck down here before in another dimension and survived."

"That's way too hard to get my head around, Secta. Alright, alright... what you're saying makes sense, I guess," Mal said, struggling with the logic.

"I'm staying as well," Hope announced with a forceful expression.

"And me," Karzoff copied. "Someone has to guard against whatever might follow Alice back through Kairos."

"That means me as well," Viktoria affirmed.

"And if something happens to Secta, only I can take over," the Professor added.

"Yes... I can," Robert countered.

"No, Robert, you collect your family and get them to safety. If everything crumbles to dust here, you at least have the knowledge to rebuild Kairos at another location," Secta advocated.

Mal raised both hands in surrender, "Alright, alright... so we're having an I'm Spartacus moment. I admire your loyalty to Alice; that's what this is all about, isn't it?" He gazed at their faces endearingly while slowly nodding. He knew he was right.

Secta opened his arms as if in surrender. "We trust Alice will get the job done, Mal. The least we can do is ensure his safe passage home."

"I know, I know, god I wish I could be here as well, but the gorillas you've assigned to me, Karzoff, are demanding I leave immediately for the old house of Parliament in Canberra."

"We understand, and so would Alice. Take Vee with you, Mal," Hope said warmly.

With his eyes welling up with tears knowing the danger these fine people were facing, he forced a smile through the angst. "Of course, best of luck, guys."

The President left them instilled with confidence.

Robert shook hands with the Professor, Karzoff, and Secta, then gave Hope and Viktoria a hug. He was hoping to see them all again, safe and sound, but at the same time understood, with the choice they had made, that they were now living on a knife's edge.

The corridor Alice was navigating had reverted to dark, sinister, and lugubrious. He'd made it through two levels and was wondering how many more lay ahead.

He asked Neit mentally, "How many levels in this joint do you reckon?"

"Can't be sure. If the demonology of Assyrian dark arts is correct, then there are twenty-three, but not all are guarded by a demon. It could simply be there are twenty-three floors to the top."

"Yeah, right."

The gradient of ascent was increasing. Alice knew if it remained consistent, then they'd soon come to another room and perhaps another demon. His footsteps were echoing off the walls of the sepulchral passageway and masking any other sound, but Alice's acute sense of acoustics caused him to stop and listen.

"What is it?" Neit asked.

"I heard something up ahead," he whispered, gripping the hilt of the Katana more tightly in his hand. Edging further along the passageway, prepared for anything, he eventually came to a door and stopped, unable to go any further. It was numbered with a seven.

"This looks like the door to my apartment," he muttered, sceptical of it.

There was nowhere else to go if they wanted to proceed, he knew he had to open it.

"This is getting weirder by the minute... I don't like it. Got no choice..."

"Be wary, Alice."

"That's the understatement of the year, mate," he said light-heartedly as he reached for the door handle. It opened.

"You didn't need a key," Neit observed.

As he swung the door open, he said mentally, "Nah, always leave it open."

He stepped inside. The bedside lamp was on. The room was exactly as he'd left it, ages ago. His bed was all messed up... his acoustic guitar was in the corner of the room with the neck broken. He listened for the sound of the Kings Cross traffic outside and heard it. Then he looked for the intermittent flashes of red neon through the window from the sign in the street outside and saw them. His clothes were scattered on the floor... the wardrobe door was ajar enough for him to see some of his stage gear. Everything was spot on... it was his flat all right. The mirrored bathroom door was pulled open, and a blonde dressed in his bathrobe stepped out of the bathroom and stopped with a surprised look on her face.

"Alice?"

He couldn't believe his eyes. It was Stained Class, his girlfriend... but she had been murdered.

Neit sensed something in his host that wasn't right... his feelings for this girl.

"Alice, listen to me... this is not real... she is not who you think she is."

"Shut up, Neit," Alice snapped, enamoured by her. "Stain."

That wonderful naughty smile that he had always found so alluring broke on her sweet face, and without hesitation, she waddled up and embraced him.

"Oh Alice, I've been waiting for you," she whispered hotly, sexily, in his ear. Taking the sword from his hand, she dropped it onto the floor and then pulled him onto the bed.

"No, Alice!" Neit protested.

Alice ignored him, his mind clouded by desire for his girl.

She forced him onto his back on the bed and then straddled him. In a flash, it wasn't Stain... she had transformed, she had red eyes with the tattoo of a spider's web around the left one... long black and red hair all the way down to her hips like a horse's mane. Two inhuman horns protruded from her forehead, and jutting out of her back were a pair of black leathery wings. Her hands and feet were clawed talons. There was the tattoo of a dragon curled around her muscly body with one of its claws grasping her left breast. He didn't find her ugly; to the contrary, she reminded him of a heavy metal magazine Gothic cover. She was a turn-on.

"Who are you?" Alice snarled.

"I am Lilitu." But her slight smile didn't do her any favours; when her lips peeled back from her teeth, they were feline-pointed. A waft of her breath hit him. It was putrid, foul.

"Phew, girl, your breath could peel wallpaper."

Her eyes couldn't find rest. They darted about, left, right, and found no comfort anywhere.

"You have to slay her, Alice... Lilitu of the dark moon is a succubus!"

Lilitu's ghoulish red eyes fixed on his, she snarled, and then opened her fanged mouth wide, ready to bite.

"No!" Alice wailed, struggling to get free from underneath her.

CHAPTER 31
THE GIG

A FLASH OF brilliant white light blinded Alice. He blinked, and once his vision had cleared, he realised he was no longer in his apartment; he found himself beneath a bedsheet on a grand, old four-poster bed. He sat up.

"Neit... Neit?" he whispered harshly. Neit didn't respond; he wasn't there.

Alice deduced that Neit must have jumped into Lilitu to save him. The sound of approaching footsteps made him alert and ready to defend. Soon, he recognised where he was, and there, to confirm it, Zule strolled into the room. She sat on the edge of the bed, slipped off her sandals, and slid under the sheet, her big blue eyes looking at him with desire.

"Did you miss me?" she purred.

"Yeah, well," Alice mumbled, confused. The last time he'd seen Zule, Queen of the Vixens, was waving goodbye to her at the Gash, in the cavernous remains of Sydney, sometime in the 22nd century after an apocalypse.

He shivered; Neit had returned.

"This time you'll have to kill her. She is toying with your memory. She is not who you think she is, Alice," Neit cautioned.

Alice realised he was experiencing an illusion, and that Zule was the same monster that had posed as Stain.

"Close your eyes, concentrate on what is real, and then open them," Neit urged.

Alice followed his instructions, and when he opened his eyes, he was facing a half-woman, half-bat monster with blood-red eyes. The illusion had vanished; the walls were now black-mirrored obsidian—Zule's bedroom was gone. His sword was just out of reach, so he subtly reached for it, but it remained too far from his fingers.

He recalled the crystal dagger sheathed on his belt, quickly drew the blade, and thrust it up under her chin into her head—black blood spurted from the wound and sprayed on his face. Her mouth opened wide in a horrific scream, freezing in a dreadful rictus filled with pointed teeth. He could see the blade inside her open mouth, and he had to use all his strength to resist her frantic struggles—she threw her hands about, and her giant bat wings attempted to flap. Then, with an almighty lunge, he drove the blade into her brain. Her scarlet eyes widened with terror, rolling back in her head.

"Hell!" he shouted, gasping after the struggle. Then, to his amazement, with a caustic hissing sound, as if she'd been doused with corrosive acid, her flesh and bone dissolved into mucus until all that remained of her was a slimy shadow on the floor. Alice was flabbergasted—bizarre things continued to happen.

"Man, this is getting creepier by the minute," Alice said, staring at the gunk.

"Creepy is an understatement," Neit admitted.

"You're telling me," Alice quipped. "Listen, we're gonna need to find a shortcut to En-Lil. I can't be fighting a freaking monster on every level; sooner or later, one of 'em will get the better of me."

"I believe there is only one way up."

"Great," he grumbled facetiously.

Unsatisfied, Alice started ascending the gradient, grumbling on his way. "Bloody ridiculous, expecting a bloke to take on a freaking army of demons on his own."

The dark corridor snaked ahead of him without any hint of what might lie beyond the next corner.

"What did you learn inside her mind anyway?"

"I thought you would never ask. There was nothing going on in her mind because it was not her mind. She did not exist," Neit said.

Alice stopped. "What are you talking about, man? Of course, she existed. If she didn't, then what did I just kill?"

"Nothing. You killed nothing. That is why it dissolved into ooze; it was only a plasma illusion… a mirage, if you like."

Alice resumed making the ascent. "So, how was it going to kill me?"

"It could have in your mind, which, in effect, could be just as fatal as if it really happened. If you want to put a label on it… she was En-Lil, or to be more definitive, a projection of his."

The concept was turning wheels in Alice's mind; he was wondering how to use it to his advantage. Mulling it over while navigating the dark corridor, he came to a dead-end where he found a dark red door with a rusted lever handle.

"Hello, this is a bit different. Sense anything?"

"No, but you will need to open it; there is nowhere else to go," said Neit, stating the obvious.

Alice grasped the lever, and it creaked as he raised it, evidently, it had been decades since it was last opened. A brilliant light radiated from the other side. Stepping through the opening, he found himself in a narrow concrete passageway, bathed in natural light at one end, leading up an incline towards what looked like a stage in an arena. It all felt too familiar; he had performed in numerous grand concerts with his band, and this seemed to be another one of them.

"I know what you're thinking, Alice, but remember, this is not real," Neit cautioned.

Despite Neit's warning, the ambient sound of a massive audience and the band tuning up beckoned him. Alice set aside his weapons and advanced up the concrete raceway towards the light.

"This is not a wise move, Alice… leaving—"

It was too late for Neit's warning; Alice disregarded it and walked out onto a vast stage, greeted by an overwhelming roar of applause from an enormous audience. The showman within him surged forward, and he strutted towards the microphone stand with the typical Black Alice swagger. To his left, the slender, raven-like Slut checked a colossal wall of amps with his black Epiphone Flying V guitar, and to his right, Ratsso, donning a red beret, tuned his starburst Fender Precision bass, supported by his SWR SM 900 head and goliath amps. Centre stage rear on a riser, Blue was seated behind a massive kit, with double kicks, the first one stencilled BLACK and the second ALICE. An electric hum of anticipation pervaded the air.

Alice discarded his jacket and headgear, leaving him in combat cargo trousers and a navy-blue shearer's singlet.

"No Alice, think this over," Neit pleaded. But to no avail, Alice was determined to perform.

Overhead reflector spotlights and beam projectors hung from the proscenium arch, scanning across the hundred thousand-plus audience. Alice gazed at the sea of faces. It was a night at a football stadium, an immense concert. Towering PA columns flanked both sides of the stage, overshadowing everything. Half a dozen black fold-back monitors lined the front of the stage, alongside an array of par cans, their power lights beaming upwards. An awe-inspiring lighting rig, suspended from trusses surrounding the proscenium, was colossal. Alice was utterly captivated; he was in his element.

He disregarded Neit, snatched the microphone from the stand, and bellowed at the punters, "Have you bastards come to see Black Alice?" He pointed the microphone at them, immediately met with a resounding wave of YES from the fans. Then, like a roaring crash of thunder, the band kicked in.

He picked up the thunderous beat, banging his head in unison with the crowd. The mosh pit at his feet was alive with energy.

Glaring at the audience in typical Alice fashion, he screamed, "Alright! Let's rock!" and then launched into the song "Wings of Leather."

A hundred thousand fists from the sea of head-banging punters promptly thrust maloik devil horns into the air. The stadium was alive with energy, and Alice was ready to give his all. He belted out the first verse...

On wings of steel I take you,
To a world beyond the skies
Where fantasy becomes reality
Life and death wear no disguise

The power cut abruptly, and the band stopped playing. The humdrum from the crowd disappeared, leaving Alice's last word hanging in the vast empty stadium like an old pair of faded denims on a clothesline. He looked up sharply, swallowing the next line in the verse. There was no audience, only empty seats... he swivelled around quickly to face his band... the stage was now vacant; they had vanished. He stood alone on the massive stage in a desolate stadium. Then resounding applause came only from a single pair of hands.

"You're hot!" A voice echoed, as though reverberating through a canyon.

Alice turned slowly back toward the mosh pit to face the voice. Standing alone was a guy clad in full-on black leather and studded metal regalia. Sporting a crimson-tipped black Mohawk, tattoos flanking his shaven head, and facial piercings that made the thin, sharp features of his handsome face look ferocious. He was well built and looked a right dude.

"Yeah, that's why they call me Mr Fahrenheit," Alice retorted facetiously. "And who might you be?" he snapped. "Where's my audience?" He gestured behind him in protest. "And my band!"

"I control all that," he smirked. "And you, Black Alice, you are my indulgence."

"What are you, a bloody promoter?" Alice squatted down to eye level with him. "Well, I'm not impressed, pal. What's your game?"

"He is En-Lil, Alice," Neit interjected mentally.

"You might well ask... indulgence? What does he mean by that, do you think? Well, indulgence because I have chosen to spare your life. But let's be serious here, you're getting way too old for this performing caper, Alice. Take a look at your hands," En-Lil said with a snide tone.

Alice held them up... they had withered and were wrinkled, but it didn't faze him.

"You'll have to do better than that, En-Lil. I've had my share of mind-games played on me... this nonsense doesn't even cut it."

"So, you've guessed my identity... clever."

"Didn't take Einstein to figure that one out, did it?"

Everything shimmered. There was a flash of brilliant white light, and once his vision had cleared, he found himself standing in a large room. Sitting opposite—in a high back chair that resembled a throne—was En-Lil. The metal garb, hairdo, and facial piercings were gone; he was now clad in a white caftan, with shoulder-length brown hair and a medium beard... Alice noticed the sandals he was wearing... the entire vision reminded him of a Renaissance painting of Jesus Christ. He looked up at a skylight high above, through which a powerful red laser pierced the dark sky.

En-Lil formed a pyramid steeple with his fingers in front of his face and said calmly, decisively, "Sit down, Alice, we have much to discuss."

"Is that beam up there the arrow of time?"

"Yes."

"I thought there were supposed to be twenty-three levels to this place, what happened? Did I get a discount?"

"No, there are only seven levels. But I decided that if you went much further, you'd be killed, and that wouldn't have been much fun, would it?"

"I don't buy it... you threw all of them at me, and I beat them hands down," he snarled, roguishly. "Why all the theatrics with the gig?"

"Look at yourself, Alice. What is missing?" En-Lil said, with a snide expression.

It was a fair point; Alice realised that in his haste to get on stage, he had left his weapons behind, thereby disarming himself. "Crap!" he snarled.

"Yes, when vanity overrides logic, mistakes are made... sometimes fatal."

"We have determined that the two rifts here in the United States are merely stems. In fact, all of the rifts globally are stems, with the exception of yours there in Sydney; it seems it's the primary conduit back to the source. So, it stands to reason that if we shut it down, then theoretically all of the others will collapse. At least, that's the counsel of our consulting scientists," the U.S. President explained.

The news wasn't welcomed by Mal, adding even more pressure to what was already burdening his mind. He knew the U.S. President felt cornered, uncomfortable with another country calling the shots, especially one as small on the world stage as Oceana. The situation was undoubtedly unnerving, with her generals and advisors pushing her to make a definitive move, hence the conference call.

As Mal contemplated how best to respond, he could see the worried look on the President's face and her demeanour reflecting the duress she was under while trying to remain composed.

Secta paced the floor, while Hope stood at the ceiling-to-floor north-facing window, gazing out at the USS Zumwalt anchored in Sydney Harbour. The Professor reclined in an armchair, sipping on a freshly brewed coffee, his gaze contemplative as he observed Karzoff and Viktoria sitting opposite him, their faces frozen in anticipation. Each person was focused on the conversation between the two leaders, wondering what Mal would say next.

Hope turned to face Mal, and all eyes were now on him. It was time to make the call.

"I'm afraid that what you're suggesting just isn't feasible. We have complete faith in our man at the source... we just need to give him time," he said, with a serious expression and as much conviction as he could muster. There was a pause while the U.S. President consulted with her advisors.

Secta approached Mal and whispered in his ear off-camera. Mal nodded in agreement with what Secta had conveyed.

The U.S. President returned, her expression sombre as she said, "I can't get my people to agree with you, Mal. There is just too much at stake here for us to depend on the success of one man."

"Yes, but this is no ordinary man, and this is no ordinary situation. We both know the beast Gaap is on the USS Zumwalt; you must have codes to disarm it... do so and move it out to sea. At least then, we will have neutralised one threat. Give our man twenty-four hours, and if he fails to succeed, I will agree to a strike."

He could tell by the expression on the young President's face that she recognised the logic in his rationale.

"I respect the confidence you have in this Black Alice... I'll put it to my investigation team... I'll get back to you, Mal."

"No problem, Oprah," Mal said, getting up from behind his desk. He stretched and then went over to the Professor.

Miss Vallins arrived with a fresh pot of coffee. "Top up anyone?" she said brightly.

"You did well, Mal," said the Professor.

Mal looked troubled. "We've given it our best shot, Vic," he sighed as he flopped into a chair. "Investigation team, huh?" he mumbled to the Professor. "They would have typically appointed a three-man team, probably back when the anomaly first appeared in the States."

CHAPTER 32
FLIGHT

THE U.S. INVESTIGATION team consisted of a brigadier general, full colonel, and a major. Brigadier Hal Bruckmaster— 'Bull' to his buddies—a tall, well-built, bald man in his mid-forties with a prominent WWII fly-boy moustache and a slab of ribbons on his chest, was the top dog. His job was massive now that anomalies had materialised in other countries, particularly in the backyard of the old enemy, Russia. The problem touched all of humanity, and government agencies from the respective countries were working diligently to keep it under wraps from the media. But for Bull, he was uncomfortable with being subordinate to a rock singer from Oceana. Accustomed to calling the shots, his attitude had become as vitriolic as rusty old metal.

The President swivelled around her high-backed chair from facing the Oval Office window that looked out over the expansive, immaculately manicured lawn, and locked eyes with Bull. "I've gotta say, I can't buy into your strategy, Hal."

A lackluster eye and a nervous tic that twitched at the corner of the big man's thin-lipped mouth, mostly hidden under his formidable moustache, greeted the statement. He folded his arms defensively, and his big bushy grey eyebrows furrowed into a frown, saying, "All I'm saying, ma'am, is we can't afford to sit on our asses being chivalrous, waiting for some dang time-travelling cowboy to solve a goddamned global emergency... Christ, if this gets out in the media, there'll be a national meltdown."

A much more demure man, Colonel Larry Freeman, added his two cents' worth. "We don't even know if these Aussies can do what they claim. Hell, we don't have time travel technology ourselves, how can they? We've got a zillion times the resources they've got."

The President studied him, evaluating the sensitive mouth, the high-bridged nose, and the dark eyes behind heavy spectacles: a man of intellect, a scientist, decisive, firm. Though his professional abilities matched his attitude and appearance, she knew he was typically underestimating the capability of another country.

"That's hubristic, Larry, you should know better. I don't have you here to make rash statements such as that," she scolded. "The due diligence of their technological claims has already been ratified by our scientists. I have summoned you here to provide counsel on how to effectively work with the Aussies on this, not to mock them like a bunch of overzealous schoolboys fighting for one-upmanship. Do I make myself clear?" The berating ended with a cold, hard, emphatic stare that itself terminated the issue. The three military men sitting opposite her nodded submissively... they knew she was right.

After a pregnant pause to let the dust settle, the President lightened her tone. "Going in to Sydney guns blazing is not the solution, gentlemen. The Russians proved that the use of weapons only amplifies the power of the anomaly... which I might add, the Aussies warned us about in the first place."

The three men nodded begrudgingly.

"I know we're not used to sitting on our hands in a crisis, and I don't intend to start now, but we must give the Aussies some latitude here... we need to consider the welfare of the whole nation, indeed, the world."

Alice checked his translator to see what language En-Lil was speaking and was surprised to find it was English. "You remind me of someone," he said, free-associating through memories. An image popped into his mind. "Got it, bloody! Nebuchadnezzar's twisted wizard."

"Oh yes," he said, as if he found Alice's revelation boring. "Over time, I have been known on Earth by many names; Amon, Set, Thoth, Apollyon, Abaddon, Adramalech, Zorlock, Beelzebub, Baal, Pluto, Moloch, Balaam, Lucifer, Baphomet, Satan, and of course the devil... the list goes on... you name it, and wherever there is a word for evil, then I have been labelled with it. That is how humankind has always perceived me... and to think, after all I have done to help fashion them into what they are today. Reprobates. Meanwhile, my brother En-Ki is granted the good god names such as YHWH-Yireh, Imhotep, Zeus, and Apollo."

"You saying this bloody drama fought over millennia is nothing more than an absurd case of sibling rivalry?" Al snarled.

"Sibling rivalry, maybe, but absurd... definitely not."

The realisation had shocked Alice. He needed to know why. "What's the beef with your brother anyway? Why have you got it in for humanity?"

"Sit down, Alice, and I will tell you."

Neit spoke in Alice's mind for the first time in a while. "Be careful, Alice, remember he is the master of deception."

Alice took a seat to hear what he had to say.

"I am the soul in raw form," he waxed lyrical. "The human body is just a carrier or a host for the soul. We are a different species: the originator if you like. En-Ki altered the human genome to accommodate the soul, which bonded humans with the universal energy—the cosmic consciousness. It was forbidden, and as a result, it diluted the purity of the consciousness. Always reincarnated, some with more knowledge of the previous life—others mutations—we are your gods. The time has finally arrived technically when humankind will discover this key and will purify souls to explore the cosmic consciousness. I cannot permit humans to time travel, they are too reckless. I have been monitoring mankind more closely since it developed the ability to destroy itself... before that, you were merely an aberration. The time has arrived for me to act. Humankind is a plague, a parasitical virus that if left unchecked will spread throughout the universe causing irreparable damage."

"That's the pot calling the kettle black if I've ever heard it... just exactly what have you given the universe other than violence? You killed your brother, waged war against humanity for thousands of years, you're the virus," Alice argued.

"You know nothing, little man," En-Lil said, doggedly. "Your lifespan and knowledge base are less than a single grain of sand in a galaxy of silica. I've experienced more in my lifetime than the accumulated knowledge of the entire human race. My brother En-Ki was irresponsible... he was given an opportunity to create a workforce to mine Earth and fell in love with his creation and procreated with it. The Greeks call it the Pygmalion effect."

"Look, mate," Alice said, getting out of his chair. "I don't have time for a philosophical debate, so how about as a sign of goodwill... you just shut down the arrow of time... then, let's talk a deal." As he proposed the idea, he plunged his hand into the left side pocket of his dungarees and found a WASP.

"You amuse me," En-Lil said, cynically. "I did not bring you here to negotiate."

Alice sneaked a little closer to him, hand in pocket on the WASP. "Then what for? Why am I here?"

"I wanted to meet face to face with the person who has made a habit of disrupting my plans... humanity's first time traveller."

"So?" He held his arms out submissively. "Here I am in the flesh... so what are you going to do with me?" He edged a little closer.

"Kill you once I've nourished my curiosity."

Alice gripped the WASP more firmly. "And where are you going to find an army in a hurry?" Alice snapped, sarcastically. He was in range.

En-Lil chuckled. "You are an impudent little man, Black Alice."

"Shut down the laser, and I'll stop. I came here as a peaceful delegate of humanity to stop the arrow of time—"

En-Lil interrupted. "No, no... that was never going to happen... just a foolish notion... you cannot defeat me? I have lived thousands of your Earth years. I have been the destroyer of worlds... others I have terraformed and helped species evolve—"

"What a joke, what are you the king of narcissists? You've got a bloody Messiah complex. I got the same crap from your clone crony Gorrick."

"So, what are you going to do, Alice: change history?"

"Mate, I change history every time I step on an ant."

"Very funny," he said, sarcastically.

"Listen, speaking of changing history, have you got a loo, I'm busting?"

En-Lil's eyelids narrowed sensing Alice was being cynical. Alice caught the look... felt for the switch on the WASP, activated it, and then whipped his hand out of his pocket and hurled it at En-Lil. To his shock, on target, it passed right through En-Lil's head, hit the high back of the chair, and detonated with a small puff of smoke.

There was a blinding flash of light...

Brigadier Bull Bruckmaster wasn't impressed at being handed the responsibility of constructing a new plan to work with the Aussies and devising a solution to the USS Zumwalt problem. He glared at Colonel Freeman, seated opposite him at the table in the small White House office they'd been allocated next door to the office of the Chief of Staff.

"Where the hell is Torrens?" the Brigadier growled irritably.

"Calm down, Bull. The major will be along soon; he's got a lot to get done."

"I don't like this at all," the Brigadier snarled grumpily.

Freeman folded his long arms in front of him. "Well, you better get used to it. The boss made the call, now it's up to our little threesome to implement it."

"Yeah, yeah, I hear you, but it doesn't mean I have to like it."

"It would make it more comfortable for us working with you if you at least tried," the Colonel said firmly to emphasise his point. He was finding it uncomfortable working with such a belligerent man.

"Keep your personal opinion to yourself, Colonel," Bull snapped.

The security door buzzed, breaking the tension. The door opened, and Major Torrens entered. He sat down. Younger by twenty years than his senior officers, he cut a fine figure in the blue USAF service dress uniform. However, the grave look on his face spelled trouble. "Sorry I'm late, gentlemen, but we have a high-priority problem. The Joint Chiefs of Staff have gone to DEFCON 2."

Bull raised a bushy eyebrow as he folded his arms defensively in front of him. "DEFCON 2... go on, Major," he spat gruffly, sitting forward in his chair.

"We've lost contact with Zumwalt, sir."

To a Navy Brigadier, this was unprecedented, and it showed in Bull's incredulous expression. Now he understood the gravity of the situation.

"Is it EMCON... have they gone black?" he questioned.

"No, sir, there is no response at all from Zumwalt's comms... Nothing."

"Did you try split key?" Colonel Freeman asked.

Split key is a secret encryption code employed when in EMCON or when emission control is enforced.

"Yes, Colonel... no response," the young major said gravely.

Bull rocked back in his chair, bristling with angst. "So, are we to presume the ship is being commandeered by a damned alien?"

"Yes, we are, sir," the major said tight-lipped.

"What do we have nearby?" Bull snapped.

"SSN-666 Hawkbill, sir."

"Send her in."

"We're unsure if the Oceana Government will permit a nuclear submarine to enter Sydney Harbour, sir."

"What! You've got to be freaking joking! Who are they to...?"

"Remember all that trouble a while back with demonstrations and all, Bull?" Colonel Freeman said, trying to remind the man of something he should have already known.

"Yeah, that's goddamn right. It comes back to bite you on the ass right when you don't want it. We need to pay these Aussies a visit, post-haste. Make it so, Major... Leave the boss to me."

Secta was at the computer, checking the automated intermittent opening of the wormhole to Eris for Alice, in case he needed to escape. He looked sideways at Dr Hope, and she gave him a small smile.

"Empty feeling just sitting and waiting," she said apprehensively.

He knew her feelings for Alice had changed; he could sense that she had fallen in love with him, but he chose to ignore it, figuring it was best to keep it quiet, just as he did with his relationship with Viktoria.

He smiled back at Hope. "Indeed, but we've got to keep the door open."

He nodded at Drs Mieko Mosaku, Ryan Clifton, Dan Weiss, Trish Scott, and Paul Sweeney, the most trusted OTT behind-the-scenes scientific staff, and Professor de Luz. Dr Mosaku gave him a thumbs-up, which Secta knew was a positive reference to a battery of tests they'd completed the previous night. Secta returned the gesture and then turned back to the console. They were all dressed in ubiquitous lab coats, which all but Secta, Hope, and the Professor would soon be shedding before evacuating to the bunker.

"What time is your flight, Mieko?" Hope asked the young, dark-haired, eager associate.

"In ten minutes, Doctor," Mieko replied, her body tense with anticipation.

Hope sensed it and really couldn't blame her protégé. "You have no need to worry about us holding the fort, guys. You've worked tirelessly over the last 24 hours to get everything in order, and we very much appreciate your efforts. Now off you go."

As the scientists filed out, an agitated Mal slipped past them and began pacing the control room like an angry lion.

"Mal, what's up?" Hope asked.

"What is it with these Yanks? Now they're flying in some highfalutin Brigadier General from Bolling Air Force Base in Washington in a bloody B-2 stealth bomber, no less," Mal growled.

The Professor rocked back in his chair and inputted some data into his cellphone. He looked up at Mal. "Hmm, around fifteen thousand kilometres from there to here. It would require a mid-air refuel... the B-2 has a range of about ten thousand kilometres... so at nine hundred kilometres an hour, give or take... ETA about sixteen hours."

Mal stopped pacing to check his wristwatch. "It's 2000 hours, so that'll put him here at..."

"Around midday tomorrow," the Professor concluded.

Secta swivelled on his chair to face Mal. "Why did she send him?"

"They lost contact with the USS Zumwalt, and Brigadier Bruckmaster will take the lead in dealing with it from here," Mal said.

"Bloody Bull!"

Mal was shocked by the Professor's impertinent response. "What do you mean, Bull, Vic?"

"I worked under Brigadier Hal Bruckmaster. He was the commander of the Desertron Super Collider in Texas... his nickname is Bull," Vic explained.

"So, you know him then?" Hope checked.

"Yeah, cranky old bastard... the obvious choice to spearhead the tactical team from the Oval Office though... sure knows how to get the dang job done, but at the expense of everyone else, I might add. Who else is coming?"

"Only three in the delegation... I didn't get the names of the others, oh, and there are two in the flight crew."

Secta swivelled back to face the computer. "Handy that you have an association with Bull. You can be the conduit for Mal."

The Professor anticipated Secta's hypothesis. "No problem."

"What's the status on Alice?" Mal inquired.

"Not a thing." Secta swivelled back to face them. "The wormhole is automatically opening and closing for Alice to jump if he needs to... I think we can call it a day here; there's nothing to do now but wait."

The evacuation of Sydney was well underway. By morning, the military expected to have established an exclusion zone within a fifty-kilometre radius of ground zero: Pelican Island.

The ominous column of fire lighting up the sky north of Sydney ensured that the residents would offer no resistance to abandoning their homes. The real challenge for the authorities was to contain the panic, road rage, and chaos. While a massive convoy of cars snaked inchmeal out of the city, looting was breaking out in some of the vacated suburban shopping centres and malls.

CHAPTER 33
EAGLE AND THE SERPENT

❝ MAYBE THIS CAT'S God?" was the thought reverberating in Alice's mind. He figured he'd get a response from Neit, but when none came, he thought Neit might not even be conscious. He squeezed his eyes tight, and when he opened them, it was as if he'd left them shut: it was as black as the inside of a stomach, and he hated it. Reaching out a hand in front of his face, he couldn't even see it. He felt around for something—anything—and crawled his fingers along the floor beside him. The surface was cold and glazed. "Glass?"

"Neit, are you there?" he whispered.

Something touched his arm.

"I am out of your body, Alice. There has been a trans-temporal event," Neit replied.

Alice sighed with relief to have company in the emptiness, but what Neit said had him confused. "Speak English, Neit."

"The flash of light, it moved you through time to another place."

"What? Aren't we inside the pyramid? Feels the same, floor is glass."

"I do not know, Alice. The sensation is strange; I sense nothing... it is like death."

"Death? Mate, I've had flashes like that before... they're like the transition between dimensions or something: an edit point on my timeline. That's all... hardly death. Don't freak me out."

"An edit point... yes, well put, Alice... you might be right... maybe the holographic projection of En-Lil was just another level you needed to progress to reach the real En-Lil, just another guardian... perhaps the discourse was only a battle of wits," Neit proposed calmly.

"Do you think I won? Doesn't feel like it."

"Perhaps, but something else has become apparent to me."

"Yeah, what's that?" Alice asked hesitantly. Quite often, Neit's thoughts were too obscure for Alice to handle. Right now, all he wanted was to get out of the pitch-black.

"This entire process is reminiscent of the Sumerian afterlife philosophy. Can you access any information on it on your implant?"

"I suppose if it helps to get us out of here... it's not online, but there's a basic wiki database... let me see, yeah... Assyrian or Sumerian... The Netherworld... Ancient Mesopotamians conceptualised the Netherworld as the cosmic opposite of the heavens and as a shadowy version of life on earth. Metaphysically, it was thought to lie a great distance from the realm of the living. Is that where you think we are... the Netherworld?"

"Yes, it emulates the Anunaki Pantheon as I thought. Go on," Neit requested.

"You sure this'll get us out of this?"

"I need more information, Alice."

"Hmm, okay... Literary accounts of the Netherworld are generally dismal. It is described as a dark 'land of no return' and the 'house which none leaves who enters,' with dust on its door and bolt... Yeah well, that adds up."

"Remember that big door, Alice... the one we went through?"

"Yeah... I don't like where this is going, mate."

"Go on..."

"It goes on about Ishtah... I remember her from the temple of Solomon in Jerusalem... It says; the seven gates to the Netherworld are protected by the demons of the dead guard. It must be emphasised the Mesopotamian Netherworld was not a hell. The Netherworld was neither a place of punishment nor reward, rather, the only otherworldly destination for spirits in search of the meaning of life... sounds like Monty Python."

"Who is that?"

"Don't worry, Neit... how about this; The goddess Inanna appears in more myths than any other Sumerian deity. Many of her myths involve her taking over the domains of other deities. She was believed to have stolen the Mes, which represented all positive and negative aspects of civilization, from En-Ki the god of wisdom... En-Ki, now this is all beginning to add up... but what the stuff is the Mes? Wait, here's something... The Mes were the blueprints to civilization: the code of how the spirit world and the physical world interacted. They are fundamental to the Sumerian understanding of the relationship between humanity and the gods. They granted power over, or possibly existence to, all the aspects of civilization (both positive and negative). The Mes were originally collected by En-Lil and then handed over to the guardianship of En-Ki who was to broker them out to the various Sumerian centres. This is described in the poem, En-Ki and the World Order, which also details how he parcels out responsibility for various crafts and natural phenomena to the lesser gods and rulers. We never learn what any of the Mes look like, yet they are represented as physical objects of some sort."

"Yes, I recall that the war of the Eagle and the Serpent was fought over ownership of the Mes," Neit explained.

"The eagle and the serpent?"

"En-Lil the eagle and En-Ki the serpent. Even until now, the countries that support the eagle have it on their coat of arms and flags. They seek to vanquish the serpent. It is the fundamental reason the Christian Church, as reformed by one of the most infamous bearers of the eagle icon, Rome, chose to demonise the serpent in the bible by making it the devil."

"So, if the eagle represents War like with the Romans, the Nazi's, the Spanish, Russia, and America... it's on all their flags and stuff, what does the serpent represent?"

"Knowledge, wisdom, the tree of life, and universal consciousness."

"Okay, so now we know all this, how is that going to get us out of here?" Alice complained.

"I first need to determine exactly what we are up against, Alice. This new knowledge renders my understanding of the challenge to get to En-Lil redundant. If the Sumerian quest to find the meaning of life in the Netherworld is a metaphor for what we are undertaking here, then we need more detail, such as how many guardians there are and how many levels. We have already confronted and defeated Lilitu, Antaeus, and Yoatl, and we do not know who the hologram was..."

"Right, I've accessed it... there are seven gates with seven guardians... we've got rid of four... the last one must have been... Utukku, a ghost... he sure was. Utukku was supposed to obey the will of Anu, the god of the heavens. At the battle of Quadesh, one was killed by the simple throwing of a stone."

"And you threw the WASP, that's what did it, Alice. You said the Utukku obeyed the god of the heavens, that's En-Lil. So, who are the three remaining guardians?"

Alice went quiet for a moment while he accessed more information. "Um... Alal, a female demon, Pazuzu with the body of a man, the head of an eagle, talons of an eagle, two pairs of wings, and a scorpion's tail... sounds like a right mess... and finally the most powerful of them all Azag the Gallu... well, they're all Gallu."

"You will need to defeat them all to get to En-Lil, and then we must find the Mes... because—"

"Wait a minute... you said you can't sense anything... the floor is glass, I bet the walls are too... the WASP went right through the ghost. That's why you can't sense anything! The flash wasn't temporal distortion... Utukku wasn't a ghost, it was a hologram, and the flash was it shutting down."

"What do you mean?" Neit queried.

"We're still in the same room... it's like the holo-deck on Star Trek Voyager."

"Star Trek, what is that?"

"A science fiction TV show... that's why the floor and walls are glass... the entire room was a hologram projected into this purpose-built room. So, all we need to do is figure out where the door is... there must be a door... wait, my Graphene lenses, I can switch to infra-red."

Alice felt released from the claustrophobic shroud of darkness. The shape of Neit's slim body generated by his body heat was illuminated red, and right behind him, he could see the faint outline of a door.

As they entered the elevator, the sound of the chopper that had brought them from the airport reverberated loudly, lifting off from the Oceana rooftop helipad.

"Where are you taking us, Agent Karzoff?" Bull grumbled in his customary no-nonsense manner as the elevator doors closed.

Karzoff scrutinised the arrogant, overweight man and his slender, balding sidekick Colonel Larry Freeman, and then choosing to reply formally, said curtly, "The President has convened a meeting in his office to discuss the situation."

"Do I detect a German accent?" said Bull, presumptuously.

Viktoria knew by the look on his face that Karzoff had taken exception to the question, and so she answered for him to avoid confrontation. "Director-General of Security Karzoff is from Germany, Brigadier Bruckmaster, and to avoid you guessing, I am originally from South Africa." It was a tactful reminder that Karzoff outranked him.

Bull raised an eyebrow at Freeman and snarled facetiously, "Figured that was pretty damn obvious."

The elevator stopped, the doors opened, and two uniformed armed officers escorted them to another elevator that would take them to the Presidential offices.

Karzoff gave Viktoria a surreptitious glance of appreciation in acknowledgment of putting the Brigadier in his place. The acrimony between the four of them was palpable. They each remained stony-faced and silent in the elevator until they reached the Presidential suites.

Miss Vallins greeted the two Americans, and then courteously ushered them into the Presidential office.

Mal was standing at the window watching the rays of sunlight reflecting off USS Zumwalt moored in the harbour. He turned to face Miss Vallins, entering with the visitors, a warm smile on his face.

"Ah, Brigadier Bruckmaster and?" he left the question hanging.

Freeman stopped dead, snapped to attention, and then saluted, "Colonel Larry Freeman, sir!"

Mal made up the space between them, holding out a friendly hand for Brigadier Bruckmaster to shake. The Brigadier saluted and then shook Mal's hand. The Colonel followed suit.

"Please take a seat everyone, we're just waiting on three more of our team to arrive," Mal said with a sly nod to Miss Vallins.

"Can I get you gentlemen and Viktoria a coffee or water?" she asked politely.

They ordered, and all sat down just as Hope, Secta, and the Professor arrived. At the sight of another woman, they all, with the exception of Viktoria, rose again, well-mannered.

"Brigadier Bruckmaster and Colonel Freeman, meet our senior scientists: Dr Secta, Dr Hope, and Professor de Luz," Mal introduced.

The Professor immediately reacted upon recognising Colonel Freeman. "Larry!" He exclaimed excitedly.

"Well, I'll be... Is that you behind those wrinkles, Vic? What in tarnation are you doing here?" The Colonel stressed happily.

"I meant to mention de Luz, Colonel," Bull started grim-faced, almost apologetic.

Vic gave the Colonel a hug, then his face tightened to shake hands with the Brigadier. "Bull, it has been a while," Vic said.

"Yes, Professor, I'm reminded that when we last parted company, it wasn't on the best of terms," the big man said snidely.

Mal felt the tension and winked to Secta, who moved into the break it by shaking hands with both Americans. He gestured, "My sister, Dr Hope."

When all seated, they got on with the business at hand. Rita soon arrived with drinks. An hour later, after several refills, they had progressed from a summary of the situation as presented by Secta (scientific) and then Karzoff (security) to discussing the purpose of the visit and the USS Zumwalt. Trouble was, by that time, Bull was even more intolerant of his Aussie allies. His impatience was telling in his belligerent attitude, an attitude Colonel Freeman was trying to defend but finding difficult to quell.

On his feet and ranting, Bull's face was blushed scarlet by hostility, so much so that the others were concerned he might suffer a seizure or cardiac arrest.

"There is no way the United States of America is prepared to just stand by, waiting for a damn rock singer you claim to be travelling in time, to save the goddamned world! Not while I'm in command!"

"That is complete madness... I expected more of the Americans than rank inflexibility!" Karzoff growled in retaliation, choosing his words carefully.

Mal raised his hands placatingly. "Everybody, just calm down. We can work this out. There's no need to get emotional. Please take your seat, Brigadier, antagonism will get us nowhere." Mal was stern but then turned his attention to Colonel Freeman, cold-shouldering Bruckmaster, who strode defiantly over to the window to peer out at USS Zumwalt, seething.

"I think at this juncture, Colonel, it might be germane for the OTT team to give you the Cook's tour of Kairos," Mal said, obviously frustrated.

"Cook's tour? Oh, yes, Captain Cook... a look... you Aussies and your rhyming slang," he said light-heartedly. "Yes, sir, that would certainly give us more insight into the science of the process," he added positively. He knew damn well that for the Professor to be involved in the project, it must have credibility, such was the genius of the man within scientific circles.

The Professor got out of his seat and, glaring at the Brigadier at the window with his back to them, said, "Some things never change. Shall we, Larry?" he said, calmly motioning for the Colonel to follow him.

The Professor knew from experience that nothing could convince Brigadier Bruckmaster to change his mind, however, the science of the Kairos operation was sure to be enough to impress the scientific mind of his old colleague, Larry Freeman. He figured that his word would be good enough for the President of the United States.

As they filed out of the office, Secta remained behind, watching the Brigadier angrily striding out last.

"I hope you're not going to give him a piece of your mind," Mal mumbled to Secta conspiratorially.

"Why not?" he quipped in reply. "He could do with it, doesn't seem to have much of his own."

CHAPTER 34
RUNAWAY TRAIN

S ECTA HAD PREPARED a demonstration for the two visiting dignitaries. He stopped in front of the secured door to the control room. The computer had confirmed his identity from his implant on approach. Two fully armed guards stood at complete attention, arms at the ready, as they flanked the door. Secta didn't acknowledge them or tell them to be at ease. As long as they stood at this station, they would not be at ease.

The door hissed and then opened automatically.

After passing through decontamination and entering the control environment, Secta could see that everything was in readiness for him. He breezed past the two Americans seated facing the opaque window to the Kairos advent room and stopped at the console. After collecting a small remote from the desktop, he turned to his audience.

"Welcome to the Kairos control room, gentlemen. I have prepared a small demonstration of time travel rather than bore you with a dreary scientific lecture."

He pressed the remote, which activated the mainframe computer and then the console. As the various technical devices lit up with an array of LED lights, so too did the Kairos advent room. Through the window, the two Americans could now see Kairos in all its majesty.

"This, gentlemen, is Kairos," Secta announced proudly.

On the one hand, Colonel Freeman found the complexity of the massive device awe-inspiring; on the other, Brigadier Bruckmaster folded his arms in front of him defiantly apathetic, convinced that the Aussies wouldn't be able to show him anything the good old U.S. of A didn't already have.

"Please observe the monitor overhead," Secta continued, conscious of Bruckmaster's disdain. "We launched a drone five minutes ago. You can see by the time code at the bottom of the screen that it is feeding us live pictures. The drone is currently hovering three hundred feet above the foredeck of the USS Zumwalt in Sydney Harbour. That's harbor with a U." He said light-heartedly, in an attempt to lighten the mood. He paused to gain the Brigadier's undivided attention... and got it. "Hope, if you would be so kind. Professor, could you take over from me."

While Hope walked Secta to the dispatch booth and then locked him inside, the Professor took Secta's place at the console.

"Secta is being prepped for time travel. Once I initiate Kairos, he will be reduced to atoms and then transported."

"He is ready, Professor," Hope said.

Freeman and Bruckmaster watched the Professor flick a switch... Secta vanished, Kairos made a whirring sound, and then the Professor pointed to the monitor.

"You can see Secta has been transported to the foredeck of USS Zumwalt."

Bruckmaster erupted, "Argh! What sort of chicanery is this?"

"I'll just zoom the drone camera and bring up the directional microphone," the Professor said using the remote.

The camera zoomed to a close-up of Secta removing the jackstaff from the bow of the USS Zumwalt.

"Brigadier Bruckmaster and Colonel Freeman, I'm just getting you a souvenir," Secta said, with a smirk.

Glued to the monitor, they watched in disbelief as Secta rolled up the small flag and then jumped into what appeared to be a small dark cloud suspended just near him and then disappeared. Almost instantaneously, Kairos fired up in the advent room, and Secta stepped out of it and unfurled the flag.

Karzoff grinned at the Americans. "Convinced, gentlemen?"

"I'll be damned!" the Brigadier spouted, totally astounded.

Colonel Freeman didn't need convincing; he knew the Professor wouldn't have attached himself to a project that wasn't legitimate. Bristling with enthusiasm, stammering excitedly, he said, "That... that was awesome, Vic... I've got a quadrillion questions... I, I..."

The demonstration had been a total success. Brigadier Bruckmaster had completely changed his attitude and bought into the project. After a tour of the Cray XC 70 Supercomputer and a further explanation of the time travel process by the Professor and Secta, which included evidence from previous missions, the two Americans were finally convinced that Alice had been sent to Eris to confront En-Lil. With that out of the way, they now focused on the hijacking of the USS Zumwalt by Gaap.

"We need to put a tactical team on board that goddamned vessel and secure it whatever the cost. I can't see any other way out of it. We might as well use your Kairos gadget to do that, as you just showed us," Bull growled in a civil tone.

"That's not possible, I'm afraid," Secta said.

"He's right, you know. That ship has the nuclear capability of taking out half a dozen strategic cities in the region. We can't afford to take the risk of leaving it under the control of the enemy," Freeman explained, fervently.

"I agree, but so far, nothing either of us have thrown at Gaap has managed to penetrate its protective force field," Karzoff submitted.

"Look, even if Black Alice succeeds, we'll still have to deal with this goddamned monster. We might as well do it now," Bull advocated.

It made sense; one way or the other, they would have to deal with Gaap, and leaving such a potent weapon under the alien's control would be negligent.

"There must be something that'll kill the thing!" Secta almost shouted as he jumped up and started pacing the control room floor.

"Yes, but what?" Bull countered.

The Professor stood up and said, "I'm not the sole repository of wisdom here, but we need to consider Gaap may not be able to survive without the rift."

The notion stopped Secta in his tracks. He stared intently at the Professor, and then a grin broke on his face. "Vic, you are a genius. There must be a distance from the rift where its influence is nullified. Can we measure that?"

"We already know what is being radiated from it," Hope added. "We can't move the rift, but we sure as hell could move Gaap."

"How, young lady?" Bull questioned.

As though a light bulb had gone on over the Professor's head, he sprouted, "By towing the Zumwalt out to sea."

"By towing it out to sea... of course," Secta copied, excitedly.

"How would Gaap react to that?" the Colonel challenged.

"We use an old tried and tested tactic... we create a goddamned diversion," Bull confidently posed.

"Where, how?" Karzoff queried.

"On board while the good ship is being surreptitiously towed out of Sydney Heads to rendezvous with SSN-666 Hawkbill," the Brigadier said with a snide smile, welcoming the challenge.

They had a plan, and all agreed it was the best they could conjure up under the circumstances. Karzoff called the President to tell him, while Bruckmaster called the U.S. President. Both were given the green light, and so set the wheels in motion by liaising with the military.

"This delay will seriously affect the construction schedule," Adamski complained to Honor.

They were standing in a large austere penthouse office suite on the 30th floor, looking through ten-metre ceiling-to-floor windows at the surrounding countryside. A long way from completion, the office would soon be Gorrick's. Zen had been expecting to move into the newly built high-rise headquarters, two hundred kilometres by road from Sydney, in three months' time, which explained its incomplete Spartan state; just a big empty grey concrete room. The only high-rise in Angel City, it looked out over the planned town and the surrounding eucalypt forested parklands. The infrastructure had been completed: roads, a subway link to Sydney and Canberra, a shopping mall, a sports arena, and housing.

Honor turned from the window and faced the smaller man. "I hope Gorrick is not expecting me to stay here while civilized accommodation is available in nearby Goulburn or Avalon."

"Did you not hear what I said, Honor?" Adamski grumbled indignantly.

"Yes, yes, I heard you, Adamski... always rattling on about your silly time travel project," she said dismissively.

"What do you find silly about it?" he snarled, finding her remark affronting.

"Nothing... nothing, it's just that I have other things on my mind," she whined, trying to make amends.

"I need the core organic chip OTT has. There must be a way of getting it... with it, I could have a matter transfer device functioning inside a month."

"Well, we had a chance and lost it," she said ruefully.

"Is Zenesis set up in this building?" Adamski asked.

"I think so. I flew here with Doctor Li. She said since obtaining some mind-boggling tech from the Tokyo office, she will have a working version of the RF series android soon. I think her labs are on the tenth floor."

Striding over to a spring water syphon, her high heels echoed in the vast concrete chasm.

Adamski followed.

"Drink?" she asked.

"Yes, thank you."

She poured two cups and handed one to the Russian.

"She gets far more support than I do," Adamski moaned, covetously.

Before she could comment, Gorrick arrived with Doctor Li.

"Speak of the devil," Honor mumbled furtively into her cup.

Both were envious of the favouritism Gorrick bestowed on Doctor Li. He knew it bothered them, but competition to increase productivity was his personal maxim.

Gorrick stopped in front of Honor and said, "I'd offer you ladies a seat, but it seems there are none." It was a feeble attempt at humour... and it didn't go down well.

"Can't we have this meeting in a more comfortable setting, Gorrick?" Honor protested.

He refrained from answering and ambled over to the window to take in the view. Then, with his back to them, he said, "Professor Adamski, your work has unavoidably been interrupted by the move here... how will that affect your schedule?" his deep voice resonating.

"Considerably, sir, but it is made more problematic by Zen's inability to provide me a faster processor... that is why OTT has succeeded—"

"We had our chance," Honor interjected to remind them.

Gorrick slowly turned to face them, his expression stolid. "How much of a delay will this cause?"

"It is the difference between weeks and years," Adamski admitted. "They would have replicated the chip many times over using 3-D printing by now."

Honor raised her eyebrows at the thought. "That chip would be worth millions of dollars."

"Of that you can rest assured, and they would be very much aware of it," Gorrick said.

"It seems a priority for Zen to obtain it. The RF series would be infallible if fitted with such a processor," Doctor Li said curtly.

"Well, with Sydney being evacuated and a skeleton staff operating OTT, there could not be a better time to waltz in and snatch one," Honor smirked.

"Do you know where they would keep them?" Adamski queried.

"No. But we could find out," Honor suggested deviously.

Doctor Li asked, "How?"

"Perhaps by using an asset as ransom," Honor said slyly.

Gorrick glared at her, "What asset do you have in mind, Honor?"

"Any one of them that you can be sure would have stayed behind in Sydney... unguarded: Secta, the Professor, Hope, Karzoff, Viktoria, or even the President or his secretary Miss Vallins."

"Clever thinking, Honor," Doctor Li muttered with a wily smile.

Alice had assumed the doorway would lead him to his objective, but instead, he found himself in a room looking down at someone in a hospital bed, dying. He stared long and hard at the woman in the bed, and then it dawned on him that she was his mother.

"Mum?" He muttered, moving up closer to the bed and taking her hand.

Her closed eyes squinted tighter for an instant, and then the eyelids batted open. Cold steel-blue eyes fixed on his, and then confusion broke on her face.

"Are you a prison doctor? Where's Doctor Riley?" she rasped.

Brimming up with emotion, Alice ran his fingers through her hair.

"Mum, Mum... it's me... your son."

"Who? Is this a mental ward or something? One minute they're telling me I've only got hours to live, and the next I've got a quack I don't even know telling me he's my son. What's going on here?" she cried out. "I'm losing it!"

The statement pretty well confirmed to Alice that it was his mother, all right; she sounded just like him. He perched on the edge of the bed, still holding her hand.

"It is just another illusion, Alice," Neit reminded him. But Alice ignored him. It was a special moment for him; he hadn't seen his mother since he was seven years old on that dreaded day of the shootout when the cops carted her and his dad off to jail, and he was left orphaned.

He squeezed her hand tighter. "No, Mum, I'm not a doctor; I am your son, Robert." It was the first time he'd spoken his real name in years.

A sharp flick irreverently cast his hand aside, and she scorned, "Don't be ridiculous, my son is only twelve years old."

Shocked, he took her hand again, but in holding it, he noticed it had changed. Then he recognised it... the hand was his!

"Huh, what the bloody hell?" he stood and questioned, confused by the bedridden person. The person was no longer his mother; it was him, but older, way older.

Through parched lips, the old Alice groaned, "Come closer... closer."

Alice reluctantly edged closer to better hear what his doppelganger had to say.

His pale blue eyes, faded by age and wrinkled, narrowed, and in the frail voice of someone on their deathbed, said, "We rocket through life towards death like a runaway train..." It was philosophically regretful. "Just know this, that I am you... if you don't dig the journey, you won't appreciate the destination. The power is in the proximity."

Before he could react to the cryptic message, an intense flash of light blinded him. When his vision had cleared, he was somewhere else. "What the hell did he mean by that?" Alice complained angrily out loud.

"What does it matter? I would be more concerned about where we are. Your other you was only an illusion, whereas this looks threateningly real," Neit protested.

He was standing in the centre of the helipad target atop the Oceana building in Sydney, facing north. Lighting up the vista of the night sky with unbridled intensity, raged a fearful column of fire; so radiant that he could almost feel its heat on his face.

"The place is desolate; they've got them all out. It looks like the end of days... and there's that bloody U.S. warship out there in the harbour," Alice said.

"It's a reminder."

"What is?"

"This... En-Lil has transported you here to remind you who is in charge."

Alice strode angrily over to the edge of the building, held out his arms, looked up, and yelled at the heavens. "I don't need to be reminded, En-Lil... I know what I have to do. Show yourself... fight me... come on, do your worst!"

Another intense flash of white light blinded him.

CHAPTER 35
TOWJOB

I T WAS JUST after dawn when Honor strode hubristically out through the entrance doors of the Avalon Motel reception towards the car park. She stopped at a black SUV and then slipped into the passenger seat.

"Jackpot," she snarled smugly at the well-built young man seated like a marble statue behind the steering wheel. In fact, she was all but surrounded by square-jawed Eastern European hunks. There was an identical pair behind her on the rear seats, and all three of them were wearing the obligatory bodyguard Ray-Ban mirrored aviator sunglasses, with a severe crew-cut and matching black suits... all were carved from the same block of Baltic ice. "Miss Rita Vallins is in room 12B," she continued. Then, leaning forward, she retrieved a small black case from the floor-well, opened it on her lap, and withdrew a small syringe gun. A twist of a knob on its grip produced a fsssssst indicating it was loaded. She handed it to the driver. "Bring her to me, Bruno." He nodded but before he could alight, she grabbed his muscly arm: she hadn't finished. "Wait..." She dipped back into the bag and came up with a pair of heavy-duty straight-cutting compound-action tin snips, which she handed over.

Bruno took both items, pocketed them, then drew a pair of black latex gloves from his inner pocket and pulled them on.

Honor watched the three big men make their way stealthily to the second-floor level of the motel complex.

Rita Vallins woke, startled by the terrifying sensation that an intruder had entered her room. She wasn't wrong; there were three of them. Before she could let out a scream for help, she was jabbed in the neck by a dark assailant. The shot paralysed her almost immediately. Screaming inside her mind but unable to make herself heard, she watched in frozen terror as the bedclothes were stripped back to expose her body in her flimsy nightie, and her ankles were grasped by black latex-gloved hands. Fear turned to dread when she recognised, in the gloved hand of the dark figure that had injected her, a pair of tin snips.

Desperately trying to struggle, but her body not responding, her eyes wide with terror, she watched the tin snips open around the little toe on her left foot. With her brain denouncing it as a dream, her senses though dulled were telling her it wasn't... she quickly learned it was real. Panic traversed her every nerve end, and then for the first time, she caught sight of the face of the evildoer holding the snips ready to chop.

He grinned macabrely... then came a loud snip; the grisly sound of her toe being amputated. She felt no pain because she was numb... but the shock of what had happened and the spray of blood on the white bed sheets caused her to pass out.

Enjoying the gruesome task, Bruno sprayed the bleeding stump of her toe with a blood coagulant, then he and his companions worked methodically to unfurl a body bag they'd brought with them. Once opened, they cocooned her inside, zipped it shut and then, maintaining the dreadful silence, two of them lugged her out of the room as if she were a corpse.

Bruno remained behind and placed the severed toe on a bloody piece of notepaper on the bloodstained bed-sheets.

It was way too early for anyone to notice the two men carrying the black body bag down the stairs and then loading it in through the rear hatch of the SUV.

With a smug smile of accomplishment on her face, Honor greeted Bruno and his confederates as they took their seats in the vehicle.

"Good. A job well done... you left a memento of our visit?"

The hint of a smile cracked on Bruno's thin lips as he handed Honor the tin snips with its sharp edges smeared with blood.

Honor took them with studied pleasure. "Excellent... her pretty feet will be far less alluring now."

It didn't take long for the President to get word of the abduction of his secretary. As a result, he immediately summoned Karzoff and Viktoria to his office.

Upon entering, Karzoff was handed the blood-soaked note. Grimacing, he read it out for Viktoria.

"'You have six hours to surrender the organic chip or another piece of Miss Vallins will be delivered.' This is the work of Honor. No-one else would be so cold-heartedly brazen," Karzoff snarled.

"Yes, I agree... it has her written all over it," Viktoria confirmed.

"Is it just a threat or—?" Mal stopped short, emotion getting to him.

"She does not make idle threats, sir," Karzoff said, dispiritedly.

Mal flopped into his favourite lounge chair and put his head in his hands. There was a pregnant pause while, with Karzoff and Viktoria remaining standing, Mal ruminated... a few seconds later, he glanced up at them. Karzoff noted the dark lines under his eyes, understandable for a person under so much stress and obviously not getting enough sleep.

"Then give it to her," Mal said reticently. "Go and explain to Secta... see if he can come up with a way of making it self-destruct or something after we get her back," he was getting angrier. "But do I t... there isn't much time."

"Yes, sir," Karzoff affirmed, equally angry.

"Sir, we can't let the chip fall into their hands," Viktoria remonstrated. "There's no telling what they'll do with it."

Mal's head slumped back into his hands.

With his face scrunched up with concern for Mal, Karzoff slowly shook his head at Viktoria, knowing full well that Mal would have taken that into consideration.

The plan to tow the USS Zumwalt out of Sydney Harbour had been deployed. Major Torrens had received orders from Brigadier Bruckmaster to assemble a small task force of Navy SEALs to be dropped onto the ship to create a diversion while it was being towed out of range of the rift. An operations centre for the task force had been set up in a large room next door to the Kairos control room. Configured with a wall of a dozen television monitors, manned by half a dozen operators, along with all that was required to orchestrate the assault, Bruckmaster and Freeman were sitting back in chairs sipping their morning coffees when Secta entered the room.

"Ah, Secta, we're all set here. Major Torrens and his assault team have boarded the chopper—"

Secta interrupted him. "Excuse me, Brigadier, but I have some bad news. Zen has abducted the President's secretary from her motel room in Avalon and is holding her for ransom."

Both uniformed men looked astonished. "For what?" Bull snapped.

"For an organic super processor I brought back from 2047."

"The thing that makes Kairos tick?" Freeman queried.

"One of them, yes, I guess you could say that."

"Is this person in serious danger?" Freeman asked.

Secta's face was grave. "They've already sent us a severed toe. We have less than six hours to comply, or they'll amputate more. I'm telling you this because it will distract us from the mission."

"Don't worry about that, do what you need to do, we can manage it from here," Freeman said, compassionately.

"If it falls into Zen's hands, we'll have another enemy as powerful as En-Lil to deal with," Secta proposed. With that said, he left them thinking and went to his laboratory.

One of the monitors was showing scuba divers coupling towropes to the underwater bow cleats of the USS Zumwalt. The other end of the massive ropes had been hitched to retractable bollards at the stern of the submerged nuclear submarine SSN Hawkbill, which while submerged, had silently made its way up the harbour and got into position overnight.

On nuclear-class submarines, the tow pad is installed forward of the forward escape trunk. U.S. nuclear submarines have specifications to be towed with a bridle flounder plate arrangement secured to a pair of SWL mooring cleats.

The countdown had started for Hawkbill to tow the USS Zumwalt out to sea. There had been no precedent of a submerged submarine towing a warship, however, Naval Operations back in the States had researched the U.S. Towing Manual for the attachment points and specifications to affect the plan. It was considered feasible, which got it the green light.

Another monitor displayed the cabin of a Chinook helicopter from the helmet cam POV of Major Torrens. They were in the air en-route to the USS Zumwalt.

It would take two hours for the Zumwalt to be towed clear of Sydney Harbour. It had already been covertly cut free from its mooring.

An hour later, Karzoff received a text from the kidnappers with the exchange details. It said, 'A chopper will deliver the hostage to the Oceana HQ heliport at 0900 hours in exchange for the chip. She will be released once the chip is authenticated. Agree by return text.'

"Have you come up with anything?" Viktoria asked Secta.

"We're not sure, but this buys us a little more time. What's happening with the yanks?"

"They're on the Zumwalt, but it doesn't look good. They're losing men," Karzoff told Secta, the Professor, and Hope.

"And the sub?" the Professor asked.

"So far so good, it's slowly moving up the harbour," Viktoria assured them.

It was slow all right. In an hour, the big warship had only moved half a kilometre towards the heads, but with the difficult part of covertly manoeuvring it out of Neutral Bay now out of the way, the sub was set to increase the towing speed.

There were six in the task force. They'd only just assembled on the stern chopper deck of the guided missile destroyer after the Chinook had dropped them and then lifted off when someone opened fire on them from inside the deckhouse. Two were killed instantly, and the others took cover. The exchange of fire provided the location of the shooter.

Major Torrens had the layout of the Zumwalt committed to memory: the deckhouse had four levels. "Shooter is on level two, the bridge." He shouted to his subordinate; his second in command had been killed in the first volley of shots. "Heads down, we need to draw him out... it'll buy time for the towing. It'd be fatal to enter the deckhouse."

The futuristic ship with its stealth design, like something out of a Star Trek episode, was moving at a snail's pace up the harbor. The sensation of it moving was hardly noticeable to those on deck. But right now, self-preservation was their primary concern.

The major slipped out from his hiding place and fired a shot at where he thought the sniper was positioned. The young officer beside him stepped out and took aim, hoping to get a bead on the sniper when he returned fire.

A shot resounded from the deckhouse, and the young officer's head exploded. The sniper's bullet had hit him in the forehead.

Back at task force operations witnessing the young lieutenant's death via the major's helmet-cam, Brigadier Bruckmaster was repelled. "This ain't kosher, Larry," he snarled.

"There's not much we can do bar sending in more support, sir," Freeman replied.

"Where the hell is the hundred and fifty-eight crew of the Zumwalt? This is the most goddamned modern ship we've got, surely we can contact someone on board?" Bruckmaster questioned in frustration.

Freeman knew they'd already tried everything. The only logical answer to the Brigadier's question was that the crew was either all dead or being held prisoner below deck. He just shook his head disconsolately in reply.

The door opened, and the Professor entered just as Torrens's voice bellowed over the monitor. "HQ, I think the shooter is a member of the crew."

"How can that be?" Bruckmaster bellowed at everyone. "Has this damned thing turned our men against us?"

"No, you'd have to think, given what we know, Gaap has possessed a member of the crew," Freeman proposed.

"How the hell are we supposed to deal with that?" Bruckmaster snarled. "It's like a goddamned horror movie!"

Vic turned to Freeman, "Not going well, Larry?"

"No, Vic. Three down. At least the towing had worked... she's almost a kilometre up the harbour. What about your end?"

"The exchange will take place soon," he checked his wristwatch, "in ten minutes."

Bruckmaster's face tightened, and he barked, "You telling me you're giving the enemy what they want?"

"There's no alternative," Vic said dolefully.

"Couldn't you have done something so the chip would fail?" Larry posed.

"You're risking millions of lives for the sake of one lousy secretary, for Christ's sake!" Bruckmaster shouted angrily.

Major Torrens was fired up. He yelled at his troops. "Jackson... here, pronto!"

A marine carrying an RPG-7 rocket launcher arrived at his side.

"Sir," the marine reported.

"Did you catch the location of the shooter?"

"Yes, sir."

"Right, put one through that dang window right up his ass, son."

"Yes, sir!"

The marine took aim and squeezed the trigger. The recoil was serious, but he handled it. The rocket hit the target, smashing through the heavy plate glass window. There was a short delay, then an explosion. A ball of fire flared out through the window.

"That would have rocked the mother," Torrens cursed.

Gripping the end of an unlit stogie cigar between his teeth, Bruckmaster punched the air. "Right on! Yeah! Yeah!"

"Haven't heard that expression in a while, Bull, but hey, the young fella iced it," Larry Freeman said with a sardonic grin.

"Surely that blew the ass of it," Bull snarled, then yelled into the microphone, "Torrens, put another one through the window for good measure."

Torrens replied, "Copy that, sir!" He glanced at Jackson beside him. "Make it a double, son!"

They watched the Navy Seal line up the window again and fire a second rocket. The explosion was equally powerful.

"Nothing could've survived that," Bruckmaster growled, chewing the butt of the cigar like it was bubble-gum.

Torrens tapped the marine on the helmet. "Well done, let's sit pat now, see what comes of it."

The marine retired to his hiding place.

A loud yell came from behind Torrens. He swung around and trained his gun in the direction of the scream. His brain could hardly believe what he was seeing. A two-metre gigantic monster had stepped out from behind the rear gun turret with one of his men held up off the ground in one hand, by the head. It was Gaap, in his monstrous form.

The marine let out a horrific scream when the monster squeezed his head until it burst. Gaap irreverently cast the lifeless body aside.

"Fire!" Torrens screamed at his men.

All hell broke loose. But the barrage of bullets from automatic weapons fire made no impact on the target; the bullets simply bounced off the bubble-like force field shielding it.

Bull was on his feet. "Get them the hell out of there!" he shouted. "Right now!"

When the dazzling light from the last flash cleared from Alice's vision, he realised he was no longer standing on the helipad atop Oceana Headquarters, but was on the aft deck of a naval ship. He immediately looked up at the sky. It was foreboding. Eerie black stormy clouds were rolling overhead, but they weren't your average storm clouds. No, this sky was reminiscent of what Alice had seen over Tokyo in 2047 when the UFO appeared in the midst of a harrowing typhoon. He could tell he was in Sydney by the skyline and swung around sharply to face the rift in the north, but the column of fire wasn't there. Instead, it was now in the northwest. He then realised he was on the USS Zumwalt, and it wasn't at its mooring. Instead, it had moved close to Sydney heads. It was then he noticed torn, bloody bodies scattered about the ship's deck.

CHAPTER 36
POWER IN THE PROXIMITY

A**LICE ASKED OUT** loud, "What the hell's going on here? What are we doing on this bloody thing? Is this real?"

"If it is me you are asking Alice, I cannot answer," Neit replied in Alice's mind.

"Nar, this has got to be another one this dude's mind games."

He walked over to the closest dead body and looking down at it said, "A Navy Seal. His head's been bashed in. There's another one over there..." He strolled over to the next body. "Something serious has gone down here."

"Gaap... he is here... I can sense it," Neit said, with dread.

Alice immediately tightened up. He didn't want to fight Gaap; the last time he almost lost his life. He noticed movement out of the corner of his eye. One of the dead Navy SEALs on the deck had twitched. But how can he? Alice thought, the guy's head is caved in like a bashed crab; his brain's hanging out.

Then the horror began to take shape. Each of the dead SEALs began to twitch as though being reanimated.

"What the—?" Alice checked around him. Four dead Navy SEALs were struggling to get up, each of them with wounds so horrific they had no right to even move, let alone live. One of them had a gaping hole in his shoulder where his arm had been ripped clean out of the socket.

Once on their feet, they all faced Alice and came staggering towards him.

"Just like the bloody zombie meatheads I fought in Japan," he barked, shaping up to take them on. "Don't even bother trying to explain these dead walkers, Neit."

The closest was only two metres away. Its eyes were glazed over white... its mouth open and drooling... a long string of gunk was hanging from its chin. Closest was the SEAL with his head smashed in. Now closer, Alice could see that half of his head was missing; there was a gross mixture of grey matter and blood oozing from the dark cavity. Wondering how to tackle him and the others, Alice quickly searched the floor for a weapon, a piece of timber... something... anything. He saw a semi-automatic assault rifle: the standard issue weapon of choice for Navy SEALs and snapped it up. He pivoted and opened fire at the closest Zombie. The quick burst took what was left of its head clean off. The headless thing took a few more steps then crumbled onto the deck. He turned the gun on the others and took out another two in the same fashion. While he was firing, a hand thumped him on the shoulder from behind. He gasped, spun around, and emptied the magazine into the last of them, blowing the SEAL's head off. The four bodies lay twitching on the deck, their legs still moving as though they were walking. Alice dumped the rifle, spent of ammo.

"Bloody hell!" he growled, puffing. "There better not be a shipload of these, what's next?"

That was a cue for the next assault. From out of the deckhouse main door poured more Zombies. The crew of the Zumwalt, all of them determined to tear Alice apart.

"Bugger!" he yelled, scanning the deck for another weapon, then sighted the RPG-7 rocket launcher. He made a beeline for it and found it armed with a rocket. A cacophonous sound of gnashing teeth and hissing was coming from the horde of Zombie sailors stumbling towards him with their arms outstretched, just like in a B-grade Zombie flick. Al fired. The rocket ploughed into a bunch of about fifteen of them and they exploded into pieces — but still, they kept coming, pouring out from the forward hold. Out of rockets, Alice discarded the RPG and frantically searched for something else. He found an M4-A1 5.56 mm automatic carbine and hoping it had a full mag, opened fire on the forty or fifty Zombies that had emerged onto the deck.

"Alice, you will need more than that gun to defeat all of them," Neit yelled, trying to be heard over the gunfire.

"Well, do something then!" Alice growled back.

Neit slipped out of Al's body and risking exposure to the light, darted across the deck like a fleeting shadow towards the deckhouse door. Kicking back Zombie sailors jammed in the doorway trying to get out, he used all of his strength to try and close the steel door against the Zombie arms clawing at him from inside. He got it shut and severed several arms and hands in the effort. He locked it off, leaving fifty or so Zombies for Alice to deal with.

Alice took out half of them quick-smart. The dead were piling up on the deck. It was a bloodbath.

Neit hurriedly scanned the deck for more weapons on the way back to help Alice and found another discarded rifle: it was an AK-47. He reached Alice just as he ran out of ammo with half a dozen Zombies only a metre from him.

The twitching mutilated bodies of the Zombies were stacked in a pile, but the remainder just kept on coming—mindlessly hungry for flesh—Alice's flesh.

The leading six Zombies reached Alice and were clawing at him. He let go a barrage of punches, breaking noses, smashing chins and teeth, but it had little effect, they were overpowering him.

Neit barged into them, wildly punching them out of the way in a desperate bid to reach Alice. They were all over him; he was going down. Neit couldn't fire the rifle for fear of hitting Alice. From the maul of Zombies ripping at Alice, a bloody drenched hand reached out through them towards Neit. An almighty lunge, and Neit plunged the AK-47 through the manic horde into Alice's outstretched hand. He got it and opened fire.

In the operations room, Brigadier Bruckmaster, Colonel Freeman, and the Professor were reclining in chairs, sipping coffees. Freeman looked up at the monitor, relieved to see the Chinook rescue mission lifting off the Zumwalt helipad with the survivors.

The monitor displaying the helmet-cam of Major Torrens showed Gaap staring up fiercely, his clawed hands fisting the air from the deck of the Zumwalt, dark that his prey had escaped him.

"Look at that thing, one F-18 could swoop and take it out in a flash," the Brigadier growled.

"Not while the force field is protecting it, nothing can penetrate it," Vic reminded him.

"It might have cost us a few good men, but the mission was a success," Bull boasted.

Freeman frowned at what he thought was an insensitive statement from the Brigadier.

The ship was about to pass through Sydney Heads.

"We estimate the influence of the arrow of time on Gaap to be around 25 kilometres," Vic said.

"How the hell did you measure that?" asked Freeman.

"We detected a significant output of muon-neutrinos from the rift. They're subatomic particles similar to electrons but with much smaller mass. We think the neutrino bursts fuel the force field protecting Gaap. We sent up a drone with a device to test the range of the neutrino output from the rift and found it reached a radius of twenty kilometres."

"Why the hell don't we just block the signal... it would have saved all this moving the goddamned ship... a bit like moving the mountain to Mohammed, isn't it?" Bull rasped, indignantly.

"There's no known substance on Earth that can block neutrinos, Brigadier. Moving the ship out of range was the only option," Vic said sternly.

Bull nodded slowly.

The drone over the Zumwalt showing the aft deck where Major Torrens and his team had fought Gaap, showed no signs of life—Gaap had disappeared Alice wasn't there fighting the Zombie hoard, that battle was happening in a different dimension though nonetheless relevant.

Alice had exhausted another clip, but had chopped down most of his opponents. Only three Zombies remained staggering towards him; the rest were piled up in a mound of twitching corpses. No longer feeling threatened by them, gripping the AK-47 by the barrel, he swung the gun, bashing the daylights out of the remaining three Zombies with its butt. They didn't put up a fight and quickly joined the mound of dead. Job done, thoroughly knackered, Alice discarded the AK-47. He was drenched in blood—on his forearms, all over his face and clothes—a right mess.

Neit was leaning against the rear gun turret, looking at Alice. "Lucky I locked the rest of them inside, that was the last weapon," he said nonchalantly.

"You're damn right," he sighed, slumping onto the deck, gulping for breath. "They didn't put up much of a fight, but it was tiring knocking the buggers over." He noticed the ship was passing through Sydney Heads. He got up, went over to the gunwale, and looked over the side into the water. "How the stuff's this thing moving? I can't hear any engines?"

Just as he was about to walk back to Neit, the door to the deckhouse that Neit had locked exploded open with incredible force. Alice had to duck the fifteen-centimetre thick two-hundred-and-fifty-kilo steel door that came flying through the air, unhinged by the blast. It smashed into the gunwale exactly where he'd been standing. The impact bent the gunwale well out of shape.

With his nerves frayed, shocked, he squawked, "What the—?" He was expecting more Zombies to come pouring out through the doorway, but instead, the creature he dreaded most stepped through, having to duck to get out. It stopped and glared at him with evil yellow eyes.

Alice stared back at the two-hundred-centimetre-tall gargoyle and rasped, "Gaap!"

Major Torrens entered the operations centre. Bruckmaster, Freeman, and the Professor immediately rose to their feet.

"Major. Well done. Sorry for your loss—" Freeman failed to finish before Bruckmaster rudely cut him off.

"Let's not focus on collateral damage, Colonel. Sit down, son."

Looking decidedly ruffled, as you would expect for someone who had come directly from battle, Torrens sank tiredly into a chair in front of the wall of monitors. The Professor and Freeman resumed their seats, while Bruckmaster remained standing.

"Now begins phase two. Is the ship's pilot on standby?" Bull questioned.

"Yes, sir," Freeman ratified.

"Right, once the towing is done, and the Hawkbill uncoupled, the sub will surface beside the Zumwalt. Then, with the force field down on the creature, Major Torrens, you will lead a larger tactical force back on board the Zumwalt to kill that thing and secure the vessel."

"Under the circumstances, I think that would no longer be the right move, sir," Freeman posed.

The Brigadier was taken aback, unaccustomed to having his orders questioned. "I remind you, Colonel, we agreed on this scenario and it was subsequently endorsed by Congress," Bull growled.

"That was before we lost men in a tactical fight with the enemy," Freeman said rationally, then eyeballed Torrens. "Major, do you think there are any survivors of the Zumwalt crew?"

"No, I doubt it, sir."

"We can assume the enemy, in an individual effort, has defeated one hundred and fifty-eight crew members and four Navy SEALs... that's quite a toll. We can't risk any more men, sir. I believe we need to come up with a better means of securing the vessel."

The Brigadier was shaking his head. To him, there was no other way than going in with all guns blazing.

The Professor interjected, "We can use a drone to check the neutrino levels once the ship is in position. Then, you'll have three choices: Hawkbill can torpedo and sink it... land another boarding party to take on Gaap, knowing his power has been reduced, or... just leave it moored out to sea and wait for a result from Black Alice."

The Brigadier threw his hands wildly in the air and bellowed, "I'm not putting the U.S. Navy at risk sitting on my ass waiting for this Black Alice character to save the dang world... nor am I going to scuttle a billion-dollar U.S. Navy warship!"

Freeman jumped up and pointed his finger at Torrens, growling with equal venom, "So you would sooner risk the lives of servicemen on a suicide mission?"

Bull wasn't impressed. There was no way he was going to cop his plan being countermanded by a subordinate officer. He was fuming.

There came a pregnant pause while they all considered the argument. Freeman resumed his seat and then said calmly, "I recommend the President be brought up to speed on the new developments so she can make the final decision."

"For what it's worth, I agree," the Professor submitted.

Torrens stayed well out of it.

Pacing the floor, Bruckmaster was so dirty they could almost see steam rising from his head. He stopped, withdrew the stogie from between his teeth, took a deep breath, and then growled hubristically, "Alright, alright, it seems I'm being overruled here. You call her,

Colonel, and explain. Give her my opinion. Call me when you have her decision." He eyeballed each of them with contempt as though he'd been betrayed, stuck the stogie back in his mouth, and then dramatically stormed out of the room.

Freeman raised his eyebrows at the two men beside him and said, "He gets like that... loves grandstanding... he'll come round."

Secta and Hope were in the shadows on the Oceana rooftop helipad, watching the black Kamov Ka-60 chopper in Zen livery land. With the downdraft from the rotors playing havoc with their hair and clothing, they made their way toward the helicopter and then stopped ten metres clear of it to wait.

The side sliding door opened, and Bruno alighted. He turned to help two men from inside manhandle a body bag out of the aircraft. The three of them placed the cargo on the ground, and Bruno unzipped the bag, then waved for Hope to inspect the contents.

Fighting her skirts from lifting in the wind, she approached the open body bag, and upon recognising Rita Vallins, shot Secta a confirming wave of the hand.

While Hope was checking Rita's vitals to ensure she was okay, holding a white envelope out for Bruno to see, Secta tentatively approached the big Russian.

Bruno opened the envelope, removed the chip contained in a plastic safety clip bag, produced a device from his inside coat pocket, and after cracking the chip out of its housing, slipped it into the device. A small window in the device registered a reading, which satisfied him. He nodded expressionlessly at Secta, and then without muttering a word, turned on his heel. Followed by his comrades, he reboarded the chopper.

Secta and Hope ducked down to avoid the rotors as the chopper lifted off with a loud roar. The downdraft very nearly bowled them over.

Without a weapon, Alice knew he didn't stand a chance against Gaap.

Neit stayed concealed but with the two combatants in sight. He scoured the deck for another weapon for Alice and sighted a pistol holstered on the hip of one of the dead Zombie sailors. As soon as he felt it was safe, he made a dash for the gun, scooped it up, and returned behind the turret.

"Alice!" Neit called, covertly. "Here."

Alice checked over his shoulder at Neit, who slid the pistol across the deck for Alice to trap under his foot. With his eyes remaining fixed on Gaap just six metres away, he slowly bent down and collected the gun.

"Don't know that it'll have much effect on the bastard, Neit, but it's better than nothing."

He raised the gun in both hands and aimed at the target. "Come on, you big bludger, make a move!"

Gaap took a step forward.

The phrase 'power is in the proximity' entered Alice's mind from out of nowhere. He repeated it out loud to himself... "Power is in the proximity... that's what my old self said, must mean something important."

Neit overheard him. "Alice, why is the ship out here, why has it been moved? Maybe to distance it from the power of the arrow of time?"

Keeping the gun trained on Gaap, Alice nodded. "Yeah, that sounds like something Secta would come up with. Maybe fatso here has lost his powers... Let's see."

Neit jumped at Alice and disappeared inside him. Alice shivered. "Damn, I'll never get used to you doing that."

Alice fired at Gaap and hit him in the thigh. The monster reeled backwards, let out a roar, and then flew at Alice. Gaap was on him in a flash and knocked the gun out of his hand before he could peel off another shot. The giant let go of an almighty right hook that collected Alice right on the chin and sat him on his butt. Struggling to stay conscious, he regathered himself, rolled onto his side, and leg tripped Gaap. The huge creature hit the deck hard, and Alice wasted no time straddling him and jackhammer punching his face with a barrage of blows. But Gaap brushed away the onslaught, reached up, and grabbed Alice by the throat. A powerful jump, and Gaap was back on his feet, choking Alice.

Blood or some black substance that looked like blood was oozing from the bullet wound in Gaap's thigh.

Alice kicked the wound and body punched him but couldn't bust free of Gaap's vice-like grip. In desperation, he reached a hand up behind him, felt for the monster's face, and using the same method he'd used fighting the Golem back in 587 BC, he felt for Gaap's eyes. Unable to see what he was doing, when he found them, he dug his forefinger into Gaap's left eye and gouged it out of the socket.

Gaap let out a deathly scream and dropped Alice.

Down on one knee, face blue from almost choking to death, Al was struggling to get his breath back. With his energy almost spent and with Gaap holding his oozing eye socket in agony, Al knew this could be his only chance. He mustered all of his remaining strength and dived for the pistol on the deck. Sliding on his side, he scooped it up, rolled, faced Gaap, and fired three shots point-blank into his face. Gaap reeled back violently with each shot, as chunks of his face were blown off by the .44 calibre slugs. After the three shots, there wasn't much left of Gaap's face. He swayed, legs buckled, and he fell backward over the gunwale into the Pacific Ocean and sank—shark bait.

Alice pocketed the pistol and snarled croakily, "That'll teach you to mess with Al." He was beat up big time with deep bloody scratches on his face, neck, and forearms. His shirt was shredded, his clothes ragged, but he was alive... and he'd defeated his nemesis.

"You did it!" Neit all but shouted in Al's mind.

"Mate, you were bloody right about the arrow of time... and thank the gods my old self warned me about the power in the proximity."

There was a sudden flash of light.

CHAPTER 37
THE SHINE

T HE U.S. PRESIDENT had consulted her staff after Colonel Freeman informed her of the situation with the USS Zumwalt. She came back with the decision to send in another tactical team to take out Gaap and secure the vessel. Her decision was based on the scientific data the Professor had provided on the range of the neutrino field suspected of feeding the protective force field around Gaap. She figured if it was no longer effective, as the science suggested, then the creature should be no match for the armament of a U.S. task force.

Freeman reluctantly agreed but made it clear he preferred the third option of waiting for Black Alice to succeed with his mission. However, when the President pointed out that the USS Zumwalt was armed with enough nuclear weapons to take out the east coast of Oceana, and then some, and that it had been commandeered by a hostile, there was really no other choice than to save it... Brigadier Bruckmaster had been right.

The decision from the Whitehouse resulted in Freeman having to eat humble pie and invite Bruckmaster back into the operations centre to brief Major Torrens on the next move.

By then the Hawkbill had reached its destination with the Zumwalt, two kilometres out to sea from Sydney. However, there was a fresh challenge on the horizon: a cyclone was approaching fast from the northeast. As a result, the rising swell caused by it would render it impossible to maintain the tether between the two vessels. With the storm forecast to hit Sydney in only two hours, it had become a race against time to get on board, kill Gaap, and secure the Zumwalt. This time the task force would consist of a hundred marines. Two Chinooks each transporting fifty troops to the destroyer.

The task force would be armed to the teeth with the very best and most effective weapons available. But there was still one problem: they were in Sydney and the nearest U.S. troops were three hours twenty minutes away at the U.S. Military base at Pine Gap near Alice Springs.

"Only option is to use the Aussie SAS," Bruckmaster said.

"Or... we deploy ten Navy SEALs we have here and thirty marines from the Hawkbill," Freeman posed.

"But isn't Hawkbill submerged?" Major Torrens asked.

Freeman nodded, "She'd have to surface."

"In a cyclone... what'll happen to the tether?" Torrens rightfully questioned.

Bruckmaster jumped out of his chair and started pacing again all fired up. "Goddamn it! There's gotta be a way!"

Just then Karzoff came in.

"Karzoff, just the man," Bruckmaster crowed, chewing on his cigar, "we need twenty crack shots of yours to go with our task force of ten or so to secure the Zumwalt, can you do that?... It's a dangerous mission?"

Karzoff wasn't expecting the question. Stammering and stuttering in his customary manner, he said, "I, I think so. We have a highly trained security team but I think most of them might have been evacuated already. Let me check."

It only took them an hour to assemble twenty of Karzoff's OTT security agents still on the premises, and ten of the remaining Navy SEALs under Major Torrens' command. Twenty minutes later, they were all geared up onboard a Chinook en-route to the USS Zumwalt to deal with Gaap.

Twenty minutes later, after probing the interior of the ship, the crack recon team declared it was all clear.

Flummoxed by the report, Bull queried Major Torrens. "Major, have they been thorough? Surely that thing couldn't have just disappeared into thin air?"

Torrens was just as perplexed by the declaration. "As you saw on your feed, sir, the recon team has been stem to stern twice for the same result, sir."

"A thing that big couldn't be hiding, could it?" Freeman asked.

"I don't think so, sir," Torrens confirmed.

They'd all witnessed the horrific carnage below decks.

"Any crew survivors?"

"Not one, sir… it's like an abattoir down there and here on deck. So much so, I don't want to expose any more of my men to it."

The Zumwalt was pitching and rolling in the swell. It was so rough Torres had to hang onto the gunwale to prevent falling over.

"Agreed. We'll fly the ship's pilot in."

"Yes, sir, I suggest as quick as possible, the storm is nearly on us and it's getting rough. I don't know if the tether's going to hold."

"Colonel, have the Hawkbill surface, give them a hand to release the tether," Bruckmaster ordered.

The assault team was forced to take cover from the waves crashing over the gunwales of the Zumwalt. It was critical for their safety for the ship to face the oncoming swell as soon as possible. One big wave amidships could capsize her.

With gale-force winds whipping the ocean into a frenzy, from the deckhouse window, Torrens watched the Hawkbill surface at midships. Moments later, a Sikorsky HH-52 Seaguard, able to endure big winds, lowered a Naval ship's pilot onto the Zumwalt helipad. He would pilot the vessel back to its mooring in Neutral Bay.

A huge sigh of relief came from Torrens, the crew, and everyone in the operations centre.

"Mission accomplished," Bruckmaster blurted out, boastfully.

"Karzoff, can you have one of your drones show us the rift? Maybe with Gaap gone, it'll be gone as well," Freeman said.

"Maybe Alice succeeded, did you think of that?" the Professor posed.

"I don't think so, Professor," Bruckmaster growled. "It was good old U.S. military ingenuity that saved the day. I'll be decorated for this."

"If it was good old U.S. military ingenuity, then where is Gaap?" Vic countered.

"What if Gaap has possessed one of the tactical teams?" Viktoria posed.

Vic grasped his chin, "Hmm, what a dreadful thought... but it's possible."

"Are you serious?" Bruckmaster interjected.

"Monitor two, Colonel," Karzoff said.

They all looked at once, hoping not to see the arrow of time, but were disappointed. There was no change; the fiery column was still irradiating the northern sky.

"Damn!" the Brigadier cursed.

Alice adjusted his Graphene lenses to enhance his vision in the dark. First to UV, which showed nothing but pitch black, and then Infra-Red, which allowed him to spot a thin red line about six metres away from him.

"I've got no idea where we are, but I bet that's a door jamb. I'm getting used to this," he remarked.

He made his way towards the red line and was rewarded when he touched it; a door slid open to reveal a staircase going up. "Do you think we're back in the pyramid? What do you suppose that was all about? Did I kill Gaap in real time, or was it an illusion?" Al asked.

"My senses were indicating it was real, but I do not understand how we were transported onto the USS Zumwalt and back," Neit replied.

Al started ascending the stairs, which were illuminated by incandescent lighting. Arriving at a door on a landing, it opened at his touch. On the other side was a large, dimly lit square room. Three of its dark brown walls were decorated with bas-relief patterns and script. Alice ran his hand over the section just inside the door, feeling the raised text.

"It is ancient Sanskrit," Neit said.

"Can you read it?"

"Yes, it tells of the cosmic egg."

Alice immediately turned his attention to an incredible device on the end wall. It was a golden clock, elliptical in shape, resembling an egg, about three metres in diameter.

"A clock?" Alice questioned.

A circular rim encased the clock, adorned with strange symbols. Around the rim were an array of wheels, bolts, and levers.

"I wonder if it works?" Al muttered.

The hour hand of the clock was on twelve, and the minute hand on the 59th minute. Circular windows above the clock and on the two sides streamed a dull red light that illuminated the room.

"I don't get I t... a clock... that obviously doesn't work?" Al pondered.

"Alice, I get the impression this is not an ordinary clock but a computer."

"A computer?"

"Something to do with the cosmic egg."

He edged closer to the clock. "Will you look at that, there's a slit in it like the one at the entrance that got us into this joint. What if..." He took the Shine from around his neck and, studying it in the crimson light, mumbled, "I wonder?"

A shrug of his shoulders, and he slipped the Shine into the aperture. It fitted perfectly, but this time it didn't come back to him.

"Bloody thing ate it!" he protested. "Last time that happened, I had to do without my bloody credit card for a week." His joke turned sour when the strange circular rim surrounding the oval clock began to slowly rotate counter-clockwise.

"Whoa! Now it's working."

The minute hand on the clock clicked into place at midnight.

"The rim moving has Cuneiform numerology on it," said Neit. "What is your Chaldean number, Alice?"

"My ex-girlfriend Stain was into all that... um, let me think... twenty-one, I think."

The rim clunked when it stopped. It was aligned with the two clock hands on midnight.

Neit said, "Twenty-one... the sign of the Crown of Magi... that is what has locked into position at midnight."

Alice took a quick step backward when the sound of a servo erupted from the gadgetry around the clock.

"Something's going on..." Alice mumbled.

Four loud clunks reverberated throughout the cavernous room... unlocking sounds from metal cleats, one at each corner of the wall. Then, all fell silent.

As though driven by destiny, Alice approached the clock and opened the face. On the other side, he found something totally unexpected.

"It looks like a giant vagina," Neit said, amazed.

"You're not kidding."

"Is it alive?"

The red light streaming through the windows changed to yellow. Another servo sounded, and four clamps like retractors extended from the sides, fastened onto the lips of the giant labia, and then retracted, opening it.

"It must be the entrance to the world egg."

Alice peered into the opening. "There's something on the other side," he mumbled.

"You need to go through, Alice. There is nowhere else to go, and besides, with you having the Shine and the correct numerological number to open the clock face, I think it is preordained."

Alice parted the giant labia lips and slipped through.

Adamski, Honor, and Doctor Li had been eagerly waiting for the chopper to arrive at the new Zen HQ in Angel City. Bruno and his two comrades stepped out of the chopper and strode across the tarmac to meet them. Bruno handed Honor the device containing the chip.

"Well done. Adamski, check it," she said, handing it over.

With Doctor Li looking over his shoulder, the nervous Russian pressed a series of buttons on the handheld device and then beamed a tight-lipped smile. "It is the correct processor."

"Good. Were there any problems? Is the city deserted?" Honor asked.

"None, the city is deserted, the column of fire still burning in the north."

"Excellent," Honor said contentedly. It felt good to be on the winning side for a change.

"I need to get this to the lab to be replicated," Adamski said.

"How will you do that, Professor?" Doctor Li queried.

"I will 3-D print it. Provided things go to plan, you will have a copy within 24 hours."

Li was happy.

Honor looked the Doctor over, reminded that she had once swiped Zanza Kew from her, and wondered how such a skinny thing had attracted him.

While Honor was busy mentally assessing Doctor Li, who was doing the same of Honor, wondering what magic she possessed that made her so alluring to men, they were so caught up checking each other out that they failed to notice they had been left alone.

Bruckmaster met with Secta and Hope to request each member of the assault task force to be screened for demonic possession, fearing Gaap might have escaped through one of them.

"With respect, Brigadier, that's more a job for a priest," Secta reacted cynically.

Seeking to avoid any further tension, Hope chimed in to prevent a potential conflict. "All we could possibly do is scan the troops for evidence of neutrinos, the presence of which would flag interference from Gaap, possibly indicating possession... but it wouldn't be definitive."

The burly man accepted Hope's proposal, though he was clearly annoyed at Secta for surrendering the highly strategically valuable organic chip to Zen. Secta, however, couldn't care less and left the task of keeping the peace to his sister.

Hope turned to the brigadier and said, "I'll have Viktoria set it up. Arrange for them, without exception, to assemble at sickbay in two hours."

The Brigadier glanced at Colonel Freeman and ordered, "Colonel, make it so."

The Colonel nodded, but before leaving, he shot a sly glance at Hope, clearly attracted to her. Hope blushed at the gesture, and Secta noticed it as well, his face breaking into a knowing smirk.

"If that'll be all, Brigadier, I have work to do," Secta said brashly.

"We still have the rift to deal with," the Brigadier argued.

"That's better left for you and the Professor to discuss. It's more important for me to continue monitoring Kairos for Alice's sake. Are you alright with that, Vic?" Secta responded.

The Professor was deep in thought, staring at a monitor that displayed the view from a drone flyover of the rift. He looked up at Secta and said, "Yes, yes... you know the rift changed colour to yellow a moment ago, and then after a couple of minutes went back to red. Quite extraordinary."

"Hmm, I wonder what that indicates?" Secta questioned.

"Intervention from Alice, perhaps?" Vic posed.

"Let's not get ahead of ourselves here," Bruckmaster interjected.

Just then, the President entered the control room.

"Well done, gentlemen," he announced. "I understand the Zumwalt has been secured."

The Brigadier quickly got to his feet and crowed, "Yes, sir, our combined effort worked with exemplary efficiency."

CHAPTER 38
REDACTED

A N ORB WAS floating suspended in the air in the centre of the room. Alice recognised it immediately as similar to the En-Ki orb but with one significant difference; omitted from the top of it up and out through the apex in the ceiling radiated a dazzling red laser beam.

"It's the source of the arrow of time," Alice said in awe, the vivid red laser so bright it was reflected in his eyes. In fact, the entire room glowed red from it, only the orb was pulsing with a white light.

"This is an ancient place, Alice... older than time. It could even be where time began," Neit explained. "Do not approach the orb; I sense it is protected by a significantly dangerous force field."

Alice tore a button off his shirt and flicked it into the orb. A loud zap! and the plastic button instantly atomised in a flash of violent purple light. For a second, the event highlighted a three-metre diameter egg-shaped force field surrounding the orb.

Alice programmed his Graphene lenses for infrared, and it allowed him to clearly see the highly charged energy field surrounding the orb in an egg shape.

"I see what you mean. What are we supposed to do here?"

"I believe the orb is En-Lil."

"So, isn't he a person either?"

"You mean is he like En-Ki? Yes, it appears so. I would venture to say that En-Lil is a computer-generated being, artificial intelligence though sentient, in that he has consciousness."

"He must have had a physical form at some time or another," Alice pondered.

"I believe he has developed beyond physical form. I think you will need to remove him from within the protective shield to shut down the arrow of time."

While Alice was contemplating that, a person materialised in front of them. He was all too familiar to Alice; it was Nebuchadnezzar's evil wizard that Alice had killed in Jerusalem back in 587 B.C. Those ghastly features: a long thin dark evil face, a body bound with dark brown bandages like a mummy. A large bright red and blue Egyptian necklace around his chest and a waist-belt that harboured a large curved pearl-handled dagger and other grisly weapons. His hairless skull, face, and pointed ears all tattooed with demonic symbolism, eyes so fierce and otherworldly red, that he looked the epitome of evil.

"Zorlock!" Alice snarled.

"We meet again," his deep voice resonated like rolling thunder.

"Yeah, thrilled," Al crowed, cynically.

"Time for revenge."

"Yeah well, good luck with that," Al quipped.

That seemed to frustrate Zorlock, and he shape-shifted into Alice's mother. She was just how he remembered her when he was only seven. Her arms opened wide to embrace him. "Son, come let me hug you," she said warm and motherly.

"No, Alice, it would be fatal," Neit reminded him.

"No mum, you're dead." He didn't need reminding after the last encounter with her. He'd come too far to be deceived by any more chicanery.

Recognising Alice's rejection, she shape-shifted into Anu Seth.

"No, no, En-Lil, try again," Alice said scornfully. "You can't get me with your sick tricks. All this shape-shifting stuff is nothing more than cheap parlour tricks. These people are all dead, especially that mug."

Again, the image morphed, this time to the very familiar form of Gorrick.

"Ah, that's more like it... so I finally get to see the real you because you cloned all the Gorricks in your own image, didn't you?"

"It is only a hologram, Alice," Neit said.

"I know, I know," Alice said with angst. He was trying to buy time to think what to do. First, he needed to determine whether the hologram was of any danger to him.

"Why should I even talk to you, En-Lil, you're just a hologram?"

"So were you once... besides, that is abstract logic, Alice, with physical outcomes. Thoughts are abstract—you must know by now that humans are nothing more than chemical computers. Existence is not just a physical existence, it is an abstract existence."

"Yeah, yeah, yeah, it is what it is... anyhow, what's existence to you?" Alice snarled, trying to keep En-Lil distracted while still formulating a plan of attack.

"You ask what is existence? Is it the realm of non-physical reality? A higher plane, that was abstract existing before the big bang, that has always subsisted? Biological life strives for the knowledge to eventually understand that abstract existence. The core of your science is imagination in alliance with perceived honesty. But being honest without being imaginative results in flawed science, Alice. Being imaginative without being honest means you're being a poet. You seek the truth of life and then you die. You, biological life forms we created, mind you, will eventually obliterate yourselves."

"Tell someone who cares, En-Lil... here's something for you to ponder, at what point does a cup become a mug?"

En-Lil stared at Alice, confused. "What does that have to do with your self-destruction?"

"Simple, what does it matter when you want to annihilate us first anyway? Look, this is not the first philosophical rave you've tried to suck me into... mate, I honestly don't give a rat's arse about what you're saying. Just pull the plug on the rift and let's get on with it; if humanity wants to blow itself away, then so be it."

"You've already done that many times over."

"Yeah, yeah, I'm sure we have, now just cut the blag and agree to call it a day, will you?" Alice was getting pissed off.

"Neit," Alice asked mentally. "Is this hologram dangerous or what?"

"He is trying to distract you from the orb. I think you have got too close for comfort... he was gambling you would not make it this far. He is going to throw everything at you any second now... I can feel a massive energy surge building inside of him. Keep him distracted, while I get the orb for you. Get me closer to it so I can jump," Neit said urgently.

But Alice wasn't having any of that. "No way mate, that force field will kill you stone dead. There's just way too much light and power... you wouldn't survive it... there's gotta be another way."

"It is a risk I have to take, Alice; it is my destiny... it is the sole purpose of my journey with you."

"No Neit, that's just crap mate... not to bloody die... not on, mate," Alice argued mentally.

But his objection had been overruled. "You leave me no option, my friend," Neit said, resolutely.

Alice shivered as Neit slipped out of him. "No!" Alice growled.

En-Lil immediately reacted to seeing Neit. "Ah, so you have an Id as an accomplice... that explains why you have been so intelligent—not a human attribute at all," he said surprised. "And so how do you think the Id can help you?" he scoffed, condescendingly.

It was a standoff: Alice with Neit beside him and En-Lil blocking the passage to the orb.

"What are you going to do, Id jump into me, I think not," En-Lil growled angrily.

Before Alice could stop him, Neit ran straight through the Gorrick hologram at the orb and then dived into the force field, which immediately erupted. When he passed through the violently reacting barrier, he began to fluoresce inside of the egg.

Infrared vision allowed Alice to see Neit's body heating up inside the egg to a deadly temperature, and for the first time, he could distinguish Neit's physical features. They were human-like. His large wondrous eyes peered back at Alice, filled with sadness. Alice knew right then his friend was saying goodbye.

Gorrick raised his hands, clawed them chest-high, and let out an inhuman growl. Glowing energy was rising within him.

Alice figured he was about to physically explode.

When Neit grasped the orb with both hands, his entire body illuminated as though it had been struck by millions of volts of electricity. The inside of the egg erupted into a violent electrical maelstrom that consumed him.

Alice watched in horror, helpless while Neit's flesh was torn from his limbs by some kind of invisible force. He was witnessing his friend's torturous death, yet heroically, in terrible agony, Neit still managed somehow to throw the basketball-sized orb through the failing force field, to Alice.

Certain that Gorrick would detonate at any moment, Alice caught the orb and prepared to make a run for it. But he wasn't expecting what happened next... Gorrick dematerialised as though he'd been simply switched off.

With the orb in his hands, Alice watched Neit dissolve into vapour—gone, forever, and a part of Alice died right then along with his friend.

A loud whoosh came from the arrow of time retracting into the egg, which then collapsed into nothing. The only light remaining was from the orb held in his hands. Alice was alone in an empty room with a gut-wrenching sense of loss. He couldn't hold back the pain and let out a blood-curdling heavy metal scream. "Noooo!"

The glow from the orb began to intensify. The white light transformed into a glowing liquid plasma that, to his horror, surged out of the orb enveloping his hands, arms, and then his entire body.

He looked at his hands and body in shock... he was glowing. Then he felt the strangest feeling inside of his body. It was as though the light was changing something deep within him at a molecular level... it was altering his chemistry.

Then came a blinding flash of white light.

Alice was standing with the orb in his hands in a room facing another orb floating suspended above the floor. The feeling in the room was way different from where he had been. Instead of evil, he felt purity.

"I have been expecting you, Alice."

The ubiquitous voice was so familiar to him. "En-Ki?"

"Place the orb above my orb."

With his body no longer glowing, only the orb, Alice walked over and did as requested. When he released the orb above the other one, it remained suspended. He stepped back. The two orbs glowed brighter and brighter until they melded into one glowing orb.

There was a blinding flash of white light.

Secta looked up sharply from the console when Kairos fired up in the advent room. Excited, he called out, "Hope, Vic, it must be Alice!"

Curled up in their chairs asleep, they woke with a start, jumped up, and half-awake, joined Secta at the window.

Alice stepped out of Kairos and immediately collapsed. That snapped them out of it.

"Quick!" said Secta.

Hope was through the pressurised doors in a flash and, together with Vic and Secta, they manhandled Alice into the control room. He was out cold. Hope checked his vitals.

"Not good, his pulse rate is poor." She forced open an eyelid and shined a pen light in his pupil to check dilation.

"What do you think?" Secta asked.

"I don't know what to think. If any of us had gone through the sort of stress he's endured, we'd be down and out for the count with PTSD for the next fifty years. I need to get him to sickbay quick smart," Hope said worriedly.

"I'll get a gurney," Vic said and darted out.

"He'll need magnetic resonance venography; there's no telling what extreme effects he's endured," Hope said.

Within minutes, Vic returned with the gurney, which they gently lifted Alice onto.

"The place is deserted out there," Vic said conversationally.

With concern for Alice showing on her face, Hope reported worriedly, "I'll need your help to get him to the MRV."

Secta pulled a phone and dialled. "Mal must be asleep... what time is it?"

"4:45 a.m.," Hope said.

It answered. "Mal... Alice is back. Can you go to your window and check the rift?" Secta asked.

"Sure thing," Mal said tiredly.

Secta mentally tracked Mal getting up from the lounge where he'd been sleeping and making his way to the north-facing window in his office.

"Nothing... it has gone!" Mal said with tears of joy and relief in his tired bloodshot eyes. "He bloody-well did it, mate! How is he? Put him on."

"Not good Mal, he's unconscious. We're taking him to sickbay for tests."

"I'll meet you there... he's going to be all right, isn't he?" Mal questioned, a tremor of anxiety in his voice.

"We don't know, he's been through a hell of a lot," Secta said optimistically.

Two hours later, the scientists were in Hope's office with test results to analyse. Mal came in carrying a tray of cups.

"No one would believe we've got the President of the country serving us our morning coffees," Vic said jokingly.

They respected the humility of the man. Mal had never placed himself above anyone else, always a humble man. He handed out the coffees, keeping one for himself, and then took a seat in the lounge setting. "Tests show anything?" Mal inquired.

"Yes, in fact, they did. It's difficult to determine the effects of it, but Al's genome has been redacted or hacked," Hope said.

"Hacked, like a computer?" Mal asked, confused by the term.

"One's DNA is not unlike code, Mal. We are, after all, chemical robots," Secta clarified.

"That's one way of looking at it, but what we can say is that his genes on a molecular level have been altered... it's referred to as Cas9 gene editing," Vic explained.

"Technically, Cas9 is an RNA-guided DNA enzyme that is clustered regularly interspaced in short palindromic repeats."

"English, please, Secta," Mal said.

"Sorry, Cas9 is a protein that can be utilised in genome engineering to induce double-strand breaks in DNA. The breaks can lead to changes in DNA behaviour... and in Alice's case, these changes would be out of the norm," Secta explained more clearly.

"So, you're saying Al's DNA has been altered but we don't know yet what affect this will have on him. Is that right?" Mal questioned.

"Correct," Vic confirmed.

"How could it have happened? Part of the teleportation?" asked Mal.

"We don't know yet," Hope said.

Nodding his head slowly but positively, Mal asked, "I suppose the most important question is; will he recover?"

"As far as the alteration to his genes... no, what's done is done. As for his wellbeing, the simple answer to that is—" Vic pulled up short of answering.

"We just don't know, Mal," Hope finished for him.

"Is this genetic alteration artificial?" Mal queried.

"Good question... we don't think so, but it does seem to be more of an enhancement than degenerative," Secta explained.

"So, it could be an enhancement to his existing abilities or senses?"

The three scientists exchanged looks of irresolution. Hope explained, "We hope so, Mal, but we won't know until he regains consciousness."

CHAPTER 39
LEX TALIONIS

BRIGADIER BRUCKMASTER WASN'T impressed when Colonel Freeman reported that the rift shutting down had been no coincidence.

"You seriously expect me to believe this guy Black Alice shut the goddamned thing down?" Bruckmaster roared indignantly.

"Yes, sir, it had nothing to do with us," Freeman said.

"Well, there's one way to check that... what happened with all the other rift sites around the world?" the Brigadier snapped.

"See for yourself, sir." Freeman pressed a remote, and a large monitor displayed a Mercator global projection showing all of the known rift hotspots. Each was marked with an X. "The X means the alert has been reduced from code red to zero, sir."

"What, all at once?" Bruckmaster snarled.

"Yes, sir, fifteen minutes prior to the arrival of Black Alice through Kairos."

Bruckmaster flopped into a chair flabbergasted. They'd had little sleep over the past few days, and their nerves were frayed, and this revelation had him even more irritated. He shoved his face in his hands and groaned.

A wry smile cracked on Freeman's face; he enjoyed seeing the Brigadier suffering being wrong for a change.

"Our President is currently on the horn with the Aussie President, sir. I expect we'll be hearing from her next," Freeman said smugly.

Bull was obdurate and let out another disgruntled groan. Having to admit to the President of the United States that he'd been wrong all along about Black Alice was way out of character for him. The phone rang. Bull looked up from his hands at Freeman, who raised his eyebrows knowingly. It would be the President, and Bull would have to eat humble pie.

Freeman thought it was terrific. He picked up the hands-free phone and then handed it over to the Brigadier.

"Madam President. Yes, it seems so. Yes, I will seek an audience with the man. I beg your pardon, Madam President... but—" His face had morphed from belligerent to dutiful. "Yes, I will, thank you, madam President." He put down the phone. "We've been ordered to meet this Black Alice character to advise him he will be honoured with the U.S. Presidential Medal of Freedom." He coughed after saying the words as they'd stuck in his throat. The decoration he was expecting for saving the USS Zumwalt now seemed unlikely.

"That might take a while, sir. He collapsed when he arrived back and is still unconscious," Freeman reported.

"Is it critical?"

"I believe so."

Gorrick was watching the break of dawn from his penthouse office window. The huge room was now furnished, though Spartanly. With his arms folded in front of him, almost defensively, a cold feeling had overcome him hours before dawn. It was as if the old saying had come true, as though someone had walked on his grave. But he knew better than that. He knew that what had died inside of him was the connection to his master, his creator: En-Lil. It meant he and the surviving Gorrick clones around the globe would now be without the guidance of their divine spiritual patriarch in their war against humanity. Gorrick needed to be strong. As soon as he felt the loss, he'd used the hive link to contact all of the other clones. There was an absolute consensus to continue the fight.

Regina Fysh brought Gorrick a coffee. "Sir, the morning news said the rift has been shut down. It is expected the President will lift the curfew in twenty-four hours for people to begin returning to Sydney."

Gorrick turned from the six-metre-high windows and took the mug of coffee from his secretary. "Get me Doctor Li, Professor Adamski, and Honor, ASAP."

"Yes, sir," the demure, elegantly dressed woman purred before breezing across the room to the door. The sound of her high heels on the tiled floor resounded in the cavernous space.

Gorrick went to the lounge setting and took a seat in a comfy lounge chair.

"Computer, activate coffee table." The glass top of the table transformed into a touch screen computer. The display on the screen confirmed what he already knew. All of the rifts around the world had shut down. He shook his head and muttered begrudgingly, "Black Alice." His nemesis had again won the battle and it irked him seriously. Not only had Alice shut down all of the rifts, but he'd also vanquished En-Lil, his father, whom he and the others believed to be immortal. For that alone, Gorrick and his cloned brothers were sworn to exact revenge. It was now imperative that Black Alice be eliminated at any cost.

Honor was the first to arrive at reception. In her characteristic conceited fashion, she breezed past Regina Fysh without even acknowledging her and pushed open the penthouse doors. Miss Fysh raised a scornful eyebrow at her arrogant manner. Following her was Doctor Li, who acted in the same way. Then came Professor Adamski, who was the opposite; overtly friendly, self-conscious, and awkward.

Gorrick waited for them to be seated.

"I expect you've heard the news? If not... the rift has been shut down. That's right, once again Black Alice has obstructed us. So, full concentration of our resources will go into eliminating him; the enemy. Do I make myself clear?"

Adamski half raised his hand nervously for permission to speak.

"Yes, Professor?" Gorrick said, laconically.

"Sir, why do we not simply hit Oceana HQ with a dirty bomb... it would—"

Honor cut him off. "Don't be ridiculous, Adamski. The underneath of Oceana is like a rabbit warren of fallout shelters, it would take more than even an A-bomb to touch them. No, we need to be much smarter than that."

Gorrick stood and with his hands folded behind his back, circled the lounge setting.

"While Sydney remains evacuated, we have a window of opportunity that is rapidly closing. We already know only the highest-ranking officials remained at Oceana, and they present a viable target." He stopped, faced Honor, and eyeballed her. "Honor, who would still be there?"

She thought for a moment, enjoying being depended on.

"I expect the President, the department heads of OTT, Karzoff, and Viktoria, Black Alice, and a modest security compliment."

"Good, then how can we confirm Black Alice is there?" Gorrick asked.

"We could overfly the building with a powerful listening device," Adamski suggested.

"No, the building has a transmission damper," Honor said dismissively.

Gorrick kept his unblinking eyes fixed on her. "In one of your reports on Oceana, particularly Black Alice, you mentioned he is fitted with an implant."

"Of course, we can scan for his implant signal," Honor said, with a smug grin.

"Is the frequency unique? Do you know it?" Adamski questioned.

"It is totally unique, and yes, it oscillates, but the core frequency is VHF 370 Megahertz, if I remember correctly."

Gorrick changed his stare to Adamski. "Can we isolate that frequency, Professor?"

"If he is the only person fitted with such a device using that frequency, then yes, I can."

"He is the only one of that I am certain," Honor barked confidently.

"Good, I need a drone to overfly Oceana to scan for it," Gorrick ordered.

"The only problem would be if he is deep inside the shelter section, say at the Kairos control centre or in the fallout shelter where the signal would be faint," Adamski said.

Honor was grinning.

"Why are you so amused, Honor?" Gorrick queried.

"The grin factor is a measurement of my mirth, sir. I believe we have now discovered the key to ridding the world of Black Alice. So simple… why had we not thought of it before?"

"Sometimes necessity is the mother of invention," Gorrick said, anecdotally. "And to that end, once we have his coordinates and can track him to a vulnerable position, how then do we dispense with him?"

A military task force, kitted out in full hazmat suits and equipped with breathing apparatus, had been airlifted by helicopter to The Lair to secure the location now that the rift had vanished. They reported no residual radiation and no signs of the rift, although the interior damage to the house was substantial.

All of the personnel from the USS Zumwalt mission had undergone screening at Oceana, and no signs of possession had been detected. The only remaining duties for Brigadier Bruckmaster and Colonel Freeman were to bring the fallen home, organise a replacement crew to navigate the USS Zumwalt to the San Diego U.S. Naval base, and to arrange a meeting with Black Alice. With everything else settled, they were awaiting updates on Alice's condition.

With the CT scanning of troops, the day had rushed by for Secta, Hope, and the Professor. Mal was paying them a visit in the ground-floor sickbay as they were unwinding after such an early start.

"You guys look shattered," Mal observed.

Sprawled out on a couch, the Professor glanced up at Mal and grumbled, "I feel more like a patient than a medic."

Hope was curled up, fast asleep in an armchair. Secta was scrutinising an iPad, alert but appearing physically dishevelled. He set down the iPad and greeted Mal with a smile, indicating Hope. "She's done most of the heavy lifting."

Mal lowered his voice to a whisper, "How's Al?"

"Still hasn't come around. I'm eager to hear what happened."

"You're not alone there... have you checked if Neit is with him?" Mal queried.

Hope stirred, groaned, and squinted up at Mal through one eye. "Hi Mal."

"So, you're not dead then?" he quipped.

She yawned, "No, just a zombie."

"You'll all sleep well tonight."

"I don't think so, Mal. I won't be going anywhere until Al's out of danger," Hope stated sombrely. "And no, there was no sign of Neit."

"When are you lifting the curfew, Mal?" Secta asked.

"I'll announce it tomorrow morning, provided I get a clear signal from everyone."

The Professor sat upright. "Best to avoid town tomorrow then; the traffic will be mayhem."

Just then, Karzoff and Viktoria entered through the doors.

"Hi guys," Mal greeted them cheerily.

"We've just come from the bookends... Brigadier know-it-all and Colonel do-it-all."

Mal chuckled in agreement with Viktoria's jest.

"They are growing anxious. Apparently, the U.S. President has ordered them to meet with Alice, and they cannot leave until it is done," Karzoff elucidated.

"Yes, they're to officially inform Alice that he's to receive the Presidential Medal of Freedom. Quite a prestigious honour: the nation's highest civilian award," Mal declared proudly.

"Wow, I wonder how Alice will react to that?" Karzoff speculated.

"Water off a duck's back, I reckon," Secta quipped, with a cynical little chuckle.

"Don't you approve of our guests, Secta?" Mal queried.

"I don't have much time for Bruckmaster," Secta confessed.

"Hear, hear," the Professor chimed in.

The wrist monitor Hope was wearing beeped. She quickly sat upright. "It's Al; he's conscious!"

They wasted no time in reaching his room, where they found him awake but bewildered by all the medical apparatus attached to his body.

Hope was the first to approach him. She peered into his eyes to assess his condition. "Al, are you with us?" she asked, offering a doctor's smile, before removing the tube from his mouth to enable him to speak.

Alice coughed once the tube was removed. "Get all this nonsense off me, will you, Hope?"

Hope began to disconnect all the now redundant monitoring and life support equipment.

Mal approached closer. "Al... we thought you'd cashed in your chips, mate."

"Nah, few more songs in me yet, mate... a couple more gigs to pull off," he grinned, in typical Alice fashion.

Even though Hope ordered Alice to remain in the hospital bed overnight, he was well enough over the next two hours to give a full account of the mission. They were all deeply moved by his description of Neit's horrific death.

The report raised more questions than it answered regarding En-Lil, Gorrick, Zen, and En-Ki, but they set it all aside until Alice had fully recovered. For now, Hope wasn't convinced about the side effects of the Cas9 gene mutation.

"So, have all the rifts shut down?" Alice asked.

"Yes, all at once and without repercussions. You did it, mate," Mal declared proudly.

"Shall I bring the bookends in for a quick visit, sir?" Karzoff asked.

Mal turned from Alice to Karzoff, "Yes, but limit the visit to five minutes."

Karzoff nodded and then went to fetch them.

A few minutes later, he returned with the three officers, donned in full military dress uniform. The others stepped back from the bed, allowing Mal to make the introductions.

"Alice, this is Brigadier Bruckmaster, the man in charge of the U.S. team that has been working with us here."

Alice reached up to shake hands.

"Brigadier."

"Call me Bull, Al..." he straightened to attention and declared, "The people of the United States of America and the rest of the world can't thank you enough for your bravery in halting the hostile attack on our planet. For such valour, I have been commanded by the President of the United States of America to inform you that you are to be honoured with the Presidential Medal of Freedom. Congratulations, son."

"Yeah, thanks," Alice retorted sarcastically, not one for accolades.

Sensing Alice's aversion to military formalities, Freeman stepped past Bull and offered his hand to Alice. "You're a credit to your country and to the human race, thank you, sir."

Alice nodded, more accepting of the Colonel.

Next to approach was Major Torrens, who bore noticeable facial cuts and bruises.

Freeman introduced him, "This is Major Torrens... he led the task force in the operation aboard the USS Zumwalt."

"I heard you killed that creature, Gaap... I fought it... a formidable opponent. You're a legend, sir."

"Too right he was, mate... yeah, I fought him, a legend no... I might have killed the brute, but it cost the life of my friend, Neit."

"I'm sorry, sir," Torrens expressed, genuinely remorseful.

"Who's this Neit guy? This is the first I've heard of him," Bull looked around with a clueless expression, realising he'd been excluded from certain information. "Does he deserve a medal as well, or what?" he queried, like a complete boofhead.

CHAPTER 40
LOST HOPE

" THERE HAS BEEN a drone flyover," Karzoff said, looking up at Viktoria from his wristwatch monitor.

"Just now?" she asked.

"Yes. It must be Zen, there was no ID signature."

"What are they up to now?"

"Hard to say, but I suspect reconnaissance. I have put a track on the drone, but it probably returned to a vehicle parked in the woods somewhere, making it too tough to find and seize."

Viktoria was deep in thought. "It could only have been taking a spy footage or eavesdropping."

"What concerns me is why now?" Karzoff muttered, pondering. "Unless—"

"Unless what?"

"What if they know Alice shut down the rift? What if they know he killed En-Lil?"

"You'd have to expect Gorrick would know that, wouldn't he?"

"What if he wants revenge?" Karzoff posed.

"Do you think the drone has something to do that?"

"It could be. But I have no idea how?"

Alice was sitting up in bed, pretty much back to normal. Hope was in a chair beside him.

"Stop being so grumpy, if the tests are clear you can get up tomorrow," she said, half joking.

"Damn tests, I feel like a bloody pin cushion... you've taken so much blood you've sapped all my energy... bloody vampire."

Hope chuckled, "Just chill Al. Are you hungry?"

"Yeah," he moaned. "I could eat the horse and chase the rider."

She beamed him a big smile. "That sounds more like the old Al. The place is empty, bar us, evacuated... but I might be able to rustle something up for you from the canteen. What do you feel like?"

"I could murder a hamburger," he said, bearing his teeth like a vicious predator and growling.

Hope got up smiling. "I'd better see what I can scrounge up before you attack me."

"Now that sounds like a good idea," he said, cheekily.

She ambled over to him, bent down, and gave him a gentle peck on the cheek.

"That's no kiss," he complained, reached up, grabbed her chin, and pulled her towards him. They kissed passionately. Holding him tight after the kiss with tears welling up in her eyes, her voice broke as she admitted, "I didn't think you were coming back..."

He touched the tear traversing her cheek and said warmly, "Hey, I promised I'd be back, besides you never finished what you were saying last time I was in hospital."

They locked eyes, and a special moment passed between them. "I think I love—"

He quickly placed his finger on her lips to stop the words coming out. "Shush, I know, I know... some things are safer left unsaid."

She sniffled, nodded emotionally, and then gave him a gentle peck on the lips. Though she would have preferred to have told him, she understood that it might not be the right moment.

She left him with a moral dilemma, should I have told her I love her? Alice battled with it for a moment and then decided, yes you idiot, tell her, it's about time you stopped hiding from love. I will, I will, he answered himself. I'll tell her when she comes back. The argument with himself was over. A smile broke on his tired face, happy to have finally made up his mind. She might be the academic type, not exactly the style of babe Alice would fall for, but there had always been a special chemistry between them, and that seemed to have blossomed of late.

Mal was treating Bruckmaster and the Colonel to a single malt whiskey in the presidential suite when Secta came in.

"Ah, Secta, care for a whiskey?" Mal asked.

"No thanks, don't drink. You wanted to speak with me?"

Mal detected in his tone that Secta wasn't happy in the presence of the Brigadier. He knew Secta had no time for Bull's arrogant, pigheaded manner.

"How's the patient?" Mal asked, trying to diffuse the tension... at the same time gesturing for him to sit with them. It worked... Secta relaxed a little and took a seat.

"He's back to himself but will need to remain bedbound until Hope gives him the all clear."

Reclining with his legs crossed, a glass of Scotch in hand, the Brigadier piped up. "Secta, I've been meaning to ask, did you get to protect the chip you gave Zen from being used against us?"

Secta was expecting the question though not from the Brigadier. He chose to refer his answer to the President. "We didn't have much time to come up with a perfect solution, but in saying that, we tried something."

"And what was that?" Mal asked.

"HSV 2," Secta said.

"Isn't that genital herpes?" Mal asked.

"Herpes?" The Brigadier repeated, sitting forward in his chair, almost choking on his drink.

"Yes, the Professor has the virus, so we isolated it from his blood sample, and because the chip is organic, we were able to infect it," Secta explained.

"But doesn't the virus only affect humans?" asked Mal.

"No, it can be sexually transmitted to animals, and the organic chip is, after all, an animal."

"So, the chip will grow warts?" Mal asked, amused by the concept.

"In effect, yes, over time, and that will cause malfunction," Secta concluded.

"My namesake... well done," Mal said, emphatically. Though it was an in-joke that only Secta recognised and chuckled at the witticism.

"You're saying the chip is diseased?" the Brigadier sought to substantiate.

"Effectively yes, Brigadier, it is diseased," Secta confirmed, a little smugly.

The lone guard stationed at the ground floor entrance to Oceana HQ failed to notice the single red dot from a Trijicon RNR on his forehead. An Osprey silencer dampened the sound of the FNX 45 tactical fifteen-shot pistol firing. The tall uniformed man's knees buckled, and he went down like a sack of potatoes.

Bruno stepped out from a recess to signal his two confederates that the coast was clear. They approached the secure doors to the upper floors, preferring to take the stairs instead of the elevator for a safer route. Bruno pressed a small device against the security module. Adamski had provided the digital device that could crack any security code for safe access in seconds. A green light flashed on it, followed by a click, signalling that the door was open. Bruno checked another device, this one on his wrist. It had located the VHF370 Megahertz signal of Alice's implant, triangulated it, and provided a map to the target, just a few doors along the corridor in the sickbay. They were outside the canteen.

Hope had managed to rustle up a burger and a coffee for Alice. Balancing it on a tray, she was just leaving the canteen when a gunman in black coveralls stopped her. With his pistol aimed at her head, he demanded, "Where are you taking the food?"

She immediately recognised him as the Zen agent who had delivered Rita Vallins in the chopper but kept it to herself.

"Dinner for me, why?"

"Then why aren't you eating it in the canteen?" Bruno asked.

"Too lonely, I'd rather eat in the nurse's room."

Bruno didn't buy it and pistol-whipped her across the face. The tray went sprawling, and she went down on one knee, seeing flying stars and fighting to stay conscious, a deep gash open on her cheek. Bruno grabbed her golden ponytail savagely and dragged her along the corridor towards the sickbay.

"Open your mouth, and I'll put a bullet in it!" he snarled, in a harsh whisper.

Hope knew the big brute meant business and could do nothing other than acquiesce.

Bruno pushed her into Alice's room ahead of him, with his arm wrapped around her throat and the silencer on his pistol barrel pressed hard against her right temple.

Alice sat up sharply in bed. He noted the dark shadows of two more men behind Hope's assailant in the doorway.

"Get out of bed," Bruno ordered.

Alice obeyed.

"Keep your hands where I can see them... up!"

He was speaking hurriedly, conscious of security guards.

"What do you want?" Al snarled.

Bruno returned serve with interest. "Shut up, or I'll drill the bitch."

"Let her go and take me."

"How heroic," Bruno snarled. He turned the gun on Alice and shot him in the right bicep. Alice reeled backward onto the bed.

Hope grimaced and squealed, "No!"

"Get up, tough guy, get up!" Bruno shouted, determined not to fail like all the previous Zen agents.

Hope's eyes were open wide with fear, her heart pounding ten to the dozen. She grappled with Bruno's grip but to no avail. "Stop it! Stop it!" she shouted, bordering on hysterical.

His hand covering the wound with blood spurting through his fingers, Alice took a deep breath and struggled back to his feet. With his right arm hung limply by his side, blood dripping from the fingertips, he knew any chance of him putting up a fight was over.

Bruno aimed the gun at Alice's left bicep and fired again. This time Alice absorbed the shot, rocking backward but remaining stoic.

Hope mule-kicked upwards into Bruno's crotch, and her boot found the mark. The agonising pain in both arms prevented Alice from taking advantage of Hope's valiant effort. Bruno recovered quickly and then pressed the pistol harder against Hope's temple. Her teary eyes met Alice's, reminding him of Neit's departing glance. Then, like a rolling crash of thunder, he realised what was going to happen, and he let out a powerful scream, "Noooo!"

Bruno fired. The bullet entered Hope's right temple. She slumped in his grip and, with her lifeless eyes still on Alice, she dropped to the ground, dead.

Hatred surged through Alice like a firebolt, permeating his body and triggering a reaction deep within him. His physical form began to transform, growing in musculature.

Bruno couldn't believe his eyes... Alice was morphing right in front of him into something monstrous. In defence, he fired two more shots into him. At less than ten metres away, the grouping was deadly accurate; he'd aimed at Alice's heart. But Alice could see the bullets coming at him as if in slow motion and leaned sideways to dodge them.

With blood still gushing from the wounds in both arms, Alice stood his ground, still growing in stature, screaming in agony... not from the wounds but from his body altering its state. He leaned forward, flexing his muscles as though doing an abdominal and thigh pose. The veins on his skin pumped and bulged, the muscles enlarged to such an extent they burst through the seams of his hospital gown. Then, he felt an innate urge to flex even harder... more veins bulged in his neck and forehead. Grimacing, he squeezed the muscles around the bullets lodged in his biceps and let out a raucous roar, pushing, squeezing, flexing... then, the slugs miraculously popped out of the wounds and bounced on the floor. The bleeding stopped, and the bullet holes instantly healed over.

Bruno couldn't believe what he was witnessing.

Twenty centimetres taller and with double the body musculature, Alice had morphed into a monster. Bruno backed into the corridor, freaked out... he didn't even have time to peel off another shot because Alice came charging at him like a stampeding rhino. Bruno's two sidekicks closed ranks in the doorway. Alice hit the first one with a lightning-fast power punch to the throat that snapped his C1 vertebra with a loud crack. He then whipped around to the second guy and bashed his face to a pulp with a barrage of jackhammer punches that could've fractured concrete. The second man dropped lifeless to the floor, pulverised beyond recognition. Bruno was next.

"Come on, you bludger!" Al snarled, his voice hoarse, venomous, different. His eyes glazed over with hatred.

Karzoff and Viktoria arrived at speed and stopped dead in their tracks. They had been alerted to the slaying of the entrance guard and had tracked the intruders. They couldn't believe what they were seeing.

"Is that Alice?" Karzoff muttered, barely recognising him with such a Herculean build.

Bruno pulled a smug face and raised his pistol to shoot Alice in the face, but like greased lightning, able to anticipate his every move, Alice grabbed his gun hand and with an almighty wrench tore the arm out of his shoulder joint. Then, wheeling the limb with its bloody jagged end, he beat Bruno to the ground with it. The Russian had no answer to the ferocity of Alice's onslaught and couldn't retaliate.

Alice irreverently cast the arm aside, whipped an arm around Bruno's throat, and then with one almighty yank wrenched his head clean off his shoulders. Bruno's headless body fell onto the floor. Alice stood over him, holding the severed head like a trophy.

It was a sight Karzoff and Viktoria would never, ever forget; their mouths were gaping in frozen terror, totally gobsmacked.

Alice dumped the head and then stormed past Karzoff and Viktoria back into the sickbay. Seconds later, to Karzoff's surprise, Alice returned with a body in his arms. He immediately noted that Alice's physical form had reverted to normal, and then the realisation struck them like a hammer: the bloody mess in Alice's arms was Hope, and she was dead.

It was the first time any of them had ever seen Secta break down. The news of his sister's tragic death devastated him. None of them were able to fully release their response to the trauma of losing Hope.

"I left Viktoria with Alice in the sickbay. He is understandably distraught," Karzoff told Mal.

The Professor was sitting beside Secta in the Presidential office with his arm around his shoulders, both of them sobbing.

Mal was physically shaken. "This... this superhuman change in Al, is it due to the gene mutation?" Mal threw out, banking on an answer.

The Professor offered one with a quiver in his voice. "There's no other logical explanation, Mal."

It was close to midnight. Gorrick was standing at his office windows, staring at the full moon. "How could this have happened?

He was in a hospital bed, half dead?" Gorrick growled so loudly it resonated like thunder throughout the large office space.

The bellowing caused Honor to shudder. Abused as a child by a truculent, molesting father, her mind became scrambled whenever she was shouted at. Sitting alone on the lounge, she began nervously wringing her hands. "Sir, you need to see the footage from Bruno's lapel camera. It—"

Gorrick turned sharply to face her, hostility burning in his eyes. "Argh!" He growled gruffly and then strode towards her. His rapid approach caused her to twitch. "I gave you free rein to select a crack team… this is not the first time, but each time your team has failed. What is it with you people?"

He stopped at the coffee table, considering her request, knowing it was logical to view the footage. "Play it," he ordered, brusquely.

Honor quickly, nervously, synchronised her wrist monitor to the computer and played the footage.

CHAPTER 41
BURNING QUESTION

T HE NEWS BROADCAST revolved around the impending war in the Middle East, a result of the escalating, perpetual conflict between Israel and Iran. Further west, there was emerging border tension between Pakistan and India, and even further north, Russia and Turkey engaged in their own chest-thumping display. For Mal, not a day seemed to pass without some sort of human conflict erupting somewhere on the globe. Aggravated by the relentless negativity, he shut off the television.

"An avalanche of negativity. The world should've revealed the truth about these rifts rather than concealing it. At least that could've provided a diversion from the constant violence!"

"When will the hostilities ever cease?"

"I can't answer that, Karzoff, all I can say is that the majority of these issues are either due to imbeciles leading nations or religious differences... in any case, greed is at the root of all evil."

"It makes our battle with Zen appear almost insignificant," Viktoria chimed in.

Leaning forward in his chair, Mal took a sip of his coffee and remarked, "If it weren't for the countless cups of coffee tonight, I'd be doing a Rip Van Winkle."

At midnight, all three of them looked visibly exhausted.

"Mal, I believe Alice will react poorly to this," Karzoff suggested.

"Yes, I expect you're correct. He won't take Hope's murder lightly," Mal retorted.

"There's a wealth of history between them. The last thing I heard when I left him with Secta and the Professor, they were arguing about Alice wanting to leap back in time to prevent Hope's murder," Viktoria informed.

"Is that possible?" Mal questioned.

"Secta said no... something about having two versions of the same person at the same place in time. Apparently, one cancels the other out, and both could potentially vanish."

"I suppose that makes sense... I wonder where they'd end up?" Mal mused, his brow furrowed.

Finding the implications of the quantum mechanics debate too perplexing, they steered the conversation towards more straightforward territory.

"So, we can anticipate Alice seeking revenge."

"Yes, Karzoff, you can bet your house on it. Let's find out before it becomes a foregone conclusion," Mal said, picking up his mobile from the coffee table and texting Secta. "One never knows how our comrades will respond when grief overwhelms logic... it can lead to irrational actions."

Before he could send the text, Alice, Secta, and the Professor walked in, their faces solemn.

"I was just texting you, Secta. Sit down, guys, fancy a coffee?"

"No, Mal," Alice replied curtly. The trio remained standing. "We've discussed how to handle this, and I'm going in to get Gorrick."

Mal was taken aback. "By your confrontational demeanour, Al, I don't understand why you're seeking my counsel; it appears you've already made up your mind."

"We can't let this slide, Mal," Secta asserted sternly. "Not only was she my kin, but Hope was also an essential member of our team... irreplaceable."

The Professor chimed in. "It was a premeditated assassination, Mal."

"I understand that your emotions are running high, but we need to deliberate on this, maintain our composure. I, I can't endorse the elimination of a public figure, guys, you understand that."

"You don't need to bloody sanction anything, Mal. We're only informing you out of obligation," Alice snarled.

"So, it's a done deal? Don't you understand that by informing me, you've already implicated me?" Mal countered forcefully.

It had been ages since Alice and Mal had locked horns. The last conflict had resulted in a physical altercation, ironically over Hope.

"Ever since the brawl on the ferry over her, you've been carrying a grudge, haven't you, Function?" Alice scoffed.

"You've got that completely wrong, Al. You don't know what you're saying, mate—"

"I know what I'm bloody saying. We're squandering time standing around here like clueless cows debating this—"

"I can't endorse it, Al, it's against everything this office represents," Mal growled.

"Gorrick is malevolent and needs to be neutralised. He ordered the hit!" Alice shouted.

Mal rose to his feet, retorting with a raised finger. "Who do you think you are, passing a death sentence because you believe he's evil? Huh? This is the very reason there are wars all over this damned planet."

"Me, Mal... me, the bloke who's battled bloody demons, monsters, you name it, mate. Megalomaniacs and cyborgs, battled the lot!... Each time, a fight to protect the likes of you and Hope. But no matter how many bloody battles I fight... no matter how many bloody victories I secure, while Gorrick clones persist on this damned planet, they will continue to execute En-Lil's evil bidding by ordering the assassination of innocents like Hope and our former president! Evil will continue to flourish... the buck has to stop somewhere, so it stops with me, Mal. Can't you comprehend that? You're quite content to have me fight and kill the enemy, but you draw the line at Gorrick... why is that, mate? Tell me? Why Gorrick?"

"Because he's entangled in too many influential spheres, that's why. His public exposure..." Mal said, dispiritedly.

"You, Mal... playing politics? Never thought I'd see the day," Alice snarled, locking eyes with his old friend.

Mal slumped back into his chair and despondently buried his head in his hands, humiliated.

"Tell me the truth, Mal," Alice said, calmly yet firmly.

Mal looked up over his hands and sighed. "Alright, alright," he conceded. "The U.S. President has asked me to lay off Zen and to let the CIA deal with them."

Alice slapped his forehead with his hand and then flung both hands in the air. "So, what, now we're subject to a government that couldn't even reclaim their hijacked ship without our assistance? You've sold out, mate. The CIA can't handle Gorrick here or anywhere else. How will they prevent him from sending someone to murder Secta... you... me... the professor, when we least expect it? Hmm? Is that any way to live?"

"You know he's correct, Mal. I understand the U.S. intelligence mandate better than you; they'll only look after their own," the Professor stated, resolutely.

"We know the Gorrick we have here is an alpha Gorrick. We have unravelled the international Zen hierarchy to discover that. We must eliminate him; there's no telling what he's planning next. He wants Alice dead, that much is clear," Karzoff chimed in, emotionally.

"So, the question is; are you willing to trust incompetents like Bruckmaster to keep Alice safe?" Secta asked, filled with tension.

Mal realised he was cornered. Though they'd ganged up on him, they were right... he was wrong. "You're right. OTT must remain independent of political interference... even from me, and if that means it having a licence to kill, then so be it," he declared.

They were in agreement.

"Then you, Mal, in the same way as us, must swear to secrecy," Alice stated firmly.

Mal met Alice's gaze, then said respectfully, "I concur."

Alice swayed, Mal sprang up and caught him by the arm. "You alright, Al?"

"Just need some rest," he grumbled.

"Karzoff, you and Viktoria escort him to the quarters below where he'll be safe," Mal instructed.

They assisted Alice out of the room.

Once they'd left, Mal asked, "Tell me, Secta, what did Hope's death mean to him?"

"Everything."

"What do you think he would do to avenge it?"

"Anything."

Mal pondered over his response before posing, "Are we certain he's rational? Does he have mastery over this extraordinary ability he now seemingly possesses?" Mal implored.

Bearing visible signs of fatigue from insomnia and the emotional distress of his sister's death, Secta stabilised himself with a hand on the chair's back. "I'm not faring too well myself, Mal. I regret this had to unfold this way, but it's been an emotional—" He started to choke up, paused, took a long, stabilising breath, then proceeded, "I too need some rest." He swayed as though on the verge of losing consciousness. "I'll let Vic expound further." He collapsed into a chair, utterly drained both physically and mentally.

The Professor took the reins, "The successive losses of Neit and Hope have severely impacted Alice. According to our test results, Alice has transformed into a homoplasmate, a human with whom a plasmate has formed an interspecies symbiosis. This plasmate, which likely originated from the orb, represents living information. It infiltrated Alice's molecular framework, navigated up his optic nerve to his pineal gland, where it uses his brain as a host to replicate itself into an active form. In essence, it stays dormant until it can metamorphose into any physical form that Alice conceives."

"But he can govern it, yes?" Mal inquired.

"As a response, I'd have to say not yet. He'll need to learn how to master it. As it stands, from our observations, it appears to be triggered by an extreme adrenaline rush, predominantly from an intense emotional response."

"That's plausible, given the circumstances," Mal conceded.

"Until we can conduct tests while he's morphing, we'll remain in the dark."

"Do you think it's safe to let him loose without understanding his capabilities?" Mal queried.

The Professor paused for a moment before responding, "If you're implying whether we can discourage him from seeking revenge, Mal, I doubt anything will dissuade him."

"He's that potent?"

"Yes," The Professor stated, glancing at Secta for confirmation.

"Yes, Mal, he's that potent... there's no stopping him now," Secta concurred.

Gorrick, aware of Alice's impending assault, began prepping his defences. The video from Bruno's lapel camera had made one thing chillingly clear to both Gorrick and Honor: Alice was now a formidable adversary, more potent than ever before.

"We need a plan to counter him," Honor proposed anxiously, "Perhaps it's safer if you go into hiding."

"Evading him would only delay the inevitable. He'd track me down eventually. It's smarter to meet the impending confrontation on my terms. Let's proceed."

Leaving his office, he led her past his secretary's deserted desk and through the doors to the elevator. During their descent, Honor asked, "Where are we heading?"

"Technology is my sanctuary," Gorrick replied cryptically.

Exiting the elevator, they followed a corridor towards the Zenesis labs. Noticing the persistent glow of lights from inside the lab, Honor commented in a sarcastic tone, "Doctor Li is quite the workaholic... it's past 1 a.m."

"Indeed, her relentless efforts and resultant successes put your track record to shame," Gorrick retorted.

Honor fumed silently at his jibe. She loathed failure and the air of superiority Doctor Li had attained over her. Upon reaching the frosted glass door to the lab, they paused for it to slide open before entering. Gorrick called out from the unmanned reception desk, "Doctor Li?"

From a nearby room, Doctor Li emerged, clad in a white lab coat with her hair neatly pinned up. "Sir, I wasn't expecting visitors."

"We're facing a situation. I need an update on the progress with the RF series since the integration of the new chip."

Doctor Li cast Honor a questioning look, then spun sharply on her heel and led them deeper into the lab. "Follow me."

The lab was faintly illuminated by the green glow from three two-metre-tall upright pods, each housing a naked man. Honor froze in her tracks upon recognising the identical faces on the three men: they all bore the face of Kew.

"Meet the new RF series. I decided on a familiar face," Doctor Li explained, noticing their stunned expressions.

"The human component in these cyborgs seems excessive, why is that?" Gorrick queried.

"Thirty percent reanimated human parts," Li explained, her tone subtly defensive.

"That's too high. Reduce it. And change the face. It needs to be more intimidating, more machine-like."

"But Sir, I... I—"

He glared at her, repeating emphatically, "Reduce the content and modify the face."

"Yes, sir," she acquiesced, visibly disconcerted.

A smug smile danced on Honor's face; she relished seeing Doctor Li chastised by Gorrick. She turned her attention to the cyborgs, scrutinising their Herculean build, and their conspicuous lack of... certain parts.

"You seem to have skipped some crucial components, Doctor Li."

"If you're shopping for a robotic lover, there are websites for that," Li retorted, causing Gorrick to chuckle.

He redirected the conversation to the cyborgs' operational status. "Where do they stand?"

"Two of them are fully functional."

Intrigued, Honor looked even closer at them. "Impressive work. But how do you prevent decay in the human components?"

"The flesh part has a blood circulation variant to nourish the tissue. The limbs, buttocks, head, and brain are all bionic. Only the torso is human."

"Why keep the human torso at all?" Honor asked.

"The human frame outperforms any that we can manufacture," Li explained.

"That's what needs to change. The Japanese branch has developed a graphene skeletal frame. We need to incorporate it," Gorrick commanded. "Meanwhile, make the alterations, equip them with full defence capabilities. They'll serve as my round-the-clock personal bodyguards. How soon can they be operational?"

"Maybe a week—"

"No. We face an imminent threat. I need them sooner. Much sooner," Gorrick interrupted.

Turning from the cyborgs, Honor added, "We anticipate Black Alice attempting to assassinate Gorrick, he could strike at any moment."

"I understand," said Doctor Li. "Okay, I will have them fully operative by tomorrow. I'll bring them to your office at noon."

Satisfied, Gorrick knew at least part of his strategic defence plan against Alice was now set.

Alice felt a longing for reconnection. He sensed that in the throes of constant conflict, he'd somehow strayed from his core self. Many battles had been personal, provoking a tumult of emotions that dredged up long-buried traumas from his childhood. Now, the loss of Neit and Hope, integral facets of his identity, only added to his disorientation. The wound left by Stain's departure was still fresh, and its healing had required a strenuous journey of self-discovery. Now, amidst self-doubt and bewilderment, he once again stood at a crossroads. His dreams, once more vivid and disturbing, woke him in the dead of the night, leaving him drenched in cold sweat and entangled in a web of confusion.

Yearning to touch base with his true self, he decided to seek solitude. It was 3 a.m., and he lay awake on his bed, his gaze fixed on the ceiling. Rising, he dressed in the clothes they'd provided him. A look in the en-suite bathroom mirror only deepened his disconnect. It wasn't him. He knew then what he needed to do. He needed to return to his roots, to his home. Quietly, he slipped out of the building and into the city street, unnoticed.

In the early hours, the deserted streets of Sydney's Central Business District seemed to echo his loneliness. Breathing in the crisp air, he felt an invigorating rush of energy. The city bore the scars of recent chaos—shattered shop windows, abandoned cars, debris strewn everywhere. It was reminiscent of the devastation of Tokyo in 2047, only this time, the streets were eerily devoid of corpses. Spotting a motorbike lodged under a taxi, he saw potential.

The bike, an 800cc Ducati Scrambler, was salvageable. The keys still hung from the ignition. He wrestled it free from the taxi's undercarriage, climbed on, and started it up. The engine's smooth purr was music to his ears, and he rode off, heading for his apartment in Kings Cross.

The wind whipping through his hair as he weaved through the abandoned vehicles brought a sense of liberation. The tension from recent hostilities began to recede. He arrived at his destination a mere ten minutes later. The ride had served as a brief yet revitalising escape from his troubles.

After parking the bike on the sidewalk outside his apartment building, he retrieved his hidden key and let himself in. The familiarity of his old abode was instantly comforting. He felt more like his old self as he swapped the alien clothes from HQ for his signature attire: black jeans, a navy-blue workman's singlet, black Cuban heeled boots, and his well-worn black biker's leather jacket. Glancing in the bathroom mirror, he was satisfied with the reflection that met his gaze—he was, once again, the authentic Alice.

CHAPTER 42
LOOSE CHANGE

K ARZOFF WAS OVERWHELMED by panic when he was informed by the security team that Alice had vanished. He feared that Zen might have kidnapped him. With Mal set to announce the lifting of the curfew, he knew the city would descend into chaos soon after, making the search for Alice an insurmountable task. In a rush, he dialled Viktoria. She took a while to answer, her voice groggy when she finally did.

"Karzoff, do you have any idea what time it is? This had better be important."

"Apologies for the disturbance, but Alice has gone missing."

Viktoria was instantly alert. "What do you mean 'gone'? As in disappeared?"

"Yes, and nobody saw him leave... Granted, we only have a skeleton staff on duty but—"

"Have you reviewed the CCTV footage?"

"Um, no... I'll check it now."

Viktoria fell silent, irked that Karzoff, despite his experience, hadn't followed protocol by checking the CCTV before raising an alarm.

"Call me back," she said tersely, ending the call and turning to snuggle into Secta.

Karzoff realised he'd acted impulsively, which was out of character for him. Again, his judgment was clouded by the aftermath of Hope's loss.

A few minutes later, in the security monitoring room of OTT, Karzoff found himself watching Alice exiting the building of his own accord.

"What on earth is he up to?" he murmured to the agent seated next to him at the control desk, replaying the footage.

A few hours later, Alice reappeared at HQ, much to the relief of OTT security. Upon hearing of his arrival, Karzoff rushed down the corridor to the Kairos control room where he found Alice.

"Alice, Alice... where have you been?" Karzoff chided.

Alice halted. "I went for a change of clothes, see?"

Karzoff gave him a quick once-over. "Ah, I see. You had us... me... worried."

"Mate, I think I can handle myself after surviving an interplanetary journey and combating demons, don't you think?"

"I am sorry, Alice. I know your ability to defend yourself is second to none, it's just my job is—"

Alice gave his red-haired friend a reassuring pat on the back. "Thanks for the concern, buddy. Now, where's everyone?"

"They're in the canteen having breakfast. Hungry?"

"Mate, I could eat a horse and chase the rider." He had just finished his sentence when he remembered he'd used the same phrase with Hope before her untimely death.

Karzoff noted his mood shift and asked, "Are you sure you are okay, Alice?"

Alice shook it off. "Yeah, yeah... I'm good, Karzoff... Let's go get some grub."

"Secta is the epitome of meticulousness," the Professor informed Viktoria. "He won't let his loss affect his work."

"But why insist on keeping her in the morgue rather than cremating her?"

"They made a pact. If one died prematurely, the other would seek ways to preserve their knowledge."

"You mean re-animation?"

"Perhaps, remember Secta is a transhumanist."

The pair were seated in the canteen, enjoying a breakfast of bacon and eggs, while Secta fetched himself a fresh cup of coffee and a packet of nuts.

"I'm worried about his mental state. He doesn't seem overly affected, maybe he's on the verge of a breakdown? He needs to grieve for his sister," Viktoria said in a hushed tone.

"We'll have to wait and see how he copes with his grief. Everyone handles it differently."

"He seemed so distant last night... no affection... is that normal?" Viktoria asked openly.

Seeing genuine concern in her eyes, the Professor reached across the table and held her hand. "It could be PTSD... He does have a lot on his mind right now. But I don't think you should worry."

"About her work?"

"Yes, it's a significant issue. Most of her work is beyond our capabilities... In fact, this morning, I was looking at the recent pathology she did on Alice, and it's quite extraordinary."

"How so?"

He opened a notebook on the table. "This is hers... It says here... 'Under the electron microscope, I detected an anomaly in Alice's blood stem cells. There's a rogue group of stem cells with a structure unknown to medical science... I placed a unit of Alice's current peripheral blood in a petri dish next to a unit of my own blood for comparison. For interest, I added some epinephrine. Alice's blood immediately transformed into my blood: an exact clone!'"

Viktoria leaned back in her chair, amazed. "Does that mean... Have you shown this to Secta?"

"Yes, he has," Secta said, arriving at the table with his coffee and three packets of nuts. "It means Hope discovered Alice can not only physically morph into a larger version of himself, as you and Karzoff witnessed, but also into another being if he so wishes. It's that brilliant, ground-breaking research we will miss without Hope," he stated matter-of-factly.

"So, Alice can shapeshift?" Viktoria queried.

"You've been reading too much science fiction, but essentially, yes," the Professor concurred.

Secta took a seat and opened a packet of smoked organic almonds.

Viktoria asked, "Can he control it?"

"We think not... but he can certainly learn to," the Professor suggested.

"From Hope's notes, I started working on something early this morning... I think the morphing can be induced by an adrenaline surge... if that's the case, there's no reason he can't be given, for lack of a better term, an antidote, to bring him back to normal," Secta offered.

"Let me get this straight," Viktoria said, "he imagines who or what he wants to become, pops an adrenaline pill... morphs into the Hulk or whoever, then takes another pill... and the process reverses... is that right?"

"Yes, eventually, he will train himself not to need the pills," Secta affirmed with confidence.

"Brilliant," Viktoria exclaimed, taking Secta's hand and giving it a gentle squeeze. "You do have a lot on your mind, don't you?" Then leaning in, she whispered to both of them, "Do you realise what this means? Alice could infiltrate Zen HQ as a member of their staff undetected and commit the perfect crime."

Just then, Alice and Karzoff entered the room.

It took a mere three days for Sydney to be repopulated. As soon as the turmoil had settled and the extensive clean-up concluded, it was back to normality.

In the interim, the USS Zumwalt had bid Sydney farewell, embarking for San Diego with its new personnel, while Brigadier Bruckmaster, Colonel Freeman, and Major Torrens had boarded the first U.S. transport aircraft to depart.

OTT had initiated a plan to seek retribution for Hope's murder, though they had yet to finalise it. Consensus was, however, that the time was ripe to attempt the eradication of Gorrick. It was glaringly apparent that OTT couldn't carry on with missions under the omnipresent threat of Gorrick and Zen's interference. The peaceful resolution had been tested and failed; the moment for direct action was now.

Neit had disclosed that a mere two thousand Gorrick clones had originally been fabricated. They'd subsequently established that this figure had dwindled significantly over time. The task now was to determine how many remained and their precise locations. The only way to achieve that would be to capture one and probe his hive mind. A scheme to execute this was swiftly concocted. With this information, they could devise a strategy to exterminate each clone. Alice vowed this to be his next quest and wasn't prepared to rest until it was accomplished.

As days passed, Al's patience began to fray. He was eager to proceed, but Secta was insistent on holding back on implementing the plan until he was entirely convinced of Alice's stabilised condition. It wasn't until he arrived early for a meeting at Secta's lab, to find the Professor and Secta taking a break, that he uncovered the root of Secta's anxiety.

"One time when we were children, as a joke, she concocted a chemical solution that turned our swimming pool water into jelly. I was eating breakfast, gazing out the window at the pool when Dad walked onto the patio for his morning swim. He donned his goggles and dived in at the deep end. There was no splash, just a dull thunk sound. Without any buoyancy, the jelly offered no resistance and he plunged to the bottom like a stone. It took a substantial effort on our part to extract him from the jelly... our laughter only made it harder."

"She did have a quirky sense of humour," Al said, joining them, aware Secta was reminiscing about his sister.

"Oh Alice, I didn't hear you arrive. Yes, indeed she did... just reflecting on old times," Secta said, mournfully.

"I keep expecting her to walk into the room at any moment," Vic admitted, sorrowfully.

They all nodded in silent agreement.

"Listening to your story just now reminded me of the unique bond you shared with her," Alice said.

"You don't have any siblings, do you?" Secta inquired.

"No, I don't," Vic confirmed.

"And you Alice, have a sister you were completely unaware of!" Secta exclaimed.

Al simply nodded his head.

"You don't seem overly thrilled about it. Why is that?" Vic questioned.

The question made Alice uncomfortable. He took a moment to answer. "I guess I don't want the liability."

"Liability?" Secta questioned.

"Mate, Zen wants me dead. If they knew I had a sister, they'd abduct her to gain leverage over me," Alice grumbled.

"Yes, I suppose they would, I hadn't considered that," Secta admitted, pensively.

"What if they already know about her? Can you afford to risk that?" Vic posed.

"True, she hasn't been in Sydney for long, but they might already be aware of her presence," Secta mused.

Alice hadn't considered that. He abruptly stood, his demeanour shifted to a man embarking on a mission. "You're right, Vic!" he snarled. "I need to fetch her... bring her here immediately, she could be in grave danger."

Secta sprang from his seat. "Wait Alice, first the test."

Alice recalled why he had been summoned in the first place. "Oh, right, the test..."

Secta went over to his workbench, fetched two small vials, and returned.

"Recall how we discussed what we thought caused your transformation?" he asked.

Alice sat back down and nodded, "Yeah."

"Well, we've concocted two tablets. One we anticipate will trigger your transformation and the other to reverse it. Have you experienced any other effects in the past few days?"

"Nah, but I've been thinking, there was something peculiar at the time."

"Go on, it could be significant," the Professor encouraged.

"When I was changing, it felt like I could perceive the thoughts of the man I was observing. It was as if a voice in my head was echoing his thoughts... sort of like when Neit was within me, feeding me information. So, when the guy decided to shoot me, I heard his internal decision, giving me time to counter it. Um, also I could manipulate time. I could see a bullet in mid-air and evade it... I could anticipate a punch because, to me, it was travelling in slow motion."

Secta and Vic exchanged looks of comprehension.

"You can read minds?" Karzoff proposed.

"Accompanied by a high fusion flicker rate," the Professor added.

"Perhaps another of your gifts is precognition," Secta speculated. "Okay, so take one of these tablets and let's observe the outcome. When you consume it, focus your mind's eye on the image of someone."

He opened the vial, extracted a capsule, and offered it to Alice. The Professor passed him a glass of water to help swallow it.

Alice ingested the pill and stood, eyes closed, anticipating a reaction. After thirty seconds, he opened his eyes and announced, "Bad luck Secta, it didn't work."

"Don't rush to judgement, Alice. Go into the bathroom and look in the mirror," Secta suggested, a knowing smile on his face.

Alice sauntered into the en-suite bathroom and peered into the mirror. What he saw reflected back completely unsettled him. It wasn't him, it was Hope.

"Jesus!" He bellowed and stormed back out to the others in panic.

Secta hurried over to reassure him. "It's alright Alice, it's alright... here, look." He showed him a newspaper with a picture of Mal on the front cover. "Become Mal."

Alice shut his eyes tight, visualised the photograph of Mal, opened them and then dashed back into the bathroom to verify in the mirror. He was looking at Mal. "I'll be...!"

Secta joined him in the bathroom and handed him another pill. "Here, take this."

Al took the pill, closed his eyes, and after a moment opened them in front of the mirror. He was back to himself again. "Incredible!" He muttered, examining himself in the mirror as if shaving.

They reconvened with the others, their minds reeling from the bizarre experience.

"I wasn't certain it would work, but it's absolutely astounding," Secta conceded.

"This opens up countless new possibilities," Karzoff mused.

"Soon you won't need the pills, Alice. You'll learn how to transform at will," Vic stated.

"Dead-set, think of what I'll be able to do."

"Yes, Viktoria suggested the same thing," Vic explained. "She figured you could become a Zen staff member walk right into Zen HQ and nab Gorrick."

Al loved it. "Brilliant. How long do the affects last?"

"We don't know yet, Alice. Give us a couple of days of experimentation and we'll have an answer to that as well as determining if there are any side effects. If it's all is clear, then I will agree to the mission," Secta affirmed.

"All right!" Alice smiled, feeling much better about things.

CHAPTER 43
LIPSTICK

ALICE WAS WITH Secta and the Professor in Hope's laboratory, everything primed to test Alice's powers once again.

"First, let's take some time to talk this through," Secta suggested. "When you initially underwent your physical transformation, Karzoff, Viktoria, and the CCTV footage indicate that you metamorphosed into an entirely different entity, not just an enhanced version of yourself. Who did you visualise to cultivate that image?"

"I was placed in my first foster home when I was nine... I'd spent two years in an orphanage before that. The foster parents were in their thirties... she was a primary school teacher and he owned and operated a swimming pool cleaning business. He had a fantastic body, always under the sun, perpetually in the gym training. In the basement of their two-storey house, there was a den, a place that was off-limits to everyone. But like all children, if it was forbidden, then my curiosity was piqued, so I stealthily ventured down to discover the reason. It was remarkable. The champions of fantasy and science fiction art of the day... the pioneers like Frank Frazetta, Boris Vallejo, and Louis Royo were celebrated on the walls with framed posters. These were the masters of Heavy Metal Magazine cover art, and some of the remarkable covers they'd done were also prominently displayed. And the women, Boris was the king of incredibly fit nude female warriors. Anyway, taking centre stage on the end wall, highlighted with its own lighting, was a large poster of The Star Lord. I don't even recall the name of the artist, the illustration was so compelling it didn't matter. A naked bloke with long white hair, seriously pumped, a killer physique, standing on top of a rock column holding up the Earth. I used to go down to the den every chance I got to sit and stare at the Star Lord, wishing one day to be just like him. The image became my role model. Much later, on stage, I'd often emulate his pose to the audience. It was the art in the den that got me into metal and bodybuilding... the Star Lord had saved me from becoming a loser I reckon. So, yeah, it was the Star Lord I imagined that day when I was being shot by that mongrel, and it was the Star Lord I became to kill him and his mug accomplices."

The Professor was engrossed in typing on his laptop. He found what he was searching for and pivoted the computer screen to show Alice. "Is this it?"

Alice was astonished. "Indeed. Haven't seen it since then."

"It's by Boris Vallejo, titled Atlas... I wonder where you got the name Star Lord from?" the Professor mused.

"So now we understand that you can create an image in your mind and then adapt your state to embody it. I think this power you possess might be connected to Neit being absorbed by the atomic reaction in the orb and the force field. He could also shape-shift, but we never delved into the breadth of his powers," Secta elucidated.

"You suggesting a part of Neit might live on in me?"

"Perhaps, you did mention that plasma emerged from the orb and enveloped your body, didn't you?" Secta asked.

"Sure did." The notion that Neit was now physically a part of him gratified Alice.

"But that doesn't clarify your ability to read minds, expel bullets, and heal," Vic contended.

"No, but I posit two possible explanations for the bullets. Either it was a coincidence that you were shot whilst transforming, and the process of changing physical form propelled the bullets out, and the subsequent molecular reconstruction simply healed those wounds, or you now possess the ability to manipulate your atomic structure at will," Secta elaborated.

Alice mulled over it. "I remember intentionally ejecting the slugs. I just focused on getting rid of them and then closing the wounds, to be at full strength."

"Alright, then what about the sixth sense?" Vic inquired.

"We'll need to conduct the tests," Secta replied.

The Professor's mobile phone rang. He reached into the pocket of his lab coat, pulled out the phone and checked the caller ID. "It's Larry Freeman," he informed them, switched the phone to speaker, and responded.

"Larry, back in the world of plush shag-pile carpets and spit-polished boots?" he teased.

"Ha! Yes, Vic, all settled into my cosy little nook at the White House. Listen, President Robinson asked me to call to see if I can persuade you to return home and lead a new division for the development of time travel."

Vic winked at Secta, he'd anticipated the call. "I've already rejected the offer, Larry. You know how I feel about working under the likes of Bruckmaster."

"I can ensure he won't be involved, Vic. Consider this, they'll pour millions into it and you... you'll be fulfilling your passion, in control... and indeed, you'll be set for life."

"I am doing what I want, Larry, I am in control and I am set for life. Say no more."

"Okay Vic, I respect that. I had hoped that when your country beckoned, you would respond."

"Larry, I answered that call while you were still in high school, and at the time when I most needed support, that call was abruptly severed. Tell President Robinson, even if I did accept a position with all the money the government could offer, we still wouldn't be able to replicate what OTT has here... You know why?"

"No, why?"

"Because without Secta and his team, there would be no time travel."

"I understand, Vic. I'll relay the message... by the way, speaking of the OTT team, is Doctor Hope there? I'd like to apologise for not being able to bid her farewell."

There was a noticeable pause from Vic. "Hello? Vic?"

"Larry, Hope was assassinated by Zen agents the day you departed," he said with a sombre tone.

"Oh God no! No, no, no... I can't believe it... I... I am so, so sorry. God, how is Secta coping? How are you all coping?... How...?" he stuttered, taken aback.

"We're all in mourning here. Three Zen agents infiltrated Oceana while security was sparse, intent on assassinating Alice, and took Hope hostage."

"Is Alice alright?"

"Yes, he neutralised all three of them."

"This is exactly why President Robinson intends to discuss with President Low about leaving Zen to the U.S. Security Service."

"That's preposterous. They couldn't even safeguard your warship against those fiends without our intervention, why on earth should we entrust our security to you?"

"I hear you Vic. I'll raise the issue with her. Please convey my condolences."

"I will Larry."

Vic ended the call and, dismissing it as inconsequential, said, "Well, let's get on with it."

They progressed with the testing. Alice could shape-shift into various forms and then reverse the process with relative ease. While in the transformed state, Secta took blood samples from Alice, while the Professor took notes. Again, the tablets worked effectively and Alice was able to control the effects. If he desired to maintain the same physical form and use the ability to read the mind of a chosen individual, he could, otherwise, he was capable of morphing into whatever form he concentrated on. One significant discovery was that the form he transitioned into only lasted as long as the body took to absorb the adrenaline released, approximately twenty minutes. The more energy he expended, the quicker the adrenaline burnt off. After twenty minutes, under laboratory conditions, he reverted to his normal form, rendering the reversal tablet superfluous. No after-effects were detected, though the main results would come from the pathology analysis. They only tested his shape-shifting twice and proceeded to examine his second sight and fusion flicker rate.

They found the second sight only worked when focusing on one individual at a time. Once he had attuned to their wavelength, he could hear the subject's thoughts as a voice within his own mind.

With the tests concluded, Alice was eager to wrap up for the day and prepared to leave.

"I think you should always carry the reversal tablets with you anyway, just in case you need to revert from whatever form you've transitioned into. Consider it a safety precaution," Secta advised.

"No sweat," Al confirmed.

They'd been engrossed in the lab all day and the positive outcome meant Secta had decided to greenlight the plan of leveraging Alice's newfound powers to abduct Gorrick. The next issue would be the method to execute the plan, and he needed to discuss that with Mal.

Simultaneously, U.S. President Oprah Robinson (granddaughter of the renowned soul musician Smokey Robinson) reached out to Mal regarding OTT. It was clear to Mal that upon his return to the White House, Brigadier Bruckmaster had informed the President about Kairos, causing a wave of paranoia to ripple through her and her cabinet. It was unlike the USA to allow a foreign nation, even an ally, to possess superior tactical technology. Hence, President Robinson proposed to Mal that OTT might consider 'lending' them Professor de Luz to aid in the development of their own version of time-travel technology. Mal had agreed to discuss it with OTT, but given the Professor's previously stated political convictions, he knew it would take more than faith in a miracle to persuade him to switch sides.

The Professor had already told Mal about the call from Colonel Freeman and that he'd already declined their offer. That, of course, put Mal in an invidious position—it wasn't going to be easy for him to say no to the good old U.S. of A.

His refusal to comply with President Robinson's request was met with some reservation, leaving him concerned about possible ramifications.

Vic took a mug of coffee from Miss Vallins and asked warmly, "How's the foot, Rita?"

"Fine, the prosthetic little toe Doctor Hope 3-D printed and fitted allows me to walk normally without any issues."

The mention of Doctor Hope caused a noticeable lull in the conversation between Mal, Secta, and the Professor. Rita noticed it and placed a comforting hand on Secta's shoulder. "I'm so sorry, Secta," she said sympathetically, tears welling up in her eyes.

Secta gently covered her hand with his.

Changing the subject back to the matter at hand, Mal asked, "So, how would you expect them to react, Vic?"

Vic watched Rita walk across the room to the door. "She still has that sexy sway even without a little toe, brilliant... oh, um," he switched back to Mal, "you can never tell with a bum like Bruckmaster."

"I agree... he's a loose cannon... can't be trusted," Secta said.

"And he has Oprah's ear. I'd just leave it be for now, Mal. Let them work out how to deal with it. If they act in their inimitable fashion, they'll offer you a few trillion dollars for the blueprints of Kairos."

"Speaking of blueprints, what if Zen is building a Kairos? They did try to steal our blueprints," Mal proposed.

"Well, if they are, you can be sure Adamski would be using the organic chip, and that has built-in planned obsolescence," Secta said with a shrewd chuckle.

But Mal wanted to know more about Alice's superpowers. "Tell me what this fusion flicker thing's all about, Secta?"

"Okay, so the threshold flicker fusion rate of a human's vision is about sixty frames a second—that's sixty pictures a second—whereas a dog is around eighty, and a cat around one hundred. When Alice is under stress, his flicker rate increases to three hundred frames a second, the equivalent of, say, a dragonfly. This means he can then, when he needs to, slow down time. For instance, he is able to see a bullet traveling through the air, so he can deflect it... or he could see someone throwing a punch and anticipate it."

"So, he's capable of seeing in slow motion in real-time," Mal proposed.

"Exactly," the Professor added. "And from an onlooker's perspective, it would appear he is moving at lightning speed, but really it's all anticipation."

"Amazing," Mal said.

"Yes, we've definitely got a superman on our hands," the Professor acknowledged.

"But for now, he needs to learn how to use the powers; they could be dangerous otherwise," Secta concluded.

"I think the knowledge of the powers would be best kept between us, do you agree?" Mal submitted.

Honor was at her desk in her makeshift office when her secretary, Layla Migden, entered.

"Ma'am, sorry to interrupt, but Sir Gorrick asked if you wish to return to Sydney HQ or remain here?" Layla inquired.

"Ahhh..." she sighed, "At last, I can take leave of this dump. Tell him I'm out of here," Honor snarled, while studying Layla's fine figure with a single raised eyebrow. Layla looked very attractive in a navy-blue knee-length skirt and a pale blue blouse. The fine lines of her delicate neck were emphasized by her short-cropped blue-black hair, worn messy with loads of product. Her black sculptured eyebrows and the square, grey-rimmed glasses framing her triangular face gave her the look of a librarian rather than a secretary. However, that appearance was quickly belied by her shiny red painted lips.

Honor rose from her desk, drifted over to the lounge setting, and slipped demurely into an armchair.

"Anything else, ma'am?" Layla asked, still displaying obvious insecurity with her job since the Black Alice fiasco.

"We are best defined by the people around us, Layla," Honor said smoothly, somewhat philosophically.

"Sorry, ma'am?" Layla said, mystified by the statement.

"Take a seat; it is you I am interested in. We should talk. Do you have a boyfriend?" Honor asked, probing.

"Not at the moment," Layla said, her body language telegraphing that she wasn't expecting such a question. However, being a shrewd millennial, she quickly sensed an opportunity to redeem herself with her boss and decided to play along.

"I admit I'm attracted to certain men, but I have a penchant for women. Mind you, I'm not looking for a relationship with either."

Honor's eyelids fluttered; Layla was speaking her language. It was just the challenge she had been craving.

The phone rang, and Honor answered. "Hello, Gorrick? Yes, sir, I will be there."

Gorrick was seated in an armchair, studying a notebook when Honor entered. In typical fashion, she took a seat opposite him and waited demurely for him to speak.

"The next phase of my plan to ensnare Alice will now be put into motion," he stated.

"Yes, sir, how can I—?" she began, but he cut her off.

"I understand you would prefer to hold office in Sydney?" he asked.

"Yes, sir."

"Right, well, that fits my plan perfectly. I want to infiltrate OTT to determine their stratagem."

"I don't think I can help with that, sir. I—"

Again he cut her short. "We will use your secretary, Miss Migden, to seduce Black Alice. Do you think she is capable?" Before she could answer, he added, "After the previous problem, she can either redeem herself by doing this or leave Zen. Which do you think she would prefer?"

Honor was shell-shocked. "I, I think she would rather stay with us, sir. Do you want me to make the arrangements?"

"Yes, and immediately... the mission is urgent, Honor."

"Yes, sir," she said, standing ready to leave.

"Oh, and Honor, you have red lipstick on your neck," he said knowingly.

CHAPTER 44
THE TRAIN

THE NEXT MORNING at 0800 hours, Alice took his usual breakfast at Café Epiphany: two croissants, two eggs sunny-side-up, crisp bacon but not burnt, and a doppio: a double espresso shot. The café was back to normal after the curfew and pretty much at capacity as it used to be at that time of day except on weekends. Alice enjoyed sitting in the corner on his own, reading the daily newspaper while consuming a hearty breakfast.

"You're Black Alice," a sexy voice purred.

He lowered the newspaper. She was dressed in Goth gear, a short tutu showing off shapely legs encased in stockings dotted with holes. She wore a black leather jacket with a flimsy black-laced blouse that displayed plenty of cleavage, black fingerless lace gloves, black lipstick, heavily made-up big blue eyes behind grey-rimmed glasses, and short-cropped blue-black hair worn messy with loads of product.

"You got that part right, what can I do for you?" Alice replied, in his inimitable fashion.

She opened a black studded leather shoulder bag, took out a photo, and handed it over.

Alice took it. It was of him doing a gig.

"Were you at the gig?"

"Yes. Can you autograph it for me?"

"Sure. Got a pen?"

She dug into her bag and came up with one.

As he signed it, he asked, "You are?"

"Layla."

"Layla... now that name has sweet action to it. There. How come you're carrying around a picture of me in your handbag?"

"I guess because I'm a devoted fan."

"Devoted?"

"Yeah, really devoted." She licked her lips ever so slightly with the tip of her tongue. He handed her back the photo with the pen.

"You got a tattoo?"

"Yes," she said shyly.

"Where?"

"I'd rather not say," she smiled cheekily.

"A picture or words?"

"Neither, but it is writing."

"What language?"

"Chinese," she said.

"Okay, what does it say?"

"I don't think I should tell you that," she said coyly.

"Thought you were a devoted fan."

"Okay," she pulled a cute face. "It says if you can see this, then you may enter."

A wry smile broke on Alice's face. "Alright, so when can I see it?"

Layla smirked, sat down opposite him, leaned closer, and whispered covertly, "Pardon the cliché, but your place or mine?"

Alice leaned close to her, placed his forefinger under her chin, and lifted it slightly to stare into her eyes. "I tell you what Layla, how about I take you somewhere really special?"

She beamed him a big consenting smile.

They left Café Epiphany and joined the crowded sidewalk.

"Where are we going? Are we going to walk there?" she asked.

Alice didn't reply; he just gripped her hand and kept walking. After a few minutes, they arrived at the entrance to a basement apartment.

"Is this where you live?"

"Yeah," Al said, opening a neglected rusted metal door.

Layla wasn't impressed by the downbeat look of the entrance, grimaced, but then followed Alice inside.

Karzoff surprised her by stepping out from around a corner. He apprehended her.

She protested angrily, "Hey, what's going on here?"

"Get inside!" Karzoff growled, having to practically force his prisoner into the elevator.

It descended to the lower security levels of OTT.

A little while later in the Kairos control room, Alice was sitting on the edge of the console, talking to Karzoff, Viktoria, Secta, the Professor, and Robert, who had just returned from Avalon.

"So, I downed a pill with my coffee and focused on her like you said, and I could read her thoughts. She said, 'I've done it... I've got him! That'll put me in good stead with Gorrick and Honor.' But hey, it was a lame attempt to fool me."

"It doesn't make any sense," Viktoria said.

"No, I agree... it has Honor's imprimatur all over it, so there must be more to it?" Karzoff questioned, scratching his head perplexed.

Secta was up and pacing, he stopped. "What security Wi-Fi system are we running now, Karzoff?"

"A new system designed specifically for OTT. It is AES or Advanced Encryption Standard using WPA2 with a daily encryption algorithm rotation that incorporates the SSID. The home network is a RADIUS server that limits the signal to OTT floors only. The same as the system used in the Pentagon."

"It has rogue-AP detection for intrusion prevention," Viktoria added.

"Why do you ask?" Karzoff queried.

Secta gave them a wry smile. "Because I think our Miss Layla Migden might be a walking bug."

"A bug? What, a snoop-type bug?" Al asked.

"Yes, but not in the conventional manner. I think she might be picking up our internal Wi-Fi by some means, boosting it to another frequency, and then relaying the data to Zen."

"But how could she get through our security encryption?" Viktoria asked.

"She doesn't need to. If I'm right, then she is simply rebroadcasting our encrypted signal for Zen to decode at their end."

"I see," said Viktoria.

"Then we had better do something about it, quick smart. But what?" Karzoff queried.

"Put her in an anechoic chamber," the Professor said. "We have one... here in this room. The dispatch room is designed to completely absorb sound or electromagnetic waves."

Honor was happy to be back at her city office desk. The desk phone rang.

"Ma'am, it's Carl at surveillance."

"Yes, what is it?"

"The bounce from the operative has paused," said Carl.

"I see, how much data have you got?"

"More than enough, I think."

"Good, then start decoding it." She terminated the call and immediately dialled Gorrick.

They concluded that the plan of having Layla captured by OTT was a success. However, somehow, OTT had uncovered that she was relaying the Wi-Fi signal a little earlier than they had expected.

Honor put the phone down. It had been an empty success. In achieving it, she had sacrificed Layla to the cause, and now she needed to set the wheels in motion to recover her.

It was 2200 hours. The city had fallen relatively silent since it had been drained of the majority of its occupants following the day's toil. But not Gorrick; this was the time he liked best, a time to attend to business in his Sydney office without interruption.

On level three of Zen HQ, Honor was also still hard at it, ploughing through numerous OTT files that Carl had enciphered and sent her. She was desperate to find a clue, anything that might give them an advantage over their rivals. Finally, she found something: an email two days old from Secta to President Low explaining his intention to commence tests the next day to determine the extent of Alice's newly gained superpowers. Further on, it explained that he would defer his approval of the attack plan until the test results were through; only then would he unequivocally sanction Alice using his powers. The information got her up pacing the floor, thinking—what are these superpowers? Not content, she rushed back to the computer to search for more but found nothing. Is it enough? She questioned herself.

Gorrick found the news of Alice having superpowers alarming. He ordered Honor to continue scouring the data for more information and then placed Zen security on high alert.

An hour later, unable to find any more relevant information, Honor had just reclined in her chair to relax when she received a security alert. The facial recognition security system (FRSS) had just granted Layla Migden entry into the building. She quickly switched to her security monitor and saw Layla's face via the elevator camera. Glad that Layla had been released, she decided not to speak with Gorrick until she had personally debriefed her.

However, immediately after Layla had been granted entry, well before Honor had viewed her in the elevator, Gorrick had been notified by the system.

The guards had been doubled on every floor, and the entire building was crawling with them.

The elevator door opened, and when Layla came out, she was immediately stopped by a guard and ordered to make her way to the private elevator to Gorrick's offices.

Gorrick had sent permission for her to be brought to him.

Layla stepped out of the elevator into the corridor leading to Gorrick's office. The two guards standing outside the suite of offices granted her entry.

Miss Fysh wasn't at her desk, and the reception area was only dimly lit. A further two sentries at the door to Gorrick's private suite admitted her.

Layla stepped into Gorrick's massive office. It had been renovated back to its former grandeur. A bubbling brook meandered through the landscaped floor space, over which a small bridge led to an island lounge setting. On the island was a fully-grown Blue Gumtree that reached thirty metres up to the ceiling skylights. There was floor lighting behind and around flowerbeds and other small trees and plants, presenting an Arcadian ambiance. A white path with LED lights spaced along it, like in the aisle of a passenger jet, meandered through the gardens to the bridge. The path reminded Layla of the Wizard of Oz. Perhaps Gorrick envisioned himself as the Wizard.

"Come, Miss Migden," Gorrick's voice bellowed from his lounge chair on the island.

The sound of running water and native bird calls provided a calming effect, even though the birds were obviously digital.

As she crossed the white bridge that arched over the brook, she noticed guards stationed in the shadows around the room.

Gorrick remained seated with a notepad balanced on his knees. In the dim lighting, the lucent screen of the notepad was reflecting on his face, giving him a sinister appearance.

When Layla sat down, he looked up and leered at her. "So, Black Alice, what do you intend to do now that you have gained entry to my inner sanctum... kill me?"

In an instant, Layla morphed into Black Alice.

Gorrick slow-clapped. "Oh, very good, very, very good. I'm impressed... you look terrific in drag. Did you pick up the morphing on Eris?"

Alice looked down at his clothes. He was still dressed as Layla, in a tutu and a leather jacket that had burst at the seams. Even the boots he was wearing had burst open. It was the downside of the morphing process.

"Hmm, that needs some work, but hey, you ain't seen nothing yet, Gorrick. I've had a gut full of you and freaking Zen Corporation. I'm here to put an end to it."

"I have no idea what you mean," Gorrick said cynically.

"You see... I ask for Rob Halford, and I got Rick Astley. Don't talk crap, Gorrick. Why do you think we've been having these ongoing battles?"

"I've got no idea what you're talking about, Alice... I can call you that, can't I? Maybe all the radiation you've been exposed to has affected your rationale?"

Alice climbed out of the seat. He was pissed off and wasn't about to get into a slagging match with him. Then he noticed Gorrick was glowing. His Graphene lenses were detecting Neon, which meant he wasn't En-Lil. It was too late for that anyway, as he'd already dispensed with En-Lil, but still, it was nice to know the lenses did what they were designed for.

"You walked right into my trap, Black Alice. You can shape-shift all you like, but you won't be getting out of here alive."

Secta was in his lab, working when the door hissed open and Vic entered.

"I think we might have a problem, Secta."

Secta turned sharply. "To do with what?"

"Pathology just came in... and, well," he handed Secta the report. "I decided to see what would happen if I took Alice's blood sample that had morphed and then I artificially morphed it a second time."

Secta read the report. "So, he morphs once, then morphs back to himself, and then, say he morphs again... is that the premise?"

"Yes. What the test revealed is that after he returns to himself, if he morphs a second time within a window of two hours, when he tries to morph back to himself, the lymphocytes, such as B-cells and T-cells, begin attacking and destroying the red cells."

"So, in effect, trying to morph back to himself could kill him?" Secta clarified.

"Exactly. If Hope was here, she'd be able to explain it better, but..."

Secta was on his feet, disturbed by the revelation. "Damn! We should've checked this..."

"I know, I guess in the rush, and like I said, if Hope was here, she would've—"

"Not only will it kill him, but this means his superpowers will only work twice within a given space of time."

"It looks like that's two hours, then. If he waits a further six hours, he can morph again."

Secta was worried. "I think Alice is planning to morph more than twice with Gorrick."

"It will kill him," Vic said gravely.

"What can we do? He needs to know," Secta urged.

"Can you get a message to his implant?" Vic suggested.

"Yes, yes, good thinking... we'll have to try."

Two cyborgs were restraining Alice by the arms. They'd come out of the shadows and seized him. A third cyborg was standing by to guard against him breaking away.

Gorrick rose from his seat and snarled, "These handy bodyguards of mine might not have the superpowers you do, but they do possess the strength of ten men. On my order, they are going to tear you apart. First, they'll rip your arms out of the sockets, and then they will beat what's left of you to a pulp; fertiliser that I will be able to use on my plants here as blood and bone."

Alice was straining against the vice-like grip of the two seven feet tall robotic-looking cyborgs, each stretching an arm to the max. But contrary to his predicament, Alice remained composed.

"You see... that's the sort of crap I expect from you. A dude comes to pay you a visit, and what do you do? You threaten to rip his arms off. Now, I'm not Carl Jung, but these must be symptoms of a seriously deranged mind."

Gorrick snapped, "Hit him hard in the solar plexus, number one."

Alice tensed up to take the hit.

The cyborg guarding, light glistening off his chrome exoskeleton, swivelled, and then let go of an almighty punch into Alice's gut, the force of which knocked the wind out of him and caused his knees to buckle. The two cyborgs held onto his arms taunt to stop him from hitting the deck.

"Ah, now I can see the light at the end of the tunnel. This is the end of you, Black Alice."

Coughing and spluttering, wincing from pain, Alice still managed a cheeky grin and grunted cockily, "Mate, the light at the end of the tunnel is a train coming right at you."

Gorrick's face tightened, and he yelled, "Rip his arms off! Kill him."

CHAPTER 45
CLOCK DRIVE

THE **SLENDER SCIENTIST** with a high forehead approached the lab doors at a quick clip, barely noticing the fully armed guard there. With his mind somewhere else, the guard was almost invisible to him, just part of the fabric of OTT these days.

The pneumatic doors to Secta's lab hissed open, and Professor de Luz went through.

"Did you get a message to him?" he asked.

Secta looked round from his computer monitor. "As you know, we don't use his implant for communication, just as a translator and for referencing." He pointed at the screen, and Vic approached to look. "I used the unique frequency to send him a visual text, see here."

Vic looked at the screen and read the text out loud. "Danger - you can only morph twice - first to whoever, second back to yourself. If you morph a third time within a two-hour period, you cannot morph back to yourself - it will kill you. Secta."

"We've not done this before, we can only hope it works," Secta said.

"It was well articulated, Secta. I do, however, have a backup plan."

The Cyborgs had Alice's arms stretched ready to wrench them from the sockets when Alice morphed into Gorrick. It was a desperate part of the plan designed to get him out of the building, not to stop a pair of Cyborgs from ripping his arms off. He was banking on the Cyborgs being fitted with facial recognition software that would be programmed to prevent them from harming their master: Gorrick. Just as the morph completed, a text tracked across from right to left in Alice's frame of vision. He got the message and added it to his problems.

Upon recognising him as Gorrick, the Cyborgs immediately stood down. Alice seized the moment and let fly with a massive kick into the chest of the Cyborg that had punched him. The blow caused the Cyborg to stagger. He tripped and went over backwards, landing with an almighty splash in the brook. Alice turned his attention to Gorrick, and they faced off.

Gorrick recoiled. There was nothing he could do to override the programming of the remaining Cyborgs: they wouldn't attack Alice while he looked like him.

"Now, you have another clone... arsehole. How about I rip off one of your arms, eh?" Alice snarled. "Let's see how you like it? Yeah! Not so tough now these mechanical mugs are standing around like a pair of bookends, are yer?"

When Layla failed to arrive at Honor's office, Honor deduced she might have been intercepted by Gorrick and immediately set off to investigate.

As soon as she stepped inside, she was gripped by an uneasy feeling. Across the room, she could see two Cyborgs standing statue-like on either side of someone. This individual, dressed as Layla, was obviously an imposter. Honor was certain of this due to the acerbic banter she could hear, prompting her to unholster her pistol. With discreet movements, she edged towards the security alert system on the wall and hit the red button. The security guards would be there in mere minutes.

Before their arrival, Honor resolved to take matters into her own hands in her unique, bold fashion. Pistol at the ready, she skulked through the room's deepest shadows towards the bridge.

"You can't possibly think you'll get out of here alive, no matter what face you're wearing. Look at you. I'm not known for dressing in drag," Gorrick gloated, his face displaying a smear of arrogance.

"No, you're going to take me over to your en-suite and get me a change of your clothes, then we're going to walk right out of here."

"Two of me? You've got to be out of your mind."

"What are your guards going to do, arrest us?... I don't think so. How will they know which one of us is the real deal?" Alice said smugly.

Karzoff and Viktoria were parked in a black van outside the side entrance to the Zen building, waiting for Alice. Karzoff's phone rang, he answered. Secta filled him in, and Karzoff recognised the enormity of the problem. Secta had received no confirmation from Alice that he had picked up the text message. If he hadn't and he morphed back into his own form as planned to leave the building with Gorrick, he would die.

"We need to go in... it is the only way to ensure Alice's safety," Karzoff said to Viktoria, gravely.

He terminated the call and further explained the situation to Viktoria. There was no backup and no time to wait for any. It meant the two of them would need to fight their way through Zen security in the lobby to the elevators and then up to Gorrick's office before Alice could start down.

Pacing the Kairos control room, Secta was worried the exit strategy wouldn't work. Robert was at the console. "This isn't going to work. If Alice didn't get the message, we can't bank on Karzoff getting to him. The odds are stacked against them."

Vic burst into the room in a flurry and bellowed, "Hold everything... I have an idea!"

Karzoff and Viktoria were preparing to leave the van when Karzoff's phone rang again.

"One false move out of you and I'll belt you, now, lead me to your ready room," Alice ordered Gorrick.

The two of them walked past the Cyborg staggering out of the brook. Just when they stepped onto the bridge, Honor emerged from the darkness with her pistol aimed up and yelled, "Stop right where you are!"

She was confused by which Gorrick to aim at and shouted, "Which of you is the real Gorrick?"

They both answered at the same time, "I am."

Gorrick quickly yelled, "It's Black Alice, shoot him. He's wearing Layla's clothes for goodness sake!"

Honor swung the gun on Alice and fired. Alice could see the bullet travelling towards him in slow motion and leaned to one side to avoid it.

Honor peeled off another shot.

Again, Alice saw it coming and dodged it.

With Alice outfoxing her, Gorrick shouted, "Cover him Honor, I'll call Li to change the Cyborg's protocol."

Honor kept her gun trained on Alice. "Don't worry sir, I have alerted security, the place will be crawling with guards any minute."

Alice was receiving another text as he snarled, "So you've got a new face Honor! No improvement, you're still an ugly bitch."

"You have no chance Alice, it is finally all over for you," Honor yelled back, angry as a cut snake. Just then, a dozen guards burst into the room with weapons raised. The odds were now seriously stacked against Alice.

Gorrick was thrilled. "Honor is right Alice, it's all over for you!"

"Never over till the fat lady sings, Gorrick, come and get me!"

"Kill him!" Gorrick yelled at the troops, who had reached the bridge.

Alice looked up at the small vortex that had appeared just near him. Everything shimmered and everyone with the exception of the three Cyborgs froze.

Secta stepped out of the vortex and while Gorrick was standing frozen on the bridge, rushed over to him and slapped a Clock Drive on his neck. "Quick Alice," Secta said.

With Secta taking Gorrick's legs and Alice his arms, they quickly manhandled him over to the vortex. Grasping Gorrick's feet, Secta stepped back through the vortex and Alice helped Gorrick through like he was a mannequin.

Half a dozen armed guards were waiting in the Kairos advent room to greet Gorrick. While they held him at gunpoint, Secta waited for Alice. After a few moments, he stepped out of Kairos, still looking like Gorrick.

"How long have I got to stay looking like this goon?" he growled at Secta, eyeballing Gorrick.

The Professor came into the room. "Another hour or so, Alice, but hey, I love the stockings."

"Yeah, well, this morphing stuff needs some work when it comes to clothing... this get-up is pretty embarrassing," Al complained.

"I think it looks great, all black, very Goth," Vic joked.

G. L. Keady

"So, you got the messages?" Secta asked.

"Yeah, but couldn't reply."

"We'll get onto fixing that as well," Vic said.

"How did you get Gorrick through without the formula?" Al asked.

"It was Hope that did it," Vic said.

"Hope?"

"Yes, she'd duplicated the Clock Drive that had come from the future with Sonoko, I guess she was about to announce it before..." Vic stopped, reminded of their loss.

"Vic found the details on her computer and managed to 3-D print one just in time," said Secta as he peeled the clock drive off Gorrick's neck.

Gorrick taunted them, "Oh, exceptionally clever of you, so what will it be now; execution?"

"No, nothing as terminal as that, you'll be my new lab rat," Secta told him with a menacing grin.

Three hours later, Vic visited Alice who was waiting in Secta's lab, still disguised as Gorrick dressed as Layla. His own clothes were draped over the back of the sofa for him to eventually change into.

"I've just rechecked my test results, you can safely transform back to yourself now."

"Great, I've been getting worried about the sly way Secta keeps pegging me. Think he fancies me?" he joked.

"No, Alice, you're not my type," Secta responded with a sinister chuckle.

Alice dropped a pill, concentrated, shivered a little, and then, before their very eyes, transformed back into himself. Vic whipped out a syringe and, ignoring protests from Alice, took a blood sample, which he then rushed over to the electron microscope to check.

"All clear," Vic said, happily.

Alice got dressed.

Alice wandered into the security offices to pay Karzoff and Viktoria a visit. At the reception, talking to Trish Boyd, the new secretary, was his sister Wyetta. She looked up sharply when he entered.

"Al! I didn't expect to see you here."

Alice cruised in and sat on the edge of the desk.

Karzoff came out of his office. "Alice, have you met our new secretary Trish?"

Alice checked her out... she was drab looking, perfect for the gig he thought. "Hey Trish, I'm Alice... I ducked in to see how Wyetta's getting on."

"Not Wyetta... Vee," Karzoff contradicted.

"Didn't ask you why it's Vee..." Alice glared at his sister.

"When I was in primary school, the kids nicknamed me Raven after a cartoon character who always wears black. By the end of primary, they'd refined it to Rave because I never said much... a bit of a loner. Then in high school, it got shortened to Vee and stuck. I prefer it to Wyetta; that sounds like a train station—Next stop Wyetta!" She crowed, imitating an announcement over a loudspeaker.

"Cool... There's something I need to talk to you about, mate," Alice told Karzoff, hinting with an eye movement toward his private office.

Karzoff led him inside.

"How did the background check on her go?" Al asked.

Karzoff sat behind his desk with a stern look on his face. "I am afraid Alice, that..."

Alice prepared himself for the truth.

"You have a sister," Karzoff finished with a big smile.

Alice whacked his forehead in exasperation. "Argh!"

"I thought you would be happy?"

Alice groaned, "It's enough trying to keep me out of trouble without having to worry about someone else, mate."

"Well, after the rigours we have put her through, no need to look after her, she is more than capable of doing that for herself."

Alice took a chair opposite Karzoff and relaxed. He knew what it took to pass the tests, which were not much different from an SAS physical and mental admission examination. They went on to discuss the assault on Zen, and Alice took great pleasure in telling Karzoff about defeating his nemesis, Honor.

Soon Secta would commence the brain scan of Gorrick to reveal the locations of all of the Gorrick clones around the world. Secta believed their beehive communications network would ultimately lead to their downfall, as it would offer the means for them to track each and every one of them.

Within days, a Gorrick replacement arrived at Zen HQ in Sydney. A Russian, he immediately called a meeting in his office with Adamski, Doctor Li, and Honor, for a full debriefing of the months leading up to and including the kidnapping of the previous Gorrick. They quickly discovered the difference between this Gorrick and the last: this one was a ruthless tyrant.

Standing and gazing out of the window with his back to the other three in the lounge setting, the imposing man demanded with a thick Southern Russian accent, "Doctor Li, explain why three RF series cyborgs failed to protect Gorrick?"

"Sir, they have facial recognition protocols with selective programming."

"Are you suggesting they are programmed to attack only specified targets?"

"Yes, sir."

"That must be changed," he said angrily and then turned sharply to face them. "Instead of pre-programming, you will monitor and adjust them on the fly. A dedicated monitor and operator will be allocated for each Cyborg 24/7. That way, we will not get a repeat of this disastrous situation. What is the point of having cyborg bodyguards if they can't protect? When will your time travel project begin trials, Adamski?"

"In less than a month, sir."

"Good. Keep me posted daily, both of you. And Honor, what exactly is your purpose? Surely it can no longer be security because your record of failures far exceeds your successes."

Doctor Li smirked, relishing Gorrick's criticism of Honor.

Honor's expression reflected her humiliation. "I am the director of ZEO: Zen Espionage Operative. It was I who secured the organic chip from OTT. Without it, we would not even have operational cyborgs or a time travel project, for that matter. That is my value!" She swallowed the last words in an effort to control her hostility.

Gorrick prowled the lounge setting like a predator, stopped abruptly, and fixed his cold, soulless eyes on Honor. There came a pregnant pause with Honor holding her breath, wondering whether she'd gone too far with her arrogant defence.

Gorrick took a deep breath and then said calmly, "Well said, Honor... had you answered in any other way, I would have dismissed you immediately."

Honor let out a sigh of relief.

"We will get Gorrick and Miss Migden back!" he said, striking the back of the nearest chair with an open hand to emphasise his discontent. "And we will rid the world of this Black Malice."

"Alice, sir," Honor carefully corrected him.

"Black Alice then... your projects, Professor Adamski and Doctor Li, will be the key to defeating him... the enemy. They will be given priority."

In the comfort of his old Kings Cross apartment, Alice was trying to get his life back in order. He'd called each individual member of his band, and one by one, they agreed to go into rehearsal for a big reformation concert. In reality, they needed the money, while Al needed to free his mind of the headaches resulting from being an OTT time traveller.

With rehearsal due to begin in a couple of days, he was sitting on his bed with a brand new Maton SRS70J acoustic guitar on his knee, putting the finishing touches lyrically on a couple of new songs.

He read the lyrics he'd written and realised they were seriously philosophical.

"Let's see here... sometimes you get it right because you believe you can do it... Other times you get it right because you just do what you believe. Some call it instinct... some call it the key... But I call it playing what's in front of me... What's in front of me... what's the difference between faith and duty?"

There was a sudden flash of bright light, and while blinded by it, he heard a familiar voice.

"Destroy the matrix: the alpha clone. It is your duty to secure the Tablet of Destinies... without it, there will be no future for humanity."

"You ask a lot of me, En-Ki."

"There is a universe of worlds for you to explore now, Alice."

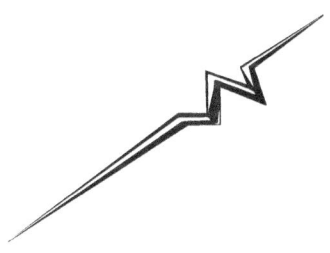

EPILOGUE
BOOK 6
THE TABLET OF DESTINIES

"DAMN!" BLACK ALICE screamed out loud. There were thousands of armed soldiers marching in a line right at him. Twenty deep, the front line was heavily armoured, with each soldier carrying a long deadly spear tucked under his right arm… aimed at him.

Standing alone in the middle of a vast barren valley surrounded by towering cliffs, the topography and the advancing soldiers were all very alien to Alice; it was like a scene from a battle in Game of Thrones. The one saving grace was that everything living had frozen the moment he stepped out of the vortex, buying him precious time to think.

"Don't like this," he mumbled, knowing the vortex was about to close. Any second now, the massive army would unfreeze and continue its march towards him. Was he just in their way, or was he their target? He had no idea and wasn't too confident about sticking around to find out. Then, as though a universal switch had been flicked, the army reanimated, and the air immediately filled with the deafening sound of thousands of marching boots and the clanking of rusted armour—the machine was in motion, and he was in its path.

The news was filled with Israel alleging it had concrete proof of Iran's nuclear capability. This escalated the existing tension between Iran and the USA, reaching an all-time high. The world was on edge, anticipating a war that had been brewing for years.

Then, a passenger aircraft vanished from radar over the Indian Ocean, and the Western world labelled it a terrorist attack, placing blame on Iran.

Within days, a UFO flap occurred over the erupting Popocatepetl Volcano in Mexico, leading to speculation that the two events might be related. Two days later, Paris suffered a massive power outage without any apparent reason. Subsequently, reports began to surface of increased alien abductions and UFO sightings worldwide.

Next, an amateur astronomer's sighting of an alien space station behind the moon went viral on the internet, diverting global paranoia from the prospects of World War III to fears of an alien attack.

Alice stumbled out of the massive, 15-metre circular teleporter, known as Kairos, with a look of pure panic etched on his face. The teleporter had signalled an incoming transit, and Dr. Secta, a lanky man sporting shoulder-length white hair on one side of his head and a clean-shaven look on the other, had rushed to the receiving room, his curiosity piqued by Alice's unexpectedly swift return.

"Bloody hell," Al grumbled. "I was lucky to get out of there with my backside intact. Wasn't the plan to send a probe or a camera ahead to ensure a safe landing?"

"Apologies, Alice," Secta responded, guiding him towards the pressurised control room door.

Once inside, Secta asked, "So, what happened?"

The control room featured an operations console, a window with a view of the advent room and Kairos, a departure cubicle, and a separate room for the Cray supercomputer tasked with processing the complex data required for teleportation. Dr. Robert James, the lead engineer, sat at the console next to Professor Vic del Luz. Together, the four were the core team of Oceana Time Travel, OTT, a secret division of the Oceana Government.

Exhausted, Alice collapsed into a chair, frustration evident on his face. After a brief pause to compose himself, he began, "I emerged right in front of an advancing army... hundreds of them, armed to the teeth. If I hadn't acted swiftly, they'd have trampled me."

"And were they aware of your presence?" inquired the Professor.

"It certainly felt that way. It's as if they were expecting me."

"But that's not possible, is it?" Robert interjected.

"Are you insinuating that they were forewarned of your arrival?" Dr Secta sought clarification.

The Professor retorted, "What other explanation could there be? Someone must have known where and when he was going."

They had utilised an ancient wood fragment from the ruins of Ekur (the mountain house) in the Kairos particle collider to fix an exact date for teleporting Alice through a wormhole to Nippur in Mesopotamia in 2500 B.C. His mission was to witness the Battle of Ekur between the Assyrian general Belit-ili and the god-monster Anzu. This conflict was about the ownership of the legendary Tablet of Destinies, allegedly stolen by Anzu from En-Lil. Alice's primary objective was to locate these famed tablet.

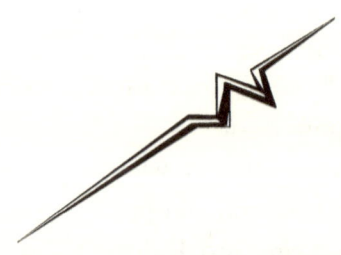

www.ingramcontent.com/pod-product-compliance
Lightning Source LLC
Chambersburg PA
CBHW020249120726
47904CB00001B/136